ALSO BY ANNE RENWICK

ELEMENTAL WEB CHRONICLES

The Golden Spider

The Silver Skull

The Iron Fin

Venomous Secrets

ELEMENTAL WEB TALES

A Trace of Copper

In Pursuit of Dragons

A Reflection of Shadows

A Snowflake at Midnight

A Ghost in Amber

A Whisper of Bone

Flight of the Scarab

ELEMENTAL WEB STORIES

The Tin Rose

Kraken and Canals

Rust and Steam

THE GOLDEN SPIDER

THE
ELEMENTAL
WEB
CHRONICLES

BOOK 1

ANNE RENWICK

To Shaunee, without whom the spider would never have crawled onto the page

Thank you to...

Shaunee Cole, Kristan Higgins, Jennifer Iszkiewicz and Huntley Fitzpatrick. You helped the plot take root, cheered me on to the end—and so, so much more.

All the wonderful people of CTRWA. This chapter and the people in it made all the difference in the world. Without you this novel would never have been born. I miss you all.

The Wiffers—all of you. You've been a part of this from the beginning.

All my former biology teachers and professors. Who knew this would be the outcome?

All my former students. Perhaps this makes up for the lectures?

My husband and my two boys who never stopped believing in this book.

My mom and dad who first taught me to love reading.

Mr. Fox and his red pen.

CHAPTER ONE

London
Fall 1884

THE HONOR OF WORKING for the Queen as a spy was overrated.

Crouched behind a burned-out steam carriage, Sebastian Talbot, the 5th Earl of Thornton, tapped on the acousticocept wrapped about his ear. The device should have worked up to a half-mile distance. He squinted through the gloom of the riverside fog. Hell, he could still see their agent. He just couldn't hear him.

"No signal," he hissed to the man beside him. Would they ever manage to make this damn device work in the field?

His partner, Mr. Black, frowned. "Same."

"Repairs." Thornton pointed across the field of rusting scrap metal before them to a derelict water boiler just large

1

enough to conceal both men in the dark of night. "There." After years of working side by side, the two men could almost read each other's minds.

Black nodded and they ran forward, tracing a winding path through piles of discarded machinery in an attempt to melt into the odd shadows the metal cast. Their agent was no more than fifty feet away, but Thornton still couldn't hear the conversation between Agent Smith and his informant. He threw Black a questioning look, but the man shook his head. Nothing.

Thornton bit back a curse. They couldn't approach Smith without blowing his cover.

Black ripped the acousticocept from his ear and twisted its dials in vain trying to increase reception. The light continued to blink red. Either the agent's artificial ear had failed or there was some fresh blunder with the receiver.

Thornton ran through the schematics in his mind. The aether chamber inside the agent's ear was sealed. Tests had proven that in the laboratory this afternoon. The next logical weak point was the needles contacting the counter rotating disks in the acousticocepts. They had a tendency to dislodge.

He wanted to growl in frustration. Henri should have fixed that problem by now. The device should be beyond field trials. They should have been sitting in a steam coach listening to the informant's tale in complete warmth and comfort, not running about a scrap yard straight from a debriefing at the opera and risking discovery in blindingly white shirts, snowy cravats, and well-tailored coats. Thornton kept a hand tightly wrapped over his silver-capped cane lest it reflect some stray ray of light and draw attention like a bioluminescent beacon.

And his leg was sending out pangs of warning. Damn sky pirate and his cutlass.

Thornton ignored the radiating pain. He pulled a cigarette case from his coat pocket as he stepped behind the metal tank. He raised his eyebrows at Black. Smith believed his informant finally had a solid lead. If Thornton didn't attempt field repairs, he and Black would be reduced to simple observation. Too many carefully woven plans had unraveled of late, and he did not relish the thought of delivering yet another report of failure to his superior.

Black nodded and angled his torso to further block any view of Thornton's activities. Flipping it open, he activated the small decilamp—its light a necessary risk—and selected micro-tweezers from among the various tools within. There was a chance he could reset the needles of the acousticocept before the agent moved to follow the informant's lead.

His cold fingers fumbled. Gloves. He'd been about to return for them when he'd spotted a determined mother steering her debutant daughter into his opera box. Discomfort, no matter how biting, was preferable to becoming trapped in such a snare. Warmth had been abandoned in favor of freedom.

Black shifted closer as Thornton pulled his acousticocept free and placed it on a steam gauge protruding from the boiler. Thornton flipped a monocle over his eye and, with only the faint blue-green light to illuminate the needles, set to work.

As always, the world about him faded as he untangled an experimental conundrum.

Moments later, the light glowed a steady green. Success, but no satisfaction. He'd uncovered yet another internal defect. Tomorrow, he would sketch out modifications to solve this issue once and for all. He handed the device to Black and set about fixing the second one. Hooking the working acousticocept once again about his ear, Thornton was drawn into the distant exchange.

"...but how is the eye doctor making contact with the gypsies?" Smith asked.

The ragged informant shrugged. "I want nuthin' more to do with this so-called doctor. Got me two young'uns, I do. Can't be found floating down the Thames." He turned away.

"Wait..."

But the informant had already disappeared into the night.

There was a crunch of shoes on gravel. A soft splash followed. Then Smith spoke as if to himself, though the information was directed to them. "I'm going to investigate."

Thornton glanced at Black in question. The man shook his head. Because of the malfunctioning device, they'd missed a crucial piece of information.

Rising from behind the boiler, he caught sight of their agent—but not his informant. Smith had climbed into a boat and was rowing down the Thames. Risky, with the Thames' kraken population on the rise. But as long as Smith hugged the shoreline and avoided storm pipes, he might reach his destination—whatever that was—before the smaller kraken swarmed and sank the boat.

But where did that leave them? There was no way to flag down Smith without compromising him. He sagged against the boiler in frustration. At this dark and foggy hour the usual clamor of steam engines, sailors' calls and horns was muted, and through the acousticocept, he could hear the sound of waves lapping at a boat's hull.

So much for simple surveillance.

"There's a dock not far." Black glanced at Thornton's leg. "Can you make it?"

He narrowed his eyes. Such concern was unnecessary. For now. "I can make it."

"Or go down trying," Black retorted.

Before Thornton could snarl an appropriate response, Black was off and running. Using his cane to counterbalance his awkward gait, he followed across the mud and rock of the riverbank, cursing as he stepped on a decaying kraken carcass and nearly lost his footing. The beasts were everywhere, the stench from their decaying bodies rising to fill his nostrils.

By the time he reached said dock, Black was already casting away the ropes. "Hurry up, old man."

Thornton leapt into the boat, and a lightning bolt of pain shot through his leg.

As Black rowed in pursuit and shook free the occasional tentacle that hooked an oar, Thornton unscrewed the silver head of his cane and pulled a glass vial as well as a needle from within. With practiced movements, he fitted the vial with a small needle. Yanking a pant leg above his knee, he injected the contents.

Instant relief. He dragged in a deep breath and shoved the empty vial into his coat pocket.

"Better?" Black asked.

Thornton reassembled his cane and gave a terse nod. As the tension melted from his muscles, he scanned the water for their man. "There, by the warehouse."

Black adjusted course.

The drug's effectiveness wouldn't last. Once, a single dose had dulled the pain for an entire month. Now he needed to administer the drug daily. It was time to curtail his field duties further. Perhaps eliminate them altogether. Before an agent fell victim to his injury.

A bitter pill to swallow for a man in his early thirties.

In the distance, Smith effortlessly dragged the boat ashore and ducked inside the brick building. His footsteps echoed in Thornton's ear.

"There's a light," the agent whispered. "A faint tapping."

There was a rustle, the sound of a coat being pushed aside and the scrape of a weapon drawn. The agent screamed. An agonizing sound that had both Thornton and Black gripping their ears. An altogether too brief scream that ended with a gurgle. There was a loud crunch followed by telling static.

Though he and Black wore the acousticocept listening devices coiled about their ears, the transmitting device, the acousticotransmitter, had been implanted deep *inside* Smith's ear.

Pulling on the oars, Black beached the boat onto the muddy, trash-laden shore. They ran to the building. Not a single glimmer of light escaped its tall windows. Thornton yanked on the rusty door handle. "Locked."

"Stand back," Black ordered, then kicked the door open, entering with Thornton at his back. Both held their weapons at the ready.

Nothing but silence and their agent, sprawled on the ground—a faint trickle of blood oozing from his ear around a protruding stiletto blade—met their entry.

Thornton clenched his jaw and bent over. He avoided Smith's vacant eyes as he pressed fingers to the agent's throat in the unlikely event that he might find a faint pulse. Nothing. He looked upward, his gaze drawn to the other horror in the room.

Black had flicked on his bioluminescent torch. The cavernous riverside warehouse was filled with stacked wooden crates. In its center, over the delivery hatch in the dock that stretched out over the river, hung a block and tackle. Suspended from the iron hook by rope-bound hands was another man beyond rescue. Blood streaked down his face and neck, soaking the front of a saffron-colored shirt. Empty eye sockets stared down at them.

"Damn it," Black swore. "Not again."

CHAPTER TWO

T HE DAY BEGAN MUCH like any other day.

Lady Amanda Ravensdale, daughter of the Duke of Avesbury, took a bite of buttered toast and a sip of cold tea before returning her attention to the femur resting before her on the polished mahogany dining table. A practical examination approached, and she had her heart set on achieving a perfect score. She scanned its surface, murmuring anatomical terms. Greater trochanter, medial epicondyle, linea aspera—

A grinding of gears and a gentle bump against her chair drew her attention. "Thank you, RT," she said to the steam-bot, lifting a china cup filled with fresh, hot tea. The roving table reversed course and whirred its way back toward the kitchens.

"Must you!" Olivia shrieked from behind her. "The horrors I endure each day as a member of this family. I will never forgive you for caving to such a base desire to mingle with the middle class in an anatomical theater. My sister in medical school. It's a social nightmare."

Amanda smirked at her sister's tantrum and twisted in her chair. "And I will never forgive you for the hours I've lost enduring soliloquy after soliloquy about the difficulties of obtaining an ice sculpture come June."

"I'll have you know planning a proper society wedding is quite an undertaking." Olivia pointed her nose in the air, and golden ringlets bounced about her face. "Carlton will one day be Viscount Bromwich."

"Children," Father warned from the end of the table. He lifted the morning paper higher. On the front page, headlines proclaimed the latest indignity: A German Imperial Fleet zeppelin had attacked what was, the British Navy insisted, a mere merchant's vessel.

"At least a wedding is a suitable pursuit for a lady," Olivia persisted as she stomped over to the buffet. "Carlton says women have no business pursuing a career."

Amanda rolled her eyes. She was thoroughly sick of hearing her future brother-in-law quoted, so she stuck in the proverbial scalpel and gave it a sharp twist. "Carlton simply wants nothing to distract you from your duty as brood mare."

Her sister's jaw unhinged, and she all but dropped her plate of dry toast on the table. "You are so crass. It's to society's benefit that you've set course to become a dried up old maid."

"If that's what it takes to be permitted to use my talents." It wasn't that she opposed marriage. Or children. It was the limitations a husband imposed upon a married female member of the peerage. Not a single man had yet met her standards. "Though Mr. Sommersby shows promise," she added aloud. He was the only male classmate who didn't sneer at her presence in the lecture hall. Quite the opposite. Not that she had *feelings* for him, but she'd promised Father she would husband hunt.

"The second son of a baron. A mere commoner," Olivia sniffed, but when she turned toward Father, her expression grew concerned. "Speaking of marriage and rotten siblings, any news of Emily?"

Another manifestation of Olivia's obsession with marrying a title. Scandal might break at any moment. The *ton* believed Lady Emily visited relatives in Italy, but if society learned the truth—that their sister had run off with gypsies to study ancient herbal lore—well, Carlton wouldn't want anything to do with Olivia.

Worse, Emily had also married Luca, a gypsy she'd known since childhood—a fact she and Father had kept from the rest of the family. No need to send Mother and Olivia into a blind panic. Though Amanda herself was proud of her sister for taking her future into her own hands, Father's response was more tempered. He respected Emily's decision, but had three as-yet unwed children to manage and a wife who valued her social connections among the *ton* above all else. As such, all communication with her sister had been severed.

Father's narrowed eyes appeared over the top of the paper. "Not a word." He carefully folded the paper, placed it on the table and pointed to an article. "Though I worry for her every day."

Amanda leaned forward, reading over her sister's shoulder. There in all its gruesome detail buried at the bottom of page eight:

South London. Another gypsy slain, eyes torn from sockets. One must wonder to what he bore witness.

A small frisson of worry skittered down her spine. Luca's family often settled in South London during the coming winter months, and gypsies traveled in tightly knit family groups. She could only hope that this year his family had chosen another city.

AMANDA STEPPED through the French windows of the library into the crisp, cool autumn air and strolled through the gardens toward the chicken coop. "A good morning to you, Penny," Amanda greeted a fat, white hen.

Penny clucked her usual cheerful response.

Eight years ago, the Town and City Food Act of 1876 had legislated that all homeowners, peers not excepted, contribute to the problem of city-wide food shortages. As duchess, Mother had decreed they would produce eggs rather than put her precious gardens to plow.

Amanda had appropriated the use of the coop's storage room as her laboratory and enlisted the orange-striped cat,

Rufus, who now twined about her ankles, as her laboratory assistant. His duties included providing her with mice suffering from spinal injuries, patients obtained during their ill-fated night-time raids on the chicken feed. The cat followed as she moved to a door in the back wall where a lock was mounted. She dialed in a ten-digit security code. Tumblers fell into place and the door swung open.

Potentially useful items cluttered the room. Shelves of glassware, bottles and rubber tubing. Boxes of clockwork components. Stacks of papers and stubs of pencils.

Yet none of the contents mattered save one. On the wide workbench before her, a single cage rested. Inside, a tiny mouse tucked into cotton batting was curled on his side as if in deep sleep. For a brief moment, she held her breath and let herself hope. Perhaps that's all it was, sleep.

She crossed to the bench and bent to examine her patient, watching for the gentle rise and fall of the mouse's ribcage but saw no movement. Still, Amanda clung to hope. Perhaps he breathed shallowly due to the pain of the surgery. That she could ease.

Except there was a smear of blood on the cotton, a clear indication the surgery had failed. Again. Her heart sank.

Rufus leapt beside her and sniffed the mouse through the wire mesh of its cage, performing his own examination. He looked up at her with mournful golden eyes and let out a gut-wrenching yowl.

Dead.

Breakfast congealed into a hard lump in her stomach. She'd had such high expectations last night. Swallowing her

disappointment and frustration, Amanda fell back on protocol. She opened the cage, scooping the small, cold mouse
from his bedding and slid him into the aetheroscope's observation chamber to seal him from the outside atmosphere. She
cranked the handle of the machine, sending concentrated
aether though its pipes and valves while activating the
vacuum chamber. The device, a birthday present from her
brother Ned, replaced oxygen with aether, allowing her to
resolve far smaller objects than her other microscope ever
had, no matter its powerful objectives.

Perching on a stool, Amanda peered through the
eyepiece and twisted the dials into focus. Rotating first one
knob and then another, she brought the neuromuscular junction of the muscle into view and sighed. The connection had
indeed failed.

Five years ago, after Ned's tragic accident stole the use of
his legs, her life-long interest in medicine had found a clear
focus. She'd concentrated her efforts on the neuromuscular
system, conceptualizing and then building a neurachnid, a
programmable, clockwork spider the size of a bronze half-
pence, one that could spin a replacement for a damaged
motor neuron following spinal injury.

It sat in a place of honor on a wooden shelf above her
workbench. Eight long, hinged legs arched out from a finely
mechanized clockwork thorax that controlled the weaving
mechanism. Lodged in the abdomen were two other key
features. A tiny slot for a miniature Babbage card to direct
the neurachnid's activities and a small glass vial, a reservoir
for a potent nerve agent administered as the spider worked.

The patient's nerve fibers needed to be quieted, but not fully anesthetized, in order for the spider to trace the pathway of the damaged neuron and, using thin gold fibers, reconnect spinal cord to muscle and restore movement.

Last night, the neurachnid had successfully replaced a spinal motor neuron in this mouse. The patient had been able to extend his lower leg. He'd walked for an entire hour. She'd returned her patient to his cage, confident she would find him walking about the cage this morning.

He hadn't. It was still the same problem. The neuromuscular junction always failed to hold. And when a mouse discovered itself unable to walk, often it reacted by chewing at the fine gold wires, growing increasingly stressed until blood loss and panic simply overwhelmed the tiny creature.

Amanda sat back, punching a button to release the gasses. The microscope hissed and spat, echoing her frustration. She wanted to scream, to fling the spider against the wall and weep for all the hours lost in her futile efforts in this smelly, dim room barely worthy of the term laboratory. She took a deep breath and pushed away the urge.

If only she had a properly equipped laboratory and trained colleagues.

Instead, she picked up the small neurachnid from its shelf and racked her brain looking over the myriad gears and pins, clicks and rivets. If she only could deduce what the problem was, she could devise a solution. But it looked as it always had. She needed fresh eyes. She needed help, competent help that could provide a leap of insight.

She'd tried communicating by post, seeking help from

notable neurophysiologists. Most ignored her missives outright, but the handful that responded suggested she abandon her project, citing its impossibility.

But it couldn't be impossible. And she wouldn't quit.

Ned *had* to walk again.

CHAPTER THREE

T HORNTON STOOD AT the front of the lecture theater frowning as students filed into the room. The men jostled and shoved, laughing and joking as they crashed about, eventually managing to land in seats. He supposed he'd been much the same as them. Once.

Lister University School of Medicine, founded by the Queen as a co-educational institution to seek out the brightest young medical minds, had not yet managed to find an equal number of women who were capable of passing the rigorous academic exams required for admission. Only three women, all dressed in dark hues, filed into the back row of seats, perching there stiff and solemn, staring down at him intently, like a murder of crows. He distinctly recalled being told there were four women in this class. One of their number was missing.

What had the dean been thinking forcing him to take on this task? Thornton belonged in his laboratory, pressing the boundaries of neuroscience, consulting with the Queen's agents to stop a murderer who sought to turn Britain's own technology against them. Not stuffing anatomical facts into impenetrable brains.

Ordered by the Queen to the Orkney Islands to investigate a sudden spike in reported sightings of selkies off the coast, Corwin, professor of anatomy, had headed north late last night. The suspicion was that Iceland was dispatching altered Inuit for reasons yet to be determined. Thornton didn't envy the man the dark and cold October nights he would spend perched on the rocky coast. Nevertheless, it meant Professor Corwin required a replacement for the term, and Thornton's physical injuries were no longer considered sufficient excuse for him to avoid teaching obligations.

But lectures were just the start of it all. There would be students in his office asking all manner of questions. Most of them would be ridiculous. Both the questions and the students. So many of them couldn't think their way out of a paper bag. Even worse, there would be exams. Exams he would have to grade. Thornton sighed thinking of the sheer quantity of red ink he would require in the near future. Waste of his time, all of it.

He walked to the podium where the limelight lantern rested, glass projection slides of the human nervous system at the ready. He twisted the gas lines providing both oxygen and hydrogen into "on" positions, picked up the striker and lit the cylinder of quicklime.

There was a lull in the conversation. Thornton cleared

his throat and looked up at his audience, expecting all eyes to have focused attentively upon him. Instead, he saw the backs of fifty odd heads and only one face.

A very beautiful face. One with deep pink lips, high cheekbones and a dainty nose between wide eyes that had just a hint of an exotic tilt. Smooth skin, all surrounded by elaborately coiffed hair the color of midnight. Unlike the crows in the back who rolled their eyes in disgust, this woman was garbed in the latest of fashions, a tightly corseted and bustled teal gown with a low cut neckline that had all the men leering.

All but him, of course.

Striking blue eyes met his gaze.

He lifted his eyebrows and drew out his pocket watch to consult the hour. It was five past. She was late.

Her lips curved upward at his obvious reprimand, but she made no effort to hasten her steps. A gentleman in the front row stood, gesturing to a vacant seat he clearly intended for her to occupy. She nodded in greeting, then with the twist of a knob at her waist to collapse her bustle, she removed her feathered hat and settled into the chair beside the smug-looking gentleman.

Instinct told Thornton she would be a problem. A woman with such obvious physical charms expected attention. Best to not provide it. He waved his hand at his assistant and the room plunged into darkness. Sliding home the first glass plate, an illuminated image appeared on the large screen hanging at the front of the hall.

Tomorrow, he would not wait. If she could not manage

to arrive promptly, she could damn well stumble her way down the stairs or sit in the back.

"Neurons and glial cells," he intoned. "Later in the laboratory you will closely study the features of both."

AMANDA LEANED FORWARD in her chair, entranced by the deep, booming voice of this new professor. The light cast by the limelight lantern threw his angular face into sharp relief. What captivating facial bone structure. Prominent zygomatic arches and a long square jaw made the planes of his face appear wide and harsh. Between his dark eyebrows, nasal bones stretched into a long, straight and distinctive nose. Damp hair severely slicked back from his forehead betrayed the man by daring to curl at its tips. Full lips formed words in a tone that made the features of a neuron sound utterly entrancing.

She rather thought she could be content to spend the entire morning listening to him read the index of her anatomy text. Clearly brilliant, he was also the best physical specimen she'd laid eyes on in a long time. Too bad about that clause in the school's charter forbidding professors from entering into relationships with their students.

A flush rose upward across her face. Such thoughts. She forced her gaze to the projection on the screen. *Focus, Amanda.*

He was proceeding at such a rapid clip that she would

soon be left behind if she could not pull her head out of the aether.

Though she put pen to paper, she could not stop herself from asking. "What happened to Professor Corwin?" she whispered to Simon, or Mr. Sommersby as she addressed him in public.

Simon shifted to lean his shoulder lightly against her own. Male instinct, she supposed, to mark her as his own. Behavior she'd encouraged. "No idea. But it seems Lord Thornton is to finish the lecture series."

Her indrawn breath was audible.

Lord Sebastian Talbot, Earl of Thornton and renowned neurophysiologist teaching a course! She'd known he was on staff, but it was rumored that he never lectured. Whatever forced him to the podium, she did not care. Fortune had finally smiled upon her. He might have ignored her attempts to open a scientific correspondence about the possibility of using gold filaments to conduct neurological impulses, but he could not ignore her physical presence in his office as his student.

Excitement must have shown in her face as she contemplated this unexpected windfall, for Lord Thornton's eyes flickered toward her. Did she detect surprise in the slight drawing together of his eyebrows? Hard to be certain, for his words never slowed. She had to convince him of the merit of her work. Convince him to allow her to demonstrate the function of her neurachnid, for his insight would be profound.

He'd already taken notice of her. Twice.

She winced. Not the best first impression. She had been late, and he'd sent quite the scowl in her direction.

If not for the overturned horse cart in the street—horses and steam coaches did not mix well—she would have been punctual. Amanda hated arriving late, enduring the disapproving stares of the other women, the speculative leers of the men. She'd fully intended to politely perch in the back. But when this new professor had met her gaze, seeming to challenge her right to enter, neither fire nor brimstone would have kept her from her usual center seat in the front row.

It was a matter of principle. She'd set a precedent she intended to uphold. Amanda was polite and collegial, stubbornly refusing to be relegated to the dark edges and corners of the room where most male classmates seemed to think she and the other three women belonged.

If only they'd join her.

Betsy, Joan and Sarah clung desperately to the notion that the best manner in which to succeed in medicine as a woman was to efface their sex with severely tailored dresses. Dark colors, long sleeves and high necklines revealing only the oval of their faces. They worked diligently at making themselves unpleasant and uncomfortable. Amanda saw no need to dress the dowd. She took pride in her appearance, and if her ladylike and professional behavior set her apart from others, so be it.

Lord Thornton paced back and forth across the dim lecture hall, a slight hitch to his step, while expounding upon the wonders of the neurological system, changing glass slides with astonishing speed.

Like her classmates, Amanda wrote furiously, her hand cramping. But instead of directing her eyes to the projected images, she stole glances at the man.

With an emphatic wave of his arm, a lock of his hair began to free itself. Another followed. Curls began to assert themselves, twisting tighter and sending waves along each strand. Lord Thornton's hair took on a life of its own, falling across his brow in playful waves.

Though they'd never met, he was *ton* and rumors reached her ears at the various society events she'd been forced to attend. He'd been involved in a terrible dirigible accident, no doubt responsible for the slight limp she detected, but most of the gossip had centered upon his new-found eligibility. For unknown reasons, his long-time fiancée had jilted him mere months before their wedding. Not that any hopeful brides cared why. He was titled and therefore a matrimonial target.

Another slide change. More words rumbled from his throat. His voice was pure intellectual delight. She wrote faster. Really, she must start focusing on the images and not the man. But pressing concerns about the neurachnid's design rose to mind. Here was opportunity. What questions might she put to the great neurophysiologist before her? What flash of brilliant design might she reveal? What was the best path toward winning his regard?

Suddenly, the opportunity was upon her.

The screen went dark, and the room brightened. "If there are no questions," Lord Thornton began. "Tomorrow I will discuss..."

He would send them on their way with no opportunity to engage? She added arrogance to the list of his defining traits. "Professor, with regard to the ganglion, would you consider it possible to transform neurility into electricity via a rare earth metal?"

As intense, blue eyes turned to stare at her, Amanda fancied she'd caught the slightest slackening of his firm, square jaw before it tightened so much his lips thinned. She waited for his answer in breathless anticipation.

"My dear Miss...?" His eyebrows rose in both question and challenge.

"Ravensdale," she supplied. Something in his eyes crystallized, not into ice, but into something much harder and denser, something with razor sharp edges, and she met that piercing gaze with the uneasy sensation in her stomach that things were about to go badly awry.

"Miss Ravensdale. From your... fantastical question, I can only conclude that you have spent far too much time reading texts beyond your comprehension without adequate guidance. Despite their high electrical conductivity, insertion of such elements into the human body would be ethically reprehensible."

Amanda inhaled sharply at the implied reprimand. There were several smothered snickers behind her. Her eyes narrowed as they caught Lord Thornton's gaze. No. She was right and he knew it. With great deliberation, he'd chosen to belittle her hypothesis before her classmates. All hope of a demonstration of her neurachnid followed by his assistance evaporated like a drop of water falling on a hot coal. She pursed her lips, and his eyes flashed with victory.

The arrogant bastard.

Beside her, Simon drew an indignant breath. Amanda pressed her gloved palm to his arm, stifling his impulse to rush to her defense.

Then without further acknowledgement of his audience, Lord Thornton strode from the room.

CHAPTER FOUR

THE FLAME OF THE GAS lamp blurred as Amanda stared at it, chin propped on her hand. Her elbow slipped along the library table. Her torso swayed in exhaustion. On the brink of falling asleep atop her notes, her mind could absorb no more. With a sigh, she closed her books and rubbed her eyes. Evening social obligations were incompatible with exam preparation.

The dinner party Father insisted she attend had been horrid. At best, two potential husbands had been eliminated from consideration.

Lord Guntwaithe, seated to her left, had informed her with a leer that, as his wife, her marital duties would leave her no time to practice medicine. Lord Lowsley, seated on her right, had droned on about a new, silver-coated cloth that the company Airship Sails was employing to make their dirigible balloons impermeable to aether.

A bell rang behind her, the steambot alternative to

knocking. "Lady Amanda," Burton intoned in a formal, flat monotone overlaid by a horrible metallic screeching sound. His jaw hinge was acting up again. "Your father requests your presence in his study."

"It's nearly midnight," she objected, but found herself speaking to the clock for Burton had already spun about and wheeled away. She pushed to her feet. One did not ignore Father's summons, no matter the hour.

Heavy footfalls passing down the hallway had been what snapped her back from the edge of unconsciousness. Not that she'd paid them any mind. The Queen's men came and went from Father's study at all hours. The family had learned long ago to pay no attention to such activity. And to ask no questions.

She staggered into the hall, pausing before a large mirror to re-pin a few stray locks of hair and smooth her crushed skirts, but there was not much to do for her tired, rumpled appearance. Why would Father summon her at this hour?

Emily.

Fear crystallized in her mind, shocking her awake and quickening her steps.

Burton held the study door open.

"Father?" she asked, crossing the threshold. Her eyes quickly sought out his face, but he looked unconcerned. "Is anything wrong?"

"That remains to be seen." Father rose from behind his desk. He waved toward an empty chair. "Please, have a seat."

That was when she saw *him.* The entirety of her body tensed, refusing to bend itself to a chair. Her stomach clenched like a naughty schoolgirl called before the head-mistress, though she'd done nothing more than ask a question. "Lord Thornton." She forced herself to politely incline her head. She very much doubted he would seek her out in her own home to apologize, to admit he was wrong.

"*Lady* Amanda," he scolded without rising.

She met his gaze. "Your assumption, not mine."

His eyebrows rose as he scanned her from head to toe, as if her appearance justified his mistake. It irritated her that despite the slight shadow darkening his jaw, his hair was neatly combed, his clothes were unrumpled and his eyes were bright and alert.

She narrowed her eyes in return. Unfair. "But under-standable, given your known indifference to *ton* affairs."

"It's true. I have no interest in the marriage mart." His voice, low and gravelly, rumbled across her skin. "Though some might think medical school provides... alternatives."

She inhaled sharply. Did he dare suggest her sole purpose in attending Lister University was to find a husband? Meeting Mr. Sommersby was a happy coincidence. Her eyes widened. No. It wasn't possible. Certainly Lord Thornton had not presented himself to Father as a suitor for his daughter's hand? A smart retort eluded her. She told herself it was the hour.

Something must have shown in her face, for she caught a faint twitch of Lord Thornton's lips before they regained a bored expression. All that remained was a speculative glint in his blue eyes.

Father cleared his throat. "Amanda, Lord Thornton has

come to me with an interesting request. He wishes to view your... spider."

"Neurachnid."

"Yes, exactly," Father said.

Lord Thornton's expression hardened, his stare intensified. She stiffened her spine. Perhaps he could bend his minions to his will with such a look, but not her.

"No."

The flicker of surprise in Lord Thornton's eyes was unaccountably rewarding.

"Excuse me?" Surprise echoed in Father's tone. Not because she refused to comply with a lord's implied command—he was accustomed to her arguments—but because she'd used Lord Thornton's presence at Lister University School of Medicine as one of her arguments for matriculation at that school.

A co-educational school. One at which she'd expected to be treated equally.

She looked at her father. "No. Lord Thornton made it clear today that he believes my design unfeasible. So he told me and my entire class." She paused to let that sink in. "Clearly, his curiosity indicates that is not the case, and his presence in your office at this late hour implies that he is not interested in collaborating but, rather, in forcing me to his will." She crossed her arms and turned her stare upon her professor. "So, no, I will not hand over a device I have spent the better part of five years developing."

Father nodded, leaning back on his desk and regarding his visitor in the light of this new information. "I will not force her, Lord Thornton, unless you can provide an extremely convincing argument in your favor."

Lord Thornton rose stiffly to his feet. "I fear I cannot." His pant leg caught. A flash of something metallic at his ankle. With a quick movement, he twitched the material, concealing what must be a brace.

Could not, or would not? Remembering his limp, Amanda wondered. Could his interest in her neurachnid be of a personal nature?

"Please, forgive my intrusion at such an hour. I'll see myself out."

With concern—of a medical nature, of course—Amanda followed his steps with her gaze, analyzing his peculiar gait. An injury to the fibularis muscles of the lower right leg prevented him from properly flexing his foot. Walking on uneven ground, climbing stairs, dancing across a ballroom floor, all would be negatively impacted.

Not that the man had ever been sighted in a ballroom. It would have caused quite the stir.

The door closed firmly behind him. Only then did she realize she'd been holding her breath.

Father frowned. "Antagonizing the prominent and influential men in the medical community is not a path to a successful medical practice, and given your research project—"

"I know, Father," she said, daring to interrupt the one man who could put a swift end to her career. "But the humiliation—"

He lifted a hand. "Before you say anything more, to me

or to Lord Thornton, I would urge you to carefully consider your course as well as your own arguments for attending medical school. What matters more, your pride or your brother's future?"

Amanda stalked upstairs, fuming that she should have to make such a choice. The hallway lamps were dimmed, the house far too silent. She wanted to grumble and grouse and be heard. How dare he disrupt her day. Her night.

Lord Thornton would not have treated a man so. She was willing to wager a great deal that a male classmate would have been praised for his insight and offered a position in the great man's famed laboratory.

Why work in a co-educational school if female intelligence offended him? Was it his mission to strip female students of any useful and novel ideas before too much education addled their minds?

As she passed her brother's room, light filtered out from beneath his door. Ned, it seemed, was still awake.

She hesitated. How could she possibly vent to him? Guilt washed over her. If not for her and Emily's teasing, her research project would not even be necessary. Her shoulders slumped. As Father had pointed out, it *was* his future. Perhaps it was only fair to present the possibilities and let Ned decide. She knocked at his door.

"Come."

Amanda opened the door and poked her head through the crack, prepared to leave if he was already in bed, but he sat in his wheeled chair before the grate, staring at the fading light of the coals, a folded piece of paper in his hand. The faint sound of a waltz issued forth from a wooden box on his writing desk. Lines of worry creased his forehead. "Is something amiss with you as well?" Amanda slid into the chair beside him. She kicked off her slippers and tucked her feet beneath her skirts.

Ned's jaw flexed as he tucked the paper into the pocket of his dressing gown. She saw pain in his eyes. "Georgina has received an excellent offer. Her father is pressing her to accept it."

"Oh, Ned. I'm so sorry." Her need to vent evaporated.

Ned rarely accepted invitations to visit friends anymore, but a year ago, he'd agreed to attend a small house party at an old school friend's family estate where he had fallen helplessly in love with his friend's younger sister, Georgina. Except her father refused to consider the suit of a man who could not walk without mechanical assistance. Not when his daughter had so many other titled gentlemen who were healthy and hale pressing their suit.

Amanda well understood the pressure to marry that could be brought to bear upon a young woman of good social stature. She herself had avoided marriage longer than most, but the relentless pressure from her parents had, in the end, won. Though she'd bargained ruthlessly with Father for a small concession. In exchange for her enrollment in medical school, she'd agreed to marry within the year.

Most young women gained no such concession from their parents. "It must be so hard to let her go."

He looked up sharply. "Who said anything about letting go?"

Oh dear. That calculating look told her drastic measures were being plotted. Amanda squeezed her eyes shut and squashed her pride. "Lord Sebastian Talbot, Earl of Thornton has asked me to share the neurachnid with him." His indrawn breath made her rush on. "He is the most domineering, self-important, puffed up..." She shook her head. "All of which has no bearing on a decision I—we—must make. He sees potential in my project." She opened her eyes.

Ned stared back in amazement. One hand gripped the arm of his chair, steadying himself as he leaned forward. "This could change everything. It's what we've been hoping for."

She nodded slowly. "I wanted to work *with* him, but he wants it for his own. If you think it best, I'll hand everything over to him. Perhaps with his resources..."

"...he might find the solution," Ned finished. "Or he might not. Either way, you lose control of the project." He paused, thinking. "Worse, there would be no guarantee he would allow me to be an early test subject. Likely he would refuse to experiment on a future duke." Ned shook his head and sat back. "No. I think you should continue your work on your own. You're so very close. Perhaps if you start anew. Let me look over the Babbage card again."

Relief swept over her as she forced herself to ask, "You're certain? It may take months. You might have to let Georgina go."

Ned set his jaw, his voice a low growl. "I'm certain. And I will never let Georgina go."

THE SUN WOULDN'T RISE for hours, but sleep was impossible, what with the myriad thoughts whirling through her brain. She might as well accomplish something beyond watching the moonlight move across the floor.

Amanda rose from her bed and crossed to her wardrobe, then selected a simple blue gown that didn't require much lacing or tying of tapes. Its bustle was a collection of ruffles that draped over the skirt, and the leather straps and brass buckles of the bodice made a corset unnecessary. Given the hours she was about to spend stooped over her workbench, the ability to bend at the waist was a priority.

As she strode through the garden, Rufus appeared, greeting her with a long, silent stare from his golden eyes. Both he and she were creatures of habit, and her appearance at this dark hour was a dramatic break from routine. Yet still he followed her on silent paws as she stepped into the coop. The hens slept in peaceful repose, barely shifting in their nests as she crossed quietly to the laboratory door and dialed the necessary series of digits.

Her earlier anger had faded, to be replaced by renewed determination. The great Lord Thornton had tipped his hand. He saw something in her project. She must be close.

Rufus settled in his favorite corner, on alert for cheeky mice, as Amanda lit an oil lamp and pulled a stool forward. She spread a soft cloth across the workbench and arranged her tools.

She would dissect the neurachnid, spread each gear,

each pin, each spring across her workbench. She would study its mechanisms with a critical eye and then make improvements.

Her gold threads did not work in the same manner as biological neurons. They weren't designed to. They made direct contact with both the spinal cord and the muscle in order to transmit electrical impulses, but as the muscle fibers contracted, the threads inevitably pulled free. Rare earth metals would cement the connection, at least in theory, but were also hard to come by—and expensive.

For Ned, she'd find a way.

She reached for the neurachnid stored on the shelf above, but her hand met nothing but air. She looked up. Had Rufus knocked it down? She scanned the empty space, then dropped her gaze to the surface of the workbench, searching.

Her heart beating faster by the second, Amanda lifted rags. Shifted bottles and tin canisters, looked under notes and papers, hunted behind her microscope.

It was... gone.

She leapt to her feet and spun around, searching the small room for any signs of intrusion and found nothing. Everything was exactly as it had been when she left.

Someone had stolen her spider.

Though no one had the combination, her security was minimal, designed more to discourage nosy children, curious family members and cleaning staff. Until this moment, she'd never considered medical espionage.

Amanda pressed a palm to her chest, willing her heart to stop pounding. She needed to think. And clearly.

Five years she'd poured into that neurachnid. Could she rebuild it? Certainly. But many fine parts were special order or handcrafted. It could take her months to construct another. Longer, if someone had also appropriated her designs.

With two long steps, she crossed to a metal cabinet in the corner. Twisting the dial first one direction, then another, and back again, she spun the combination. With a click, the lock released, and she yanked out a drawer.

She heaved a sigh of relief. All her notes, all her schematics were still there. She gathered them up and pressed them to her chest. Her laboratory was no longer secure.

Only one person she knew possessed the motivation and the mentality, the will, and the resources to infiltrate her laboratory.

Lord Thornton.

CHAPTER FIVE

AMANDA MARCHED DOWN the empty hallway past numerous doors, her back ramrod straight. She'd spent the last twenty minutes tracking down his inconvenient location. The man seemed to have deliberately removed his name and location from all directories.

If a student managed to locate Lord Thornton's office in the meager half hour he grudgingly allotted to office hours each week, he—or she—would have but mere minutes to pose a question. Perhaps that was the earl's goal. On this point, at least, he did not discriminate; he hated all students equally. She came to a halt, stopping before an enormous iron door at the end of the hallway. Its lock defined security.

She stared in amazement, studying the mechanism. Several large gears would—with the right combination—pull the thick iron teeth from their sockets in the iron doorjamb. An ominous red light glowed steadily from a box that also housed a screecher. Anyone who attempted to guess at the code would deeply regret their actions. She glanced upward, half-expecting to find a portcullis installed to trap the offender.

"*This* can't be his office," she murmured, her voice hushed in amazement.

"No, Lady Amanda. *That* is my laboratory."

She'd recognize that voice anywhere. It ruffled her feathers. She turned on a heel to glare at him. It figured the man would work in an impenetrable fortress.

Filling the doorway to her right, Lord Thornton stood looking every inch an earl, a man whose actions were not to be questioned. Yet upon closer examination, he did seem a bit pale. Were those dark shadows beneath his eyes? Though he wore exactly the same clothes from his late night visit, his creases were no longer sharp, his shirt had lost some starch, and his cravat hung loose. But there was not a stray feather or cat hair to indicate he'd spent any time inside a chicken coop.

She narrowed her eyes. Then again, a man such as this would have minions to send to such a task. Did he ever get his own hands dirty?

He tipped his head in question, giving Amanda a glimpse of a strong, corded neck that stretched down to broad shoulders. She frowned. How did a scientist come by such a physique spending long hours in a laboratory? His lips twitched and for the slightest of moments, his gaze slid below her chin, and she was glad she'd taken the time to don the armor of high fashion and impeccable grooming.

A flush rose to her cheeks. What might have passed

between the two of them had they met in society rather than as academic adversaries?

Adversary. The man was a liar and a thief. Amanda had not sought him out for a social call. She focused her anger on her target. "Give it back."

His eyebrows rose, but his voice was irritatingly calm. "Give what back?"

"My neurachnid."

"A clever name but, as you'll recall, not something I've laid eyes upon." He turned his back on her and stepped into a small side room that must be his office, leaving her standing in the hallway.

The effrontery! She snapped her jaw shut and followed him, refusing to accept his clear dismissal.

Lord Thornton stood at the wall, twisting a dial that would allow him to communicate with a person at the other end of the speaking tube. "I require your presence in my office. Now. She's here."

She bristled. He'd been expecting her? Yet denied involvement with the neurachnid's theft? Had he been *here* all night, waiting? Had he and his minions already trialed the neurachnid and found it wanting? Well, he had another think coming if he thought she was going to help him, or anyone else amenable to such underhanded methods.

"On our way," a voice over the tube crackled back.

In the oppressive silence, Amanda studied his office.

A carved mahogany desk nearly buried under a mountain of papers and books sat on a threadbare rug. Against the wall behind the desk was a bank of shelves covered in yet more books and papers. She glanced over the curiosities tucked among them. A bird skull. An oversized wax model of the human ear. Vacuum tubes. A two-headed snake floating in preservative. On another wall hung an extensive anatomical chart detailing every nerve in the human body.

A single, solitary chair—unrelieved by any cushion—sat before his desk. Anyone so unfortunate as to be offered that seat would soon hasten to leave. Rather the point, she thought.

Lord Thornton moved to sit behind his desk without so much as offering it to her.

She stood behind the chair, her fingers gripping its back. Tightly. Much like they desired to grip his neck. "You deny it then?"

His face impassive, Lord Thornton leaned back in his chair, steepling his fingers across his chest. "Deny what?"

Amanda wanted to smack the flat of her hands on his desk and growl. But Father's words came back to her, and she controlled herself. Barely. "That you sent someone to appropriate my neurachnid. I would not hand it over willingly, so you resorted to force."

"The low opinion you must have of me." Lord Thornton clucked his tongue. "Let me assure you that while I would like very much to have possession of your contraption, I do not."

"So you admit the rare earth metal might work?"

His face darkened. "I admit nothing."

A perfunctory knock sounded behind her. Amanda spun around. Leaning in the open door was a man of medium height and medium build. He had brown hair and brown eyes. All the usual features in all the usual places. A face so common that most would immediately forget it.

"So this is the student of the hour," the man said. "Thornton didn't mention you were beautiful as well as brilliant." A playful grin so altered his appearance that Amanda immediately warmed to him.

Confused, but flattered, she was about to reply when a petite blonde woman, no more than five feet tall and attired in black mourning, shoved at the man's back, knocking him off balance and into the office. "Mind the manners your mother taught you."

"Follow the customs of my mother?" the man quipped. "You might regret that."

"There is much about you to regret," the lady retorted.

The man's grin widened as she stepped around him and pierced Lord Thornton with a look. "You bellowed?"

Lord Thornton showed no inclination to rise. "Lady Amanda, may I present Lady Huntley and Mr. Black."

Mr. Black bowed, then quietly shut the door behind him.

Lady Huntley inclined her head. "We've met." Her light green eyes studied Amanda through long, kohl-darkened lashes.

Indeed, they had. Lord Huntley had once courted Amanda herself. They'd spent hours in each other's company discussing any number of topics, including her work on the neurachnid, and developed a comfortable kind of friendship. Amanda had been expecting a proposal at any

43

moment when Eloise Kale, now Lady Huntley, made her dramatic entrance into the social whirl of the *ton*.

Her heart-shaped face, Cupid's bow lips and the angelic color of her hair had men falling over their feet to make her acquaintance, Lord Huntley among them. Several months later, when Amanda wished him happy on the occasion of his wedding, he'd still only had eyes for his beautiful bride.

But he'd died, tragically, not too long after their wedding. On his way to Brussels to attend a scientific conference, airship pirates had attacked his vessel. Lord Huntley had been a good friend and scientific ally, and she'd privately mourned his death. She glanced at Lord Thornton. He'd also been aboard when that dirigible crashed but survived with a mere injury to his leg.

"You'd best take a seat," Lady Huntley said. "He'll not offer one and this may take some time."

"What will take time?" Amanda asked, disinclined to sit. She glanced from one face to the next. If this was about her missing neurachnid, it was causing quite a stir.

"She accuses *me* of stealing it," Lord Thornton said.

Mr. Black crossed his arms and leaned back against the door. "Well, you do have motivation."

Lord Thornton growled.

"This device of yours," Lady Huntley began, "that can repair a damaged motor neuron by spinning gold fibers from the central nervous system to the muscle, what is your current success rate?"

Amanda stiffened. This *was* about her neurachnid. It

hurt to think of Lord Huntley sharing her research with a woman he'd married instead of her.

"Let us save the details for later, Lady Huntley." Lord Thornton turned his intense gaze back in Amanda's direction. "Where were you last night?"

She took exception at his accusatory tone. "Excuse me? What business is that of yours?" Her voice rose with each word. "Why are you treating me like a suspected criminal? As if I would steal my own spider."

"Just answer the question," Lord Thornton insisted. "Where were you last night?"

Spite made her answer, "With you."

Mr. Black snickered.

Lord Thornton frowned. "Before," he clarified.

"At the Townson's dinner party."

"Can anyone bear witness to that?" he asked.

Amanda rolled her eyes. "Have you never been to a dinner party?" The lines around Lord Thornton's mouth deepened further. "Generally, a large number of people sit about a long table for several hours of inane conversation."

Lord Thornton's jaw clenched.

Mr. Black pressed, "Names, if you please, Lady Amanda."

Amanda refused to look away from Lord Thornton as she answered. She'd count it a small victory if she could make his teeth grind. "Lord Guntwaithe visually calculated the depth of my cleavage, while Lord Lowsley employed his voice to its full soporific effect."

Mr. Black spoke. "As verified."

"And after I left?" Lord Thornton leaned forward over his desk. "What of the early morning?"

Amanda sucked in an outraged breath. "I was in my bed." That, for the most part, was the truth. "Alone, of course. How dare you suggest otherwise." She stepped toward the door, waving at Mr. Black to move. "I'll not spend another minute answering these offensive questions. Expect to hear from my father. Please step aside."

But Mr. Black continued to block her exit, his face expressionless. "My apologies, Lady Amanda, but we simply cannot allow you to leave."

"There was a situation last night." Lady Huntley's tone was conciliatory. "At the Queen's request, Lord Thornton and Mr. Black were on hand to assist. Aside from the brief stop at your town home, they spent the early hours of the morning here. As a result, their manners are strained."

"A situation?" She tipped her head, intrigued.

Lady Huntley nodded. "Despite all evidence to the contrary," she shot a dark look at Lord Thornton, "we would very much like to enlist your help."

Amanda crossed her arms, suspecting they were about to confirm her earlier suspicions. "With what, exactly?"

"I'm afraid we must have your agreement first," Lady Huntley said.

Amanda looked about the room from face to face to face. It seemed they had reached an impasse. All were firmly closed, though she was certain they knew something about her spider. If they didn't have it, they knew who did. She would have it back, and it seemed the only way to that end was to agree to assist them.

Concern warred with curiosity, but not for long. "Fine," she bit out.

"I like her," Mr. Black said to Lord Thornton, his mood lightening once more. "Not at all like you described." Then, throwing her a wink, Mr. Black turned and exited through the door.

"*This* is a bad idea," Lord Thornton grumbled.

"Not at all," Lady Huntley replied. "It's our *only* idea."

CHAPTER SIX

"SHALL WE ADJOURN to the morgue?" Lady Huntley gestured toward the door.

"Leave off that ridiculous hat," Thornton snapped at Lady Amanda. "It has so many feathers it's about to take flight." Feathers that brushed against the nape of her neck, much like a man's kiss might. An irritating thought he swept aside.

Lady Amanda's mouth dropped.

"You'll have to excuse Thornton," Lady Huntley said. "He's rather cranky today. Your hat, however, may indeed prove an inconvenience."

Lady Amanda cast him a dark glance. She pinched a hatpin between thumb and forefinger, sliding forth the long, sharp implement and dropping it upon his desk. The hat followed. "If he's capable of being pleasant, I've yet to experience it," she said, then turned on her heel to exit his office.

Her angry steps made her hips sway beneath her bustle in the most distracting manner. Why was he wondering what the real woman looked like underneath? Better that she found him cold and unbending and harsh. She might be his social equal, but here, at Lister University School of Medicine, she was first and foremost his student. Admittedly, one whose home he'd invaded in the dark of night, upsetting her equilibrium with the merest of glances and allowing her, for just a moment, to think he was there to play suitor.

He was still trying to interpret the resulting look upon her face. Shock and horror? Surprise and hope? He wasn't certain. Either way, they would be in close proximity for the foreseeable future, and Thornton would need to maintain professional distance from this woman. Theirs would be a working relationship, not a personal one.

Of all the times for his libido to reawaken.

Thornton ran a hand over his face, then forced himself to his feet and reached for his cane. He needed rest, needed sleep. Two nights, two murders, two autopsies. And his leg was killing him. But increasing the dosage of the medication would only hurry along the inevitable. Already the painkiller was at sixty-two percent purity. According to his calculations, the fibular nerve would begin to erode at seventy-four percent. He had a week, maybe two before the brace would no longer suffice.

Relegated to desk duty, the murderer might well escape his grasp. He couldn't allow that to happen.

He followed the women to the ascension chamber, climbing inside when the doors slid open to stand stiffly beside Lady Amanda. The room was not made to carry three, and the ladies' skirts made it a tight fit. Warmed by the angry heat of her skin, a faint floral scent drifted past. Orange blossoms? Thornton gripped the top of his cane tighter and fixed his gaze on the doors. He had no business wondering.

"What can you tell me about this *situation*?" Lady Amanda asked as the doors closed and the chamber's engine engaged. "And how can it possibly relate to my neurachnid?"

As they dropped downward, Thornton answered, "It appears we may have a lead on who has stolen your spider. We require your... expertise to examine the evidence."

The doors slid open once, disgorging them into a cool, subterranean room.

"An autopsy suite!" Lady Amanda glanced about with interest, then pressed a hand against the metal wall. Her voice held a note of amazement. "I've heard of the novel cooling systems, water pipes providing a continuous flow of cold water to refrigerate bodies and prevent their decay."

"Slow their decay," he corrected. "We are one of the first facilities to install one. An important step to preserve evidence."

It was a far cry from the traditional dissection theater, one that was lined with wooden benches and tall windows with a table in the center from which the surgeon would perform his autopsy, often over several days as the stink rose, all the while describing with clinical detachment exactly what he found. Here they became intimately involved with those murder victims who caught the eye of the Queen's agents.

Three walls and the floor were lined with mint green tile. A large circular grate covered a drain in the floor. Much easier to keep clean. One wall contained a supply cabinet and a sink. Another wall contained metal doors covering six storage slots around which the pipes ran. Over the central table hung harsh, bright lamps, the better to ferret out evidence of wrongdoings.

Thornton crossed the room to one of the doors in the wall and twisted its handle, yanking it open. "Are you aware of the recent string of murders?"

"The gypsy murders?" Lady Amanda asked. "I am. There was mention of one in the *London Times* the other morning."

Lady Huntley shot him a grim look before turning to Amanda. "Often the most curious news is covered in a mere sentence and never expanded upon. This particular bit of news happens to be our concern."

Thornton tugged on a metal shelf within and the gurney rolled forth, its contents discreetly covered with a white cloth. "This is the sixth such murder. We suspect there will be yet more. Prior to this murder, we have had few leads. Lady Huntley and I have already examined this latest victim and made our observations. Now, we require yours."

"Mine?" Lady Amanda pressed a hand to her chest where leather buckles encircled her torso.

An interesting and practical alternative to a corset. He imagined it wouldn't take much time to remove such a bodice. He forced his gaze away; staring at her figure was improper, and her attire did not require his attention. This victim did. "Until now, the victims, all gypsy, have had their eyes removed with surgical precision, as if the perpetrator was deliberately practicing—unsuccessfully—a specific technique upon them. What that is, exactly, has been unclear."

Each death weighed heavily upon his mind. Sleep no longer came easily.

"But now?" Her eyes were fixed expectantly on the white sheet.

He pulled the cloth away from the victim's face. A disconcerting sight, a human face without eyes. But Lady Amanda didn't scream or turn away. Her face didn't take on a tell-tale green pallor. No bucket was necessary. Aside from a noticeable swallow, one might be convinced she dealt with such sights daily.

Thornton supposed she did. The cadavers in the dissection theater were often grislier displays. Still, her composure impressed him. "This time a different approach has been used," he said. "A technique much like the one you described in your communication to me. It uses fine gold threads—"

She looked up. "You *read* my letter?"

He had indeed. And recognized brilliance immediately. "Your work is promising."

"Yet you couldn't be bothered to respond?" Ire laced her voice. Fire flashed in her eyes. "Five years I've been working on this project. Struggling. Was it too much to expect a few words of encouragement? Of insight?"

It was indeed. Her approach to nerve repair so closely

paralleled his own research it had been unsettling to learn of another mind that traveled the same path. But his work was the property of the Crown, and protocol dictated he offer her no help. "Those of us who work for the Queen are not permitted open exchange of ideas with..."

Lady Amanda's eyes narrowed. "With a woman."

"Not at all." Lady Huntley spoke up, saving him from swallowing his foot. "How else do you explain my presence? Communication with anyone outside of Lister Laboratories is not permitted unless sanctioned by Queen Victoria herself. Our research ensures the safety of our shores and our citizens. At the time of your missive, you were not even an applicant to medical school. *Any* medical school."

In truth, any other person would have been immediately recruited. But her work had been dismissed, not because she was female, but because she was *ton*. As certain as the turning of the tides of the Thames, the daughter of a duke would marry and abandon any academic pursuits, no matter the raw talent she possessed. The Crown refused to invest time or funds educating such women.

That Lady Amanda matriculated at Lister University at all was... extraordinary.

"If not for your current status as student and the strings the Duke of Avesbury tugged on your behalf, you would not be here," Lady Huntley said bluntly.

Lady Amanda blinked, her expression incredulous.

Lady Huntley opened the supply cabinet doors and withdrew a simple linen apron. "Please examine the interior of the eye socket. You may recognize the work."

After a brief hesitation, Lady Amanda nodded, taking the apron, tying it about her neck and waist. "I'll do what I can." Pushing her sleeves above her elbows, she collected several tools and donned a pair of magnifying goggles before approaching the body. Delicately, she probed the empty sockets. Then she bent, peering closely. "This man was found last night?"

"Hours before my arrival on your doorstep," Thornton said.

"I see now the reason for your visit. The weave of the gold fibers is exactly what my neurachnid is programmed to accomplish. Except my spider is designed to work with *peripheral* nerves, not *cranial* nerves. There are significant differences between the two in terms of how they originate from the central nervous system. The nerve involved here is the oculomotor nerve, the third cranial nerve. It controls a key muscle for eye movement. It appears the murderer severed the oculomotor nerve in both eyes before attempting to reconnect it to..." Lady Amanda straightened, pushing the goggles onto her forehead with a bare forearm. A few dark locks escaped their pins to brush against the side of her face. Concerned eyes met his across the body, and she tipped her head in question. "To what?"

Behind her, Lady Huntley shook her head. Lady Amanda wasn't cleared for that information.

"That does seem to be the key question here," he said. "We have our suspicions, but would like to hear yours."

"Well," she began. "It certainly isn't punishment for what the gypsy has seen, as the newspapers speculate. Since someone went through the trouble of stealing my neurachnid, there must be a defined goal."

"Go on," he urged.

"Given the third cranial nerve originates in the mesencephalon, the midbrain, could this be an attempt to access its functions? Vision, hearing, temperature regulation?" Her cheeks pinkened but she did not glance away. If anything, her eyes darkened. "Arousal?"

Had her mind slid away from the cadaver? To him?

Yes, it appeared the attraction was mutual. Contrary to Black's hypothesis, neither the accident nor his former fiancée, Lady Anne, had castrated him. He'd simply needed time. How inconvenient that a student should reawaken such an overwhelming sense of need.

A problem that would have to be handled delicately given she was the daughter of the Duke of Avesbury.

"An impressive analysis," he said, offering her a rare compliment in his most professorial voice, hoping to dampen her interest, but her flush only deepened.

He was in trouble.

There was no denying her keen mind was part of her attraction. Students in their first year rarely knew anything about cranial nerves. It seemed Lady Amanda had made a considerable effort to self-educate before enrolling at Lister University. If he were a betting man, and he wasn't, he'd guess medical school to be a mere formality. The poor woman must be terminally bored in lectures.

But fortunately for him, in this case, she was far off the

mark. "But no one is certain, Lady Amanda," he said. Practice made the lie fall easily from his lips.

Without meeting his gaze, she began setting aside the steel tools. "How did he die? These injuries are awful, but given the care taken to cauterize the blood vessels of the eye, not fatal."

"Violence." He waved at the sheet. "Go ahead, look." He'd want to know as well, and it was best she realize the full extent of what they faced.

She lifted it clear of the body. And stared at the gaping hole in the thigh, the massive damage done to the femoral artery. The final—and fatal—injury.

"He was found tied to a chair," Thornton said. "Shot in the leg. He bled out."

"A horrible way to die." Only the slightest of tremors shook her voice as she spread the cloth back over the victim and turned to the sink.

He slid the gurney back into the wall. He and Lady Huntley waited silently, giving Lady Amanda a chance to collect herself. Contrary to common belief, scientists were not cold-blooded, emotionless creatures. It took effort and practice to suppress the instinctive reaction to blood, pain and death, to push aside the worry, the fear, and the horror so that one might *do* something to prevent such occurrences. In this particular case, murder, so that they might work to prevent it from happening again.

For a few minutes the only sound in the room was the sound of running water as Lady Amanda scrubbed her hands mercilessly. Finally, she turned around, drying her hands upon a linen towel and removing her apron. "There's one other feature of my neurachnid I should mention, one I did not divulge in my communications with other scientists."

"Yes," he urged.

"The procedure will not work on a fully anesthetized patient. During surgery, the neurachnid must constantly probe and test the nerve remnant to ensure a proper electrical connection is being established. To accomplish this, my spider contains a vial in its abdomen that injects, via a small needle, a mild nerve toxin that quiets, but does not fully numb, the nerve."

"A nerve agent?" he asked, his ears pricking. "Which one do you use?"

She shook her head. "Not one you are familiar with. My sister, Emily, concocted a novel agent. Unfortunately, the stolen device contained the last of the toxin."

"Have her make more," he said.

"I'm afraid it's not that simple." She looked pained. "My sister is... traveling."

"Contact her." He threw a hand in the air. "Have her send the formula. Our chemists will reproduce it." Enough dithering. This nerve agent needed to be analyzed. Immediately. It could be the answer to so very many of the issues they faced in his laboratory.

"Thornton." Lady Huntley's voice held a note of warning.

"I'll try," Lady Amanda said. Her fingers fiddled with one of her buckles as if this request presented an enormous obstacle.

What could possibly be the problem? He wanted to bark that she'd do more than try, but Lady Huntley shot him a pointed look, and so he bit his tongue. His assistant knew all too well why word of a novel nerve agent would spike his interest out of all proportion. He was willing to try anything that might dampen the persistent pain in his leg.

"Then I believe we're done here." He moved toward the ascension chamber and jammed his finger on the button.

"Without the neurachnid, the nerve agent is... pointless." She glanced at his leg.

She'd taken note of his brace the night he appeared at her house. Now she wondered if he had other uses in mind for the nerve agent, personal uses. Of course he did. But he hated that everyone was forever considering the state of his damaged leg. Hated the way they tiptoed around the topic.

He turned to face her. "Yes, it would be nice if somehow your device, your nerve agent could fix my injury, but know that I place the lives of other men, even gypsies, far above my own problem. We must stop this murderer." He paused. "The stolen spider was unable to accomplish the man's goal, a goal he will not abandon. At this point, we have no other leads. You will build another neurachnid, one that is better, one that can connect to the cranial nerves, one we will use to lure him out of hiding."

Her face fell. "Building another will take months."

"We don't have months," he said. "We may only have days before he chooses another victim upon which to experiment." God forbid the murderer succeed in his efforts before they could locate him.

Lady Amanda's eyes grew large. "We? I'd... I'd need resources. Assistance."

"You'll have them," Thornton promised, climbing into the ascension chamber, pressing one hand against the doors to hold them open as the women stepped inside. "As the newest member of my laboratory."

Somehow he'd keep his distance.

CHAPTER SEVEN

AMANA CLUTCHED HER leather satchel, her skin pricking with excitement as she stood before the enormous iron door. Mr. Black stood beside her, providing her with detailed instructions as to how she must enter and exit.

Two long days it had taken for this moment to arrive; time they didn't have. She'd done her best to gather what supplies she could to rebuild her spider, even starting on some of the simpler mechanisms in her laboratory under the watchful eyes of Rufus. She'd befriended a small gypsy boy, promising him unlimited clotted cream and scones in her kitchens if he could find Emily and deliver Amanda's letter.

"Now, slide your right index finger in that slot." The sound of Mr. Black's voice jolted her back to the present.

Amanda lifted her hand hesitantly. "It doesn't use blood as an identifier?"

Mr. Black said, "No. Only the epidermal ridges of your finger."

She complied, cringing as a soft, gelatinous substance oozed forth from several small pores in the metal cylinder surrounding her finger. There was a tiny jolt of electricity— enough to make her inhale sharply—and it was done.

"Oops." He smirked, passing her a handkerchief. "And galvanic skin conductance."

"You nasty man." She laughed. "You only wanted to see me jump."

"Caught," Mr. Black admitted.

She wiped her finger clean and entered the code he'd had her memorize earlier.

The screecher flashed green, and gears the size of dinner plates began to turn. With a click, a hiss and the sound of rushing air, the lock disengaged.

"Shall I set aside my paltry manners and allow you to open it yourself?" Mr. Black asked.

He was suppressing a grin. Laughing silently at her awe. Was her excitement that obvious? She supposed it was. She nodded, reaching for the bold, brass handle. The well-balanced door swung open with her slightest touch. Not a creak or a groan issued forth from its hinges.

The smell of acetic acid and neuroglycerol met her nose as Amanda stepped into the room—the best-equipped laboratory ever. Yet her eyes were immediately drawn to Thornton himself.

A protective leather apron covered his shirtsleeves. Thick gloves and brass goggles protected his hands and eyes.

He stood before a long bench, amid shelves of glassware and tubing, flasks and beakers filled with various liquids. A rack held vials containing an array of powders. His head was bent over the bench as he and another similarly dressed man manipulated an oddly shaped device beneath a high-powered microscope.

She would not gawk at Lord Thornton like a lovesick debutant, no matter that his very presence made her heart beat faster. She pulled her gaze away and examined the rest of the laboratory.

Windowless walls were covered in shelves from floor to ceiling. One wall held a variety of instruments. The usual balances. A tritrometer. A fuge. A large incubator in the corner. But the function of many was a mystery to her.

Two other technicians hurried about, one mixing solutions, and the other bent close over his own work. A scurrying, scratching sound and a distinctive scent drew her forward, and as she stepped about the bend in the L-shaped facility, a wall of wire cages met her eyes.

She estimated fifty-two. Inside each one was a rat. *Rattus norvegicus.* Though with all the wires and tubes and gauges sprouting forth from their heads and bodies, a novice might be forgiven for thinking them an altogether new species. Larger than mice, rats made better medical test subjects, but they were—thankfully—harder to find near her chicken coop. Known to hold grudges, they were also known for a tendency to bite. Hard.

Stepping closer, Amanda peered into the nearest cage. The rat lifted its hardware-laden head from its nest and peered back. A twist of fine wire coiled about its left ear. Enhanced hearing?

Suddenly, Mr. Black was at her elbow, clucking his tongue. "Not functioning so well, the acousticocepts, though the transmitter works fine once the patient recovers. Thornton keeps muttering something about needles not tracking right, but every time he fixes them, they go wonky again."

"Wonky?" She smiled. If there was a receiver, there must be a transmitter. She looked along the rack of cages, searching for the rat to which this one was paired.

"That's the scientific term." Mr. Black leaned against the wall. "That's what they're busy with over there." He jerked his head toward Thornton. "The sooner they fix the problem, the better."

"Thornton's invented an artificial ear that transmits sound?" She heard her own voice rise in excitement.

"Quick study, aren't you?" Mr. Black affected a leer. "Omitting the 'Lord' already, *Lady* Amanda?"

Her cheeks grew warm, but attributed it to the heavy jacket she still wore. She busied herself by pulling it from her shoulders and draping it over a nearby stool.

But Mr. Black wouldn't let it go. "His first name is Sebastian." His voice dropped to a low, conspiratorial level.

She cleared her throat, gathering what she could of her dignity. "Lord Sebastian Talbot, Earl of Thornton. I am aware of his name and status. I only thought to address him as Lady Huntley does. I had no intention of taking... liberties." She risked a glance in Thornton's direction as doubt crept in. "Should I not address him so? Are he and Lady Huntley...?"

Mr. Black threw his head back and laughed as if the very idea were absurd, but Lady Huntley was young and beautiful and perfectly suited to become the wife of an earl.

"No. No they aren't," he answered after he'd caught his breath. Laughter still danced in his eyes. "Lord Huntley was Thornton's closest friend. To court his widow..." Mr. Black shook his head. "No, Thornton's interests lie... elsewhere. Please accept my apologies, Lady Amanda. I only meant to tease. By all means, call him Thornton. Everyone who works in the laboratory does indeed do so. And, please, call me Black."

An interest elsewhere? She wondered what lucky woman had won his regard.

She nodded. "Very well."

"That should do it," Thornton said to his assistant. "Once the chamber fills with plasma, the perilymph helix should take care of the rest." He stepped back, pulling off his gloves and dropping them to the bench top. He pushed his goggles onto his forehead, the India rubber band twisting locks of hair in every direction. He looked every bit the brilliant, but mad, scientist. Quite the contrast from the proper gentleman who lectured on anatomy with hair carefully combed.

Passionate scientist or rigid gentleman? Or perhaps both? Each had their appeal. She pressed her lips together. Either way, it was not she who would win the chance to peel back the layers and discover the truth.

"Thornton," Black called. "Your newest assistant has security clearance."

Both men turned in her direction.

Thornton yanked off his goggles and ran a hand through his hair. "Lady Amanda Ravensdale, may I present my assistant Mr. Henri LaFevre. Mr. LaFevre, Lady Amanda, my newest student."

The blond man sketched a bow. "Henri, please," he said, his accent French. "This laboratory is most... informal." Henri's pale skin and red-rimmed eyes suggested long hours spent in the laboratory, but his light blue eyes were alive with keen intelligence. Thornton would work with no less.

"Then you must call me Amanda." She inclined her head politely.

"I'll leave you to your introductions," Black interjected. "As much as I wish to stay, duty calls." With a last wink, he strolled out the door.

"Lady Amanda brings a new project to our lab," Thornton said. "She will be indirectly involved with the acoustico work. Her original prototype, a clockwork spider designed to spin gold fibers to replace a nerve for an individual myomere, showed promise. Regrettably, it..." Thornton trailed off.

Was stolen?

Was used to commit a crime?

She jumped in. "It fails to maintain a connection with the individual muscle fibers. I'm convinced that with the right rare earth metal—"

"You can convert neurility into electricity and establish a

tighter bond," Henri finished, a wide grin on his face. "Brilliant!"

"Yes, exactly." Amanda grinned back. After years of solitary work—well, with only the company of Rufus and his hens—she at last had a colleague. Someone with the knowledge and experience to help her evaluate the rush of ideas that sprang to mind.

"Establishing a lasting connection to the myomere is only one of several problems to overcome," Thornton instructed Henri, all business. "The new spider must be able to connect to the *cranial* nerves, not just the peripheral nerves. Additionally, Lady Amanda has knowledge of a new nerve agent, one which quiets a nerve without numbing it."

"If I can obtain the formula," Amanda reminded him.

Henri clapped his hands together. "Most excellent. That would save our agents much agony and suffering when the acousticotransmitter is installed."

"The acousticotransmitter is implanted directly into an agent's ear?" she asked. To drill into the skull... Her stomach flipped. General anesthesia followed by effective pain management would be essential.

Henri nodded. "An artificial ear of sorts, one undetectable to the enemy, that both enhances the range of human hearing and can transmit sound to a receiver, allowing a second agent to listen."

"I'm afraid I must impose upon you, Henri," Thornton said, preventing Amanda from asking further questions.

"*Oui?*"

"While the acoustico work must continue apace, Lady

Amanda's project must take equal priority. Please orient her to the laboratory and its resources. Introduce her to our technicians, Samuel and Robert."

Thornton didn't look at her as he spoke. He barely acknowledged her physical presence. From the way he shifted away, it was clear he wished to be elsewhere.

Despite his earlier compliments, disappointment and self-doubt flooded her. She'd been under the impression that Thornton himself would mentor her, assist her in redesigning the neurachnid. Instead, he was foisting her upon another, interested only in her ability to help solve the mystery of the tortured and executed gypsies, a goal to which she felt equal commitment. It seemed she was nothing more to him than a tool to accomplish that end.

Henri smiled at her. "It will be a pleasure and an inspiration."

"Well, then." Thornton nodded, not meeting her eyes. "I'll leave you to it." He turned and limped to a door in the far wall. Amanda watched as he pressed his entire hand into a depression, and the door swung open.

"Another laboratory?" she asked, attempting to hide her disappointment.

"*Oui*. One that only he and Lady Huntley may enter. A top-level clearance research project that is, of late, making Thornton rather... tense."

Did the research conducted within have any particular connection to the recent gypsy deaths? Or perhaps the tension in his shoulders came from the sheer number of demands upon his time. Multiple research projects, teaching, a new student research assistant and, of course, the pressure brought by the Queen to assist in solving the gypsy murders.

Not to mention his pronounced limp.

"It seems his leg causes him considerable pain." She was careful not to phrase it as a question. "I understand airship pirates were involved." Would Henri tell the story to a new laboratory member?

Henri sighed. "A tale of bravery and heroism. Exciting and thrilling but for Lord Huntley's resulting death."

"Will you—can you tell it?"

"Truthfully, there is not much to tell. Thornton and Lord Huntley were traveling to a neurotech conference in Brussels via airship. Ropes appeared, seemingly from the clouds, and pirates dropped onto the deck." Henri glanced at the door behind which Thornton had disappeared. "The two men were caught in the middle of the attack. They attempted to escape, but as they jumped onto an evacuation glider, a cutlass caught Thornton's leg and Lord Huntley's throat. By the time they touched down, it was too late for Lord Huntley."

With the slice of a blade, Lady Huntley became a widow.

A moment of silence hung between them as Henri allowed the information to sink in. He continued, "This is how I met Thornton. They brought him to me, the only doctor able to concoct a potion to counteract the poison coating the pirate's cutlass. He was grateful and brought me here, a foreign physician, to work in this great laboratory."

Henri began to clear the surface of a workbench. "I am most fortunate."

Poison-coated cutlasses? Amanda's eyes were wide. She wanted to pry, to inquire about the specifics of Thornton's injury, but she'd already overstepped her place. His leg was not her affair. If she wished to help, focusing on her assigned task was the best route. She would work, as assigned, to make her neurachnid establish connections with cranial nerves and to locate her sister and the formula for the nerve agent. Perhaps it might ease his pain.

If, in her limited spare time, she managed to recreate the original spider's ability to repair peripheral somatic nerves, she would press Henri for details, and then, if warranted, broach the possibility of repairing Thornton's leg as well as her brother's.

She focused on the task at hand, lifting her satchel, unbuckling it, and drawing out its contents. "Along with what parts I could procure, I brought a copy of the original design sketches and all my notes." She spread out her sketches and waited as Henri fitted a monocle to one eye, lowered himself onto a laboratory stool, and bent close. Amanda held her breath. This was the first time anyone besides Ned had examined her clockwork mechanism.

"Clever, most clever," Henri murmured, scanning the pages, his finger marking his progress. Then, he abruptly stood and tucked his monocle into a waistcoat pocket.

"Did you notice any improvements I must make? Alterations?"

"Ah. Yes. A few. Come. We will discuss them as we

walk." He crossed the room, tossing aside his leather apron. He pulled on a coat and set a bowler hat atop his head. "A beautiful fall day. The sun shines. We must not waste it. Too many days I have not felt the sun on my face. England, the weather is so contrary."

"Where are we going?" Amanda pulled on her own jacket, her hat and, adjusting the bow beneath her chin, somewhat reluctantly followed Henri from the laboratory.

"To begin, a visit to Clockwork Corridor is called for," he announced. "These parts you have need of, they are not here. I take you to a favored horologist who has only gears of the highest quality. The gypsy Nicu will have what we need."

"Nicu Sindel?" Amanda asked in amazement, warming at the prospect of greeting an old mentor and friend.

He paused, lifting an eyebrow. "You know this man?"

"I do indeed." She took a deep breath, but stopped herself. A lady did not publicly claim gypsies as relatives. At least, not when she'd promised her father she wouldn't. Announcing that Nicu Sindel was none other than grandfather to her brother-in-law would generate more questions than Amanda was prepared to answer. "Years ago, his family camped on our estate. Nicu gave me—and my brother and sisters—our first lessons in clockwork."

"Ah, the inspiration for your spider." Henri nodded. "I take you then, to a reunion of great minds."

CHAPTER EIGHT

"MORE ANESTHESIA," Thornton instructed when the rat's foot twitched.

"Informality does not preclude basic manners," Lady Huntley stated.

She reminded him of his mother. He heaved an exasperated sigh. "Please."

With practiced movement, Lady Huntley placed the small rubber mask over nose and whiskers and turned a knob. With a hiss, the machine delivered a measured dose of chloroform. Enough to keep their small patient unconscious.

There was a faint snick of a lock disengaging. Only one other person besides Lady Huntley and himself had unlimited access to this inner laboratory. About to insert the lens with microtweezers, Thornton paused, his hand hovering over the rat, and addressed Black. "Any leads?" Deftly placing the lens, he nodded to Lady Huntley. The surgery was complete. Tomorrow, they would test focus length and aperture. Thornton set down the tweezers and turned around on the stool, giving his fellow agent full attention.

Black was their only hope of obtaining gypsy cooperation. With a gypsy mother, he had been raised in caravan, constantly on the move. While his heritage brought a variety of unusual skills to the agency, the ability to speak the Romani language and move about the gypsy camps with ease was why he had been tasked with solving these particular crimes.

"I did manage to find the victim's family. They're Romanichal gypsies camping on Putney Heath for the moment, but I was able to obtain little more than the victim's name," Black said.

"Which was?" Lady Huntley asked in a hushed voice.

"Marko Blythe. His family will be by soon to collect his remains if you've no objection."

"None," Thornton replied. "Perhaps his relatives will find some peace in their traditions."

British gypsies called themselves Romanichal. In the late fall, starting about this time of the year, various groups converged upon cities for the winter, many upon London's outskirts, including Putney Heath.

"A mother, a father, several brothers and sisters and not one of them can think of a single thing that would have made him a target of our murderer," Black said.

Gypsies moved about the edges of society, performing essential, menial everyday jobs—farm work, scrap metal hauling, horse trading. Only their clockwork skills attracted notice, their mechanical contraptions—available to all for the right price—were highly prized. For this, they were tolerated.

On the surface, gypsy life seemed unconnected to direct government concerns. But gypsies were known to go to great lengths to avoid the law and had the habit of slipping past borders unnoticed, habits that caused the government great concern as any number of unwanted foreigners might—for the right price—cross with them. Black was often tasked with looking into their movements.

Black sighed heavily. "In any case, we've nothing else to go on from that end. Best to focus on the..." He snapped his fingers. "Neuro spider contraption."

"Neurachnid," Lady Huntley offered.

"Exactly," Black said. "Where is she? Any progress?"

"Lady Amanda will be in later. It's been all of two days." Lady Huntley stood to shift her patient onto his cotton bedding where the rat would recover comfortably from general anesthesia. She latched the cage. "We can only claim her spare time after lectures and dissections."

"So that's a no?" Black asked.

"She's made progress," Thornton snapped.

The irritation in his voice surprised him, but Lady Amanda had been weighing on his mind. He felt guilty for not mentoring her directly, but with thoughts of her disturbing his dreams with activities that had nothing to do with research, he needed to keep his distance. Even in the lecture hall—especially in the lecture hall—he avoided eye contact. The pull he felt toward her might lead him to cross a line, and then what? He didn't want a woman in his life. At least, not one that would expect an offer of marriage. The life he led was incompatible with matrimony.

He continued, "Henri examined her plans and helped her assemble all the necessary parts and tools. It took her six months to build her last neurachnid. Let's give her the better part of a week, shall we?"

Black held up his hands. "You're the one running out of time with that leg of yours."

Thornton ground his teeth together. "Rushing the project will only result in an inferior device."

"The nerve calming solution might prove a problem," Lady Huntley added hesitantly. "The Duke of Avesbury has indicated that his daughter, Lady Emily, cannot be contacted."

"Ran off with a man, did she? And now they don't know where she is?" Black looked from her face to Thornton's. "What? I cracked that code among the *ton* long ago."

Thornton narrowed his eyes. Though Black was likely correct, it was not his place to speculate, but to solve the problem. "While we pursue that avenue, we'll try alternatives. Somnic may work." He named the very drug that kept his injured leg functioning.

"Is that wise?" Misgiving laced Black's voice.

"You doubt my ability to control my dosages?" he asked, his voice hard. He hated that Black felt the need to watch for addiction.

"What if I do?" Black countered, refusing to back down. "At some point, your condition will cause problems in the field. Pardon me if I watch for signs of imminent disaster."

"It won't come to that," Thornton bit out. He was a physician. He could manage his own care.

"How can you be certain?"

"Gentlemen," Lady Huntley snapped.

They glared at each other for a moment.

"Moving on," Black ground out. "None of the technicians have been able to figure out if, or when, the security for this inner laboratory was breached."

"So the murderer may be using his own eye technology?" Lady Huntley asked.

"Perhaps," Black answered. "Unless he leaves behind evidence either way, which would be unaccountably sloppy, we can't know for sure."

"Then we can do nothing but press forward on this project," Thornton said. "Continue to refine the acoustico work."

"Both of which are progressing quite nicely," Lady Huntley added. "Despite a number of small setbacks."

Thornton wouldn't quite classify the recent death of their agent as small, but he said nothing. "Another agent has volunteered. He's waiting now in the outer laboratory." The acousticotransmitter trials were too valuable to discontinue.

The device required surgery to connect it to branches of the eighth cranial nerve. Minor surgery, to be certain, but surgery nonetheless. As this nerve controlled both the vestibular system and the auditory system, there were occasional side effects. Tinnitus. Vertigo. Nystagmus. And no one escaped the three-day period of adjustment.

As such, most agents balked at the suggestion at first. But with German hostilities on the rise, the idea of having several agents listening in and ready to provide assistance at a moment's notice was appealing to all the Queen's agents.

Not only did the artificial ear provide superior hearing and the ability to send a signal to a nearby acousticocept— provided the needle issue remained resolved—it also provided an amazing sense of balance. The last agent had described it as providing the ability to stand on the edge of a wooden fence, like an alley cat. The enhanced hearing, Smith had insisted with a grin, would likewise provide him with an additional eight lives.

If only.

"Henri's prepping the agent volunteer in the other room as we speak," Lady Huntley said, bringing him back to the moment.

"We're done speaking." Thornton rose and crossed to the door. He slid his hand into the receptacle. Not only did you need clearance to enter, you needed it to exit.

"The Queen thinks it's best if you sit out the next mission," Black said, pitching his voice at a low level as he followed Thornton.

Thornton stiffened. He'd been expecting this. "I agree. I'll work the field only as necessary to wrap up the gyspy murders."

"Won't you miss it?" Black asked.

Working in the field? *Terribly*. "Does it matter?" Thornton answered. "I belong in the laboratory for now."

Black snorted. "Never thought I'd see you caged."

"It won't be forever." As if willing it could make it so. Thornton didn't look behind to see if Black agreed.

WHEN THE CRANK HACKNEY ARRIVED, Mother and Olivia were paying calls, and Amanda was at school. Father had left hours ago and was likely closeted in some windowless room with officials, protecting Queen and country.

This meant no one left behind dared voice objection to Ned's odd departure in a public form of conveyance not used by future dukes. With a twist of his wrist, he increased the torque on his mechanical leg braces.

He hated them, these artificial legs. Hated the clunkiness of his movements, the steam that billowed forth, his dependence on a fuel source. As much as he loved his automatons, he did not wish to be one. And these damned legs kept him from his greatest desire: Georgina.

His heavy, metallic footsteps rang out as he clanged down the broad steps to the street. The driver, hearing his approach, leapt down from his seat. With great bulky arms, he began to wind the spring tight.

Crank hackneys had sprung up all over London. With no horse to feed or water, a driver strong enough to use his own muscles to power such a conveyance—hour after hour, day after day—soon felt the effects of pure profit. So much so that they'd become quite the dandies. Sleeveless shirts under double-breasted leather vests to show off their bulging arms. Form-fitting, black pants to advertise thick, strong thighs built by the constant work of shoving home the hackney's braking mechanism.

Ned tore envious eyes away and glanced up at the gray sky. Crank vehicles and clockwork horses had decreased the quantity of horse droppings in London. Now, if only something could be done about the coal soot and the ever-thickening sulfurous fogs.

A pea-souper was in the making. Tonight or tomorrow, dirigibles would be grounded. He pulled up his muffler to keep from inhaling the particles that hung in the air. Soon the smog would become unbearable, and the *ton* would retreat to their country estates. As soon as harvest was complete and the great hulking farm machines were heaved into stone barns for winter storage.

The hackney door swung open, and Tony leaned forward to call a greeting, making no offer to help Ned climb aboard. Despite the mechanical legs, his body was in topnotch form. Thanks to Tony.

Tony had been at Ned's side for five long years now, the closest thing Ned had to a friend. His therapist, the man in charge of keeping his leg muscles from atrophying, knew him far, far better than any nurse, nanny or tutor. How could he not, given that every intimate, minute detail of his health and hygiene had once required Tony's assistance?

But not today.

Ned hauled himself into the hackney and dialed down his legs.

"Any problems?" Tony tipped his head at the townhouse as the hackney jerked forward.

"None."

From the way Tony's foot shook, the man was fighting a bad case of nerves, but not Ned. The nerves that brought him forth this day were long past calming. They were all but dead.

He'd spent yesterday putting his affairs in order, leaving one note for his family, another for Amanda. If the doctor offered, Ned would proceed with the surgery immediately.

He leaned back and closed his eyes, forcing himself into a model of genteel repose. After some time, an assault on his nose snapped him from his trance. Scents of boiling tripe, melting tallow and slaughterhouse cast offs announced the East End. Twisting through crooked streets, they came to an abrupt stop at a Georgian-terraced house, one which had long since left its good days behind. Soot covered the brick surface. Drunken shutters hung from lower windows. The front door stood ajar.

A hollow-eyed man stared at them from the street corner as a weary, hunch-backed woman carried a basket of wilted flowers. Others moved about, in and out of uneasy shadows cast by buildings that only managed to remain standing by propping each other up.

A sinking feeling tugged at Ned's stomach, but he twisted the knob of his artificial cage legs. He climbed awkwardly from the hackney and clomped across the road, its surface slick with slime.

Tony pushed the door wide. "It's empty!"

"He's gone?" Ned shoved past him and stepped into the foyer.

"I was here. Four days ago." Tony waved his arms about, gesticulating wildly as only an Italian could. "This room was filled when I dropped off the spider."

Dr. Millhouse had been called away, but left a note instructing Tony where to secure the neurachnid. The doctor had later sent a note praising the device, expressing his complete confidence in a good surgical outcome and designating the day and time Lord Ned was to arrive.

They'd been hoodwinked.

"It was filled with bottles and steel instruments. Medical equipment." Tony raged on. "An operating table right there. I swear it."

Ned laid a hand on Tony's shoulder, quieting him. "We'll find him," Ned said, turning back.

He made every effort to project the quiet assurance of a gentleman, when, in fact, he felt anything but. Frustration. Anger. A need for revenge. All swirled around together. Guilt and regret followed swiftly.

A woman with sunken, black-rimmed eyes and tattered, soot-stained clothes passed.

"You... missus," he called, uncertain how to address such a creature.

Her pallid face turned upward.

"There was a doctor here," he began. "Dr. Millhouse. Any chance you know where the good doctor went?"

She stared back, unresponsive.

Ned dug in his pocket and produced a silver coin.

A smile—one with but a scattering of rotted teeth— formed on her face as the coin disappeared into the folds of her skirts. "Weren't good. Nor a doctor. Never fixed no one. Broke 'em's more like. Packed up 'n left. No idea where. Three days past?"

Three days.

"Broke?" Tony repeated. His eyes all but bulged as he glanced at Ned.

She nodded. "People went in. Din't come out."

Ned frowned, wanting to press for more, but interested faces were eyeing his legs, trying to decide if they were a weakness or a strength. Some shifted out of the shadows, oozing in their direction. "Let's go," he said, climbing quickly into the crank hackney. Once seated, Ned rapped on the roof, jerking them into motion. "We'll need to track Dr. Millhouse," he stated. He wanted—needed—that spider back. Amanda had counseled patience. He should have listened. "I'll hire a private investigator."

"I'll find my original contacts. See what they know." Tony hung his head. "I'm sorry."

"It was a risk," Ned said. "I knew that when I asked you to find a doctor. I take all responsibility." The only thing that kept him from howling like a caged beast was the knowledge that Lord Thornton had invaded his sister's life and dragged her into his laboratory, demanding she build a new and better neurachnid.

Amanda would have killed him. Still would if she found out he was the one who'd cracked the combination of her laboratory door to hand her precious spider over to a man he didn't know on a mere promise.

But if there was no surgery—and soon—Georgina would be married, and life would no longer be worth living.

CHAPTER NINE

WITH A SUDDEN start Amanda sat upright, horrified to realize she'd fallen asleep on top of her notes in the laboratory—Thornton's laboratory. She'd been so very tired. After too many late nights studying into the early morning hours, frustration finally gave way to exhaustion. She'd been simply too tired to identify the problem with the neurachnid. Only a moment's rest, she'd promised herself, a moment to close her eyes and rest her mind. Instead, she'd ended up napping.

Leaning closely to the side of the polished incubator, she checked her reflection. Her cheek was red and imprinted with the lace pattern of her sleeve. Several strands of hair had pulled free, and the scooped neck of her bodice had shifted.

She clapped a hand to her chest, adjusting her neckline and tucking the escaped locks behind her ears, then, her face burning with embarrassment, glanced discreetly across the room, praying none but the nearby rats had been provided with an interesting view.

Henri's coat was gone. She'd chastise him later about leaving her to sleep the evening away on a workbench.

In the far corner, Thornton's human volunteer, now with advanced hearing, slept on a cot. Earlier she'd seen the man clutch a bed pan to his chest, moaning as his eyes rolled backward. Now he slept the sleep of the heavily sedated. Samuel, one of the laboratory technicians, sat in a nearby chair, head bent in slumber over a loosely clutched book.

She pulled out her pocket watch and gasped. Quite some time had passed since she'd closed her eyes. It was nearly midnight.

Rats moved about their cages with a soft rustle, going about their nocturnal business, gnawing on seeds. Her own stomach complained in sympathy, but she couldn't leave the laboratory yet. Already, mental clarity was returning, and she felt the sharp edge of a breakthrough scraping her mind.

She spun on the laboratory stool to face her research notes and grabbed a fresh sheet of paper. Her hand moved as if of its own accord, sketching out the image forming in her mind. She added lines and notes and details as to which pins, gears, springs and guards to use. Several minutes passed before she set down her pencil and sat back to stare at the plans for a new—and better—neurachnid before her.

It just might work. Satisfaction tugged her lips into a small smile. Wait. She tipped her head and sighed. In that position, the reaper guard might fail to catch. Unless she—

"No. That won't work." Thornton's voice wrapped

around her, deep and dark. More than just the thought forming in her mind melted.

She froze. She'd been so lost in thought that she'd failed to note his approach. Despite his limp, the man moved as quietly as a panther on the hunt.

For all the long hours she'd spent in his laboratory over the past few days, she'd seen precious little of the renowned Thornton outside the lecture hall. Now, here he was, standing so close she could feel his body heat. So close that as he reached past her to place a finger to her sketch, his arm brushed hers and a thrill ran through her, settling low inside.

She risked a glance, then found herself staring. The shadow of a beard darkened his jaw. Wild dark curls fell across his forehead. Wide, soft lips pursed in thought. Her heart tripped before picking up its pace, disregarding her mind's insistence that theirs was a purely professional relationship. Would that it was her right to reach out, to run her fingers over his rough beard and into the tangle of that hair, to pull those lips to her own.

Her breath caught, and she dragged her gaze away. "What won't?" she asked. They were colleagues, that was all.

Focusing on the benchtop didn't help. Thornton's shirtsleeves were rolled back, exposing a scattering of dark hairs across strong forearms. As his large hand snatched up her abandoned pencil and began to modify her design, joints and tendons and muscles flexed and shifted in a strangely alluring manner.

She closed her eyes and inhaled deeply, forcing much needed air past the struts of her corset and into her lungs.

Then, with a large quantity of willpower, she opened her eyes and began to objectively evaluate his alterations and his comments.

"If you move this spring and connect it to this gear instead..." He went on at length, pinpointing every issue before solving it with ease.

The small, simple adjustments would allow the thoracic gears to turn unimpeded and increase the angle to which the spinnerets could bend as they wove. The hardest to reach parts of the central nervous system would now be reachable. The man was breathtakingly brilliant, his mind an intricate seduction. She wanted... what she could not have. Time to leave. Flee.

"I'll start on the changes tomorrow." Amanda looked up. "Thank you." The words fell automatically from her lips, but came out as a whisper.

For his expression was unreadable, his eyes different somehow. Darker. More liquid. Then he blinked and addressed his next words to a space over her left shoulder. "I'd like to apologize," he said, straightening. "For the public set down I gave you that first day in class. A knee jerk reaction, I'm afraid, when one works too secretively for too long. To discover an untrained student's work might very well hold the key to solving a long-standing problem..." He cleared his throat. "This neurachnid, along with the nerve agent, might very well improve the acousticocept surgical process and resultant outcome." He waved his hand over the papers. "You've done impressive work here."

Amanda nodded, accepting both the apology and the

compliment. She had a feeling he rarely delivered either. She swallowed, gathered her nerves and pressed her advantage. "Working together, we might well be able to speed the process."

He nodded. "I've not been much of a mentor, I'm aware." He glanced at the door to his inner laboratory. "There's been a pressing issue with other research... but now, I find I have some time."

Her heart sank. He wasn't here of his own accord. At best, her project was a way to fill his free time. At worst, Lady Huntley had badgered him into fulfilling his duty toward his student. Possibly both. Either way, she'd best set her girlish infatuations aside and focus on the task at hand. She directed her words to the sketches before her. "I'd quite welcome the assistance."

"There's one more thing." His voice held a note of warning.

She held her breath.

"Mr. Simon Sommersby appeared in my office yesterday, petitioning me for a place in my laboratory."

Amanda's jaw tensed. Not only had she won a coveted laboratory position, she spent many long hours in here, out of Simon's view, out of his reach. With so many laboratories to choose from, why this one? Classic male territorialism. Simon perceived Thornton as competition for her hand. Perhaps he would be right to worry, if only his perceived opponent demonstrated any interest. Both of them frustrated her to no end.

Thornton gave her a significant look. "It seems he thinks

I have need of a nerve calming agent. I realize that the two of you have something of a personal relationship—"

"We've made no promises," she objected, then, her face flushing, realized his true concern. With wide eyes, Amanda shook her head. "I've told him nothing." Simon knew of her work. They'd discussed their respective research interests in vague terms over tea, but nothing specific. "He knows only of my interest in using clockwork devices to repair nerves, nothing more."

His eyebrows rose. "Really? Interesting."

Her stomach clenched into a tight knot. There she'd sat, wondering if such a man could be romantically interested in her, quite possibly jealous of Simon, and all the while he'd actually been wondering if she was betraying him, leaking laboratory secrets. Then a thought occurred to her. "Your... your injury is common knowledge. Perhaps—"

"Yes, perhaps." Thornton rolled down his cuffs and lifted his coat from a nearby stool. "Now, the hour is late," he said, once again all stiff formality. "I'll escort you to your carriage."

They walked in uncomfortable silence down the stone-paved hallway, the only sound the rhythmic tap of his cane, his movements easy despite the small hitch in his step.

Amanda had to ask. "Has there been any progress on the gypsy murders?" She waited as his lips twisted in consideration. Would he still tell her? Still include her in the investigations?

"None," he said. "Though I'm afraid it's only a matter of time before another victim is found, Black works diligently to make it otherwise." His steps paused and he turned a thoughtful stare upon her, then seemed to come to some kind of decision. "Black's mother is gypsy. He was raised in a caravan, around campfires. He speaks Romani. If there is anything to be learned among them, Black is our best chance to ferret it out."

"Gypsy," she repeated. That would explain his dark, swarthy looks and the distinct air that he was anything but a gentleman.

"Do you have a problem with that?" Thornton's eyes grew hard as they searched her face.

"No! Not at all." But this new knowledge left her no choice. She had to tell him, before Black discovered her family's secret and told Thornton himself. She would not have him looking upon her with suspicion again. She desired his respect. "There's something you need to know, something you must keep in the utmost of confidences."

With so many lives at stake, it was past time to break her promise by telling Thornton.

His eyes narrowed, promising nothing. "Tell me."

"My sister, Emily, eloped some months ago. With a gypsy. A childhood friend named Luca."

The great country estates of the peerage relied heavily upon gypsy labor and their finesse with clockwork-driven machinery. Most *ton* children were forbidden to visit their camps, to befriend the gypsies, but Father had waved aside Mother's concerns. Once merely a distant relative of the former duke with no expectation of inheriting the title, Father had not been raised as an indulged elite. He'd worked

—at the docks, in the fields, in trade—and believed in personal industry. As such, Amanda, her brother, and two sisters had been actively encouraged to seek out knowledge wherever it resided, and the gypsies on their country estate had had much to offer.

His permissiveness—resulting in Emily's elopement—was now the source of a deep rift and a festering argument between her parents.

Emily's actions, were they to become publicly known, would have deep and lasting social ramifications for Amanda's family. Mother had great marital aspirations for her remaining daughters, particularly Olivia. Even Ned needed to marry well, and the pool of acceptable brides was already greatly reduced due to his injuries. Father's post was a political one, easily lost to social opinion. No, Emily's marriage to a gypsy needed to remain a secret from society.

"Emily does not wish me to visit," Amanda said. "I don't know her whereabouts. We communicate by letter, one gypsy after another passing along our messages, hand to hand. Sometimes days pass, sometimes weeks, before a letter returns. I've written her about the formula, but," she shook her head, "I've had no response yet."

"So Lady Emily could be anywhere." Thornton's mouth was a grim line.

"Yes. But Nicu Sindel, the gypsy who often sets up shop in Clockwork Corridor? He is my brother-in-law's grandfather."

"And would likely know Lady Emily's whereabouts,"

Thornton concluded, his eyes lighting with interest. "Henri took you to his caravan for parts."

Amanda nodded. "He did."

Nicu had folded Amanda in his arms, welcoming her like family, inquiring about her own. Emily was fine, more than fine, he'd whispered in her ear. Yet when she'd discreetly inquired as to her sister's whereabouts, Nicu shook his head. He'd make certain Emily knew of Amanda's desire to visit, but a gypsy guarded privacy above all else. Emily herself would have to extend the invitation. Amanda might be family, but she was also *gadji*—an outsider.

She told Thornton as much, then finished, "Every day I go to Clockwork Corridor, but Nicu has yet to return. Perhaps Black can help?"

"Of course." Thornton began to walk down the hallway once more. Faster, as if eager to be rid of her. "I'll set him to it. Immediately."

At this speed, his limp was far more pronounced, the earlier ease of his steps, gone. The man's leg hurt him far more than he was willing to admit. As a physician, he would be using medication in addition to the brace, but there was more to be done. She had studied traditional Oriental pressure points and thought they might provide him with some relief.

She grew warm at the thought of wrapping her hands around the man's leg and thought better of extending the invitation.

Together, they stepped out of Lister Laboratories onto

pavement. A line of stately gas lamps attempted to cut through the gathering fog.

She made one last attempt to ask. "Does it hurt?"

"Hurt?" he asked.

"Your leg."

He sighed. "You're not going to let this go, are you?"

She waited.

"Yes, it hurts. With every step, a thousand tiny needles pierce my foot." A one-shouldered shrug. "The drug keeps the damaged nerve from deteriorating further. It dulls the needles. The brace stabilizes the muscle damage already done. What is there to do but carry on?"

Carry on, indeed. Build a better neurachnid and obtain the formula for her sister's nerve agent. If that could be accomplished, many problems might be solved.

They turned a corner and her waiting steam coach came into view.

"Tomorrow, we will redouble our efforts," he said. "I will set aside the entire afternoon to work with you on your project."

Amanda's heart leapt. "That's most generous of you." Did that mean she was forgiven for her secrets, her suitor and her questions?

"It's the least a mentor should do." Thornton handed her into the carriage. "Good night, Lady Amanda," he said, and firmly closed the door, giving her no chance to reply.

Thornton turned and strode back in the direction of the laboratory, leaning a bit more heavily on his cane. Did the man ever rest? For she had no doubt he would be summoning Black to his office in the small hours of the night to send him in pursuit of Nicu Sindel and his granddaughter-in-law, Lady Emily.

IT WAS NEARLY midnight when Wasp turned slowly around, eyeballing the warehouse. It would do for the interim. Moving was such an inconvenience, but what choice had there been? Wasp had known the lordling and his minion would not give up easily.

So now only the essentials, easily carried, remained.

A bioluminescent lamp hung from a pulley over an old door propped on two barrels. An assortment of ropes and straps rested on its surface. It would serve, though the easy adjustments provided by the mechanized operating table would be missed.

A nearby crate held the required tools. A rust-stained enamel ewer and basin provided a place to scrub. A copper cauldron hung from a cast iron hook. Underneath, a gas jet burned, the water slowly coming to boil, though it almost seemed a waste of time, sterilizing the tools, when the patient was unlikely to survive the surgery.

It was time to get back to business.

Lifting the spider from a small, velvet-lined case, Wasp peered at the glass vial encased within the abdomen. Nearly all the numbing agent was gone. Certainly not enough for the next patient. Wasp couldn't afford to have it chemically analyzed, but more was needed.

Pain. Screaming. There were ways to deal with that.

But the extreme delicacy of the weaving process made the formula a key part of the procedure. Most nerve agents paralyzed the nerve. This one only calmed the damaged root allowing the spider to test the efficacy of the newly woven nerve, making minute changes to the final structure before completing its task.

Fortunately, the source of this nerve toxin had been located with relative ease and a delivery was due momentarily.

There was a rapping at the door. That should be it now.

Wasp crossed to the thick, wooden door, sliding it open a crack. A gypsy, one who looked to be about seventeen years of age, stood on the threshold. "You have it?"

He pulled a small vial from his pocket. The liquid had a greenish cast, similar to that inside the spider. Excellent.

"Come in," Wasp pushed the door wider.

Warily, the gypsy stepped just over the threshold, holding the vial tight. "Five pounds."

"Five! I only agreed to four."

"Five." Dark brown eyes blazed back. Blue would have been better, but there was no need to be choosey.

"Fine," Wasp sighed, holding out a hand as if about to drop a pile of coins into the gypsy's palm.

As the young man handed over the vial, Wasp pressed a hand—and the device strapped to it—against the gypsy's chest, directly over the heart. A bolt of electricity discharged, shock barely registering on the man's face as he slid bonelessly to the floor.

CHAPTER TEN

S ATURDAY AFTERNOON, Olivia lifted the calling card from the silver salver Burton presented. "Mr. Simon Sommersby," she announced, casting a sly sidelong look at her.

"Thank goodness," Amanda muttered. Mother was indisposed and Ned had grown moody, sulky and uncommonly melancholy as negotiations for Georgina's engagement progressed. Today, he'd refused to leave his room, leaving her alone to endure Olivia's brainless chatter over tea. She raised her voice. "Please show him in, Burton."

The butler rolled away to retrieve her visitor.

Olivia planted herself on a nearby chair. "This is the tenth time he's come to call."

"You're counting?" Amanda eyed her sister with suspicion. It had been a long time since her sister had taken any interest in her life.

"Of course. His intentions are quite clear, and he is a gentleman, if untitled. Tell me, dearest sister, has he proposed yet? When he does, will you accept?"

"That is yet to be determined," Amanda replied. But it wasn't. Not really. Simon was her only suitor. Unless another gentleman took an interest, and soon. She tried hard to envision Thornton in that role and failed.

Thornton had made it quite clear he wouldn't be pursuing her. Nevertheless, Simon was jealous, and if she wished to advance in medical school, she needed to encourage his affections before they were diverted elsewhere.

Married within the year.

One of two conditions Father had placed upon his agreement to allow her to attend medical school. She'd already broken the second, by telling Thornton about Emily, but perhaps that wouldn't count, provided Black was able to locate her with utmost discretion.

"Carlton believes a husband such as Mr. Sommersby would provide you with respectability. An unmarried woman acting as a physician is a breech of propriety."

Amanda gaped at her sister. *Carlton approved?* Words failed her. And then it was too late to reply.

Simon crossed the parlor and bent, kissing the air above her glove. "Lady Amanda." He turned and bowed again. "Lady Olivia."

Olivia flashed him a smile, then rose in a graceful rustle of ruffles. Crossing to the speaking tube, she pushed a button. "Fresh tea, Steam Mary, and an abundance of cream cakes."

Carlton approved? Well, that certainly explained Olivia's reformed attitude, and Amanda's sudden urge to toss Simon out the front door. But that would be cutting off the nose to spite the face. No. Better to rid herself of a problematic sister.

Observation of patterns was a strength any scientist possessed. Given that Olivia had remained for tea the past nine times Simon visited, Amanda employed her not-so-secret weapon. She lifted her copy of *Gray's Anatomy* from the settee beside her and smiled invitingly at Simon. "Shall we begin with the muscles of the upper or lower extremity?"

"Oh, dear." Olivia snapped open her fan and waved it at her now bloodless face. Scarlet feathers struggled to keep pace with the speed of her flapping wrist.

Perhaps the words *muscle* and *extremity* were too much. Amanda certainly hoped so.

Simon caught Olivia's elbow as she swayed. "Are you quite all right, Lady Olivia? Shall I call for a footman?"

She simpered. "I'm afraid I've a most delicate constitution, and topics such as...." There went the feathers again. "I must go."

Enough with the theatrics. "If you will excuse us then, Olivia," Amanda said, "we've much to study for the upcoming exam. There are more than twenty muscles in the human arm and numerous blood vessels."

Olivia swallowed hard, yet clung to protocol. "A chaperone?"

"We'll leave the door open," Amanda said.

"Very well," Olivia said, then fled.

"Not the nicest way of dismissing a sibling, but effective." Simon's knowing smile showed off his perfect teeth as he settled onto the settee beside Amanda, his leg brushing against her skirts.

She allowed it. It was, after all, the point of choosing a seat built for two.

"Shall we begin with the rotator cuff?" Simon asked, leaning closer yet to view the book on her lap. The warmth that rolled off of him smelled of soap and starch. All perfectly pleasant. What other man was willing to court her by reviewing the origins and insertions of various muscles?

Not a one.

Why, then, could she not push away thoughts of another man?

Simon dropped a finger on the page, his arm pressing against hers. "The supraspinatus abducts the arm and is innervated by the suprascapular nerve. Its origin is the—"

A clanging at the door announced the arrival of the roving table. RT rolled to a stop before them emitting a soft hiss as he powered down. The tea tray, laden with cream cakes, scones and cucumber sandwiches, beckoned.

"Perhaps we should continue after tea?" Amanda asked, marking their place in the book.

"Very well," Simon agreed, moving not an inch from her side.

As she poured, a topic nagging at the back of her mind demanded to be broached. "Lord Thornton informs me that you wish to work in his laboratory. I'd no idea you were interested in developing novel nerve agents. What happened to your interest in vitreous humor?"

Though she could think of many practical uses for developing an artificial vitreous humor—the colorless gel that filled the back part of the eye—she wasn't convinced there was a reason to determine the specific chemical reaction that led the gel to liquefy under certain pathological conditions.

"Professor Stonington declined to support my project." He shrugged. "So I thought, given the long hours you now spend in Lord Thornton's laboratory, it might be nice to work together."

"Except neither his work nor mine encompass nerve agents. Wherever did you get that impression?" Amanda tried to project innocent curiosity into her voice, but acting was not one of her talents.

"No?" Something flickered in Simon's brown eyes. "I could have sworn a classmate mentioned something to that effect. I was hoping I might find a new chemistry project." He leaned closer, and his blond hair fell across his forehead. "Tell me, how were *you* so fortunate as to gain entry to his laboratory? Especially given how exasperated he seemed by your question that first day."

"Yes, well." Amanda sat back and sipped her tea, stalling. Black had warned her she could no longer discuss her spider. She cast about for a likely explanation. "Lord Thornton was rather... forced into accepting me as a research assistant. I became eligible when... well... the last anatomy exam, I—"

"Top student in anatomy." Simon sat back. "I should

have known." Except, instead of looking proud, he looked wounded. Some men had such fragile egos. "Will you talk to Lord Thornton on my behalf?" he pleaded.

Amanda set down her teacup. "I don't think he's interested in taking on another student, Simon, regardless of the project. Besides, I've only just begun working in his laboratory. I don't have any influence."

Simon's face fell. "You'll put in a good word, right?"

"I will," she agreed.

But she wouldn't. Working in Thornton's laboratory was too precious. She intended to hug it tight, not to share it. Even if that made her an awful person. Simon would have claim on enough of her attention if—when—they married.

"I'm sorry. I guess the idea of you spending so much time with Lord Thornton when you could be at my side, makes me realize how jealous I am of your free time. There's so very little of it."

Her lips parted. *Jealous?* Covetous of her dowry or her position in Thornton's laboratory perhaps, but not jealous of her time. She tilted her head and studied him, somewhat suspicious, but he seemed serious. "No need to feel so, Simon." She smiled her reassurance. There wasn't. Thornton was all that was professional. "I spend most of my time working alone, under the supervision of another research assistant."

"Well, then," he said, sounding mollified, "at least tell me what projects the great Lord Thornton is working on in his laboratory. I hear he's developing cranial nerve prosthetics?"

Amanda's brow furrowed. It was uncanny, the degree to which Simon seemed informed about Thornton's work. Then again, if he'd been to Thornton's office seeking out a research position, Simon would have to arrive prepared. Nothing he'd said spoke to any deeper knowledge than one could arrive at by reading Thornton's published papers or listening to *ton* gossip about his injury. "Simon, I'm sorry. If you could only see the confidentiality papers I signed. I'm afraid I can't tell you anything about Lord Thornton's laboratory or his research."

He grinned. "So the man's a spy, an agent for the Queen?" His voice was light and teasing. "Do promise not to let him take you out into the field, on dangerous assignments."

"Don't be absurd." Amanda laughed. "Lord Thornton is merely a research scientist. At most, the Queen reserves first right to any of his inventions."

He might surgically implant his invention into an agent's ear, but neither that nor consulting for the Crown on various murder investigations as a medical scientist made the man a spy. Now, Black, *he* could very well be a spy. Except he answered to Thornton. Which made Thornton... No. Not possible.

Was it?

Simon reached out and lifted her hand. His palm was warm and soft as he stroked his thumb across the surface of her knuckles.

She pushed Thornton from her mind and looked up into his eyes, doing her best to appear charmed. His eyes were so bright, so earnest. Was he about to propose? Would she accept?

Please, not today. She wasn't ready to commit to marriage. Not just yet.

"What I really want is your permission to formally court you. To know I have a right to a portion of your time. Promise me a waltz at every ball, a drive in the park every Sunday afternoon while the weather holds." Simon's thumb picked up its pace while he waited for her answer, brushing across the surface of her hand.

She should be pleased. This had been today's goal, had it not, to encourage his pursuit?

Simon shifted closer, the length of his leg pressing against hers. "I want to take tea together. Regularly. In this parlor. Alone." The fine golden hairs of his beard were visible at this range. He lifted his hand to cup her jaw. A kiss was imminent.

She'd allow it. If she agreed to marry him, kissing would be a regular event. Best to determine if his initial advances were tolerable, for his lips were rather thin.

Other lips rose to mind. But as professor and mentor, he was forbidden. Nor had he given the slightest indication that he was interested in anything more than her mind.

That, perhaps, was one of his biggest draws.

Parting her lips, she leaned forward in invitation, and Simon covered her lips with his. Unexceptional, but adequate, she decided. Pulling away, she made an attempt at a demure nod and a coy smile. "Of course I welcome your attentions, Simon."

Who could be better for her than a peer who was also a future physician? With this first declaration of intent, they could finally begin to negotiate the terms of any relationship their future might hold.

Why, then, did her stomach hurt?

CHAPTER ELEVEN

THE FEW TIMES THORNTON had taken on a student he'd been the one giving the orders. Yet, for the second day, he sat beside Lady Amanda in *his* laboratory taking orders from his student, helping *her* assemble the complicated network of gears, pins and springs.

Working with such a quick mind was pure intellectual pleasure. Together, they'd sunk deeply into the hands-on technical work of building the new neurachnid while continuing to verbally explore more improvements, often finishing each other's thoughts. Progress was swift, and at this speed, they should have a working neurachnid by week's end.

Not since he'd collaborated with John Huntley had he worked so seamlessly with another. The memory brought pain, like a wound that would not heal. Much like his leg. He pushed the thought away into a deep corner of his mind. He had no wish to explore it further.

Amazing, what she'd been able to accomplish on her own. A shame her formal training had been delayed so many years. The blame was partially his. Had he not ignored the missive she'd sent some two years past, this neurachnid might already be operational. Thornton regretted losing even the few days Lady Amanda had worked in his laboratory. Though she'd been in Henri's capable hands, he should have expressed more immediate interest in this project.

He set down his tools and turned to look at Lady Amanda. Really look at her. Not only was she brilliant, she was beautiful. Even though she wore a stained canvas apron and clockwork grease covered her long, elegant fingers. Even though strands of dark hair floated about her face, catching on magnification goggles that made her eyes seem twice their normal size. As she reached for one tool after another, tweaking and adjusting the tiny creature's mechanized legs, she bit her lip in intense concentration, and Thornton lost all interest in the task before him.

All he wanted at this moment was to reach out with his thumb and forefinger to tug her lower lip free from those teeth. His hand twitched as he imagined cupping her jaw, drawing her face across the space that separated them and claiming those soft, pink lips with his own crushing need.

His mind screamed that this was a horrible idea, a clear abuse of his position. Another, much lower portion of his anatomy disagreed, urging him to take immediate action.

This wasn't like him. It had been a long, long time since he'd felt such an uncontrollable rush of desire. So long, in fact, that he'd allowed his mother to arrange a suitable marriage to one Lady Anne Grimwauld, a match that had fulfilled everyone's expectations until his injury. At which point Lady Anne had cried off. It seemed she had received a more enticing offer, one from an uninjured viscount.

Marriage, he'd decided, could wait. There were other ways to meet basic, biological urges, but not with the woman beside him. No matter the inviting glances she threw him, her eyes dilated with desire. No matter the racing pulse at her throat when he returned her stare. No matter the dark satisfaction his primitive brain found in eliciting such reactions.

What reaction might a simple touch unleash?

But not only was she his student, she was the innocent daughter of a duke, a duke who had the ear of the Queen. A duke who, as Thornton's superior, had ordered him to report to his side this very evening. It seemed Lady Amanda's father, citing his family's involvement, had been granted oversight of the gypsy murders.

Thornton closed his eyes to block temptation from view, but her very image was burned into his retinas.

In his mind's eye, he could still visualize her as she donned her apron, covering her very generous bosom. Covering the rust and caramel leather of her corset. Covering the wide straps and gold buckles that cinched her waist.

His hands insisted they could easily span the width of that waist and lift her onto the workbench. His fingers, also traitorous, demanded permission to free the prong from each buckle's hole, after which they planned to hunt for buttons among the white frills of her shirtwaist. His palms then insisted they must explore the soft curves beneath all those layers. Together, hands and fingers would fondle and stroke and tease until they managed to coax an uncontrolled gasp from her throat.

Thornton stifled a groan and opened his eyes. There'd be no rising from his stool anytime soon. Mentoring her might prove an impossibility.

Lady Amanda pushed her goggles onto her forehead, pinching the bridge of her nose between thumb and forefinger. Tiny lines of worry creased her brow.

"Headache?" he asked, surprised to hear his voice sound normal while the rest of him throbbed.

"A bit," she admitted. "Mostly from worry. Has Black had any luck locating my sister?"

Thornton shook his head, grateful for a topic serious enough to distract his unruly mind. "Not yet. Nobody will admit to Nicu Sindel's whereabouts, and not a single gypsy has seen Luca Sindel or his *gadji* bride."

Her face fell. "Not surprising."

"No. Black did report, however, that the gypsies camped on Putney Heath seem unusually agitated. It seems a man has gone missing. One whose return was anticipated for reasons the gypsies decline to disclose."

Lady Amanda frowned. "That does not bode well."

"Not at all."

It had been over a week since the last gypsy murder. Given past patterns, Thornton feared another death was imminent. It was agony to sit helplessly in his laboratory, banned from fieldwork due to his damned injury.

He looked at the partially assembled mechanism before them. Not entirely helpless. Once complete, there was a chance—a very slim one—that the neurachnid could be programmed to repair his own leg. What would it be like to experience movement via gold threads and rare earth metals? Not that he cared, so long as he regained full function of his leg, of his foot.

He tucked a loupe into one eye and picked up a screwdriver. Work was one way to dispel the sense of dependence upon others, and an excellent way to avoid staring at Lady Amanda's form. "What inspired the idea of this neurachnid?" he asked.

"My brother," she said, pulling her goggles back over her eyes and lifting her own tools once more. "We were at a house party some five years past. Ned accompanied Emily and me, but only because said party was at Nellie Atwater's manor."

"I see." Lady Nell was a beauty, and lust was a powerful motivation.

Her hand stilled. "We teased Ned awfully, insisting he could never steal a kiss for her mother kept her under close watch during the day, lock and key at night, and the trellis outside her bedroom window was covered with thorns of the sharpest variety." She paused. "Ned took that as a dare."

Thornton remembered twenty-five. An indestructible age. Though, at the time, he'd yet to do anything requiring nerve repair. He waited, guessing at the ending before it was spoken aloud.

"The wood was rotten. He fell, landing on a stone planter below."

The wrong angle and just enough force and a man's life was altered forever.

"I'm sorry," he said, pausing at his task. Guilt too was a powerful motivator. In the years that followed, Lady Amanda had designed and built the neurachnid, while Lady Emily toiled to concoct a drug that met the needs of the procedure. "I gather that Lady Emily, despite finding love among the Romani, continues to assist with your project?"

She nodded. "By letter. Though, as I said, I haven't heard from her in some time. Nor did I expect to. The last batch of nerve agent should have lasted months, provided the largest test subject was of the murine variety."

Mice would require significantly less of the drug during the procedure. To calm a grown man's nerves long enough to perform the surgery would require much, much more nerve toxin.

"There's still hope," she said. "Ned's injury is not as severe as most imagine. The fall damaged the L4 and L5 nerve roots." Her lashes fell. A slight blush tinged her cheeks. "However, the father of his would-be fiancée has expressed concern."

So Ned's spinal cord was not severed. Fatherhood was still possible. But the nerve roots emerging from beneath the fourth and fifth lumbar vertebrae provided a large portion of motor input to the legs. He understood, but the *ton* at large would not. "I see." He paused, then discarded delicacy in favor of bluntness. "I gather there are no bastard children to prove otherwise?"

Her cheeks flamed and she kept her eyes firmly on the work before her as she shook her head. "No."

Lord Edward, Ned, might be heir to a dukedom, but if it was suspected he could not produce an heir, no decent father would approve a match. Despite the availability of numerous artificial solutions to cope with such leg injuries, a young lady's family preferred her affianced to have an unaltered, intact, and fully functioning human form.

If this procedure succeeded, there would be no surface trace of the repair beyond a scar. Ned would be considered "cured", and young ladies would throng to his side, hoping to be asked for a dance.

Dance.

That was something he himself could no longer do. Not that he wished to attend a ball. The opera and the theater were risky enough, but to attend an event where mothers herded flocks of young available women in the direction of the nearest eligible title... Well, his limp and his cane would only provide him a modest amount of protection.

Lady Amanda cleared her throat and spoke, seeming to read his mind. "If the neurachnid can fully restore a spinal nerve, its Babbage card can be programmed to restore a partially damaged nerve."

"Thank you for your consideration, but the procedure would likely fail."

She looked up, meeting his eyes as she pulled the goggles from her face. "Why?" Her direct approach—where others tiptoed—was almost a relief.

So he told her. "The German cutlass that cut through my leg was coated with a particularly virulent bacteria. Its toxin immediately began to destroy my nerve." Her eyes grew large with concern. "Henri does what he can to stop the damage from spreading, but I'm not certain if enough intact nerve remains for your neurachnid to trace." Not that it would stop him from trying.

"Oh, Sebastian," she murmured.

The sound of his given name on her lips shocked them both so much they jumped as the clock on the wall chimed the hour.

Eight o'clock.

"I must go," she said, leaping to her feet and hastily arranging her work space. "Father extracted a promise that I would attend the Whitmore's ball."

He reached for his cane. "I'll see you to your steam carriage."

"No, please." She glanced at his leg. "I must hurry."

He cringed. He hated being viewed as damaged, as requiring repair. But before he could force his stiff leg to bend against the weight of the metal brace, he found himself alone. Staring at his great iron door.

AMANDA TURNED SIDEWAYS, admiring the brocade gown she wore in the mirror. The bodice, the draped overskirt and bustle might be black, but the teal underskirt with knife pleat ruffles provided a dramatic flash of color. Yet the color wasn't the reason she'd chosen this gown. She'd pulled it from her wardrobe because of its bodice. The décolletage was deeply cut, yes, but the eye-catching feature was that it was only held in place by a black silk cord laced through tab accents in a pattern reminiscent of corset lacings.

It was a stunning gown designed to snare a man's attention. Unfortunately, the one man whose dark, tortured glances she craved wouldn't be in attendance at tonight's ball.

Simon would be there, of course, and Amanda would try to feel something more for the man than mere friendship. A proposal would not be long in coming; she would soon need to make a life-altering commitment to a man who did little to evoke strong emotion.

Not long ago, such a marital prospect would have suited her. Now, her thoughts and emotions were in such a tangle, she wasn't certain she'd be able to work the knots free.

It had been easier when she'd thought Thornton a soulless, if darkly beautiful, scientist, but there was more—much more—beneath the composed exterior he presented to the world. Unless she missed her mark, he too fought to untangle instinct and duty where she was concerned. She wanted *him*, not Simon.

Earlier in the laboratory this evening, she'd felt his stare, felt that intense blue gaze on her face. She'd bitten down on her lip. Hard. She'd needed to do something to keep from looking up, something to keep her breathing slow and steady even as her heart raced.

She agreed—in principle—that their emotions were inappropriate and misplaced. The deep attraction developing between them, if allowed to surface, would jeopardize everything. Her schoolwork. Her research. Her marital prospects.

She was a fool.

If his stare invited such thoughts, what urges would his touch unleash? For already she longed to press her palms against the rough surface of the beard that darkened his face, to slide her fingers into his inky locks and pull his mouth against hers.

Staring in the mirror, Amanda traced a finger over the exposed curves of her breasts, her nipples tightening as she imagined how Thornton's calloused hands might choose to explore her intricate bodice. If given license, would he skim the surface, trace the lacings? Delve beneath the edges? Or would he drag her into a shadowy alcove and work the knot free, pulling the cording from their tabs?

Amanda pressed her hand to her stomach and forced her breath to slow. The man who haunted her thoughts wasn't coming. Lord Thornton had yet to be sighted in a ballroom—and wasn't likely to be.

With the deteriorating condition of his leg, dancing would be difficult. Soon, it would be impossible. She'd been so moved, so distressed when he'd confided in her the extent of his injury that she'd forgotten herself and whispered his name in sympathy. That whisper had torn through a nameless barrier, shocking them both. Unable, or rather, unwilling to explain her impulse, she'd made her excuses and fled to the safety of her waiting coach.

"Daring, but effective," Olivia said, snapping Amanda from her thoughts. Her sister stepped into the reflection of Amanda's mirror. Behind Olivia followed her lady's maid, Steam Cora. "In that gown, you'll have a proposal by the end of the night."

With a proposal, with an acceptance, her world would narrow. "And if I don't want one?"

"Then you'd best wear something else."

"Something like yours? Pink ruffles to hide every feminine curve?" Amanda asked, raising her eyebrows at Olivia's choice.

Her sister sighed. "Carlton hates to see other gentlemen looking at me. Until the final contract is signed...."

"And after, Olivia? What then?"

Olivia shrugged. "The usual. A wedding. Babies." Her sister turned away and fiddled with a number of ribbons laid out upon Amanda's dressing table. If Carlton's controlling nature bothered her, she did not wish to discuss it. "Black velvet, I think. Sit. Let Steam Cora wind this in your hair."

Olivia handed the ribbon to Steam Cora whose finely articulated fingers began to twine the velvet around locks of Amanda's hair, creating an updo to rival all others. Many of Olivia's friends begged her to share the Babbage cards that created the hairstyles for which she was famous, but she guarded them closely, lest they reveal her secret, that she herself was the designer. A lady didn't dabble in programming.

Amanda met her sister's eyes in the mirror, noting her drawn face. There was something more on her mind. "What's wrong?"

Olivia sighed. "Father summoned me to his study. He received some distressing news today. He told me he suspects Emily has taken up with Luca."

"Has married Luca, you mean." Father must be preparing Olivia for the worst case scenario: discovery.

A derisive snort. "You know as well as I gypsies refuse to take out a marriage license. Not that that would help. Mother has taken to her bed. If this becomes public..."

"Carlton will set you aside," Amanda finished. Since Olivia seemed set on Carlton, she prayed for both her sisters' sakes that Emily was nowhere near London or its outskirts. "Father will keep this quiet." She hoped.

"Speaking of which, Father is to escort us to the ball tonight."

"Not Ned?" Amanda frowned.

"He's already at the Whitmore's, preparing the orchestra."

"I see." Occasionally, Ned would accept a private commission. He would then spend the entire evening behind a stand of potted palms, ostensibly overseeing his clockwork musicians.

"I can't blame Ned for hiding." A flush crept up Olivia's neck. "I suspect from the foul mood he's been in that he's had more... inquiries."

Olivia referred to certain young ladies, having had no luck on the marriage mart, who offered their hands in marriage to Lord Edward. Marriage to a cripple in exchange for a future title. Many hoped to be relieved of their marital duties. A few, however, had been so bold as to offer, with Ned's permission of course, to produce an heir outside the marriage bed should he prove incapable.

Horribly embarrassing, all of it.

Amanda closed her eyes for a moment. "While that may be, his mood is more likely due to the speed with which Georgina's marriage contract negotiation is proceeding."

"Faster than mine." Her sister sighed. "Carlton keeps negotiating for more. He wants the house in Kent."

Carlton's demands were like his opinions: ridiculous and selfish.

Amanda couldn't shake the feeling Ned was avoiding her. Her request this evening, that he program a card that would instruct the neurachnid to repair Thornton's fibular nerve, had been met with fierce refusal. Ned could not see past his own problems. But Olivia, she also had talent. If she could overcome her aversion to anatomical images... "I wonder if I might convince you to program a Babbage card for me?"

Her sister blanched. "For your spider?"

A minor lie and a major sacrifice would be necessary to cajole Olivia's help. Worth the price if she could erase the look of despair she'd read on Thornton's face when he admitted his leg was likely beyond hope. "Ned lacks a certain... finesse with needles." Olivia swayed. "If you'll help, I'll promise to keep my books and specimens from the breakfast table."

Speculation lit her sister's eyes. "And the parlor?"

Amanda grimaced, but nodded her agreement.

"Then I'll have a look. Tomorrow. On an empty stomach."

CHAPTER TWELVE

W ITH THE HOUR OF receiving lines long past,
Thornton finally dressed for the night's ball.
He climbed aboard the steam carriage that bore
his family crest and directed it to the Whitmore's London
home.

Earlier, he'd made final adjustments to the newly
implanted acousticotransmitter in an agent's ear, then
watched, not without envy, as Black left with the man—still a
bit unsteady on his feet—to take to the dark, foggy streets for
a bit of practice with the new device.

An evening wandering the streets of East London held
more appeal than any *ton* ball. Especially as both Lady
Amanda and a particularly irritating student, one Mr. Simon
Sommersby, would be in attendance. Likely Sommersby
would be found no less than an arm's length from her side.
Thornton didn't trust the man. Under a seemingly carefree

demeanor, Thornton recognized a streak of possessiveness. Sommersby was also annoyingly persistent.

Lady Huntley had called Thornton to her side after Lady Amanda's departure. "You should know," she began, "that Mr. Sommersby managed to track me down outside of Lister Laboratories to press his case for a position in your laboratory."

Thornton frowned, knowing Lady Huntley valued her privacy. "Inappropriate."

"Very," she replied. "However, the man is highly recommended by his professors. He may only be an adequate medical student, but I'm told he has a decided talent for chemistry. Are you certain you wish to dismiss him out of hand?"

"Yes," Thornton replied without hesitation. Sommersby rubbed him wrong. Why, exactly, he couldn't say. Certainly, his pursuit of Lady Amanda played a part, but there was something more about the man, something he couldn't quite pinpoint, that set his teeth on edge.

Yet Lady Amanda *encouraged* Sommersby's attentions. Why? She could reach much higher.

His hand tightened on the top of his cane. The thought of Sommersby winning such a woman as his bride elicited many foreign emotions. Among them, jealousy was the one Thornton least enjoyed. He had no wish to see her in another man's arms.

His steam carriage stopped before the Whitmore residence. The broad marble stairs that led upward were alight with the latest in proximity-sensing bioluminescent lanterns, their blue and green lights flashing and swirling as he passed. Inside the great hall an automated coat rack held out an appendage of sorts, and Thornton hung his hat on the outstretched hook, but held onto his cane. A tell-tale ache was settling into his leg. Soon, it would require another injection.

He greeted familiar faces with a mere nod and side-stepped a giggling flock of young ladies in a cloud of pastels and white lace who eyed him with unconcealed interest.

Skirting the ballroom, he passed down a long hallway and through a door into the library. The Duke of Avesbury sat in a shadowed corner holding court in a wingback chair. He caught sight of Thornton and crooked his finger. The duke's men scattered as Thornton approached, providing them with a moment's privacy.

The man's face was grim. "I understand you need to speak with my daughter, Emily."

Thornton nodded.

"A headstrong child. Short of locking her in a tower, there was little to do to stop her from following an unusual path."

"Are you certain you don't speak of Lady Amanda?"

Lord Avesbury barked a laugh. "Perhaps you'll have more success directing her future than I."

Thornton doubted that.

"Emily is at Putney Heath," Lord Avesbury continued, his voice low as he revealed the location of his potion-brewing, runaway daughter. "She stays with her new family, living a quiet and unremarked life. Am I clear?"

"Indeed." Thornton could speak with her only, revealing her location to no one. The social implications for the duke and his family, should Lady Emily be discovered not to be in Italy as supposed, were dire.

He would await Black's return before departing to question Lady Emily. They could be at the campsite by dawn.

"My daughter, Amanda, is she useful?"

"Very," Thornton replied. And a terrible distraction.

"Good." Lord Avesbury stared at Thornton, his eyes seeming to bore holes through his skull as if it would allow him to read his thoughts. His next words caught Thornton off guard. "Amanda has waited too long to marry. As have you. I would advise you both to choose carefully."

Thornton blinked, and hesitated, both uncertain how to respond and why the duke would concern himself with his marital status. Did the duke issue a warning? Or a suggestion?

Another gentleman drifted silently to Lord Avesbury's side. "Keep me apprised," the duke said and turned away.

His time was over. He bowed his goodbye and stepped aside.

For some time, Thornton remained in the library, speaking with a number of other gentlemen involved in government affairs, discussing the recent German atrocities and the likelihood that the King of Iceland would seek to interfere in European affairs.

As the hands of the clock approached midnight, Thornton's leg could no longer be ignored. Each step he took sent pain radiating behind his calf and spiraling down to his ankle. At least the pain reassured him the nerve still worked. When the numbness began...

Thornton stepped into the hallway, searching out an unoccupied side room. When the pain reached this level, it was time to administer another dose. He'd calm the nerve, then return to the laboratory to await Black.

He stepped into a darkened room containing a couple of chairs and a sofa. Perfect. He closed the door softly behind him. The injection would take mere minutes. He'd taken not more than five steps into the room when the door behind him opened again and slammed shut. He heard the key turn in the lock.

Spinning, he turned to find Lady Amanda leaning against the door.

She gasped, her eyes growing wide with surprise as they met his, and pressed an index finger to her lips.

Not that she needed to ask for his silence, for he was struck dumb. The lacing of her bodice snared his gaze, focusing all thought directly upon a portion of her anatomy where his eyes ought not linger. He swallowed, the pain in his leg forgotten. Black silk cords crossed repeatedly over her chest, twining their way down her bodice to form a knot at her narrow waist.

"Lady Amanda?" a confused voice called from the hallway.

Sommersby.

Thornton raised his eyebrows.

She shook her head, her eyes begging him to say nothing.

The footsteps moved on, and Amanda exhaled in relief,

brushing past him as she crossed to stand beside the window. Moonlight flooded in, setting her skin aglow. "Thank you," she said. "Mr. Sommersby is overly solicitous tonight. I'm afraid we're trapped for a few minutes. I hope you don't mind."

Mind? He minded quite a bit. "Not at all, Lady Amanda," he said. Then moved, flinching, to a nearby chair.

"I'm surprised to find you here. To think I envied your ability to remain in the laboratory, to work late into the night." She flicked him a glance. "Though I don't suppose you're here to find a bride."

Did she pry? Or merely state the obvious, for he would not seek a wife among young women who viewed his injury as an opportunity to easily acquire a title. "No."

"Mr. Sommersby is a good man, if predictable," she said. "I could do worse."

"You don't sound convinced." He shouldn't care. Shouldn't encourage this discussion.

She sighed and sank onto the chair across from him. Thornton struggled to keep his eyes on her face. "I'm not a fan of society's expectations. Nor of balls, teas or garden parties. The privileges of a peeress are many, but the expectations are constrictive."

If she did not wish to marry, why was she here? "As an earl, I concur." Rather contradictory, her behavior. Encouraging Sommersby one minute, hiding from him the next.

"Ah, but you have many years before society will force a woman into your arms."

"Force? Am I that distasteful?"

"Not at all." She leaned forward, her breasts straining against the silk cords that bound them.

"No?" He leaned forward as well, lowering his voice. "I must warn you, locking me in a darkened room might not have been the wisest choice. For I'm anything but predictable."

Her smile fell away. The tip of her tongue darted between her lips. "You certainly aren't," she whispered, her gaze alighting on his mouth. She turned her head quickly to look out the window and into an empty garden. "What drug, may I ask, do you use to calm the nerve in your leg?"

"Somnic," he said, naming a powerful nerve agent that was as damaging as it was effective. A muscle in his foot twitched, a reminder of the reason he'd entered this room.

"But the side effects are irreversible!" she exclaimed, her eyes wide with concern. Lady Amanda knew her nerve agents.

"They are," he said. "But every other available drug no longer has any effect." Thornton watched her mind run through the implications, watched as it pounced on the inevitable conclusion.

"The neurachnid might still work," she said. "If completed before the drug loses its efficacy."

He nodded, acknowledging her conclusion, and began to unscrew the silver cap of his cane. Let her know the worst, know the dosage upon which he now relied. He needed an injection now, or he would be incapable of leaving the room under his own power. The cap came free in his hand and he swore.

"What's wrong?"

He held up an empty vial. Henri had assured him that he would refill the vial. Clearly, he'd forgotten. And he had failed to check—an inexcusable mistake that could well cost him his leg.

Still, there should have been enough residual medication for at least a half dose. Was he really using such a large quantity of Somnic? Tipping his head back and glaring at the ceiling, Thornton swore again. At this rate, he calculated, the drug would become ineffective in less than two weeks.

There was a rustle. A whiff of roses. A light pressure against his knee.

He looked down, and his jaw fell slack.

"Let me help. I've been studying the Oriental practice of using pressure points to relieve pain." In a rumple of brocade and silk, Lady Amanda knelt on the floor before him. Her fingers pressed through his woolen trousers around his brace, expertly seeking out the damage.

"I don't think..."

Her finger found a pressure point. He gripped the arms of the chair, sucking in his breath at the sudden piercing pain, then exhaled. Slowly. And found the pain had lessened.

"Where did you learn to...?" Her fingers deftly landed on another pressure point, and his jaw clenched. He hissed on an indrawn breath

"Does it matter?" Her fingers moved behind, then beneath, his brace.

Thornton was incapable of response. Not since the

initial injury healed had anyone touched his leg. There'd been no need for a second opinion. Already the top physician in his field, Thornton knew exactly what to do, knew exactly what was to come.

Her fingers still moving, she tipped her face upward. "Which nerve? Only the superficial fibular affecting the lateral component? Eversion and plantarflextion?" The superficial fibular nerve innervated the lateral muscles of the lower leg responsible for turning the foot outward as well as pressing the foot downward.

The pain was less now. He unclenched his teeth and exhaled as slowly and as calmly as he could manage. "No, the deep fibular nerve as well," he answered, closing his eyes, lulled by the decreasing pain. He'd not experienced this kind of relief since the very first dose of Somnic. How long would it last?

Thirty minutes or three, he didn't care.

Her hands moved, lifting the hem of his trousers, sliding underneath. Upward. To his knee. She pulled his hose free, baring his skin to her cool fingers.

"So dorsiflextion as well," she stated.

"Yes." At times he also found it difficult to lift his foot. Soon, walking would become difficult. Running, impossible.

"Better?"

"Much." The near-constant pain in his leg had faded to a distant ache. He relaxed his grip on the chair and slitted his eyes, finally able to enjoy the close-up view as she leaned ever closer, still on her knees before him. It was difficult to stop his mind from drifting down erotic pathways.

No. It was *impossible.*

Dark eyebrows arched over half-closed eyes. Long lashes fanned over pink cheeks. A delicate nose rested above full red lips. All that attention focused directly upon his person.

Other parts of his anatomy began to ache, every instinct insisting she returned his interest despite her now intimate knowledge of his weakness.

She shifted and her breast brushed against his knee. There was a slight catch in her breath, the slightest hesitation in her touch. About her face, dark locks of hair were twined with black velvet and pinned into submission. All but a single lock that had worked itself free and skimmed over her cheek.

He reached down, gently tucking the strand of hair behind her ear.

Her hands stilled, then released his leg.

With one finger, he traced a path down the side of her neck to rest where her pulse beat strong and fast. It echoed his own racing heart. He watched the rapid rise and fall of her chest, waiting. Her lashes lifted, and two dark pools met his eyes. Her lips parted, and her breath hitched. Something between them shifted. He slid his gaze to her lips, making clear his intent.

Yet still he waited, giving her a chance to stop him, to back away, but desperately hoping she wouldn't. Anticipation burned in his chest as he reached out with both hands to capture the base of her skull, tugging her upward. His fingers slid into her soft hair as she rose to meet him halfway. He tilted her mouth to his, the warmth of her breath a soft caress, and her eyes fluttered closed as he claimed her lips.

Lips that were warm, soft and inviting. They parted, inviting him in. She tasted of champagne and strawberries, of longing, of a future he'd not dared to hope for in years.

Her hands gripped his thighs. He deepened the kiss, pulling her closer against him, driven by a primitive need to claim her as his own.

Beyond the rushing of blood in his ears, Thornton became aware of a commotion in the hallway. He released her, already missing her warmth, and left desperately wanting more.

Breathless, they stared at each other for one long incredulous moment. Then the realization of what he'd done crashed down upon him.

"I... we..." she began.

Now was not the time.

"Shh." He held a finger to his lips, then offered a hand. She accepted. Thornton pulled her to her feet as he himself stood. Together they crossed the room, stopping before the door.

He heard the deep timbre of Black's voice. Black would know Thornton was here at the ball. His carriage waited outside. If his partner had tracked him to a society event, it followed that there was pressing news. Likely of the bad variety.

He would have opened the door immediately, but for the presence of Lady Amanda. To be seen emerging from behind a locked door with a man would expose her to scandal. He turned his gaze on her. A rare combination of beauty and intelligence, one to which he was not entitled. He ran a hand through his hair in frustration.

"You go first. I'll delay." Amanda did not meet his gaze. "I understand the potential repercussions. Romantic liaisons between female students and staff is forbidden and grounds for my immediate dismissal." She spoke the very words about to form on his lips then, passing him his cane, reached for the key and unlocked the door.

He waited for relief to follow as he stepped into the hall-way—and kept waiting.

One kiss and he was perilously close to tossing aside those cursed rules and regulations, damn the consequences.

CHAPTER THIRTEEN

DECIDING SHE CARED more about learning the cause for commotion than she did for her reputation, Amanda waited mere moments before emerging from the room.

She followed the deep rumble of Thornton's voice to the library, where he stood beneath the low haze of cigar smoke beside both Black and Father. "Father. Mr. Black." She swallowed. "Lord Thornton."

"Amanda." The corners of Father's mouth pulled downward. His eyes narrowed and his bushy eyebrows drew together. She knew that look. It always preceded a reprimand and certain dismissal. "What are you doing here?"

Black gave a slight snort, but when she returned his look with a glare, every hint of troublemaker fell away, leaving behind only the gravest of expressions.

She lifted her chin and returned Father's stare with the knowledge that she had every right to be included. "If this concerns another gypsy, under similar circumstances, my consultation is required."

Thornton nodded his agreement and, despite knowing another man might be dead, a certain thrill ran through her at being treated as a professional.

"My men have sent word that another body has been found," Black said. "Putney Heath."

Putney Heath, a known winter stopping place for gypsies, was a distant part of southwest London.

Father shot Thornton a dark look.

Thornton nodded slowly. What had just passed between them?

Emily.

Emily and Luca were there. Thousands of icy spider feet ran down her spine.

"Word is the gypsies call him the eye doctor," Black continued.

"Wonderful," Father grumbled. "Let's hope the newspaper men don't catch word of that sobriquet." He waved a hand. "Go. Sort this all out. And fast."

Eye doctor. Her device and Emily's potion were now at the center of it all. Amanda desperately hoped the discovery of the latest body had nothing to do with Emily herself.

"What of our test subject? And the device?" Thornton asked Black, ignoring Father.

"For the moment, both transmitter and receiver are in good order. The man, however, is a bit green. I sent him home. Came directly here."

"We'll take my carriage," Thornton said, turning for the door.

"There's a faster way," she said, and all eyes focused on her. "Lord Whitmore keeps a dirigible. On his roof. Sparrow class. Designed for two." She paused, tipping her head. "Assuming someone knows how to fly one."

Black scoffed. "Permission to commandeer the airship, Lord Avesbury."

"Permission granted," Father answered. "I'll sort it out with Whitmore."

"I'm coming," she stated, in case she'd not already made that clear.

Voices rose in dissent. "A lady... that dress... campground..."

"It's *my* neurachnid." The grumbling subsided. "We've spent the last week improving upon the design. Who's to say this eye doctor hasn't been doing the same thing? The sooner I evaluate the body, the sooner you may have leads. The Sparrow class has a jump seat in the tail." She crossed her arms and sized up Black. He wasn't short, but Thornton was a good six inches taller. "You'll fit."

"Me?" Black's voice objected, but his eyes took on a teasing gleam, and Amanda knew she'd won an ally. "You're the shortest," he retorted.

She returned his sly grin with her own, gesturing to the volume of her skirts. "You'd consign a lady in a ball gown to the jump seat?"

With a stage-worthy roll of his eyes and a theatrical sigh, he conceded. "Let's go."

"Wait." Thornton pulled off his coat and held it out to her. "In that dress you'll..."

Amanda raised her eyebrows. "Be a distraction?"

Father frowned, as if reconsidering the wisdom of allowing his daughter to go.

"Be cold," Thornton finished.

She pulled the coat over her bare arms. The shoulders hung loose and the sleeves extended past her fingertips. Still warm from his body heat, it smelled of him, like soap and exotic spices and something that was uniquely male. It was probably the closest she'd ever get to having his arms wrapped around her.

"Button it," Father grumbled as she passed by him.

She ignored him.

Minutes later, the three of them stepped out onto the dark roof. The blue light from the phosphorescent lamp Black swiped from a hallway sconce struggled to illuminate their path. Thick fog obscured everything more than five feet away.

She hoped the men were capable of instrument flight alone. She glanced at them. They seemed unconcerned. Nervous excitement coursed through her. She'd ridden in dirigibles, but never in one so small. Never at night. Never in a fog. Never with a man who made her lose her grasp on proper behavior.

She was certain, absolutely so, that Emily was at the Putney Heath encampment. She missed her sister fiercely. Emily had been her only ally in a house full of people hell-bent on societal acceptance. Only because of her sister's flight had Amanda found it within herself to challenge Father, to threaten him, to bargain with him so that she might achieve *her* dreams, and not Mother's.

So, while a man might have died and died horribly, the life Amanda had dreamed of was finally in reach. Not just medical school, not just research, but the field application of both. Emily would be there. Emily would understand. Emily would help.

But first Amanda had to get to her.

Small, light and brown, Sparrow class dirigibles were designed for gentlemen of business—and the occasional passenger or two. With a streamlined open cabin and a narrow, cigar-shaped balloon, the Sparrow class carried a bare minimum of fuel and water. With a maximum range of eighty miles, they traveled easily from London rooftops to country manors, and could do so in a quarter of the time it took a steam carriage to negotiate the crowded, sometimes poorly maintained, roads.

Neither man spared her a glance—or offered assistance—as she stuffed herself and her voluminous skirts into the passenger seat.

Thornton and Black worked together seamlessly. Without so much as a word or a look, each pulled on leather gloves and set about preparing the Sparrow for flight, a task usually seen to by servants. Black checked the water level in the boiler, adding several buckets from a nearby cistern. Thornton spread a bed of lamp-oil soaked charcoal and flicked in a safety match before laying in a bed of coal to heat the water.

These two were no strangers to piloting a dirigible.

That Black knew how to fire a steam engine did not surprise her. Even with all the trappings of a gentleman, the man had certain rough edges. Rough edges he would need with a habit of running about the streets of London at night.

That an earl—a neurophysiologist—should know how... that he was comfortable taking to the skies in a fog...

Tipping her head, she studied the man in question, considering the conversation she'd had with Simon days earlier.

A spy?

Thornton's shirts stretched and pulled across his broad shoulders. If his arms were as strong and solid as the thighs she'd gripped... Amanda's face grew warm. She should feel shame. Humiliation. Kissing a professor was forbidden.

Instead, she wanted nothing more than to try it again. That kiss, sudden and unexpected, would have brought her to her knees had she not already been on them. The brush of his fingertip along her neck had sent shivers across her skin, but it was the touch of his lips that turned her muscles to liquid.

For hours during class, she'd stared at those lips as the deep timbre of his voice set her body aflame. While he lectured about how myelin wrapped about the nerve axon forming a sheath, she'd fantasized about wrapping herself around him, fantasized about how his lips might feel pressed against hers. Now she'd had a tantalizing taste. It was enough to drive a woman mad.

But from the moment he'd drawn back, she'd glanced

into his dark eyes, seen the inevitable rejection. Such an entanglement would jeopardize everything. Were they discovered in a compromising situation, only she would pay the price. The rules of society favored men.

Amanda strapped on a pair of goggles and fixed her eyes on the steam gauge. She would not think about such things now. A man had died. As pressure began to rise in the boiler, she took to calling out its progress. "Fifteen psi. Eighteen. Twenty!"

"All aboard!" With a mighty heave, Black spun the propeller into motion and leapt into the rear jump seat, rocking the dirigible. The netted balloon swayed overhead as the engine roared to life with clangs and hisses, as the cylinders and pistons and rods and gears set up a comforting rhythm.

The dirigible tipped again and Thornton was beside her, his hands expertly working the various levers even as he folded himself into the pilot's seat. Between his size and her skirts, it was a tight fit. His thigh bumped hers, and their shoulders pressed tight. Every inch of her skin tingled with awareness.

Though his leg didn't seem to trouble him for the moment, pressure point massage only worked a few hours at most before the pain returned. The key to preventing the muscles from seizing, from pinching the damaged nerve, was repetition. Though it would only continue to work so long as the nerve retained a minimum of function.

What dosage had Thornton used? How much longer could he sustain its use?

Pulling on a pair of goggles, Thornton called, "Cast off!"

Black tossed away a final rope, and the dirigible began to rise. Tendrils of fog swirled about them.

Amanda ignored the warm, solid thigh pressed against hers and instead stared determinedly into the gray night.

Moments later, Thornton glanced at the altimeter. "We're clear of the chimneys!" he called to Black. Then he turned to her, a glint in his eye. "Ready?"

If not for their destination and purpose, she could think of no better way to escape the tedium of a ball. She threw him an answering grin. "Ready."

Thornton reached forward, and threw the throttle wide open.

She shrieked—from surprise or fear, she wasn't certain—as she was thrown back into the seat as the dirigible shot clear of the roof out into the dense fog. For the first time, she heard Thornton laugh. Deep and dark and decidedly dangerous, it scraped across her skin. For once, she felt truly alive.

CHAPTER FOURTEEN

T HE THRILL OF LEAVING solid ground behind, of being unfettered, quickly faded. Flying nearly blind made for a tense twenty minutes in the sky. Hazy lights and shifting shadows made Amanda feel as if her sight was failing even as she kept her eyes wide open.

There'd been a couple of near misses that had sent her heart racing. Thank goodness other airships carried bright lanterns, providing precious seconds to avoid collision. But nocturnal pteryformes, a bird-like creature that glided over London at night, made no sound and were as dark as the night. The brush of leathery wings across the balloon of their dirigible had set her every hair on end. Much effort was necessary to keep her respiratory rate in normal range.

As the dirigible began its descent into Putney Heath, Amanda kept a white-knuckled grip on a nearby brass handle. Beside her, Thornton's lips pressed into a thin line, and his hands moved rapidly over the various controls. He had a close eye on the altimeter, but the evening's fog made choosing a clear landing site impossible. The dirigible veered.

"Trees!" Thornton yelled. "Brace for impact!"

Her eyes were wide, her heart pounded. Tree branches meant the ground was close.

Branches reached out with malicious intent, snagging on the balloon's netting. A jerk, an ominous ripping sound, and the airship careened wildly.

A scattering of lights emerged, rushing up at them.

Campfires!

Thornton swore.

They were landing directly on the gypsy encampment!

Below them, dark forms scattered, screaming and yelling.

Thornton throttled back the engine and shouted commands to Black.

A loud crunch—one felt more than heard—signaled they'd landed. Hard. Lord Whitmore would not be pleased.

There was a moment of stunned silence. Then the yelling began. Harsh angry words in the Romani language filled the air. Gypsies pointed and waved.

"Fire!" Black yelled from behind them. "Get out. We've landed on a campfire." He leapt from the jump seat. Thornton followed, vaulting to the ground. All while she still struggled to stand—the wire of her bustle was wedged in her seat.

"Jump, Amanda!" Thornton yelled.

There was a sudden whooshing sound and flames licked

up the hull and climbed the ropes toward the balloon. Smoke swirled upward to twine with the fog.

"I'm stuck!" she yelled. But over the roar of the fire, had anyone heard her? Frantic, she yanked harder at her skirts, trying to rip them free. Did hydrogen or aether fill their balloon? She couldn't remember and didn't want to be in the dirigible when the answer became apparent.

"Amanda!" Thornton appeared at her side, balancing precariously on the wreckage. His hands pulled at her waist, wrenching her free. They dropped to the ground and, though Thornton hissed at the pain, he didn't set her down as he ran from the flames. Amanda wrapped her hands about his neck, glancing back over his shoulder as he carried her to a safe distance.

Gypsies glared at them. Their dramatic entrance had won them no friends.

"Thank you," she whispered, as he set her down onto her own somewhat unsteady feet, shaking from the aftereffects of too much adrenaline. With her bustle bent out of all proportion, her skirt sagged in odd places, promising to drag in a most unbecoming manner over the dew-dampened dirt.

"You're bleeding," he said and pulled a handkerchief from his coat pocket. He wiped blood from her cheek while keeping a steadying hand at her elbow.

Several yards away, Black and another man gestured broadly with their hands, arguing in Romani. No need to understand the language to know they argued about the damage caused and how the gypsies would be compensated.

As the fire intensified, a crowd gathered about them

emerging from the fog in all the colors one might find in a Turkish rug. Scarlet. Magenta. Saffron. Cobalt. Ochre. Gold. Brighter and more vibrant than anything one might find at a *ton* ball.

The men stood in front. Women clustered behind, babies in their arms, smaller children peering from behind their wide skirts. Older children shoved and pushed, vying for the best view. A hush fell over the crowd as the flames reached the skin of the balloon, licking across its surface.

"Hydrogen or aether?" she asked, this time aloud.

Left unsheltered and unattended and frequently unused on rooftops, personal dirigibles often sustained damage from the elements. In short, they tended to leak. Aether was stable, but expensive. Hydrogen was abundant and cheap but extremely flammable.

"Hydrogen," Thornton answered. "This should be quite a show."

The fabric of the upper fin began to flutter. There was a muffled explosion, and yellow-red flames jumped into the air, spreading, eating away the fabric as black smoke poured into the sky. The exposed underlying girders, weakened by the intense heat, collapsed over the hull of the airship as the fire dropped to a low smolder.

Amanda forced herself to breathe deeply and slowly, to slow the shaking that persisted in the face of a horrible demonstration of the dangers of in-air collision.

Men carrying water buckets rushed forward, dousing the flames as a multitude of faces with accusing, narrowed eyes turned in their direction. Not an ideal first impression.

"Amanda?"

She turned, searched for the source of the voice. "Emily?"

Men hissed in disapproval, moving quickly aside as an obviously pregnant woman pushed her way forward. Fog swirled around her skirt as its folds shifted; to be brushed by a woman's skirts made one *marhime*, unclean.

A dark-haired woman with a cerulean blue shawl draped about her shoulders stepped forward.

"Emily!" Amanda cried. She rushed forward to clasp her sister's hands and scanned her from head to toe. Her sister glowed—and was further along in her pregnancy than Amanda expected. Details that had clearly been kept from her. "You have no idea how badly I've missed you."

Emily squeezed Amanda's hands. "I feel the same. Your latest letter—"

A man emerged from the crowd, scolding Emily in Romani. Luca. Private concerns would have to wait.

"Your sister?" Thornton stood behind her. She nodded.

"Disaster always seems to follow you, Amanda," Luca growled.

"Not true. Disaster arrived before me." Dispensing with formalities, she tipped her head at Thornton. "We're here about the body."

There was a moment of startled silence.

"Tova?" Luca asked.

"If that is the name of the boy found in the ditch," Thornton answered.

"What might you and Lady Amanda have to do with Tova?" Suspicion laced Luca's words.

"This is about the clockwork spider, isn't it?" Emily said, her face pale.

From Amanda's letter, Emily would know it had been stolen. What she didn't know was its involvement in the gypsy murders.

Luca's face darkened. "Your work?" He glanced from Amanda to Emily. "You refer to the spider?"

"Yes," Amanda answered. "And Emily's nerve potion."

"Why is your contraption being used on my people?" He glowered. "Don't answer that. It's because we are disposable."

"We're here to try to stop this man, this eye doctor. Better to ask 'who would do such a thing' and 'to what end?'" Amanda suggested. Though annoyed at her brother-in-law's hostility, it was understandable, given the chaos their arrival caused. "Which is exactly what we hope to discover, Luca. By viewing the body."

Emily laid a hand on Luca's arm, her eyes large with worry and concern.

"Follow me." Luca turned and led them into the heart of the encampment.

They trailed behind him across the damp ground, leaving Black to conclude his negotiations with the men whose property had been demolished in the flaming wreckage of the dirigible. Thornton was limping again, his cane forgotten in the crash. At the doorway of a makeshift tent, Luca exchanged a few tense words with an older man who glowered at the visitors. Finally, a terse nod granted them access.

Tova lay stretched upon the ground, covered with an old, wool blanket.

"Where was he found?" Thornton asked.

"Beside a road. Any number of wagons traveling by could have dumped him there," Luca answered.

Thornton bent to lift the makeshift shroud. A single, unseeing eye stared back. Beside it was a socket filled with congealed blood.

Emily moaned. Luca murmured in Romani, trying to pull her away, but she shrugged off his hand, shaking her head.

Thornton pointed. "Look at his wrists, his ankles." Red, raw marks encircled each.

Tova had suffered greatly just prior to death.

"There was only enough nerve agent in the abdominal vial for one procedure," Amanda said. "And that was used on the last victim. The eye doctor must have attempted this procedure without any nerve agent."

Emily gasped and covered her mouth with her hands. With a slight mewling sound, she rushed from the tent.

Thornton straightened and turned to Luca. "I need to take him back to the laboratory for a complete examination. There are tests—"

"No. Do it here."

"Impossible."

Luca shrugged.

Thornton swore. "It's your people who are dying! I'm trying to stop this."

"It's being handled."

"Hardly. How many bodies now? Six, now seven, have been brought to my attention. You need help."

Luca crossed his arms.

"I will send the police," Thornton threatened.

"They will find nothing," Luca fumed, his eyes narrowed, "but the wreckage of your dirigible."

"Gentlemen!" Amanda interrupted. "There must be some way to compromise. Luca, we need special tools, magnifying lenses. Intense, strong light. We need to determine what this eye doctor has done."

"Bring them here," Luca said.

"We can't. Come with him," she offered, pleaded. "Come with Tova. The examination will take..." She looked at Thornton. "Thirty minutes? An hour?" He nodded. "When we're done, Tova comes home—immediately—for his funeral.

"Is that a promise?" Luca directed his question at Thornton.

"Only if you arrange *immediate* transportation."

"I'll see what I can do." Luca looked at Amanda. "Now would be a good time for a *brief* conversation with your sister."

She stepped from the tent, leaving the men to make their arrangements. Outside, Emily stood, her arms wrapped across her chest, her shoulders shaking, still overcome by the sight of Tova. Amanda put her arms around her sister, pulling her close, holding her until the shaking stopped. "Six months?" she guessed.

Emily sniffled. "Yes."

Father must know about the baby, must have known months ago that Emily's departure had been motivated by more than love alone. It would be the only reason he'd left Emily to Luca instead of dragging her home.

Emily caught Amanda's hand and pressed it to her rounded abdomen. There was a soft thump against her hand. "Can you feel him kicking? He's strong."

"Or perhaps *she's* strong."

"Or she," Emily agreed, grinning.

"Will you come home, for the birth?"

Emily shook her head. "No. He'll be born here, as is tradition."

Amanda drew breath, about to launch into a list of reasons why a physician should be allowed to attend.

"Stop. Don't waste your words. This is why I didn't dare tell you." A faint smile tugged at Emily's lips and she began to walk, pulling her sister across the campsite, weaving between campfires, tents and vardos, the gypsy name for their caravan homes. "Mother would be horrified if I were to return now, with nothing but the story of my gypsy wedding. Society would view him—or her—as a bastard. Olivia's wedding plans would go up in flames much like your dirigible."

Amanda made no comment. It was all—unfortunately—true.

"Have Olivia and Carlton set a date?"

Amanda snorted. "Hardly. It's ever-shifting. They're on the fifth version of a wedding contract."

Emily laughed. "I never cared for Carlton. Such a pompous ass."

"Olivia quotes him endlessly." She paused. "I'll worry now. You'll let me know how you're doing? Will you allow me to attend the birth?"

"You'd come here?"

"In a heartbeat," Amanda said.

Emily considered the idea for a moment, then nodded. "I'll have Luca send for you. Only you. Alone."

"Agreed."

They'd arrived at a smattering of vardos tucked among a few sparse trees, a good distance from the now smoldering dirigible. Emily stopped before a yellow vardo with a red door and green shutters. An inviting ladder curved gently down from the base of the door. Baskets and cages and pots and pans and all other manner of household implements were strapped, tied or hooked to its side. A short distance away burned a small campfire with two overturned buckets beside it to serve as seats.

"Yours?" The caravan seemed familiar.

Emily nodded. "Yes. And Nadya's."

"How is it she's still alive?" Amanda wondered aloud. The old woman had seemed a hundred years old when they were in short skirts and braids.

"Shh!" Emily swatted, pressing a finger to her lips. "She is Luca's great aunt. Have some respect. She's taught me so much these past months, and I've still so much to learn." Her visage sobered and her voice fell. "However, this is not a social call. It's about the nerve agent. Given what's happened, you need to know."

All the tension that had evaporated during their sisterly chat dropped once more onto her shoulders with a heavy thud. Amanda stared back into the fog, searching for a form that resembled Thornton.

"Tell him later. She won't speak if he's here. You, she knows. Me, she trusts."

Amanda followed Emily up the steps. A single lantern illuminated the interior and she could see all the usual gypsy comforts. A small stove. A table affixed to the wall. Built-in benches covered in colorful patchwork pillows served as both storage and seating.

On a bed built into the back wall of the caravan sat a tiny old woman wrapped in shawls. Fringed curtains concealed all but her face, a face so wrinkled and weathered that she resembled nothing so much as an apple left to sit in the sun untouched for a year. Or ten.

Emily crouched beside her, scooping a small, withered hand into hers, whispering in Romani to the old woman.

Tears escaped, running over sunken purple half-moons beneath her eyes and over her cheeks. She shook her head. Emily murmured more insistently. At last, the woman nodded and pulled her hand away, agreeing to whatever it was her sister requested.

"Tova was her grandson and Luca's cousin," Emily said. "He was sent to deliver the nerve potion. And never came back."

"Excuse me?" Amanda's eye grew large. "Are you telling me you gave nerve agent to the eye doctor yourself?"

"We didn't know," Emily said, her voice defensive. "A letter came, offering a grand sum for a serum that would calm, but not numb a nerve. But it wasn't *the* formula. The batch you had, I expected it to last longer."

They both had. There'd been no reason to think that her neurachnid would be tested so soon—and unexpectedly—on a human.

Emily continued, "But the nerve potion you use requires the flower of a plant that's not in bloom, not in October. Nadya and I, we've been trying to find a replacement for that sole ingredient, something available year round."

"In the event my spider suddenly began to work," Amanda finished her sister's thought. "Why didn't you tell me?"

"Because the nerve agent is my duty." Emily's part of the burden they'd both assumed after Ned's accident. "When your note arrived, I knew you needed more." She swallowed. "We brewed a new batch, one we thought likely to work."

A sick feeling settled into Amanda's stomach. "And gave it to the eye doctor. How could you?" First the spider, now a potion. The murderer collected their secrets too fast.

The old lady rocked and moaned.

"We didn't know!" Emily objected, but a tear ran down her cheek. "I sent a message with the potion, warning that it should be tested first, but..."

Nadya pulled a shawl over her head and wept.

But the eye doctor took it upon himself to test the formula upon the handiest subject—the delivery boy.

"There's more." Emily's voice was nearly a whisper. "There was a note pinned to Tova's shirt demanding that we produce a working potion or... there would be more needless suffering." Tova's body had been returned as a warning, detailing the pain the eye doctor was willing to inflict upon an innocent.

"Send it where?"

"He didn't say. I assume instructions are to come."

A sudden chill ran through her. She gathered Thornton's coat more tightly about her. "You'll need to let me know, let Thornton know, when he contacts you again. Immediately."

Emily glanced away.

"Don't." Amanda grabbed her sister's arm. "Don't try to manage this on your own, with only gypsies to apprehend the eye doctor. Working together, we all stand a better chance of ending this without more boys losing their lives."

Luca appeared in the doorway. "Lady Amanda, transportation has been arranged. Time to leave." Emily murmured in Romani. Luca frowned. "Five minutes," he said, stepping back outside the vardo.

"Before I go, I need the formula," Amanda said. "There are talented chemists at my school who might be able to help."

Emily nodded and turned, rummaging through a wooden box filled with scraps of paper. She held out a page. "I'll write out what modifications we've tried and send a boy."

Amanda tucked it into her bodice. "You're not safe here, Emily." She glanced at Nadya. "Neither of you are."

Emily's hands clutched her shawl about her chest. "Without us, the eye doctor cannot obtain more nerve agent. He'll leave us be."

"For now. But for how long?"

"If I flee, if I run and hide, more gypsies will suffer for certain." Emily shook her head. "No. I'm staying here. I'll work on the formula. Let me know what your chemists say."

There was no budging Emily once she'd made a decision. "Only if you agree to let me know when the eye doctor contacts you. The very minute he contacts you."

The old woman pulled away the shawl and spoke clearly despite the tears streaming down her cheeks. "The very minute. This man will pay for what he has done."

CHAPTER FIFTEEN

T HORNTON WAS AT his breaking point by the time they reached London's streets. Gypsies and their aversion to steam power.

He'd been on this mechanical beast for over two hours, and each step the clockwork horse took behind the heavy, old crank wagon coiled his impatience tighter. Two long hours in a hard leather saddle fitted to an iron horse with no saddle blanket to compensate for its unforgiving flesh, whose gait jerked and jarred his leg. Two long hours with Amanda sitting sidesaddle in front of him, her leg pressed against his knee, her arm and shoulder bumping against his chest every time the beast lurched right.

And the horse lurched every sixteenth step, yanking on the reins he held.

At first he'd thought the road back to London rutted and littered with oddly shaped stones. Then he'd noticed a pattern and begun counting. It was the horse, not the road.

The dense fog had provided yet another problem. There was little to fix his eyes on and so they kept drifting back to the view in front of him.

Her teal skirts were torn and sagging, her bustle bent into an odd shape. His coat, oversized on her frame, kept slipping from her shoulders and catching about her elbows.

The twists and loops of her hair would have fallen long ago, but for the black ribbon that tangled about them, keeping her hair perched precariously off center above her right ear, presenting him with a tantalizing view of the bare nape of her neck. From that long, elegant neck, it was but a short slide to the magnificence that was her bosom, still lashed in place by those black cords. With agony, he kept his gaze trained on the sway of a pearl earring that dangled from the gently curved shell of her ear.

He closed his eyes, willing himself to think of her in anatomical terms. Her earlobe was but a pinna. Her neck merely the delineation of the sternomastoid muscle running from the base of the skull to the clavicle. The sternum and ribcage defined her upper thoracic cavity over which lay... the most splendid breasts he'd ever seen.

Thornton groaned.

"Does your leg pain you?" she asked. "Pressure points only work a short while at first. I could—"

"No." He wrestled his manners into place. "Thank you. We're almost there. I can manage until we reach the laboratory." Where a dose of Somnic waited.

He'd argued against sharing the clockwork horse with Amanda, claiming impropriety. Something for which his current companions cared little. Luca insisted upon traveling with the body, muttering about promises and honor and tradition. Black only laughed and shook his head before climbing onto the bench beside Luca.

It boggled the mind how the man could be so cheerful when he was en route to inform Lord Avesbury of the demise of Lord Whitmore's dirigible after promising the gypsies restitution that was nothing short of extortion.

The horse lunged right, jarring Amanda against him once more. A special sort of hell this evening was. He'd lost control and kissed a student and this was his punishment, to be forced into close proximity and endless temptation.

Now, in the small hours of the night, he was dragging her and a body and a gypsy—one who was effectively the duke's son-in-law—to the morgue. With luck, they might finish their examination and send Luca on his way, only hours before he was due in the lecture hall to expound upon the chemistry of nerve impulses.

Could the night possibly worsen? Amanda shifted in her sidesaddle and cleared her throat. Yes, it seemed it could. He could be expected to make conversation.

"Emily gave me the formula," she said.

Thank God.

"Unfortunately, it requires a specific flower not currently in bloom. It can't be replicated. Not until spring."

He swore.

"Emily has promised to send me every variation they've tried."

"I'll have the chemists review the formula." They were

the best in the country. If anyone could replicate the nerve agent's effects...

She nodded, her expression grim. "There's more." She told him how the eye doctor had known to contact Emily for additional nerve agent. How, not knowing with whom they dealt, Emily and another gypsy woman sent a vial of the new formula to the murderer himself for testing. How the eye doctor had kept the delivery boy, Tova, to do just that. "The eye doctor has demanded more."

"Is it too much to hope he provided a location?"

"It is. Emily promised to inform me the minute he contacts her."

"She's in danger. So is this woman, Nadya."

"I know. Yet they've refused help."

The traditional gypsy way of dealing with danger, with confrontation, was to fade away. To shift their tents and caravans to new locations, hoping to find safety in relative anonymity. Only when backed into a corner would they fight, but when they fought, they fought brutally.

Thornton liked having Black on his side; he knew where the man's loyalties lay. But he wasn't certain the gypsy tribe, for lack of a better word, would cooperate. He was wrapped up in thoughts of how to work with gypsies when her question caught him entirely off guard.

"So how does a prominent neuroscientist find himself working for the Queen as a field agent?"

Tonight's activities had given her a peek into his life outside Lister University. "Are you asking me if I'm a spy?"

"I'm not really asking." She gave him a knowing look.

"Your average professor would not be charged with the task of catching a murderer."

A smile tugged at his lips. "Spy might be somewhat inaccurate, but one thing leads to another. A useful invention catches the attention of the Crown, much like yours has, and before long, one finds himself in the field."

She glanced over her shoulder, eyebrows raised. "Does your field work often involve mad scientists?"

He barked a laugh. "Quite."

"What other device are you currently testing in the field besides the acousticocept?"

Easily answered. "None."

"No? Perhaps you and Lady Huntley are close to starting field trials?"

"I am not at liberty to discuss my other project with you, Lady Amanda." He said it as kindly as he could, but her back stiffened at the rebuff.

Still she pressed. "I think you've a vested interest in this case, that your expertise is required in the same manner that mine is required. In which case, it would help to know exactly what the eye doctor stole from *your* laboratory."

He stayed silent. He couldn't tell her, but if she guessed...

"Your refusal to inform me of the particulars of your research into an artificial eye may hinder the investigation."

She knew. Not that it surprised him. She had a sharp mind and an instinct for ferreting out the truth. Only Black and Lady Huntley knew the particulars, but she had been let closer to the truth than anyone else who was not directly involved. "Can you explain how you have arrived at such a conclusion?" He asked out of curiosity, wishing to follow the path her sharp mind had taken whilst piecing the facts together into a whole.

"Three things, Lord Thornton." She held up a finger, a long, slender, ungloved finger. "First, you have already created an artificial hearing device which connects directly to the vestibulocochlear nerve, the eighth *cranial* nerve. This you have already implanted into more than one agent of the Crown." A second finger. "You are investigating the gypsy murders, all of which involve missing eyes." Another finger rose. "And the first body I examined involved a severed third *cranial* nerve, a nerve entirely devoted to the movement of the eyeball."

He waited, impressed.

"Therefore, it stands to reason that you and Lady Huntley are in the process of developing an artificial eye which, as our murderous villain has demonstrated, is *not* ready for field trials."

It certainly wasn't.

"Tell me, am I warm?"

The sweet smell of her perfume—overlaid with coal smoke—rose to twine about him. He wanted to drop the reins and once more pull her lips to his. She was more than warm. Brilliant and beautiful, he'd not yet met a woman her equal.

He caved, not to his physical impulses, but to his intellectual ones. "The device was not stolen from my laboratory," he said. "No one could pass the multiple levels of security."

"The pirate attack," she asked, surprising him with her leap. "Not so random?"

"No," he admitted, his hands tightening on the reins. That attack had cost him far more than his best friend and his leg. "The men masquerading as pirates were trained German agents. They knew exactly where to locate the prototype."

Lady Amanda fell silent, digesting this new revelation during which the mechanical horse clopped another fifteen steps. He braced for the lurch, then grimaced at the burst of electrical pain.

The horse straightened. The pain in his leg would fade once they reached Lister Laboratories. The pain of Lord Huntley's betrayal would not.

The two men had competed for highest honors in medical school, but rather than becoming enemies, they'd become fast friends. Their combined brilliance had quickly come to the attention of the Queen, and they'd found all manner of honors and privileges and responsibilities draped about their shoulders.

"Lord Huntley?" Amanda asked, her voice barely a whisper.

"Who else?" he answered, his voice bitter. "It seems his debts were extensive; more than Lady Huntley's dowry was able to repair."

"Greater than his loyalty to his country."

He nodded. Or his friendship. Every single memory poisoned by one act of betrayal.

"I'm sorry," she said. "Lady Huntley must have been devastated."

"Her entire world destroyed," he agreed. "It was how she came to work in my laboratory."

"An attempt to make amends?"

"A kind of indentured servitude in service of the British Empire. The only condition under which the Queen agreed not to revoke the title. His entire family is required to make similar amends."

"Even though they share no guilt?"

"Even though."

She tipped her face upward and caught his gaze. "How can I help?" she asked.

"By continuing your work," he answered, making a snap decision. The relief he felt in allowing her to help shoulder the burden was palpable. Black and Lady Huntley wouldn't like admitting another to the inner laboratory, but what she said was true. The more she knew about the artificial eye, the better prepared she would be to analyze the bodies and therefore the eye doctor's knowledge. "As you well know, there are two kinds of cranial nerves. The sensory nerves—those which convey information to the brain alone, and the motor nerves—those which convey impulses away from the brain to control muscle movement."

"Yes."

"The acousticotransmitter connects to an existing, undamaged sensory cranial nerve. We do not replace the ear so much as we enhance it. Information travels from the device into the brain for processing. There is no need to re-wire the nerve."

"I see."

"In the case of an artificial eye, installation requires severing the connecting cranial nerves, both the sensory nerve—the second cranial nerve, the optic nerve—and those motor nerves that control the movement of the eyeball, cranial nerves three, four and six."

"The oculomotor, the trochlear, and the abducens. Plus, the optic nerve. Four nerves in total. I can't imagine agreeing to such a procedure." She shuddered. "Much more compli-cated and invasive than installing the acousticotransmitter."

And gruesome. He did not look forward to removing a man's eye, but at least he would have their informed consent and the hope of improving their lives. "We will recruit volunteers, veterans who have lost their vision or their eye in its entirety," he reassured her. "At this point, we are only able to successfully connect to the optic nerve. We have restored vision, of sorts, but not the ability to move the eye itself."

"In the first victim, there was no attempt to reconnect the sensory nerve—the optic; what you say has already been done. The eye doctor attempted to rewire only the third cranial nerve, a motor nerve." Then she gasped with sudden insight. "He must be trying to use my spider to reconnect the three motor nerves to the eyeball itself. To control the move-ment of the artificial eye internally." She shifted in her saddle, twisting in his arms. "If he manages that, all eye movement will appear normal. Provided the prosthesis itself does not readily stand out, an artificial eye might well be undetectable without close examination."

"Precisely," he said, reveling in her quick mind. "No external indication is the clear goal, but we've had no success rewiring nerves to muscles. *You* have."

"Temporary success only," she pointed out. "And cranial nerves are vastly different from the peripheral nerves emerging from the spinal cord. Cranial nerves originate from multiple locations within the brain and from within the skull. Peripheral nerves have but one origin and lie outside the central nervous system where my spider can easily access them." She shook her head. "Both cranial nerve origin and accessibility make the prospect difficult if not impossible."

"Exactly," he said. "Once your neurachnid is rebuilt and functioning, the addition of rare earth metals to the golden fibers will stabilize the artificial nerve's connection with the muscle."

"Leaving the problem of the diffuse origin and accessibility to be solved." She looked up, and her gaze locked with his, flashing insight. "Which must be the very problem the eye doctor is attempting to remedy."

"So I suspect. The Germans have had their hands on the prototype now for nearly a year. They have competent neuroscientists. Once the problem of connection is solved, they might very well employ our own technology against us."

She hesitated, fought the temptation to ask—and lost. "What does the eye enhance? How does it form images using the visual cortex? Will you show it to me?"

For the first time in what seemed like forever, Thornton

wanted to laugh. Wanted to trust the woman in his arms and tell her everything, but something held him back. Could he trust his own judge of character? After all, he'd trusted Lord Huntley and that had ended... badly.

As his assistant, Lady Huntley would need to agree to sharing such information, but was she any better judge of character? No. Better to seek the opinion of the one man whose judgment never failed.

"I'll speak with Black about your security clearance," he said.

Her eyes sparkled with excitement. Just as his once had at the promise of ground-breaking advances. If only treachery and betrayal and death hadn't followed... leaving him dependent upon the help of others, upon Somnic. Somehow he needed to find a way to recapture the exhilaration of discovery.

They fell silent. The clockwork horse's hooves pounded out their lurching cadence on the streets as they picked their way through street traffic. Before them the crank wagon rumbled along. At last they rounded the final corner. The building housing the morgue drew into view as the first faint rays of dawn crept around the edges of London's buildings.

They'd arrived. Holding Amanda in his arms was torture, but letting her go was worse.

CHAPTER SIXTEEN

T HE PAIN OF DISMOUNTING from the horse nearly
brought Thornton to his knees. Black caught him
at the last second, saving him from collapsing on
the flagstone walkway outside the laboratory complex. There
was no way he could help Black carry the body into the
morgue. Not without more Somnic.

Black assisted Amanda with her dismount, then turned
to Luca. "If you'll assist me with the body."

Luca narrowed his eyes and pointedly crossed his arms,
not moving a single step.

Thornton let loose his fury, words tearing from his
throat. "Do you think *you* are safe? Perhaps. But what of
your *wife* and unborn child?"

Luca's hands curled into fists.

"That's right. The eye doctor believes Lady Emily can
brew him something he needs, something he wants badly. A

drug to assist him with his macabre surgeries. He's *not* going to leave her alone."

Luca's eyes grew wide with alarm. His gaze shifted to Amanda who confirmed his testimony with a grim nod.

"Do you understand now?" He pointed at his chest. "I'm your best hope of ending this." He pointed at Black and Amanda and once more back at himself. "We're your best hope at stopping these murders and keeping your family safe. So stop acting like we're desecrating your dead and start helping."

Amanda laid a calming hand on his arm. "Enough," she said, then turned to Luca. "Please, Luca. What Lord Thornton and I glean from a scientific examination of Tova may very well be key to preventing another gypsy death."

Silently, the gypsy turned and helped Black carry the litter toward the morgue.

"Was that really necessary?" she asked curtly.

"Yes," he bit out, wiping a hand over his face, over the rough stubble of a long night and wondering if he had the strength to reach his office. He'd lost his cane in the crash, but what were his options? Stand about like a stork until Black thought to come back with a litter for him?

"Your leg," she said. "Lean on me." She draped his arm about her shoulders. "I'm stronger than I look."

He gritted his teeth and swallowed his pride. With slow, painful lurching steps, he made his way into the building and down the hall to his office. At least at this hour there was no one to witness his humiliation.

Inside, he dropped heavily onto the nearest chair and began tugging at his pant leg, exposing the metal brace to her view. Not once—not since the brace was fitted—had another individual viewed his infirmity. But she'd felt the brace, threaded her fingers beneath its bars to bring him relief. The pain had grown so debilitating he could no longer hide his agony.

"I could—"

"Not necessary," he cut her off, declining her touch. "I keep a supply available there." He indicated a carved wooden box sitting on a shelf.

She retrieved it, but her hand hesitated. Thornton snatched it from her and flipped the lid open. He snapped the tip off a glass vial and poured the entire dosage into a glass syringe, tapping away the bubbles. He plunged the needle into his leg, the sting barely registering over the nerve that screamed in agony.

Slowly, blessed numbness spread across the side of his lower leg, from his knee down to his toes. Six hours of relief. All that was left was the mental exhaustion that gnawed on his brain. He rose, limping across the room to grab an old cane.

"Shall we?" He indicated the open door, gesturing for her to precede him. There was a gypsy to examine and, hopefully, a spy to thwart.

"Just like that?" She didn't take a single step toward the door, instead she planted two fists upon her hips. "As if you didn't just inject yourself with five milliliters of the most powerful nerve agent available when, at the price of five minutes, pressure point therapy would have provided you with nearly four hours' relief."

"One."

"One what?" she snapped, her body vibrating with frustration.

He needed to push her away. "One hour, Lady Amanda. It only worked for one hour. If that. Now. Your impatient and irate brother-in-law waits below." He waved toward the door again.

"Later, then." With clipped steps, she brushed past.

"No."

"No?" She froze, her back stiff, her chin high. Without looking back.

Though it would pain them both, it needed to be stated aloud. For him as well as her. "Let us be clear," he said. "The last few hours may have created an artificial sense of... intimacy, but it's not your place to direct my actions with regard to my personal health. We must remember that we work together in a professional capacity alone."

"Is that so, Lord Thornton?" She strode from the room without a backward glance. Leaving the room feeling decidedly empty.

Thornton followed, knowing she would make him regret those words.

In the morgue, all was in readiness. The bright limelight burned over the examination table, casting Tova's maimed face and neck into stark relief. Luca, pale and drawn, stood with his back pressed to the wall as far as he could remove himself from the body.

Lady Amanda wasted no time beginning her examination and the incongruity struck him as surreal. She pulled a stained canvas apron over lace and silk, then twisted her hair tightly behind her head, pinning it in place with a number of tongue depressors. His lips twitched, trying to form an unwelcome smile. She snapped magnifying goggles into place and bent over the body to probe the empty eye socket.

She asked for no assistance, and he offered none. He set about collecting a variety of blood and skin samples, studying the hands and nails closely for any clues they might reveal. Wrists and ankles were rubbed raw where they appeared to have been restrained by a coarse grade of rope. The forehead also showed indications of restraint. All marks not found on earlier victims. The eye doctor was operating in less than ideal conditions.

Fifteen minutes later, his samples were labeled and stored for later examination. Lady Amanda also declared herself done and began her report, speaking in the general direction of his left shoulder.

"Only one eye was removed. Likely the eye doctor realized that nerve agent was ineffective and aborted the procedure. However, there are, now that I know what I'm looking for, indications that he successfully interfaced with the optic nerve."

Black shot him a dark, pointed glare.

"She figured it out on her own. I did not *tell* her about the phaoscope."

Black's jaw clenched.

Lady Amanda ignored them both. She continued, "From

the location of the gold fibers in the superior orbital fissure, he attempted to establish a connection with the trochlear nerve, the fourth cranial nerve—and failed."

He nodded. "Consistent with our expectations."

"There's more. Look." She ripped the magnifying goggles from her head. Tongue depressors clattered to the ground as long strands of wavy hair spread wildly across bare shoulders. He felt a pang of regret as she handed the goggles to him. "Here." She lifted a blunt-nosed probe and indicated a bit of the gold wire she'd teased free of the congealing tissue. "Remember from the last victim how the threads wove together in a tight concentric pattern?"

"Yes." He pulled the lenses over his eyes and studied the gold fibers. "The weave pattern is less compact. Almost web-like."

She began to pace. "It's exactly as we feared. The eye doctor *is* making his own improvements to my neurachnid." Her eyes blazed with insight. "It's genius. The eye doctor may be evil, but he's also brilliant. If... I need paper." She crossed the tiled room to the sink, her ruined gown dragging behind her. She washed her hands with determined concentration. Meanwhile, he pulled open drawers, dragging forth a dull pencil and autopsy forms. The backs were blank.

"Thank you," she said, accepting the pencil and paper. Standing at the cold, steel counter, Lady Amanda began to sketch. He watched, entranced, as her idea took form before his eyes. She paused, tapping the pencil against the paper in irritation. "It's missing something. How can we connect the..."

He plucked the pencil from her hand and added a small modification. "With an extension of the pin here and a size three spring there."

"That would do it." Her voice was tight, her gaze fixed upon the design.

The gears and pins and rods modified as she indicated, along with some programming changes to the Babbage card, would adjust the pincers so that they could angle through the supraorbital fissure in a manner that would allow wires tipped with rare earth elements to penetrate the brainstem in multiple locations, thereby tapping into the diffuse elements of the cranial nerve.

It was nothing short of brilliant, but he kept his admiration to himself. She was a member of his laboratory, nothing more.

"*That*," she stabbed the paper with a finger, "is what our eye doctor is attempting. His modifications are incomplete, and the ineffective nerve agent sabotaged his most recent effort to test his spider improvements."

"Unfortunately," Thornton said, "we're no closer to discovering who the eye doctor is, or where he conducts his experiments."

Black spoke up. "Nevertheless, his failure buys us time."

Luca shifted, drawing attention. "But at what price?"

CHAPTER SEVENTEEN

AMANDA DIDN'T CONSIDER a chaperone necessary for an afternoon walk with Henri along Clockwork Corridor. It was a public thoroughfare. If the still-burning gas street lamps only served to give the fog that swirled about her skirts an otherworldly glow, she could at least claim the street was well lit.

They passed a number of storefronts that possessed such parts as were required for the neurachnid's modifications, but few possessed them at both the minuscule size and the quality required. Such was the ostensible reason they searched for Nicu Sindel's vardo.

The other reason was personal. She worried for her sister's safety. For the safety of her impending niece or nephew. For Luca, for Nadya, and even Nicu himself. Though most of the eye doctor's targets had been young and male, knowing what she now did, there was no reason to think the murderer would not select a different target.

Perhaps, now that they were on alert, the eye doctor would avoid gypsies altogether.

After rushing home to attend to her appearance, she'd attended classes then reported to the laboratory—attempting normalcy—to find the great man himself cloistered within the eye laboratory and unavailable. Though disappointed, Amanda knew proper channels must be followed before the Queen's agents and Black would grant her permission to view the phaoscope.

The idea intrigued her more than she cared to admit. She was desperate to know the details of this ground-breaking research. That the phaoscope was a more advanced eye providing its user with super-human visual acuity was certain—as was its secretive nature, but from the look of pride on Thornton's face she *knew* there was more.

But Henri had been awaiting her arrival.

With a broad, welcoming grin, he'd clapped his hands and rocked back on his heels. "I hear a brilliant modification is to be made to the neurachnid?"

She smiled in return; it was impossible not to return such a greeting. "A breakthrough, perhaps. A modification of the pincers should allow us to access the very origin of the cranial nerve inside the brain."

"Ah, we will slide inside the very fissures and foramen of the skull."

"That is the plan." She had pulled the sketches from her satchel and handed them to him.

Henri stroked his goatee as he perused the pages and noises of pleasure escaped his throat. At last he spoke. "Brilliant. A vast improvement over our method for installing the acousticotransmitter. It might prevent all the resultant intense nausea and dizziness." His gaze rose. "Once again, we need supplies. Have you a list?"

"Of course." She waved a long strip of paper.

"Only Nicu will do. Shall we?"

He'd offered his arm, she'd accepted, and they had set out on their quest into the gloom of London's streets. Last night's fog had yet to lift.

They searched the entirety of Clockwork Corridor without success and began turning down narrow side streets. Nicu was proving elusive as he had for the past several days. Amanda hadn't seen him in the camp on Putney Heath, but the fog and the trees and the time pressure hadn't allowed her to search for him there. But perhaps he was, perhaps he remained for the funeral services, in which case their search was in vain.

"Pardon me," Henri said. "You look tired, my lady. Too many late hours working on your invention?"

Chasing after it, rather. "It's exhausting," she admitted. "Living two lives."

His eyebrows lifted.

"The social expectations of a lady of the *ton* do not mesh well with that of medical student."

"Ahh. Yes. It is hard for Lord Thornton as well."

"Hard?" she scoffed. The man *wanted* no social life. "He buries himself in his work. I don't believe he has ever been sighted on a ballroom floor or on Rotten Row. Not even before his injury."

"He broods too much over things he cannot change. You are good for him."

Her head jerked in his direction. "Good?"

"You bring him out of his shell." Henri's voice radiated approval. "He attended a ball last night, did he not? The man could use some feminine distraction."

It was not her presence at a ball that had drawn him there. Realizing two of his daughters were now involved in the gypsy murders, Father had taken it upon himself to personally oversee the situation. It seemed Father was Thornton's superior, though the hierarchy eluded her. In any case, the Duke of Avesbury crooked his finger and, quite probably against his will, Thornton appeared.

It annoyed her to no end that Father had seen fit to give Thornton Emily's location directly, an attempt to keep Amanda herself from visiting the gypsies. If not for Simon's overzealousness in his suit and Thornton's injured leg, they would not have found themselves locked in a dark, moonlit room where, for a moment, she'd glimpsed cracks in the man's hard exterior.

"I don't think he wishes to be distracted," Amanda answered. "Not by me. He scurried quickly back inside that shell." The moment rational thought returned and he realized he'd kissed a student.

"A shame. If that's what you want, leave him there. Otherwise, lure him back out. The man, he has inside such life and loyalty if only..." Catching sight of a vardo, Henri trailed off, but it was not the one for which they searched.

Despite Thornton's clear determination their relationship would remain professional, she'd no intention of ceasing her attempts to break through the man's hard exterior. During that brief experience, when all of that passion had been directed at her... Something inside her had certainly cracked.

Her world had shifted and now hung askew, and the easy assumption that she would marry Sommersby had grown exponentially harder. Not only did that man have two left feet—one of the many reasons she'd thought to hide—but he lacked vision, drive. Passion.

Once she'd thought to content herself with a permissive, passive husband. One she could control. One she could predict.

Now she wanted something... more. She wanted a husband whose touch sent blue flames jumping across her skin, a husband whose mind and ambitions were equal to her own. She wanted a partner, not simply a spouse.

"He's shown incredible loyalty to Lord Huntley, agreeing to keep his wife on as an assistant in his laboratory after he committed such treachery."

Henri laughed. "Is that what you think? My dear, Lady Huntley is no burden. How do you think she met Lord Huntley? I am told he was no more inclined to attend a ball than Thornton. That he attended through duty. No, they met through a shared passion for science."

"Really?" Misplaced envy flared.

He nodded. "A sad, sad tale. The long-distance transmitter was her invention, you see. Without her invention, the acousticocept would not be. I am told it was a whirlwind romance, a swift wedding and, dreadfully, a marriage cut short."

They ought not be gossiping so, but if Amanda was going to pursue Thornton, the more information she had... "I'm told Lord Huntley sold a device under development to the Germans, a prototype."

"When Thornton was brought to me, he'd lost quite a bit of blood. That was bad enough, but the infection, the bacterially secreted toxins, left him raving. From what I could piece together, Lord Huntley transmitted their location to the Germans the entire time they were in the air. Airship pirates, ha!"

"Yet they killed him, Lord Huntley," she said, forcing her feet to move again.

"So they did. Sliced his neck the moment they had what they'd come for." Henri paused a moment. "Thornton rewarded those who were faithful. He saved Lady Huntley by making her his most trusted assistant, and he opened opportunities for me. Here, I am compensated well enough to take better care of Mama. She is ill."

Amanda glanced at Henri. "What ails her?"

He shrugged. "No one can say. Not even the best physicians Thornton makes available. Yesterday a letter arrived informing me she has taken a turn for the worse."

"Can she not come here?"

"Will not." He shook his head. "I make plans to visit her. Soon."

"Henri! Old friend," a voice hailed. In the fog, Nicu's

figure shimmered before his maroon vardo. Behind him stood his grumpy apprentice, Milosh.

"At last," Henri said. "So, enough of what is past. The present is enough for now. We will find the parts for this newest spider modification and do as we must to access the cranial nerve roots. Still, I think, you and I will work to be certain that one day soon, your neurachnid can spin a fila-ment that will repair Thornton's leg."

"We will." Even if it meant she did not sleep for the rest of the month.

They climbed the stairs into the caravan, exchanging greetings, politely declining Nicu's offer to have Milosh serve tea and biscuits, and moving swiftly to business.

"Those fish claw pins you asked for, Henri, I have found them." Nicu pulled a wooden box from a shelf and handed it to him.

"Wonderful," Henri exclaimed. Monocle in place, he began to pluck through the various pins, muttering excitedly under his breath. Then, suddenly remembering himself, he looked up. Beneath his crooked top hat, his magnified eye seemed to bulge in alarm. "So sorry, Lady Amanda, let us first attend to your list." He lowered the box.

She fought the temptation to laugh at the picture he presented. "No, Henri, find what you need. Take your time."

"Milosh," Nicu said. "Please see to Henri's needs. I have some very special pieces I wish to suggest to Lady Amanda."

Milosh glowered, but moved to stand beside Henri.

Nicu took her list and drew her aside, deeper into the

vardo near a wooden partition that divided the business half from the living half. The door providing entry was ajar, beyond it nothing but a simple bed and a small table and chair.

He spread an array of clockwork components before her, his smile fading. "Lady Amanda, the Romanichal currently of Putney Heath are in disarray. My sister, Nadya, despairs. She is certain your chemists will not be able to replicate the formula without the bloom of the *amatiflora*. The elders wish to move on, immediately. The younger men wish to seek vengeance and actively hunt this eye doctor." He shook his head. "Now there are *gadjos* living among us, desecrating our camp. These men claim to be there at Lord Avesbury's request, yet refuse to tell us anything about what is happening. Is any progress being made? Any hint as to who this murderer might be?"

Father had inserted guards at the gypsy camp? She shook her head. "None. We know only that he is very clever. And German, or likely so. He seeks to use my clockwork spider and Emily's formula to his own government's end." Guilt tightened her chest. Even sharing this much felt like a betrayal. "As to the potion, I've heard nothing."

"Yet you continue to build another spider and ask Emily to continue her work on the formula." His voice was bitter. Unlike Amanda, his loyalty was not divided. "It seems to me, that like the Germans, the British have their own nefarious goals."

"Those of self-preservation," she replied. "We do not, will not, resort to such unethical means to make scientific progress. The eye doctor, he has no such scruples. Will you help?"

Nicu shook his head. "Not directly. We claim no citizenship. We only wish to live in peace."

"The eye doctor is unlikely to allow that."

"Nor is the British government."

Amanda sighed. "Then we must all do what we think is best and hope to end this soon."

"Guard this device well." His expression was stern. "I did not teach you all I know only to see it turned upon my people."

"I will." Every day she regretted not installing a more secure lock upon her laboratory door. "You will guard Emily?"

"Of course. We all will," he said. Nicu pointed to a golden gear. Back to business. "This one. The cogs are tempered with iridium and will not bend."

CHAPTER EIGHTEEN

WITH THE PARTS they required in hand, Amanda and Henri returned to the laboratory and set to work. The afternoon hours melted into those of the early evening. The great iron door opened and closed as laboratory technicians departed one by one, until only she and Henri remained.

Then Henri too reached for his coat. "It is late. Perhaps that is enough progress for today?"

Amanda sat back, flipping up the lenses of her glasses. Her eyes were dry. Her neck ached. And she deeply regretted her fashionable choice of attire. The too-tight corset she wore dug into her ribs, but she'd wanted Thornton to look at her again with heat in his eyes, now more than ever. There was more between them than work alone, and Amanda intended to explore those possibilities. She didn't care that his leg was failing. She could help, if only he'd let her. If physical beauty was the key to drawing his attention...

Amanda sighed. She'd seen neither hide nor hair of the man she'd worn it for, not since this morning's anatomy lecture. Even then, he refused to so much as look in her direction. She flirted with disaster, but for a man like Thornton, she would take the risk.

If only he would return the sentiment.

Alas, all he seemed interested in pursuing was the neurachnid and the nerve agent. Yet even after the spider was rebuilt, even after the formula was reconstituted, how would it bring them any closer to catching the eye doctor?

She wanted to *do* something. Something to lure the eye doctor from his lair, but she couldn't act on her own. So, until Thornton or Black saw fit to include her... She glanced at the tightly closed door to the inner laboratory.

"*Oui*. He is inside. It may be hours before he emerges."

"I'll just adjust the tension on this spring then..."

"*Bien sur*. Do as you think best." He gave her a knowing wink and exited the lab.

Amanda sat there, screwdriver in hand. Was she being tested to see if she could continue working for him after their... moment? Or punished for daring to confront him? She looked around the empty laboratory. Or perhaps just forgotten.

Whichever it was, she'd had enough. Under the watchful eyes of the rats, she locked the neurachnid in its safe, along with the as yet unused clockwork pieces, and reached for her cape. The rats suddenly froze, every whiskered nose pointing toward the door at the back of the laboratory, every sensitive pink ear on alert. The door's many gears began to turn.

Lady Huntley stepped from within, her face tight and unreadable. "Amanda, if you're ready, Thornton and Black have arranged for a one-time visit to our interior laboratory. If you'll place your hand here." She gestured to a security pad much like the one used to unlock the laboratory's great iron door.

Her exhaustion forgotten, Amanda crossed the room and placed her hand on the glass plate. As Lady Huntley made adjustments in the device, she studied the woman. Dressed in full mourning, the absence of color only highlighted the woman's bright hair and pale complexion. An ethereal beauty. The moment a full year had passed, the moment the color of her attire lightened, gentlemen would be in pursuit.

"I was sorry to learn of your... situation," she offered. All too easily it could have been Amanda in her position.

Lady Huntley's fingers paused. "You refer to my indentured servitude? I understand Thornton informed you of my husband's traitorous acts."

Delicacy was not her strong suit, but Amanda tried. "Is it so very awful? The conditions?"

"Working here, with Thornton, is everything a neuroscientist could dream. Any resource I desire, I have only to ask. Socially, my life is a nightmare. When I leave the laboratory, I return to my husband's town home and stay there—alone— until it is once again time to return here."

Amanda felt an upwelling of sympathy.

The only daughter of a wealthy industrialist, Lady Huntley had stayed at her father's side, caring for him. Though instead of needle-pointing pillows, she'd experimented with magnetic aether waves and, over time, developed the transmitter now used in the acoustico work. Upon her father's death, she'd done the near impossible—she'd put *herself* on the *ton* marriage mart and managed to land an earl in less than a month.

"May I ask a personal question, Lady Huntley?"

"You already have." Lady Huntley did not meet her eyes. Instead, she pressed a heavy metal plate onto the surface of Amanda's hand, pushing her palm into an odd pliable substance. "You may feel a slight tingle."

"Do you wish you'd never married?" A faint electrical pulse ran through her fingers.

Lady Huntley's hand shook as it hovered above a lever. "Our marriage was mutually beneficial, my dowry for his title—and the ability to continue my work. It wasn't love at first sight. Although, in the short time we had together, a certain... understanding developed."

"Would you... recommend marriage?"

"That is two questions." Lady Huntley pulled the lever. A final gear turned and the lock released. "If you'll follow me."

A sore point, Amanda realized. She'd overstepped her bounds, but it was hard not to compare herself to Lady Huntley. They were of a same age and had similar interests. A husband was a complicating factor, and she wasn't certain how one would alter the equation of her life. Lady Huntley was the only one she knew who might be able to shed light on the matter.

Perhaps—scientist or not—the widow of a traitor was not

the woman she should ask.

She stepped through the door.

The inner laboratory space was much like the outer one, only smaller. On a miniature operating table lay a white rat, his nose connected to a miniature ether mask. Lord Thornton sat on a stool beside his patient, manning the anesthesia. He nodded a greeting, barely glancing at her.

The rat's foot twitched. "A few minutes more. While we wait, Lady Amanda can inspect the device." He indicated a small metal tray holding a number of tools and, nestled in gauze, a small pink glass sphere with a long wire protruding from its center.

"The phaoscope?" Amanda did not touch the sterile object. "It's so small." She looked at Thornton. "This cannot be the device the eye doctor is attempting to activate."

"Of course not. This is not much more than a tiny lens, a simplified prototype." His voice was dismissive. "The wire inserts directly into the optic nerve, sending electronic impulses to the visual cortex for interpretation. The human prototype is far more complex. Lady Huntley, if you will."

The widow handed her a wooden box. "*This* is the human prototype."

Amanda opened the lid and peered inside. A blue eye peered back from a nest of cotton batting. "May I?" she asked, her fingers already reaching.

He nodded.

She lifted the surprisingly light glass sphere, marveling in its human likeness. Pliable strips attached to its sides in strategic positions. "Artificial muscle," she marveled, remembering the substance that had molded to her hand. "Capable of responding to electrical impulses. It contracts?"

"It does."

"Amazing."

"So it is," he said. "We call it myotech. As you are aware, muscle attachment to the cranial nerve and, therefore, control of eye movement is our current stumbling block. At present, all movements must be controlled by external wires and an impulse generator. Though if the myotech could be connected to the original nerve..."

"There would be no external evidence that the eye is artificial."

"Exactly. Unfortunately, so far our attempts to connect existing cranial nerves to myotech have failed. Your device could provide the perfect solution."

She was missing something. True, having both eyes track together would provide the individual with both natural appearance and greater visual acuity, but... No. This device was not simply an artificial eye. A spy would be after something like enhanced vision. "There has to be more," she said, turning toward Thornton. "Does it provide the wearer with unusually keen vision?"

Thornton's eyes lit up.

"Look closer," Lady Huntley prompted.

Amanda rotated the glass eye in her palm, examining the iris. The radial striations were convincingly real and even contained small flecks of brown and gold, but the pupil was not perfectly round. "A hexagonal aperture. It adjusts to varying light levels?"

Impressive.

"If I may?" Lady Huntley held out her hand for the sphere. With a gentle twist, the eye fell open into halves. Inside was an exquisite piece of machinery. "With this lens installed, an agent could read a document over the shoulder of a man standing one hundred yards distant."

Amanda gasped. That alone explained the interest in the artificial eye. "How is the focus mechanism controlled?" She leaned closer, tracing the pathways of the wires. "The muscles!"

"Exactly," Thornton confirmed, pride melting away his icy demeanor. "With a series of preset eye movements, the agent will be able to focus at superhuman distances. What's more, the artificial eye is a camera."

Eyes wide, Amanda followed Lady Huntley to a wooden box. It was plain, but for the slots carved in one end.

"This is the receiver. Much like a traditional camera, you prepare the plate and slide it in here." Lady Huntley indicated the slots. "Either the agent or the person manning the camera can initiate exposure. In a matter of minutes, we can see whatever the agent himself is viewing."

Unless one stood nose to nose with said agent, the eye would appear so real, no one would know images were being taken and transmitted. It certainly explained the over-the-top security.

Lady Huntley walked over to the operating table and pinched a tiny pink foot. "No response. I believe we're ready." She lowered herself to a stool at the head of the table, and together, she and Thornton bent over the rat, working seamlessly.

The small wire of the tiny, glass sphere was inserted into the optic nerve. Moments later, after a few well-placed stitches and an injection of morphine, the rat was returned to a small cage to recover upon a rubber flask filled with warm water.

"As yet, we only have daguerreotypes from a rat's-eye perspective. There have been no human trials yet," Lady Huntley stated.

"By you," Amanda pointed out. "Though the eye doctor is doing his best. On gypsies. Against their will and with no regard for their life."

"Do not compare us to him," Lady Huntley snapped. "Not in any way. Our techniques are always brought to perfection first." She gave Amanda a level stare. "You can rest assured all our human patients—veterans or agents— arrive here voluntarily and already missing an eye."

Amanda tried to apologize. "I didn't mean to...."

Thornton understood. "She's not criticizing our research, Lady Huntley, merely observing that all this," he said, waving a hand, "gets us no closer to catching a murderer. Nor will her completion of the redesigned neurachnid." He stood, unbuttoned his laboratory coat, and hung it from a peg. "Lady Huntley is merely feeling the pressure of another investigation into her husband's activities."

The woman in question crossed her arms and gave Thornton a pointed look. "I don't appreciate the Queen's agents once again combing through John's possessions. They didn't find his contact last time, what makes Black think they'll find him now?"

Thornton stabbed his fingers through his hair. "It's an avenue that cannot be ignored. You know as well as I that John once courted Lady Amanda. He knew about the device she was developing."

Amanda's heart jumped, picking up its pace. "You think he told the Germans about my device?" It had been nearly a year since she'd spoken with Lord Huntley, and then, only to wish him happy in his new marriage.

A tight nod. "It may very well be his contact who sent the eye doctor to London, to seek out and secure the means and ability to install the phaoscope."

A dark cloud settled over Lady Huntley's face. "If this gets out, my reputation—what little I have left—will be destroyed."

"We've no choice. No other leads," Thornton countered. "Black and his men have found nothing but rumors and vague descriptions of the eye doctor that fit nearly half of London's inhabitants. Beyond gypsy bodies, he leaves no evidence of his... work." He released a long, burdened exhalation. "I won't sit idly by waiting for him to make a mistake at the cost of more lives. If he manages to connect the cranial nerves to the myotech, he'll disappear. Once the phaoscope is operational in German hands, it will be used against us. Against our own agents. Against our own country. We must do something."

"Fine. Do as you must." Lady Huntley turned away and,

with abrupt, angry movements, began to set the small laboratory to rights.

"What of his knowledge of the nerve agent?" Amanda
asked. She was almost certain she'd not discussed *that* with
Lord Huntley.

A clang rang out as Lady Huntley set down a tray with
more force than necessary. "It seems my husband paid court
to quite a number of young ladies before we met. Why not
your sister?"

Why not? Emily had danced with Lord Huntley on more
than one occasion.

Thornton looked pained. "In any case, your father has
taken steps to ensure his daughters' safety. Even now, agents
posing as gypsies are in her camp. You will find agents by
your side as well. Please show your newest footmen kindness. They are not enamored of the required uniforms."

CHAPTER NINETEEN

THE NEXT MORNING, Black stopped him with a yell in the hallway outside the lecture hall. "Lord Thornton!"

Several of his students cast curious looks in their direction. Neither of them were at their best and, quite possibly, looked every bit like dissolute peers. Black sounded harassed; his face was drawn and lacked his usual cheeky grin. Thornton himself had glanced in the mirror earlier and noticed a gathering darkness beneath his own eyes.

Unpleasant thoughts raced round his head constantly—Amanda. The eye doctor. His failing leg—and sleep eluded him.

"Find anything new?" Thornton asked, referring to the search of the Huntley townhouse.

"Nothing."

"I suppose it was too much to hope John kept a hidden diary with details of his German contacts."

Black didn't smile. "He left nothing behind. I begin to suspect he didn't intend to return."

That surprised Thornton. With his debts cleared, Huntley had plenty to return to. A beautiful wife, his estates, his research, his family. Perhaps John had intended to leave on the pirate airship after all. Though the way the short, burly pseudo-pirate had sliced the neck of his former friend certainly didn't indicate he was interested in a new alliance.

Thornton ran a hand over his eyes. He'd dragged John with him, into the evacuation glider, the extra time devoted to saving his friend earning him a cutlass slice to his leg. John hadn't lived long enough to reach the ground, despite Thornton's attempts to save him. If not for a kind farmer in the fields below who bound his leg and delivered him quickly to Henri, he too would have died.

He'd certainly felt like dying. What with the infection raging through his bloodstream and the new knowledge that his closest friend had turned traitor. They'd been en route to a conference on nerve conduction, all research prototypes left securely behind on British soil. The discovery that Huntley had been transporting the phaoscope prototype had shattered five years of companionship and trust.

"The Queen asks too much of you," Thornton said, dragging his mind back to the present. Helping the agent adjust to his new acousticotransmitter and all its accompanying abilities, reopening the investigation into Lord Huntley's treasonous activities, forcing the gypsies to accept the presence of government agents, and overseeing Lady Amanda's protection.

Black sighed.

"Leave Lady Amanda to me." He could at least coordinate the guards that stood watch. He wouldn't put kidnapping beyond the eye doctor, not if the man thought he could harness and direct Amanda's clockwork skills.

"That would be a great help," Black said. "I'll tell them to report to you."

"Good. Now, I've a class to euthanize." Leaning on his cane, he turned to go.

"Wait." Black reached inside his coat and pulled out a brown paper-wrapped package. "I'm not certain how much longer I can obtain extra doses. The pace at which you are consuming this has caused eyebrows to rise."

"Thank you." With thinly veiled relief, Thornton took the Somnic and tucked the package of vials inside his pocket. "I won't need it much longer."

"How soon to failure?"

"A month or so," Thornton lied. Until the eye doctor was caught, he couldn't admit the truth to Black. Not if he wished to be allowed even the rare moment of fieldwork in pursuit of the eye doctor. According to his calculations, he had less than a week.

Thornton made his way to the front of the lecture hall. In large letters he wrote the day's topic on the chalkboard: Theory of Synaptic Transmission. He didn't need to turn and look to confirm when Lady Amanda entered the lecture theater. A certain heated and hushed whispering always accompanied her arrival. Today there were even low whistles of approval.

His hand paused not one bit as he finished sketching a chalk outline of a nerve. Beside it, he wrote the central theorem that was today's commonly accepted explanation for nerve conduction and began a list of supporting evidence. At the end of the lecture, he'd throw in a few ideas that most thought to be mere hypotheses or far-fetched possibilities.

They weren't.

Perhaps a bright student would see though his abstruse and cryptic comments to divine the truth. It was the purpose of Lister University to find those brilliant minds, to harness them in service of the Crown. Such students, like Amanda, promptly found themselves sworn to secrecy and working in a secure laboratory.

Thornton knew the moment she took her seat, the empty one next to Sommersby, for it didn't require extraordinary powers of hearing to regret overhearing their conversation.

Sommersby sounded wounded. "You were much missed at last night's dinner party. Though our hostess was grateful to Lady Olivia for making up the numbers."

"My apologies, Simon. A breakthrough in the laboratory occurred, and I simply couldn't tear myself away. Please, allow me to make it up to you."

Her conciliatory tone irritated him. As did her use of Sommersby's given name. Thornton snapped the stick of chalk he held. He set aside half and continued with his list, grinding the calcium carbonate into the board somewhat more firmly that perhaps necessary.

"Your research consumes all your attention," Sommersby

whined. Thornton's hand paused. "You are forever in Lord Thornton's laboratory."

"Not on Sundays."

He could hear her eyelashes bat.

"Excellent." Sommersby's normal cheer returned. "I'll pick you up Sunday afternoon then. I've a new phaeton I'm dying to take out."

She giggled.

Giggled! He threw aside the piece of chalk he held and spun to face his audience—and had to clench his jaw to keep it from dropping. He shouldn't have looked. That was his first mistake. Ever since the kiss they'd shared at the ball, he'd made a concerted effort to keep his eyes firmly above her neck. For it didn't seem to matter what the woman garbed herself in, his mind immediately began plotting the most satisfying method of removing it.

Today, she'd outdone herself.

Though a brown velvet jacket covered her from neck to wrist, it cut away in front just below her shoulders. This allowed the cream ruffles of her shirtwaist to emphasize the fullness of her bosom above a striped, wasp-waisted cincher that itself served only to outline and uplift two particularly large and round feminine assets.

A few snickered. At him.

His teeth ground away a millimeter of enamel as he realized he'd just been reduced to the level of his students. He cleared his throat and fixed his eyes on her face, but that was no better. Her eyes sparkled with amusement and knowledge. She'd caught him staring at her chest and not even discreetly. From the faint curve of her full lips, he wondered if perhaps that had been her very goal.

She was going to be his undoing.

His face carefully impassive, he launched into his performance, concentrating instead upon searching the faces of his students for sudden insight and understanding of his cryptic comments—any face but hers. "And that is why Johannes Webber speculates that the constant factor of stimulus places a significant limitation on the magnitude..."

All his students were scratching notes, looking thoroughly confounded. Among them, only Lady Amanda sat immobile and serene. She wrote not a single word. She alone saw through him. It was unnerving.

Nevertheless, he had an hour to fill.

As he droned on, in the back of his mind, he evaluated the irrational emotions that coursed through him. It seemed women were fickle, even the bright ones. At the ball, Amanda had hidden from Sommersby. Today, she encouraged him. Yet it was Thornton she'd kissed. His laboratory that took precedence over a dinner party.

Insight struck like lightning.

He turned his gaze in Amanda's direction, careful to prattle on. Her lips twitched. He was right. She'd purposefully encouraged Sommersby here, in his presence, her intent clearly to annoy. She dressed not for Sommersby. She dressed for him, her anatomy professor. She was toying with him.

Yet it was a husband she needed, not an illicit affair with her mentor.

Unless she intended to have first one, then the other.

That thought made him bristle. The rules clearly stated that there were to be no romantic liaisons between male professors and female students. They were not permitted to openly court. But the statute was vague about marriage.

Marriage.

Thornton tripped over his words, losing his train of thought for a moment and stringing together unrelated words to resemble a sentence until he recalled the point he'd been about to make. Of course, he would one day be forced to wed in order to produce an heir, but his responsibilities to the Crown, the school, his laboratory were all-consuming. He had no actual desire to take a wife.

Did he?

He turned back to the board and began to sketch. "So, with regard to the tactile experience, the phenomenology of impulse resists quantification." He spun back to the audience, jabbing a finger in the air as if he made a key point. "What if it could be linked to a specific application of pressure and electrical current?"

Amanda lifted a hand, the back of her gloveless fingers pressing against her mouth as if holding back a laugh—and he knew *she* knew he was making this all up. Did she realize she was the reason behind the words that popped to mind?

Tactile. Impulse. Pressure. Current.

For he felt all those in her presence. Even in the labora-

tory when he watched her nimble fingers make fine adjustments to the clockwork spider, wondering how those same
fingers would feel moving over the fine hairs and nerve
endings of human skin.

His skin.

He turned away. Now was not the time for such imagin-
ings. He shoved the annoying thoughts and feelings into a
corner of his mind for future examination and walled them
off through sheer force of will and finished his lecture.

"A word, Lady Amanda," he said, as the other students
shuffled from the room, concern over solving the assigned
electrochemistry problem clear on their faces and in their
subdued voices.

She took her time gathering her things, stepping down to
stand before the podium. From the intent look on her face,
he thought it wise to keep the piece of furniture between
them. "Yes, Lord Thornton?" She leaned forward. Ruffles
shifted. He kept his gaze carefully on her face.

"Do you think it wise to abstain from laboratory work on
Sundays?"

Her back stiffened. "Jealousy does not become you, Lord
Thornton. You made your lack of intent clear."

"Jealousy has nothing to do with it," he lied. "You. Are.
Needed. In the laboratory."

She climbed up one step, then turned around, bringing
her eyes level with his own. "But not desired?"

He glared at her, exasperated. There was no way to reply
to such a question.

"I have very specific social requirements laid out before me by none other than my father, the Duke of Avesbury. Since it seems you report to him, perhaps you'd like to address this issue directly? You might manage to chase away Simon, but then my social obligations will only increase as someone will have to replace him." A coy tip of the head. "So unless you know of any volunteers?"

He stayed silent. Increase? Was her father forcing her to husband hunt? That might explain the duke's strange comment at the ball. Thornton was socially eligible for her hand. Nevertheless, he had no plans to take a wife.

"I thought not," she said, and began to turn away.

He didn't want her to leave. "The chemists, they say the formula is useless. That there's no such thing as *amatiflora*."

Like sunlight through a magnifying lens, all her attention focused on him with burning intensity. "Perhaps it is the gypsy name for the flower."

It was his turn to shrug. "Perhaps it is a weed."

Her lips parted on a gasp. Then closed, pursing at the perceived insult.

"Lady Emily has been asked, of course, but is able to shed no further light on the plant."

"Then it seems we must wait until spring."

His hands gripped the side of the podium. "We don't have the luxury of time."

"It's not as if we were going to hand over the formula and the ingredients to the eye doctor." Her voice softened, wordlessly acknowledging his personal situation. "There must be other avenues to pursue. Do your chemists have any suggestions on how to recreate the effects?"

"None," he answered.

"Well, then. It would seem we have reached an impasse," she said. "On many fronts."

He crossed his arms. "So it does."

CHAPTER TWENTY

T AKING TEA IN THE parlor with Mother and
Olivia on Sunday afternoons was always a trial. It
was especially painful today.

"I don't want to live in Cumbria," Olivia whined to
Mother. "It's too far from London."

"The manor has a lovely view of the lake," Mother
replied, placidly continuing to ply her needle, forming
Prince Albert's distinctive nose. Another needlepoint
portrait pillow. It was all the rage. Queen Victoria, Mother's
most recent project bolstered Ned. Amanda found it
disturbing that so many familiar faces looked back at her
from every available sitting surface. On the other hand, it
kept Mother occupied.

"But a pencil factory?" Olivia moaned.

"Yes," Ned quipped with a roll of his eyes. "How
lowering to have that in one's dowry."

Pencil.

One should be in her fingers now, working equations that would further refine the neurachnid's movements. Amanda might not be able to work in the laboratory today, but that didn't mean the gears in her mind weren't turning, examining and reexamining the plans they'd made to connect the gold threads to the diffuse nuclei of the brain.

Where was the promised missive from Emily containing her research notes? It had been several days. Thornton wouldn't admit it, but she'd seen it in his eyes. The inability of the chemists, of the botanists, to identify the *amatiflora*, had punctured his hopes, not only for her project, but for his leg.

If he was using Somnic, he'd run out of alternatives. It was an effective, but harsh drug, often leaving its users worse off than when they'd started. She wished she knew how long Thornton had been reliant on the drug, how long he had until its effectiveness wore off. He might have months, or weeks, or merely days.

She stared at Ned and frowned. Time was not on his side either. He was quiet and distracted, his infrequent comments more biting than humorous. He seemed smaller somehow, as if he'd started to sink into himself. Dark circles emphasized the pallor of his skin beneath vacant eyes that would not meet hers.

Georgina's wedding contract negotiations must be going well.

Unlike Olivia's. Which had been under discussion for the better part of the last hour. Carlton would not agree to exchanging a larger estate in Cumbria for a smaller one in

Essex. It had something to do with the Scottish border and pencils, but Amanda had long since stopped listening.

Enough.

She slid a hand behind the throw pillow and under the seat cushion, pulling free the small notebook she kept hidden for emergencies. Given her state of mind, this qualified. Careful to keep the notebook buried in the folds and ruffles of her skirt, she flipped to a blank page and began to sketch out her predictions.

From the chair beside her, Ned snickered.

"Do not mock me." In truth, she was relieved he'd even noticed. "Tea is a form of torture. The technicalities of Olivia's marriage are tedious, and as there are no other conversational topics to distract me..." She gave him a significant look.

"Sorry. I'm... preoccupied." He sighed. "What do you wish to discuss?"

She closed the notebook and lifted her tea cup. "Have you had a chance to punch that new Babbage card I requested?"

"No." He looked away.

"Olivia," she said, raising her voice. Time to make a point. If Ned wouldn't help her, she would find someone else who would. "Have you made any progress with that Babbage card I asked you about?"

Her sister's face paled. "I'm... working on it," she answered, glancing at Mother. "The technicalities are something I've not considered before."

Mother's lips pursed. "Proper young ladies don't punch

Babbage cards. They don't program steambots, no matter how badly they desire a new and intricate hairstyle to impress their friends." Mother looked up from her pillow to throw Amanda a pointed stare. "Please don't make such requests of your sister. Place an order with our modiste. The stylist will punch you a card."

"Perhaps you can help me place that order later, Olivia?"

"Of course," her sister replied, color returning to her face now that she was certain Amanda wouldn't boldly inquire about the peroneal nerve over tea. "We'll discuss the details tonight."

Mother quickly turned the discussion to the number of tiers required to hold sufficient confections at the wedding breakfast.

Ned leaned forward, speaking under his breath. "You asked *her*?"

Amanda shrugged. "*You* won't help."

He huffed. "I'm still contemplating the adjustments and their relevance to my situation." An eyebrow went up.

"The muscle attachment problem has been solved," she said, her words clipped in irritation. "The new neurachnid will be able to weave a number of nerve patterns but not without the proper Babbage cards." It was true. Though her ability to invest significant time on Ned's specific issues were hampered for the moment. "Remember, it *is* a complete rebuild. The theft consumed three months of effort."

Ned looked away, a shadow falling across his face. Perhaps thinking that in another three months, Georgina would be another's wife.

She continued, "Despite current appearances, outside of studies and... certain social obligations, I am devoting every available hour to perfecting the neurachnid."

"I'm aware of the bargain you struck with Father." Ned rolled his eyes. "Can you do no better than Sommersby?"

She drew back as if slapped.

"What about Bloxham? Didn't he offer for you a good two months past? If you'd only accepted, by now you'd have no social obligations. Plenty of time to devote to the neurachnid."

"You selfish twit." Amanda leaned forward on her chair, narrowing her eyes and lowering her voice so only he could hear and spoke words she hoped would shock him. "Yes, he offered. Because of my advanced age, he offered to keep me tied to the bedposts and well ridden until I produced his heir."

Ned's face flamed.

"Having only *you* in mind, I declined. With the time constraints imposed by Father, I reasoned Mr. Sommersby, a man of medicine, would be more inclined to allow me to continue my research after a wedding."

"I didn't..."

Her brother's apology, if there was to be one, was interrupted by the arrival of RT. His wheels clattered across the floor toward her. On the flat surface of his head rested a silver salver bearing a single calling card.

Simon. At last.

"I'm afraid I must go," she said to the room at large, rising. "Duty calls. Mr. Sommersby awaits." She met her brother's eyes. "I will try not to inconvenience you with too long a courtship. Or," she glanced at Olivia, "a protracted negotiation." With a deep breath, Amanda forced a pleasant smile onto her face before stepping from the room. She did not dislike Simon. He was... adequate.

Her arrival in the front hall was heralded by the sounds of a strident shouts.

"I said, put me down!"

A small boy wearing torn and patched trousers, a scarlet waistcoat, and an oddly misshapen hat dangled from Simon's outstretched arm. The boy's skinny legs and arms were churning furiously. In one clenched fist, the boy held a thick packet of crumpled papers.

The first sign her day was improving.

Simon looked up, his face tight. "Look what I caught slipping in through the front door behind me. Your butler didn't even notice his presence."

Indeed, Steam Mary stood idling by the door, holding Amanda's hat and cloak, oblivious to the chaos. Their butler, Burton, was rolling away having left the front door wide open to the public.

"It's quite all right. You may put him down. He's merely a delivery boy."

"He's a gypsy."

"But still a delivery boy." She smiled her assurances at Simon. One had to make allowances for such a widespread prejudice. She could disabuse him of his misconceptions at a later time.

Simon lowered the boy to his feet, and he bounded to her

side, sliding a dark glance behind him at Simon, who glowered back with suspicion.

"I'm to deliver this directly into the hands of Lady Amanda Ravensdale."

"That would be me."

He held up the folded, sealed packet and bowed with a flourish.

"Thank you, young man." Amanda stuffed the letter inside her reticule and pulled the drawstrings tight. "Now I must pay you for your troubles.

"Steam Mary," she called. The maid rolled over to her. "Please take this young man to the kitchens." She turned to the boy. "Will you accept payment in apple tarts?"

The boy gave her a gap-toothed grin and nodded.

Steam Mary puffed off down the hall, and the boy trotted behind her.

SHE FLUTTERED her lashes and tipped her head with a smile like Olivia was wont to do in Carlton's presence.

It did not have the desired effect.

Simon frowned as she took his proffered arm. "Does it not worry you to have a gypsy running free about your home?"

"Not in the slightest." Perhaps now was as good as any to introduce the concept of having one in the family. "Growing up in the countryside, I spent quite a lot of time with them. Most of my clockwork skills originated under the tutelage of an old clockwork tinker." Simon was still frowning. "My brother's as well. He used to call us his apprentices. If not for that old gypsy, there would be no London Steam Orchestra."

"Ah, I see now," he said, his voice haughty. "A refinement and elevation of tinker technology."

It was Amanda's turn to frown. She didn't think of it that way at all.

She tucked her hand around his elbow and allowed him to lead her from the house. Outside, the sun shone brightly. Such a day was rare.

"May I inquire as to what model butler you have?" Simon asked, handing her into the phaeton runabout. "He could barely speak. His gears ground and his joints screeched, and all he did was drop my card onto a kind of... table."

"Burton is an old family favorite. *Father* is quite attached," Amanda replied politely as Simon settled beside her. She couldn't afford to alienate him. So she invoked the duke, a sure way to trump any argument.

"I see," Simon grumbled.

Amanda pressed her hand to his arm and leaned in close, attempting to lighten his mood. "Besides, RT—the table— seems quite fond of you, delivering your card directly to my side."

His free hand caught up hers, and his brow unfurrowed. "I've been anticipating our drive all day. There's something I've been wanting to ask you."

"Of course, Simon." But the look in his eyes as he

squeezed her hand tightly—as though she might suddenly slip away—gave warning. "Oh! Are those twin compound steam engines for the drive wheel?" Amanda exclaimed, pulling her hand free. She reached for the steering handle and uttered words designed to prick the pride of any man. "May I steer?"

Her suitor was suitably distracted. Grasping the handle, he stammered excuses and began—without drawing breath—to point out and manipulate the various gadgets and improvements that had inspired the purchase of this particular model while Amanda made appropriate noises of appreciation.

Then, as the engine chugged to life and lurched into motion with a puff of smoke, Simon crammed his hat down upon his golden curls and grinned at her with bright blue eyes and two straight rows of white teeth, inviting an answering smile.

She did her best, but therein lay the problem, did it not? Rather than a whole, Simon forever appeared to her as a collection of items on the list of husbandly requirements. Handsome? Check. Intelligent? Check. Kind and thoughtful? She thought of the gypsy boy. Simon only thought of her safety. Check. Dependable. Check.

Soon they were deep in the throngs, amidst all the other *ton* out to see and be seen. The latest models of steam carriages were everywhere, polished and painted to showroom perfection, their engines clicking and clacking and chugging along, forced by the crowd to throttle back to a crawl. From time to time, a gentleman passed by riding a clockwork horse. But none lurched to the right on the sixteenth step.

She'd felt Thornton tense just before each lurch and knew his leg pained him, diminishing the initial thrill of having his arms wrapped about her as he held the reins. She suppressed a sigh and glanced at Simon, determined to focus on the man she was with. It was possible her future sat beside her.

Why, then, did her stomach churn?

Overhead, colorful balloons floated in the clear sky above Hyde Park as groups of young people went up to take in the view. Up high, away from chaperones, they could flirt with the dangers of the sky, though carefully tethered below. Enormous, oblong silver balloons of transport dirigibles hovered in the distance as backdrop. All serene and calm. No airship pirates ever threatened London airspace.

What did it say about her that she'd rather be in the windowless room of a laboratory than outside on such a crisp, fall day?

She tried reducing Thornton to a list. Handsome. Unruly curls. Unreadable sapphire eyes. Wide lips. A strong chin. A deep, rumbling and entrancing voice.

But there was much more to admire.

Brilliant. He was the most intelligent man she'd met. Brave. She thought of the confidence with which he'd launched into action at Black's side. Loyal. He'd stood by Lady Huntley even when her husband proved a traitor. Kind. He'd brought Henri into his circle. Fair. He respected her work, acknowledged its uniqueness and treated her as a colleague, not a convenience. Direct. She knew where she stood.

Amanda sighed. She knew exactly where she stood, and it was not close enough.

Was Henri right? Should she attempt to pry Thornton from his shell when he'd made it quite clear her attempts were unwelcome? Could it even be done?

Yes. She'd felt his resolve weaken during their last conversation. The man was not immune to feminine charm —or dress. Once, he'd even been engaged to one Lady Anne Grimwauld. How *had* the woman managed it? Amanda might have been tempted to ask did not Lady Anne openly pity Ned's injuries.

Her hands tightened about her reticule, feeling the papers tucked securely within. Riding about in Simon's phaeton seemed a sorry use of her time. She desperately wanted to review Emily's work. Perhaps she had noted something that might be employed as an alternative to the *amatiflora*, something the chemists at Lister could substitute. Something that might help Thornton.

Even a sketch of the "gypsy weed" would be progress.

"Amanda," Simon spoke, breaking into her reverie. He reached out and traced the path of her bonnet ribbon under her chin, his eyes searching her face. "I'm worried about you, about the vast number of hours you spend in Lord Thornton's laboratory. Lately, you've seemed so... distracted. Tense. Is he making demands you can't meet?"

No.

And wasn't that the problem? He wasn't making the kinds of demands she wanted to meet.

His demands on her time were extensive, but she relished those hours. On the rare occasions they worked together, side by side, the hours flew by, their like minds finishing each other's thoughts as the new neurachnid took shape. Never had she made such swift progress. Yet there was something more between them, a spark that flashed every time they *accidentally* touched. But while she stood ready to fan the embers, Thornton carefully doused every flammable moment.

Simon was still speaking. "Ever since you became a student research assistant in Lord Thornton's laboratory, it seems as though you barely have any time for me." He was jealous, and rightfully so.

Smoothing his ruffled feathers seemed the wisest course. "It's not that I do not wish to spend time with you, Simon. I..."

He silenced her by reaching out with his hand, pressing it over her gloved one. "Then know I'm looking forward to our evening together at the Symphony House."

She'd forgotten. Ned's latest program for the Steam Orchestra was scheduled to debut this week. *And* he was to unveil a new row of automusicians. *That* was why she'd heard him muttering about the delayed coal shipment.

Simon sighed. "Please don't tell me you planned to spend that evening in the laboratory? I won't chance another breakthrough keeping you from my side."

Ned was surly enough. She couldn't risk missing this

performance. "Of course not." She did her best to smile reassuringly.

He squeezed her hand on the seat between them. "Would you mind if I seek an audience with your father?"

Panic fluttered in her stomach, and she tugged her hand away. No. Not yet. She did not want her marriage contract to be the topic of conversation at next Sunday's tea. She needed time. Time to consider other possibilities. "So soon?" she asked.

Irritation flickered across Simon's face, but he mastered it. "Yes."

Perhaps she could delay. "Shouldn't we set aside a time to discuss our career expectations first?"

He glanced at her in confusion. "You *want* to finish medical school?"

Amanda had expected to negotiate the hours she would divide between her career and home life, but not this. Did he think her years of study, her years spent building the neurachnid nothing more than passing fancy? Did he think she'd cast it all aside to be nothing more than his wife? Did he know her at all? "Of course," she answered. Then took a deep breath. "I intend to practice medicine as well as continue my research, though I'm prepared to make certain concessions to the demands of family. A small family."

Simon yanked on the steering stick, just missing a lamppost as he steered the runabout onto a quieter street. His face was flushed.

"Simon?"

He shook his head. "My apologies. I was under the

impression that medical school was a way for an intelligent woman to fill her time while waiting for marriage."

She swallowed hard, trying to think of a way to salvage this conversation and failed. She'd horribly misjudged him. "You thought..."

"All those fashionable clothes. Silly hats. Your insistence upon sitting in the front, clearly an attempt to attract attention. Male attention."

"You think I enrolled at Lister University to husband hunt?"

Simon sat straight and stiff now. "It is known for accepting a large number of gentlemen. Spare heirs, as it were."

It was as if someone yanked her corset too tight. She couldn't breathe. Her stomach hurt. The indignity. The embarrassment. It was too much. Did all her classmates think her nothing but a flirt? Did Thornton? "Please. Take me home."

CHAPTER TWENTY-ONE

B ETWEEN EMILY'S NOTES, thoughts of Thornton, and the aftershocks of Simon's not-quite-a-proposal, one that he'd all but retracted, Amanda was unable to sleep, so she wrapped her dressing gown tightly about her nightdress, grabbed the notes and, throwing discretion to the aether, padded down the darkened hall.

Minutes later, she arrived in the distillery, hunting for the dried blooms of a plant Emily had suggested and therefore worth a try. The dried flowers still on their stems hung exactly where Emily had indicated. Amanda doubted anyone had entered the room since her sister's departure some five months past.

She gathered the blooms in a sack and, barefoot, padded outside into the garden. Tonight, she would distill their essential oils, praying time had not destroyed their potency.

Shadows shifted beside her, and her heart skipped a beat, but it was only one of Thornton's agents stepping forward into the moonlight, nodding briefly to let her know of his presence before melting once more into the background.

She entered the chicken coop. The hens barely acknowledged her arrival beyond lifting a head to point a gleaming eye in her direction in hopes of a midnight snack, only to tuck their beaks back in warm straw the minute her hands fell on the new, more secure locks Thornton had ordered installed upon the doors of her makeshift laboratory. There were no safer hens in all of London.

As she worked through the complicated steps to free the deadbolt, she heard a squeal which cut off abruptly. Rufus, wearing his night-vision monocle, rounded the corner, a terrified, half-dead mouse hanging from his jaw.

She held the door wide for the orange cat, and he trotted in, dropping his offering at her feet as he passed, then leapt to the counter where he sat with his back to her, tail twitching, his displeasure at her recent neglect clear. Only when she produced—and opened—a tin of sardines, were her recent absences forgiven.

Amanda pulled dusty boxes of Emily's chemistry equipment from their storage space beneath the workbench and set about converting her workspace into a makeshift apothecary. Then, as Rufus curled into a ball on the discarded packing material, she followed Emily's specific directions, setting about the tedious task of distilling the oils from the dried flowers.

With nothing left to do but wait, she sat down on a narrow cot she'd set up in the corner of her laboratory to review Emily's notes again. It was late. Really late. The words of Emily's notes began to blur and run off the edge of the page as she read. Her head jerked, and Amanda realized she'd nearly nodded off despite the chill in her laboratory.

Emily's knowledge of plants was extensive. Nadya's even more so. It appeared they'd tried nearly every bloom that might be related to the *amatiflora*, and some that were clearly not. Still, the original formula had flaws that went beyond a specific, unavailable flower. Several.

The protocol Emily had sent was maddening in its complexity, and there were non-standard measurements, chemicals named without their ionic states indicated and, most baffling of all, a host of Romani superstitions. Those, at least, she could discount. What potency could picking the *amatiflora* flowers during a full moon possibly impart?

As the hours passed, Amanda napped on the cot, managing to rouse herself every hour or so to check on the small glass still. The distillation of essential oils from flowers was a long, slow process. Several small, controlled flames burned beneath various pieces of glassware, concentrating liquids and speeding along chemical reactions.

Dawn was still a good hour or more away when, blinking the sleep from her eyes, Amanda pushed herself up from her makeshift bed and stretched away her stiffness. She bent close to the glassware. Finally, enough oil had collected in the amber vial. She could attempt the final step.

With a pipette, she dispensed the oil into the burette positioned above a flask containing a thick orange-red liquid.

Drop by drop, the oil fell. The oil became sulfurous, then several drops later, shifted color to glow a sickly green.

She closed the stopcock. Retrieved the limp mouse from its cage. Filled a clean syringe with the green fluid. And injected the nerve agent near the injury site.

Now came more waiting. Hoping.

Smoothing loose strands of hair from her face, she sought out her cot once more. Just as she began to sink into sleep, a knock sounded on the door.

Amanda's heart stopped. Then thudded back to life as she recognized her brother's voice.

"AMANDA?" Ned called. "I know you're in there. Open the door." Hens rustled in their nests. Dawn approached. He was out of time.

He'd lost track of how many hours he'd been standing outside her laboratory, his forehead pressed against this new door, ringed with gears and pins and deadlocks. It was an intimidating door. More because it seemed a symbol of all the secrets he kept locked within himself. Ever since he'd made the mistake that ended with him in these monstrous mechanical legs.

It gnawed at him, his sister's angry confession that she sacrificed all hope of marital happiness in the practical pursuit of a man who would allow her to continue to labor on his behalf.

What right had he to ask that of her? Particularly when

his own impatience had sabotaged her project. He knocked again, harder this time and the gears began to turn, pulling iron bolts from their slots.

"Ned?" Amanda's face was pale and drawn. Dark circles beneath her eyes echoed his own. Except guilt kept him awake through the wee hours, while worry for her brother and a need to solve his problems kept his sister awake.

It needed to stop.

"May I come in?"

She opened the door wider.

Ned stepped—or rather his mechanical legs stepped—into a mad scientist's laboratory. Gone was the familiar clockwork. Instead, bottles of all shapes and sizes held liquids of colors that defied description. Brass scales and weights were poised ready to measure out undefined white powders resting near a porcelain mortar and pestle. A small glass still dripped a viscous liquid into an amber vial.

A little brown mouse, eyes unblinking, lay upon a cloth pad, the slow rise and fall of his chest the only hint he still lived.

"I thought you were working on the spider."

Amanda sighed. "Not here. I can't. Because of the theft, my neurachnid work is confined to Lord Thornton's facilities." She waved her hand at the apparatus before them. "This is an attempt to recreate Emily's quieting nerve agent."

He nodded, unable to tear his gaze away from the mouse, hating that he needed to add to her burdens. "I've something to confess."

"Confess?"

He ran both hands through his hair, tugging at the roots. "I'm the person who stole your spider. There was a physician, a Dr. Millhouse, who promised..." Ned swallowed. "Promised I would be his first patient, but he disappeared. Took the spider with him. I've sent runners looking, but none return. I'm so very, very sorry, Amanda."

Her jaw dropped and her knees folded as she dropped abruptly and heavily onto a rumpled cot. "You?" She choked the word out.

"It was wrong of me."

"Oh, God," she breathed, then shook her head. "Ned, it wouldn't have worked."

"How can you know that for certain? For Georgina I'm willing to risk it all. Please. I'm begging you. I don't need *this*," he waved his hand at the chemicals. "I'll endure whatever pain is necessary. Just please don't let me miss the only opportunity I'll ever have to bid for Georgina's hand. I need to be a whole man."

"I can't." Her voice was a whisper.

"Won't." Yes. He was being selfish again, but he only wanted this over so they could both lead the lives they were meant to live.

"No. Can't." Amanda dropped her face into her palms, her hair falling forward to hide her face. "The neurachnid isn't ready, and the procedure will not work with an unquieted nerve."

"You've every right to be furious."

"Oh, I am." Her voice hardened. "How could you?"

"It's been five years, Amanda. How much longer am I expected to wait?"

"As long as it takes!" The orange cat his sister favored raised his head at her exclamation, fixing his malevolent gaze on Ned. Amanda threw her hands in the air. "You have no idea what you've done! None."

"What?" His own voice rose now. "I said I'm sorry. I'll talk to Father about moving his deadline. You deserve better than Sommersby."

She gaped, then shook her head.

"What?" he asked.

"Are you aware of the recent rash of gypsy murders?"

How could this possibly be relevant? But he nodded. "The one the papers call the eye doctor?"

"The very one." She paused. "I can't divulge details, but we know what he's trying to do."

"We?"

"We, Ned. I'm involved. Ever since the eye doctor stole my neurachnid." She stood now. "He's experimenting on them."

"Altering their eyes?" *Oh, God. No.* "Using the spider? How? Why?"

She shook her head. "I cannot share any more details."

His blood ran cold. His fault. "How close is he to succeeding?"

"Is that all you can think about!" Amanda yelled. "Yourself? And whether or not a *murderer* might have perfected what I could not?" She fixed him with a glare, then turned her back on him. "Leave. I need to think."

"No, that's not what I meant," he objected. Bitter bile hit the back of his throat. How many gypsy deaths were on his shoulders? "If he's close... if he succeeds, he'll stop."

"Yes, Ned. If he succeeds, the gypsy murders will likely stop. But this device? In the hands of our enemies, many more lives will be destroyed." Amanda turned and lifted the limp rodent. "And he's not likely to share any progress *he* makes on the neurachnid."

She slid the mouse into some kind of examination chamber. She turned a series of dials, bringing the animal's wound into graphic view. She pushed a button and flipped a lever. There was a loud, electrical zapping sound. Several of her loose hairs lifted away, floating in a charged cloud about her head. She bent close to the monitor, her face hopeful. Then her shoulders sagged.

"Amanda?"

"It didn't work," she muttered.

He watched as she grabbed a packet of papers and began leafing through its pages, grumbling. "Amanda," he said again.

"Why are you still here? Leave. I have work. Without a functioning nerve agent, the neurachnid cannot properly spin its web."

He couldn't leave. A sneaking suspicion had crept upon him as she worked. "There's more."

She ignored him.

"Tony has been searching for Dr. Millhouse. He thought he was getting close."

Amanda looked up.

Today, for the first time in five long years, Tony had failed to arrive for work. Ned had sent round a footman to his lodgings, but Tony was nowhere to be found.

Only now did the full significance register.

Ned shut his eyes and swore. "Tony's missing."

BRILLIANCE COULD NOT BE RUSHED. A grim smile pulled at Wasp's lips. Still, it had taken Lady Amanda long enough to figure it out. A spider able to make diffuse connections was finally under construction.

When Wasp had first learned of her device, then beheld its brilliance, it was clear Lady Amanda Ravensdale was nearly a mental equal. Worth watching. Worth keeping close. Worth prodding into reaching her potential.

She suspected nothing. For now, Wasp would continue to employ only soft suggestions, gentle assistance, and careful watchfulness to nudge her along while maintaining a normal routine.

Annoyance had surged when Lord Thornton became involved in her life, pulling her under his wing and into his laboratory. Seeing her eyes shine for the titled lord was an irritation that was a struggle to bear, but it seemed her infatuation was to be to an advantage. Wasp certainly couldn't have foreseen the enormous investment of time and effort she would devote to her clockwork spider, all to please a man.

Such cliché.

Though Lady Amanda labored diligently away, it was bad form not to attempt independent modifications to the neurachnid.

A rotating blade was not the solution. Attempting the procedure on the other eye had not been worth the bother. Wasp had chosen instead to send a message to the old gypsy woman that her efforts did not suffice. Yet today, Wasp had new hope. This new pin and spring might allow the neurachnid to make the multiple insertions necessary to connect to the entire cranial nerve root.

But all this work would be wasted unless the old gypsy provided the necessary numbing agent. The green fluid that had filled the neurachnid's abdomen was key and long since depleted.

Diethyl ether left a test subject unconscious but also made the nerve root incapable of responding to the spider's gentle probing. The resulting gold web was too diffuse and often misdirected. Accuracy was required.

If Nadya did not produce a new sample soon, Wasp would be forced to provide motivation. Discovering that Lady Amanda's sister lived among the gypsies as one of them had been... revelatory.

It was an effective screw to turn.

CHAPTER TWENTY-TWO

AT THE END OF THE last lecture for the day, a selection of students was called to the front of the lecture theater to stand before Professor Quimbly for a public shaming. Amanda was one of them.

She deserved this. In favor of spending more hours in Thornton's laboratory—and now in her own—she'd neglected her studies. In this particular case, her failure was to review the slew of assigned histological slides in the microscopy facility. Now, like the others at her side, she was being taken to task for failing an unannounced quiz.

Exhausted past the point of caring, she kept her gaze downcast. She'd taken on far too many tasks for one woman and the balance had finally tipped against her. School, the neurachnid, the nerve agent. Husband hunting.

She glanced at Simon.

She'd arrived in the lecture theater to find he hadn't moved from his usual seat. She hesitated, but only briefly.

Amanda refused to let the end of their courtship displace her. Sitting in the back with her female classmates was not an option. Nodding in greeting, she'd settled herself beside Simon. He was all that was polite, pleasant and proper, though her arrival had been met with a noticeably cooler reception.

Eventually, Mother would comment to Father that Mr. Sommersby had ceased to call on Amanda for tea and her social obligations would increase.

Amanda closed her eyes while Professor Quimbly began to berate her along with her fellow students.

What to do about Ned? Worry churned her stomach, making her feel she'd swallowed the contents of a bottle marked *poison*. Thornton needed to know. That Ned had been the one to steal her neurachnid, to deliver it to the eye doctor. That, while searching for the eye doctor, Tony had gone missing. That her own brother was the one who put her and Emily—his own sisters—at risk.

She dreaded the look that would cross Thornton's face when she informed him. Her own brother, and she'd missed every sign of his guilt.

Worse still was knowing the nerve agent was a failure. It pained her to admit—even to herself—how much hope she'd pinned on last night's distillation. For future patients. For her brother. For Thornton's leg.

The packet of Emily's notes weighed heavily upon her mind. She would turn a copy of them over to the Lister chemists. Whether or not they dismissed the work as "gypsy snake oil" was irrelevant. It was the correct thing to do. Not that it would stop her from continuing to work on her own to find possible alternatives to the *amatiflora*.

All these painful tasks to accomplish as soon as Professor Quimbly dismissed her.

"Do you think that your gross anatomy studies are sufficient to prepare you for the identification of all a patient's diseases?" Professor Quimbly railed. "Do you intend to simply cut out the offending organ for study when a man arrives in your surgery?"

Condescending laughter from her classmates filled the room. Particularly cutting was the nasty tittering that came from the back of the room where her female classmates roosted.

"No!" Professor Quimbly shouted, his face growing red as he answered his own question. "There is so much to be learned from tiny scrapings, from the most infinitesimal..." His rant continued for quite some time, finally concluding with a tirade against those who might dare think themselves privileged. "No consideration will be given to rank." He surveyed those among their small number descended from peers, then fixed Amanda with a look. "Or sex."

He spun to face the audience catching Simon in his sight. "And no excuses will be offered on their behalf. Balls and teas and garden parties and drives along Rotten Row... pfft."

Simon stiffened and his face grew red, but he did not move to defend her.

Amanda's face grew hot with embarrassment. She did not wish for—nor had she ever asked for—special treatment from either her professors or her classmates. She was, however, sorry for the impression Simon had formed from her behavior. Perhaps her female classmates had a point. She would reconsider her wardrobe.

"Class dismissed." Professor Quimbly waved a hand in the air.

Elbows jabbed, heads bent toward each other, and whispers filled the room, speculating on the current state of the class romance.

Amanda walked past her classmates with all due speed toward the exit. She had no desire to hear their relationship pronounced as alive as their cadavers. She strode down the hall, bypassing the histology room. She was in no frame of mind to spend her afternoon peering through a microscope. For that matter, she was in no mood to work on the neurachnid either. Thornton's impersonal company would be too much to bear.

She'd not abandoned her plans to bring him around to her point of view on how an intellectual partnership could involve both romance and maybe even marriage, but today was not the day.

This day called for a retreat into her chicken coop laboratory, a soothing afternoon in Rufus's silent, uncondemning company where she could apply herself diligently to her studies as another plant's blooms distilled. She would hand a packet to the footman standing guard among the hens. He could carry Emily's notes and Amanda's excuses to Thornton—along with the news of her brother's treachery.

Cowardly?

She preferred to think of it as efficient. If she failed to attend to her studies, she would be sent down from Lister University and no longer available at all for work in Thornton's laboratory. If he wished to discuss anything with her, he could come to her.

"Lady Amanda!" Simon called. "Wait."

She didn't. Her quota of rejection and humiliation for the week had been met. Tired, frustrated, and despairing of her future, she stepped from the building into a gray, drizzling afternoon. No matter, her personal bodyguard—disguised in gold-trimmed livery—stepped from her waiting carriage, opening an umbrella as he approached.

"Please." Simon's hand caught at her elbow.

Her extremely tall and well-muscled footman loomed over them both, glaring at the placement of Simon's hand. "Lady Amanda, is this gentleman troubling you?"

Amanda's elbow was hastily released. "Not at all. A moment please," she said.

The footman handed her the umbrella, bowed and stepped a few feet away.

"Really, Amanda, your servants—"

"How may I help you, Mr. Sommersby?" She'd rather had enough of his opinions.

"So formal, Amanda? You have to forgive me," Simon began.

Amanda frowned. She had to do no such thing.

"About this evening's concert..."

She sighed. Amanda had intended for the London Symphony Orchestra performance to fulfill her weekly social commitment. Without Simon—or any male escort—at her side, Father would discover her lack of a suitor sooner than she hoped. She saw more balls in her immediate future.

"...I apologize."

"Excuse me?" She returned her full attention to the man before her.

"I humbly admit that I did not expect a lady of your station would wish to pursue a career in medicine."

Something inside her twisted in agony. She didn't want his apology. If he weren't constantly at her side, it might be easier to convince Thornton to reconsider his stance. "There's no need to revisit our last conversation. I release you from your obligation as my escort."

"No." He shook his head. "I do not wish for you to think me such a small-minded man. If you want to work, then so you shall."

"What if I want to work in a research facility?"

He stiffened, but quickly relented. "Then we will make that happen." He glanced warily at her glowering footman who had somehow managed to inch closer. "Perhaps we should discuss this at another time?"

It was wise of him to worry. The agents Thornton had assigned to guard her were both over six feet tall and solid muscle. They seemed to have two states, watchful and menacing. She only wished she could say for certain Thornton cared more about protecting her safety than he did for catching the eye doctor.

Though Simon didn't—and couldn't—know, the guards both had implanted acousticotransmitters. Anything said in their presence was immediately relayed to another listening agent and, ultimately, to Thornton.

A smile tugged at her lips. The idea that Thornton would receive a report on her ongoing courtship with one Mr. Simon Sommersby amused her. She'd plan on providing Thornton with an earful.

Perhaps the evening would prove more entertaining than she'd hoped. "Very well," she conceded defeat. Besides, she could not afford to blithely toss aside Simon's regard. Not without a drastic realignment of her life's goals.

She found herself deeply resentful of her father's condition of marriage, even though she herself had initiated the bargaining process with blackmail.

What kept Thornton from pursuing her romantically?

Amanda couldn't believe it was from a desire to honor the rules set down by the school's board of directors. Thornton didn't strike her as a man to blindly follow rules unless they suited him.

Perhaps he had no interest in a wife. Or perhaps as an earl, he wanted nothing more than a wife who would produce children at regular intervals, tend to the comfort of his home, and make no demands on his time, leaving him free to pursue his passions.

If so, that certainly wouldn't be her.

"I'll see you tonight, then?" Simon asked.

But neither was Amanda ready to consign herself to a tepid marriage where her husband tolerated her career. True, she'd been resigned to such a marriage, but that was before she'd stepped behind the great iron door that separated Lister University, School of Medicine from Lister Laboratories, a place where technologies that physicians couldn't even dream about were already in development.

No, she was not at all resigned.

"Yes, Simon. I will see you tonight."

Hours later, Amanda paced from one end of the room to the other.

She'd spent the afternoon as planned, studying and distilling more plant essential oils. Though she was now considerably more on top of her coursework material, the oil from the alternate plant's bloom hadn't worked, and Thornton hadn't seen fit to reply to her missive, let alone pay her a visit.

Evening invariably arrived. Trussed in a peacock blue gown with the accompanying feathers sprouting in all directions, some doing their best to conceal the deep vee of her plunging neckline, Amanda stopped pacing and crossed the room to greet Simon. She placed her hand in his and allowed him to hand her into his carriage. If Simon thought it odd that her statuesque footman rode on the back, he didn't comment. Father must have had words with him earlier.

The ride to the Symphony House—short though it was— was an exercise in endurance. Simon was overly solicitous to the point of being outright annoying, offering her a heated foot warmer, a fur blanket and a glass of champagne.

Amanda declined them all.

He might be celebrating their reunion, but she only found his romantic overtures irritating. Even worse were his attempts to engage her in a conversation about how the cellars of Seymour House—the property his father had allotted him—might be best retrofitted to incorporate her laboratory needs.

Could he not hear himself? He may have taken her off a marble pedestal, but instead of imprisoning her in an ivory tower, he proposed to lock her in a dingy, dusty, subterranean dungeon.

"Thank you, but no." Her words were clipped as he again held out a box of chocolates. "Please stop, Simon. While I appreciate your efforts, I'm not yet convinced we suit."

"I shall convince you otherwise," Simon replied, his jaw tightening.

Amanda suppressed a sigh and turned her face away, glancing out the window, wondering if her footman was close enough for his enhanced ear to register Simon's fawning words.

At last they'd arrived.

The steam carriage stuttered to a stop before the wide granite stairs leading into the Symphony House, and they joined Mother and Olivia in her family's private box. Father —if he bothered to show at all—would be late. Carlton was reportedly en route.

While polite conversation circulated around her, Amanda studied Ned. He stood, mechanical legs engaged, in the orchestra pit beneath his mechanical orchestra. He'd designed the pit to be deep and shadowed, to conceal his legs from the public's view.

"Amazing." Simon leaned in closely, continuing his campaign, she supposed. "Every year, your brother outdoes himself."

"Always," she agreed politely. If only Simon spoke of her own work with such admiration in his voice. She'd not spoken to Ned since his revelation in the chicken coop. The orchestra was tuned and ready, small wisps of steam escaping from the musician's various valves. There were several minutes before the concert commenced, and she was restless. She rested a few gloved fingertips on Simon's arm, then rose. "If you'll excuse me, I'll be just a few minutes. I'd like to wish Ned luck."

Simon rose with her. "Allow me."

"Thank you, but it's better if you don't come. He's terribly sensitive about his legs. It's best if I go alone."

Amanda made her way down the hallway, accepting compliments and congratulations on Ned's behalf. It seemed half of London had turned out for this latest concert. If only she could feel proud. At last, she reached the corridor that led to the orchestra pit, but as she pulled back the black velvet curtain that marked its entrance, she froze.

Ned was not alone, and he was not addressing a stage worker. Those were the distinctly higher tones of a woman's voice. They were huddled together out of sight and out of hearing of the audience.

"How much longer can you delay?" Ned asked.

From a dark corner, a trembling female voice replied, "A

week more, maybe two. What happened with Dr. Millhouse?"

"There are... complications," Ned answered. "The spider requires further modifications."

Georgina stepped out of the shadows to lean her forehead on Ned's chest. Her brother caught her by her waist and pressed a kiss to her hair.

Amanda's heart ached for them.

"The spider may never work," Ned admitted. "I've already scheduled a surgical replacement for next week. If you can hold out for two weeks..."

"No! Please, no." A tear ran down Georgina's cheek. "Not for me."

Ned pressed a handkerchief into her trembling hand. Georgina dabbed at her damp eyes. "How can you say that? I'll risk anything for you," Ned insisted.

"Don't. Please. We'll elope," Georgina begged.

Amanda wanted to add her pleas to Georgina's.

A strident female voice hallooed from the corridor. The young couple stiffened.

"It's Mother. I'd best go," Georgina whispered, tipping her pale face upward. Ned pressed a kiss to her lips.

A replacement! Amanda turned her back, giving the couple their moment of privacy, but the rustle of her feathered skirts gave her away.

Georgina gasped, brushing past Amanda without a glance as she made her escape.

"How long have you been standing there?" Ned demanded.

"Only a moment." Amanda turned to see her brother giving her a knowing look. She let the curtain fall, stepping forward to stand at his side. She kept her voice soft. "But long enough. Ned, please don't. Ferrous replacements... the risk..." She pressed a hand to the wall to steady herself. She'd studied this surgical procedure. If you could call such a procedure surgery. More like butchering. Limbs were removed, the controlling muscles scraped away from the bone of the pelvis to make room for bolts and hinges and pistons... Her stomach turned.

The list of side effects and complications were numerous. Death being a particularly worrisome one. Impotence from nerve damage another.

"I'm done living my life in hiding. Others have replaced a limb and found acceptance in the *ton*. One day, I'll be Duke of Avesbury. If I can pass for normal, her father might accept my suit."

"And if something goes wrong?" For years she'd worked on her neurachnid, hoping to avoid exactly this eventuality. "If you can't give her children?"

Ned looked away. "At least I'll have tried."

"Please. Don't." She added her appeal. "I'm so close. You're young. You have plenty of time. There will be other women."

"I don't want other women!" His voice hardened. They'd had this argument before. "Five years I've stalled. I'm done waiting. So unless you're ready for human trials..."

She snapped. "Stop!" she hissed. "*Your* actions set me back. *Your* actions have consequences."

"Incredibly unfortunate ones," he countered, his face impassive. "But they also drew the attention of the great neurophysiologist Lord Thornton. Is it too much to hope that his vast resources would hasten your progress?"

She sucked in a deep, indignant breath. "Lord Thornton's resources are not mine to command. We're. Working. On. It." She leaned forward, shoving a finger into Ned's chest. He inhaled, perhaps to defend his decision, but Amanda cut him off. "Has it never occurred to you that you put *me* at risk?" She paused for effect. "If my spider is not functioning properly, who better to fix it than the inventor *herself*? Or the woman who can brew the numbing agent?"

To his credit, Ned blanched. "Kidnapping? Has—"

"No," she said. "However, as there are many who worry that it is a distinct possibility, I am well guarded. As is Emily."

"I—"

She held up a hand. "If you want to help, convince Father to release me from my social responsibilities. The hours I spend sipping tea, flirting and waltzing are hours lost."

The curtain separating them from the corridor twitched. A pair of intent eyes glanced inward. Satisfied, the man let the curtain fall back.

"My guard," she informed Ned. She had a highly trained government agent to keep her safe. Suddenly, Amanda felt the need to be anywhere but trapped in the Symphony House making not the slightest bit of progress.

"I'll try," Ned said.

"You'll do more than try," she retorted. "You can start now. I need to go."

"Go where? Now? What will I tell Mother? Or Mr. Sommersby when they come looking for you?"

She shrugged, not entirely certain where she was headed. Out. Away. "What you tell them is your concern. I won't be back."

"What of your safety!"

"My assigned guard will keep me safe."

She left Ned sputtering.

CHAPTER TWENTY-THREE

Amanda's feet made no sound on the burgundy carpet as she crossed the gleaming white marble entryway of the Symphony House. Beside her, two-storied columns rose upward to support a dome from which an enormous crystal chandelier glittered. Gilded iron railings wrapped up the sides of the curved stairs that led upward to the private boxes. The Queen had spared no expense. No wonder Amanda's brother thought so highly of himself.

"Good evening," she greeted her guard.

He nodded politely.

She closed the gap between them and leaned close to his right ear, whispering into the acousticotransmitter. "And good evening to you as well, whomever you are."

The agent's eyes narrowed with annoyance.

"We'll be leaving shortly," she said. "But first I need a moment."

He stiffened.

"I won't go far."

Yet.

It was time for her to go. The question was where. Home to her own laboratory to pursue the reformulation of the nerve agent? What progress could she hope to make where her sister had failed? When the chemists at Lister University had dismissed the formula?

She would return to Thornton's laboratory. The rebuild of the neurachnid was nearing completion; there she could make progress. Yet without a working nerve agent, ultimately her spider would fail.

"Beautiful, isn't it, Lady Amanda? This monument to music."

"Lady Huntley," Amanda said with surprise as she turned toward the voice.

"A rare outing," Lady Huntley explained. "A command performance to maintain the illusion." She detached herself from the gentleman in evening wear who stood at her side. The man seemed familiar. Tall. Blond. Privileged. Overconfident. "Have you met my brother-in-law, Lord Huntley?"

Ah. That explained the familiarity.

"You look much like your brother," Amanda addressed the new viscount. "May I offer both my condolences and my congratulations."

The man bowed. "A pleasure to make your acquaintance, Lady Amanda." His words drawled as his eyes raked approvingly over her form, resting on the swell of her bosom.

Lady Huntley rolled her eyes. "Come. Walk with me."

She tugged Amanda away. "The man is a determined rake and not worth your notice. Besides, we need to speak." She set a leisurely pace. "You were missed today."

Amanda had no doubt. "Was Thornton upset?"

"Rather." Lady Huntley glanced at her. "He told me about your brother. I'm sorry."

She nodded. What more was there to say?

"Those notes you sent, they're most impressive. Your sister would have made an excellent botanist. Still could."

"Emily would tell you she already is. That gypsy lore is worth a lifetime of study, one that she has already commenced."

"Love does tend to make one blind. And impulsive." Lady Huntley's eyes saddened.

They'd reached the far side of the entryway. From a short distance, Lady Amanda's guard followed at a respectful distance, keeping close watch.

"I'm sorry I was short with you the other day," Lady Huntley said, turning to face those still arriving through the entryway.

"I understand," Amanda said. "Having one's personal privacy invaded does not make for a cheerful mindset."

"It certainly does not." Lady Huntley paused. "I spent quite some time combing through your sister's notes, and it just now occurred to me to wonder. Do you think it possible that Lady Emily could sketch the plant? Perhaps it is not a mere weed. Perhaps it grows in the greenhouse. They do maintain an extensive selection of plants, many are medicinal."

A greenhouse. Amanda had not known Lister University maintained one. "And given the correct conditions, blooms can be forced," she said, brightening. "I'll send a note to my sister straightaway."

"Eloise!" The new Lord Huntley stood at the base of the stairs, looking rather impatient.

"I must go," Lady Huntley said, turning away. "Duty calls."

"Lady Amanda." Her guard appeared beside her. "You'll need to return to your box."

"I think not," she replied, striding past him out onto the broad steps of the Symphony House, searching the street. She could find a messenger boy, but given the time it took to send and receive a response, it would be faster for Amanda herself to carry the message to Emily.

Despite the assurances Thornton and Black had given her as to her sister's safety, Amanda needed to be at her sister's side, to see for herself. To *know* Emily was well-guarded.

Besides, there was the matter of Ned to discuss.

"No. I need to be somewhere else entirely."

The agent sighed in resignation and followed in her wake as she descended the stairs. She shivered, missing her warm wrap as a gust of cold night air reminded her that autumn quickly progressed into winter. A gypsy campfire would warm her, but first she had to get to Putney Heath.

Several steam carriages lined the street, their engines idling as drivers reclined on their seats or gathered about lampposts, puffing on cigars. She had no money and without funds, no driver could be convinced to abandon their employers. Amanda eyed the many conveyances, searching for the Avesbury carriage. It was here. Somewhere.

She took a step forward, intending to search it out, but was caught mid-step as hard fingers dug into her arm.

"Where might you be headed?" Thornton growled beside her.

She tried to yank her arm away. "What are you doing here?"

"Stopping you."

She glanced behind her, looking for her guard. "What have you done with my agent?"

"I dismissed him."

She spun to face Thornton and was struck dumb by the striking figure he cut. He was every inch an earl out for the evening. A tall top hat. A new, silver-capped ebony cane. A snowy cravat tucked into a maroon brocade vest and pinned with a ruby. Tailored black evening attire engulfed the rest of him in darkness. No beard shadowed his face tonight, not a single strand of hair curled free. His lips were pressed into a hard line. The harsh planes of his face and the ice blue of his eyes warned he was a dangerous man to cross.

He turned his head and a tiny pinprick of green light winked on the device fastened about his ear.

"*You* were monitoring me?" Her words sounded outraged, but then it struck her. Thornton exhibiting possessive and protective behavior while she was out with Simon. The corners of her lips curved upward.

"This is not a joking matter." His eyes sparked in anger.

"After your failure to report to the laboratory and the information provided about your brother's activities, I was concerned about your mental state."

"I'm fine."

"Then why do I find you running from the building alone?"

"I wasn't going anywhere alone," she objected. "I had a guard."

"Now you have me."

"Do I?" Amanda leaned close, rising on her tiptoes and all but pressing her lips to his ear, she whispered, "Is such a thing possible?"

"Amanda." His voice held a note of warning.

"For I think I've made my interest clear. Next time, you could dispense with all the technology and simply request to escort me yourself."

He released her arm, shifting away. "Not here, Amanda."

Exactly as she'd expected. "Let me know if you ever figure out where." Then she started down the stairs, suddenly feeling very alone. "I need to speak to my sister." She scanned the waiting carriages. "Which one is yours?"

He followed, leaning on his cane. "Emily is safe."

"In a dark field? Surrounded by trees? Near a road that anyone might travel at any time?" She scanned the street and spotted his vehicle.

He'd brought his own personal carriage, his family crest displayed in all its glory on the sides. The best disguise tonight was none at all. She stalked forward. As no one made a move to assist her, she yanked open a door, scooped her skirts up about her knees and climbed inside.

"Take me to Emily," she commanded Thornton.

"My lord?" Thornton's driver asked.

Thornton sighed with resignation. "Kensington Gardens it is."

"Yes, my lord."

Thornton pulled himself inside, landing heavily on his seat. Already his leg throbbed and it was only four hours since the last injection. He gripped his cane tightly; he'd checked its contents twice before beginning this evening. It wouldn't do to find himself low on cartridges again. He stared at the beautiful, headstrong problem across from him as she shivered in the cold moonlight.

Her iridescent blue gown was designed to showcase her assets, not to provide warmth. A profusion of peacock feathers fanned across the bodice and fluttered from shoulder straps, creating an illusion of sleeves. A shimmering blue bead necklace wrapped tightly about her throat once, dipping deep into her cleavage on its second circuit. It was impossible not to look, and, therefore, impossible to think.

Resigned, he pulled off his coat and passed it to her as the carriage jerked into motion. She murmured her thanks, and he knew a moment of gratitude as the black wool swallowed her form. Thornton let the dark and the silence wrap about him.

She cared so very deeply about her sister, about her family. What would it be like to have someone care so deeply about him?

Mother viewed him only as her duty, the required son, necessary only to pass on the Thornton name. He had no siblings. Lady Anne had agreed only to a marriage of convenience; it had hurt not one bit when she cried off. Only Huntley had ever really known him.

Or so he'd thought.

John had been the brother he never had. Theirs had been an instant friendship, borne of shared interests and shored up by long hours in a laboratory. Together, they'd been a driving force behind the establishment of Lister University School of Medicine.

The thrill of discovery and invention drove him, but Huntley had lost direction, succumbing to one of the many opportunities London presented a young, unmarried earl. Gambling. He'd been so convinced his mathematical formulas would win back the small fortune his father had squandered. They hadn't. Then, with a mountain of debt confronting him, Huntley had eyed Lister Laboratories with greed and sought profit by turning traitor.

His betrayal had cut Thornton to the quick.

Ever since, he'd been careful to keep acquaintances and colleagues at a professional distance. His caustic reputation and scathing remarks in the classroom kept students at bay. Fellow scientists regarded him with awe, but steered clear, seeking him out only when necessary. Black and Lady

Huntley were the closest he had to friends, and theirs was a working relationship.

Lady Amanda alone refused to honor his boundaries, constantly pushing for something more. When she looked at him, it was as if she could see into his soul. Such easy familiarity was unsettling. The hours they spent together were the best hours of the day. He was drawn to her in a way he'd felt with no other woman.

Yet one didn't trifle with a duke's daughter. So he held himself apart, kept her at safe distance.

"Why," he spoke into the shifting gray shadows. "Why are you so intent on Mr. Sommersby?" Thornton had been treated to a nauseatingly detailed account of the modifications Sommersby was willing to make to his home in order to accommodate Amanda should she agree to be his wife. But she sounded unconvinced.

Amanda's eyes grew large, then, perhaps remembering he'd been listening through the acousticocept, narrowed. "Why do you care?" she asked.

"Humor me."

She hesitated so long, he thought she would decline to answer, but the dark of night made confidences easier. "I must marry," she said at last.

"Must? Most practicing female physicians remain unmarried."

"Most practicing female physicians do not have dukes for fathers who make their continued enrollment in medical school conditional. I have the rest of the academic year to become engaged." Her face fell flat and her voice lost all color as she spoke. "Should I wish to return to Lister University next fall, a wedding is required."

"That seems... unfair."

It was more than unfair. That a mind as brilliant as Amanda's should be placed under the control of a man whose medical career would be middling at best did not sit well with him. Aside from the man's talents in chemistry, Thornton was at a loss as to why Sommersby had been recruited. Should Sommersby, as her husband, forbid her to practice medicine, or to conduct research, Amanda would have no choice but to obey.

"It was the bargain I made," Amanda said. "I am allowed to attend medical school, provided I marry." She laughed bitterly. "At the moment, Mr. Sommersby is the only one in pursuit of my hand. What choice have I but to accept his attentions?"

Thornton swallowed and looked away. His initial assumptions had been correct, but only in part. She was indeed husband hunting, but only under duress. Someday he would need to take a wife. But now? He was willing to do much to further her career. But marriage? No. Marrying her was not the right solution.

Why, then, did it sound so appealing? To have a woman like her in his life. By his side in the laboratory. In his bed.

He cleared his throat; it felt oddly constricted. "What you need is not a husband, but independence. Or, at the very least, more time."

"I happen to agree," she said. "Father does not."

"Will you allow me to speak to him?"

"*You* intend to offer for my hand?" She leaned forward, her eyes soft and round. "I accept."

It was a punch to his gut that sucked all the air from his lungs. "I..."

"Oh, for goodness sakes, I know what you meant," she said, falling back against her seat. "By all means, try. Perhaps you might hold some influence or think of a good argument for extending my deadline."

He nodded, breathing deeply as he forcibly pushed the topic into a dark corner of his mind for later consideration. "Why must we visit Lady Emily?" he asked instead. "What can you possibly hope to accomplish?" Then repeated his earlier assurance, "Lady Emily is well guarded. *You* are well guarded. Provided you let our men—let me—do our job."

"You've reviewed Emily's notes?"

He nodded. Her sister's work was impressive. For an amateur. "They were extensive."

"Before she... left, Emily hung many plants to dry. I've tried recreating her formula using distillations of all those she thought related to the *amatiflora*. None of them work."

That explained the long hours in the chicken coop. His agents resented—profoundly—the need to brush feathers from their clothes after standing for hours in a room full of snoring hens.

She continued, "What if the *amatiflora* is not just some pretty weed? What if your botanists are growing the very plant we need in their greenhouse, but know it by another name? What if Emily can sketch the plant, its flowers?"

He understood. "Then our botanists can identify it and, perhaps, force it to grow, to flower."

"Exactly." She nodded. "Because otherwise, until the *amatiflora* blooms again, the formula is worthless."

He doubted this path was worth pursuing. Then again, the smallest of discoveries could often have great implications, and they *needed* this drug. "Very well. We will visit Lady Emily."

"Thank you." Amanda visibly relaxed, turning to look out the window and the passing landmarks finally registered. "This is not the way to Putney Heath!"

"No. It's not." He held up a hand as she inhaled to object. "We've had Lady Emily—and a small portion of her band—relocated. Your father is a very powerful man. With special permission from the Queen herself, a small number of vardos have a temporary encampment in Kensington Gardens beside the Long Water. It is there that I have directed our driver."

CHAPTER TWENTY-FOUR

IT WAS AN ODDLY picturesque and romantic sight. Five vardos formed a circle lined up nose to tail about a single campfire. Behind them, as if a backdrop for a play, a palace rose shimmering in the glow of gaslight. A man dressed in bright colors sat on an overturned bucket, swaying as he drew out a melancholy tune from the fiddle pinched between his shoulder and chin.

Though the gypsy played on, all eyes turned in their direction. As recognition dawned and their last entrance recalled, a number of mouths turned downward.

Emily looked up, and Amanda knew instant relief. She exhaled the breath she'd been holding. For the moment, her family was safe.

But keeping it that way...

Luca reached down and helped his wife rise to her feet. Together, they stepped outside the circle of wagons, crossing over the neatly trimmed lawn to where Amanda and Thornton waited.

Beside her stood a silent clockwork horse, his springs all wound down for the night. The same horse that lurched to the right with every sixteenth step? Luca's craftsmanship was impeccable and she strongly suspected he'd set Thornton atop an unbalanced horse quite deliberately.

"Dare I hope you arrive with news of the eye doctor's capture?" Luca asked, by way of greeting. "Your agents' Romani, all but Black's, it hurts the ears."

"Not yet," Thornton answered. "You'll have to tolerate their presence somewhat longer."

"Now, Luca. It's not that bad," Emily chided. "Think how horrible my Romani was once." Luca's lips tugged into a faint smile, and Emily turned to Amanda. "What brings you here then?"

"I need to speak with you," she replied. "About the *amatiflora*."

"Walk with me," Thornton said, addressing Luca. "We'll survey the perimeter while they speak." He pinned Amanda with a look. "After the two sisters have reached the safety of a vardo."

Amanda caught her sister's arm and began walking toward the bright yellow vardo Emily shared with Luca and his great aunt, Nadya. She suspected they might need to consult the old woman. "How are you?" she asked. "How is the baby?"

Emily smiled. "Fine. Kicking strongly, often keeping me awake late into the night."

They'd reached the curved stairs leading upward and inward. Amanda's lightness faded. She paused, turning toward her sister. "Before we go in, I need to tell you about a situation brewing with Ned." Amanda filled her in on their brother's plans to amputate.

Emily's face contracted with concern. "He needs to be stopped."

"I agree. I'll speak with Father, but only as a last resort," Amanda said. "The spider, if I could only focus on it alone, without worry this eye doctor might strike again at any moment..." Too many responsibilities pulled her in opposite directions. "I could have it ready for rat trials within the week. But..."

"But without a working formula, it's hopeless," Emily finished.

Amanda nodded. "I cannot make it work, Emily. I've tried every plant you suggested, but they all lack... something."

Nadya called in Romani from inside the vardo.

"There's certainly nothing wrong with her hearing," Emily muttered, waving Amanda to precede her.

Inside, Nadya, little more than a face and two gnarled hands emerging from a swirl of colorful rags, gestured to a low cushion beside her.

"Me?" Amanda was uncertain her attire was up to the descent.

The old woman nodded, pointing again and launching into a stream of Romani.

Amanda scooped her skirts with one hand and bent her

knees, aiming for the cushion, but the best she could hope for was a controlled fall onto the pillow. "Oof."

Corsets and crinolines were not meant to accommodate floor seating. Amanda thought she caught a twitch of amusement on Nadya's face, but buried amidst so many wrinkles, it was difficult to tell.

"So what do you need to ask me?" Emily asked, folding easily onto a cushion despite her rounded stomach.

"*Amatiflora*, it may grow—somewhere—in a greenhouse. If you can sketch it, I can hunt for it."

Nadya erupted into Romani and Emily reached behind her, drawing forth a scrap of paper and a box of broken pastels. Grasping the items in her gnarled fingers, she began to sketch with incredible skill. A twining vine took shape, twisting up a lamp post and bursting into white flowers. Handing the picture to Amanda, Nadya muttered.

Emily translated. "She is not at all confident the flowers will be potent if grown inside beneath a roof of glass where the moon's rays cannot touch the blooms."

Another torrent of Romani flowed forth from the old woman's lips.

"I *did* write that down in the formula I handed her," Emily replied, addressing Nadya, attempting to force the language into English.

Nadya sighed, her wrinkles scrunching into fierce concentration, as if English pained her. "You must use flowers *exactly* as in formula."

"I will," Amanda said. "If I manage to locate them."

The old woman shook her head. "I know *gadji*.

Before *me*, this girl" she pointed a knotted finger at Emily, "not know to pick flowers at full moon. Still, she resists."

Amanda gave Emily a speaking look.

Emily shrugged, managing to convey with a look that it was easier to humor an old woman than to reason with or oppose her on such a trivial matter.

"Now. You try my way." Nadya jabbed at the air for emphasis. "It will not do. Fresh picked at full moon. Tonight."

Emily's eyebrows rose.

"We cannot. The *amatiflora* is long past bloom," Amanda reminded her.

The *amatiflora* was a vine-like plant, one that curled its way up trees, lamp posts, buildings, anything that would draw it closer to the sun. In England, Emily's notes had indicated, the plant's lifecycle was brief, its blooms confined to late summer.

"There is a chance." Nadya's mouth worked. "Long ago, when I was girl, the Effra ran," her hands waved, "above. *Amatiflora* along its banks."

The Effra was one of the lost rivers of London. Forced underground, it was now little more than a sewer that emptied into the Thames near the Vauxhall Bridge. She only knew of it because of the coffin. The Effra, passing beneath a cemetery, had covertly carried a coffin and its occupant downstream into the Thames where the coffin surfaced, shocking all of London and reminding its populace of the lost rivers conscripted in the creation of the great sewer system that ran beneath them all.

The Effra had been underground at least fifty years.

"It's October," Emily pointed out gently.

Nadya's eyes scrunched. "Listen." Her voice wobbled on. "South London Waterworks, they build near the Effra, near Vauxhall Bridge. Yes?"

Companies such as South London Waterworks had once drawn their water from the Thames, but pollution had long since forced them to move operations upstream.

"The building," Nadya pressed. "It still stands?"

Amanda nodded. "Part of the building was incorporated into Airship Sails." A large factory, dedicated to manufacturing and sewing enormous lengths of silver cloth to form the balloon that held the aether.

"They have engine station," Nadya said. "Where great furnaces make sewing machines turn."

"Yes, of course," Amanda answered, as realization began to dawn on her. "You think..."

"No." Nadya shook her head. "I not think. I know. *Amatiflora*, it climbs for sun, yes, but also for warmth."

Amanda and Emily's eyes caught. Was it possible?

"Unlikely," Emily said.

"But worth looking," Amanda concluded.

With a working nerve agent, it was just possible that the neurachnid could soon re-spin the nerves Ned had damaged. It was certainly worth trying before he resorted to Ferrous Limbs.

"Last night was the full moon," Emily stated flatly.

The old woman's hand see-sawed. "Need not be perfect. Just much moonlight."

Amanda did not care about the moonlight. She cared only for obtaining the correct flowers. Or, at the very least, a length of stem to carry to the botanists at Lister University. They could use the sketch and the sample to search through what was certain to be an extensive selection of plants to determine if what the gypsies called the *amatiflora* grew within. She shoved to her feet. "Thornton will take me." He would. All she had to do was threaten to go alone.

"You can't go there looking like a peacock." Emily gave her an assessing glance. "A lord and lady skulking about the factory's premises will draw immediate and unwanted attention." She twisted onto her knees beside a trunk and began to drag forth a selection of skirts. "Strip."

No, Amanda certainly couldn't skulk about the streets of South London in silks and feathers. She complied, unhooking her bodice and stripping down to her corset and combinations. This was it, then, the end of their visit. Once dressed, Amanda would be on her way, leaving Emily alone again. Though Thornton's guards would look over her, she would feel much better if Emily were closer, where she could see her daily. "Please, Emily," Amanda pleaded as her sister loosened her corset. "Will you please move home?"

Emily held out an ochre-colored skirt, her eyes sad. "I cannot."

"Only until this situation is resolved. Never mind Mother. Or Olivia's dreams of a titled husband. She'd be better off without Carlton. You can help me with the formula in my laboratory. I could use the help. I *need* the help." Amanda tossed aside her corset and pulled on the full, ruffled skirt; its hem skimmed her knees. The last time she'd worn a skirt this short, she'd yet to pin up her hair.

"It's not just that." Emily held out a pair of high-heeled brown leather boots. Straps and buckles covered their sides. "I promised Father."

"It's your *life*, Emily. Perhaps the baby's." The boots fit snugly and rose to her knees. Likely they'd be wading through overgrown weeds. Thorns were a distinct possibility.

"So it is. I will not leave Luca. Or Nadya. Or..." She waved a hand, indicating the camp. "The rest of my family."

It was a knife to the gut, realizing that Emily trusted the men and women in this camp to look after her better than her own biological family.

"A fine gypsy woman, my Emily," said Nadya.

"Don't look like that, Amanda. Father hasn't abandoned me. Not only do we camp here because of him, but if you take the time to look, you'll find that *his* men outnumber the gypsy men two to one. I am better guarded here in this camp than I would be in any mansion," Emily said. "Now, about your attire." She lifted a short, midriff-baring white cotton blouse. It was mostly sleeves. Full, puffy sleeves. In her other hand was an equally short, sapphire blue vest. Silver chains and coins dripped from the hem.

"I don't think so."

"Come now, Amanda. I've seen Lord Thornton sneaking sidelong glances at you, but the hinges of his jaw seem bolted tight." She grinned knowingly. "I think this outfit might loosen them. Let's see if we can make the earl's jaw drop."

Amanda pursed her lips a moment, but it was as if her

sister read her mind. She reached out and snatched the blouse from Emily's hand. Turning her back to the two women, she pulled off the top half of her combinations and tugged on the blouse. It ended directly beneath her breasts. She slid her arms through the holes of the half-vest, drawing it closed with its leather buckles. The vest pushed her breasts upward against the low ruffle of the blouse, placing the deep valley between them on display. The coins hanging from chains brushed against her bare belly. She felt like a temptress; it would be impossible for Thornton not to look.

Cool metal fell around her neck. A chain with yet more silver coins. "Without a necklace, no one will believe you Roma," Emily explained.

The dressing continued. Two more coins, one each to hang from an earlobe. A green scarf to wind about her hips, an ochre one to hold back her hair, and a broad leather belt to sling over her hips, fitted with a knife and a purse.

"To harvest the *amatiflora*," said Emily. "The vines are tough. Collect the leaves as well as the flowers."

Nadya nodded her approval.

A cool breeze blew across Amanda's midriff. Into the vardo stepped Luca. And Thornton.

And Amanda had to suppress a satisfied smirk as his jaw did indeed unhinge.

CHAPTER TWENTY-FIVE

T HORNTON DID *NOT* agree with the plan.

There would be no moving Emily or her husband Luca to the Avesbury townhouse. The two were stubborn and foolish. Perhaps both. Just like Amanda's plan.

He was a fool for going along with it. A gypsy fool dressed in a crimson vest and a loose white shirt with sleeves that flapped in the wind that blew in off the Thames. A brown, woolen cap that made his scalp itch squatted on his head, well-worn leather trousers hugged his legs, and distressed boots a size too small squeezed his feet, cramping the small muscles of his feet and threatening to send his bad leg into full spasm.

Worst of all he sat atop the splintery seat of a crank wagon, driving the daughter of a duke to South London in the dead of night across a rickety bridge when nearly all her family believed her safely ensconced in the London Symphony House.

"Throw any scrap metal you find in the back of the wagon," Luca had advised. "It'll lend authenticity to your disguise."

Black had near cracked a molar clenching his jaw when Thornton informed him he'd be remaining behind at the gypsy camp on guard detail. The man clearly thought Thornton had lost his mind.

Quite likely, he was correct.

But Amanda and Emily swore up and down and sideways that the *amatiflora* was the key ingredient. The old woman insisted it still bloomed and that it must be harvested tonight.

Looking at Amanda standing there in the vardo, the flickering light of a lantern casting shadows and throwing highlights onto her curves, he'd nodded, knowing full well he was agreeing to a fool's errand. His eyes had fixed on the swell of her chest above a tightly strapped vest, then fallen to catch on the swoops of chains and dangling coins that brushed her bare stomach above her navel. He'd been incapable of refusing.

Struck mute, he'd been easily led into an adjacent vardo, easily convinced into adjusting his own appearance to match hers. All under the wry eye of Luca. Then, with much suppressed amusement, the gypsy man had wrapped a protective arm about his pregnant wife and waved them on their way.

Beside him, Amanda tensed and gripped the side of the cart as they approached Vauxhall Bridge.

"There've been no reports of any giant kraken," he reassured her. "None over five feet in length."

"It's not the kraken that worry me, not directly. Rather, the bridge no longer appears... straight."

Thornton glanced ahead out over the water. It did appear somewhat... bowed. Everything about tonight was a bad idea. "Would you prefer to go the long way around? Use another bridge?"

"No. Airship Sails is directly on the other side," she said. "But I do prefer to cross quickly."

The kraken population in the Thames was on the rise again, keeping river traffic to a minimum. Men brave enough to take on the job could easily find work perched on the front of larger boats, air cartridge-loaded harpoons in hand, watching and waiting for the inevitable kraken large enough to capsize their vessel. The smaller ones tended to swarm, but were a danger only to small boats.

For the most part, bridges were safe—except for Vauxhall Bridge. During the last infestation, an extremely large kraken queen—rumored to be some thirty feet, beak to pointed tail fin—had taken up residence between the two central piers, badly damaging the structure. Plans to replace the current bridge only fueled rumors of its imminent collapse. Traffic, therefore, was at a mere trickle.

Thornton pulled on a knob, allowing the spring to unwind faster, and the wagon shot out onto the bridge, which did indeed seem to bend in a westerly direction as the tide rose.

As the crank wagon rumbled off the bridge into South London, Amanda let out a long sigh of relief.

A few minutes later, just as the crank wagon's spring had nearly run down, Thornton pulled on the steering handle, directing them onto the side of the road. For a few long moments, he and Amanda sat quietly, studying the hulking brick factory building that was Airship Sails. It was deserted, the workers all having been sent home hours ago.

The sewing machines here were great, hulking beasts with needles the length of a man's arm to bind together lengths of sailcloth with steel threads. A feat of engineering that turned the silver-coated cloth into enormous balloons that, when stretched across their metal framework, could float an airship's hull—the equivalent of a small city—wherever its captain steered it.

There would be a watchman or two about, but no more. Sailcloth was thick and heavy, and in such lengths that theft was unlikely. Nevertheless, there were tall iron fences and stout locks that the owners assumed—in this case, wrongly—would keep troublemakers and thieves at bay.

"The gate is locked," Amanda said. "But over there, down by the Thames, there's a gap in the fencing next to..." She squinted. "Is that an old submersible chute in the weeds?"

"It is."

At one point, personal submersibles were all the rage amongst businessmen. Until the kraken infestation. Now airships were considered far, far safer. However, when progress had been made in the clearing of the river, specifically with the recent development of a TDM, Tentacle Defense Mechanism, some companies had polished up their submersible stations and vessels— wealthy stockholders often preferred to visit their investments unseen—in hopes of once again being able to travel beneath the Thames.

Airship Sails was not among those companies. Yet, if he was not mistaken, a toolbox rested beside a submersible floating in the tank beside the docking station. Perhaps efforts at modernization were underway.

"The gate is a much more direct route to our goal," he said.

His gaze traveled along the roofline of the factory, then fell upon the power house, set to the side of the main building and built of brick, cast iron and granite to alleviate fire concerns. The engines it housed generated an immense amount of power for the sewing machines by firing coal. It was a square building, small compared to the factory, and the chimney attached to its side towered over it, stretching some six stories into the moonlit sky.

All day coal burned. All day the engines churned, belching hot air and smoke into that chimney. All day the bricks absorbed heat. All night, those same bricks radiated that heat back out into the night. And, at the base of the chimney, a smattering of weeds still clung to life through the increasingly cold nights.

Did vines still twist and writhe up the brick column? Did he dare hope flowers still bloomed? He squinted, but it was too dark and too far for that level of detail. They'd have to move closer, breach the iron fence. "It would make much more sense to return tomorrow," he said. "There are strings easily pulled."

Amanda shook her head. "Best to act quickly and leave no record of our activities for the eye doctor to learn of. Besides, though it likely amounts to nothing, Nadya insists we gather the blooms in the moonlight."

He doubted very much moonlight contributed to the plant's potency, but hiding their activities from the eye doctor carried weight. "Very well." Grateful that he'd thought to administer an additional dose of Somnic back at the gypsy campground in the privacy of the vardo Black had conscripted, he hopped to the ground, dropping most of his weight onto his good leg. The brace he wore compensated for the odd twisting of his foot, but provided little in the way of power.

He lifted a hand to his gypsy woman, helping her down. She wobbled for a moment on her heeled leather boots as she adjusted to the uneven ground. Coins and chains tinkled faintly beneath the shawl she'd wrapped about her shoulders for warmth.

With a slight tug, he could pull her against his chest, let his hands wander across her un-corseted waist, her un-bustled behind. Would she slap him? Or might her own hands slide beneath his vest and invite further liberties? Losing. He was losing the battle for self-control. Reminding himself that it was a husband she sought, he released her and turned away. Her marriage to Sommersby was certain to be a disaster. What man wanted a wife who would run about London at all hours of the night risking life and limb? Lady Anne would never behave in such a manner.

But Lady Anne had never made his blood run hot.

"How do we get inside?" Lady Amanda asked, her voice hushed as they walked along the gravel road that led to the factory's entrance. Tall iron gates rose up before them. "Do we climb?" Doubt laced her voice.

Over Luca's vehement objections, Thornton had appropriated his tool belt, but only the belt. The tools within its various pouches and pockets he'd replaced with a selection of his own devices—and a few of Black's. He pulled one such item from a pouch now. It felt good to be back in the field, even if all he was after was an unlikely white bloom.

"No. We use this. Captain Jack's Tension Torque. Insert the hollow copper coil and the pick," he demonstrated, "then depress the plunger on the syringe to extrude the alkylsorcin into the lock. Wait three seconds..." He counted them off, "then use the thumb wheel to make a few fine adjustments. And with the flick of a wrist..." He twisted the device, there was a soft pop and the iron gate swung open.

"Impressive." Amanda looked up at him with admiration shining in her eyes.

It was a heady experience, praise from a lady for the most basic of an agent's skills. "The alkylsorcin liquefies in a few minutes, leaving no trace." He pushed the gate wide, its hinges protesting with a screech. "Ladies first."

She slipped inside, and he followed, nudging a large rock

against the gate, holding it in place, but not preventing a swift exit should someone take issue with their presence.

"Keep your eyes out for bobbing lanterns, they indicate..."

"Watchmen," she finished, then led the way down a well-worn path toward the power house. Weeds, some with thorns, lashed out at their legs—her skirts—as they passed.

Soon they stood at the base of the great chimney. It *was* warmer here.

A multitude of vines twisted and writhed about the structure. None seemed to possess flowers. He tugged a torch from a pocket and shook it vigorously, activating the bioluminescent organisms within. With a quick adjustment to the lens, he pointed the beam of blue light upward and handed it to Amanda.

She paced around the tower, her face tipped upward, eyes searching.

He should help. Or watch for guards. Instead he watched her.

Her hair had come undone and spilled from its scarf over her shoulders in long, dark twists, brushing against the bare skin of her lower back. Her hips and skirts swayed with each step her long leather-encased legs took. Her shawl slipped free from one shoulder, and she tied it carelessly about her hips, continuing her search.

She turned, aiming the torch higher, her back arched. Above a taut stomach, breasts thrust upward against a thin cotton blouse, tight nipples in clear evidence. He suppressed a groan of frustration and turned away, leaving her to her search, directing his gaze where it ought to be: watching for guards.

It wasn't right of him to be lusting after a woman he was unprepared to make his. She deserved more from him.

A few minutes later, when he had his lust once again under control, she stepped close, wrapping her arm about his, and spoke in a low, excited voice. "I can see them, but they're too high to reach. Look." She tugged on his arm, turning him toward the chimney and pointing with the torch. "There."

A scattering of tiny white blooms on a vine where the chimney jutted free from the building. Beneath the pitch of the roof ran a narrow bank of windows, and beneath those windows, a narrow ledge ran around the building, a ledge wide enough for a man to walk along.

He moved toward the door, readying the tension torque by inserting a new cartridge of alkylsorcin. "We'll go inside," he said. "Keep watch. I'll make my way to the windows. From there, the ledge..." He trailed off.

It could not be him making the journey. Not even with the extra dose of Somnic. He could walk the ledge, but scaling the roof, that was beyond him. Control of his right foot was too uncertain. "I can't, Amanda. We'll have to come back tomorrow." It hurt to admit, but his lower leg was untrustworthy.

"No," she said. "I'll do it."

"It's too dangerous," he objected. "How often do you walk ledges?"

She had opened her mouth, no doubt to protest, when a beam of greenish-blue light caught her in its glare.

"Well, well, what have we here?" The man's eyes were alight with glee as he waved his pistol about wildly. "Gypsies. There'll be no ledge walking tonight. Just a trip to lockup. Unless..." He glanced at Thornton, then turned a speculative eye toward Amanda's bare mid-section and waggled his eyebrows.

No one but him would be touching her tonight. In one smooth motion, he reached beneath his vest and drew his TTX pistol, shooting the watchman once in the arm and again in the neck.

"Whaaaa...." The watchman's eyes rolled back into his head as he crumpled to the ground.

"Grab his weapon and his torch." Thornton turned and made short work of the lock, forcing the alkylsorcin into the keyhole, counting off the seconds before pushing Amanda safely into the powerhouse. He bent over and, grabbing the watchman beneath his arms, dragged him inside as well. As he closed the door softly behind him, a bobbing glow appeared in the distance, weaving behind outbuildings, but drawing close. More night watchmen.

He cursed and closed the door.

Inside, the smell of coal and oil was overpowering. The building was two stories tall, its massive undecorated brick walls devoid of ornament. Tall columns supported the roof. Two silent black cast iron engines dominated the room, flywheels and belts and pistons that turned long drive shafts that extended into the factory building proper. A spiral staircase led upward to a walkway that ran around the room—and beneath the window bank that led to the roof.

Thornton dragged the watchman across the room, tucking him safely out of sight behind one of the great engines in a utility closet.

When he returned, Amanda was still staring at him with wide eyes. "Did you...?"

"He'll be fine." In another twenty-four hours or so. "The bullets are loaded with TTX—pufferfish toxin. One bullet slows a man down. Two drops him. Three kill."

"But—"

"Did you wish him to alert the other watchmen?" Not the time to be questioning his methods.

Amanda shook her head, then turned and darted for the staircase. He followed, unable to call out and annoyed that his steps were not as certain, that she refused to listen to reason. Yet, as she climbed upward, he shamelessly took the opportunity to appreciate the view of long legs extending upward into the shadow of her skirt. She strode along the catwalk that led to the windows, tugging at the casements.

He caught her as she swung one of those long legs upward. "Wait. You can't go out there wearing those boots. Take them off."

"Off?"

He demonstrated, tugging his boots off, his socks, one from beneath his brace. "Your stockings too. Bare feet will grip the slate roof tiles. Leather soles?" He made a motion with his hands, demonstrating how she would slip from the roof.

Her eyes widened. Amanda sank to the floor, loosening her boot buckles, pulling them free. Then, casting him a coy glance from beneath long eyelashes, she hiked her skirts up to her thighs, unhooked a garter and began rolling down a silk stocking, exposing more to his view than no man other than a husband ought to lay eyes upon.

He closed his eyes and swallowed his lust. Then turned to the open window. He climbed out onto the ledge and waited, his feet registering years of accumulated grit, his brace making his grip less steady than he liked. Silently, he held out a hand, helping her onto the ledge.

Together they made their way to the chimney. His gaze fell on the small, white flowers and the slick, slate tiles she would have to scale to reach them.

Disappointment registered on Amanda's face as she assessed the vines and number of blooms. "Barely enough for one batch."

Not enough to save her brother's legs *and* attempt to treat his.

Then again, he'd never had hopes. Besides, losing both one's legs entirely was far worse than losing the function of a single foot. "We'll trace the vine to the ground, dig up the plant at its source. Perhaps it can be coaxed into bloom in winter," he whispered, as she tucked her skirt into her waistband. "Be careful."

Amanda nodded, then dropped to all fours, scaling the steep roof.

At the top, she straddled the ridgeline. She pulled a knife from her waist and began by cutting the vine, yanking its suckers free from the brick chimney until the ropy twist fell into her lap. Quickly, she cut free the leaves and flowers, tucking them into the leather pouch attached to her belt and reached for another vine.

He watched as the blue light of a night watchman circled the powerhouse, as it was joined by a second light. Two men now, one gesturing wildly and pointing at the open gate, circled the building positively bristling with excitement. Likely they'd never had cause to even draw their weapons on the job and were itching to do so.

Thornton sighed silently in resignation. He recognized the Welsh Drobwll Disrupters they held, more commonly known as the Whirlpool of Death, a favorite of untrained watchmen. Its blast of electromagnetic waves wasn't deadly in and of itself, but rather left its victim so dizzy and confused they often staggered in circles, wandering into harm's way, dying from unrelated causes. One blast from the Whirlpool while on a rooftop and they would, at best, break several bones from the fall.

Would the men think to look up?

No, they did not. They did, however, stop at the door to the powerhouse. One unhooked a ring of keys from his belt. Boots and stockings waited for discovery on the catwalk inside. Would their dedication extend to the second level? Thornton had a bad feeling it would.

As the men entered the building, he quickly ran through options. None appealed as much as undetected escape. Silently, he slid the window shut. Perhaps the guards would think the boots the forgotten remnants of a workers' tryst.

Not that he was naïve enough to count on it.

Moving along the narrow ledge, he plotted a course that would take them along those lengthy drive shafts and into the main factory. He glanced up at Amanda. Her pouch was nearly full. Not a single white bloom remained on the chimney. Good. They needed to move.

He snapped his fingers, hoping the sound would not attract undue attention. Amanda looked down. "Watchmen," he mouthed silently, gesturing with his hand that she should slide down to him.

CHAPTER TWENTY-SIX

AMANDA FELT HER EYES grow round. Had they been discovered? Why did Thornton look so concerned? Certainly there were those "strings" he could pull. But perhaps not before they confiscated and destroyed the *amatiflora* in her pouch.

Unwilling to leave a single flower behind, she wrapped the final section of vine with its scattered white blooms about her neck and began to descend. Careful as she was, a foot slipped out from underneath her on the slate roofing tiles, and she skittered toward Thornton, her descent down the steep angle of the roof rapidly growing out of control. She slid past, her feet catching briefly on the ledge before the accumulation of grit and dead leaves slid from beneath her—and she felt nothing but empty air beneath them.

Right before she jerked to a stop.

Thornton had caught her belt, holding her in place, her feet dangling. The breath squeezed from her midsection as he flexed his arm, heaving her back onto the roof, dragging her tight against his long, hard length.

Gasping with relief, she pressed her face to his solid chest, her hands gripping strong shoulders. His arm wrapped about her, pulling her tight. Her heart pounded in synchrony with his.

A mind sharpened in a laboratory; a body honed in the field. How many times a week did this man pick locks, run across rooftops and save damsels in distress?

Her thought was only fleeting because he tucked his chin against the top of her head and whispered hoarsely, "We need to go. Now. There are two overzealous men inside searching for us."

"Our boots. My stockings. Your socks. The guards. They'll know."

"Yes. The watchmen have disrupters, not deadly—unless you fall from a roof once hit."

She swallowed.

"Exactly. We need to move. Now. Follow me."

Reluctantly, she let go of him.

Slowly, carefully, quietly they picked their way across the steepled roof that ran above the crankshafts that extended from the powerhouse to the main factory. When they reached the far side, Thornton pried open a small window, then clasped his hands, offering her a foothold.

She slid through, collapsing in a heap on the narrow metal catwalk that ran around the inside of the building. Thornton landed beside her.

Overhead, glass panels in the roof let in the faint rays of

moonlight and illuminated the immense room beneath them. Pulleys and cables and wires suspended giant metal hooks to lift and drag long lengths of heavy sailcloth material. Large, geared rollers fed the sailcloth into the endless lines of powerful sewing machines that stretched across the floor.

"This way." Thornton's metal brace clanged softly on the catwalk. He swore under his breath and adjusted his steps to make no sound.

Heart pounding, she followed.

Down a metal staircase, ducking beneath windows on the off chance the moonlight would cast a silhouette, they reached the oily factory floor. They skirted the machinery and iron columns, hastening through the dark shadows they threw.

Amanda had lost all sense of direction, trusting Thornton to find the way. There it was, a metal door marked *exit.*

They were only some ten feet away when it opened.

Thornton grabbed her, pulling her into a dark shadow behind an enormous spool of metal wire. His back pressed to the wall, her back pressed against his stomach, his chest. Thornton's arm wrapped tightly beneath her breasts, silencing the tinkle of chains and coins, holding her securely in place. He slid his other hand beneath his coat, drawing forth the pistol he'd used earlier and pointing it in the direction of the watchmen.

She swallowed hard, willing the two men to walk away.

"We should go back, search the powerhouse again, top to bottom," one watchman grumbled.

Several heavy, clattering thuds sounded.

"Trysting lovers aren't worth the effort," snorted the other watchman. "'Sides, you've got their boots now. Sell 'em. We'll split the profit. Take the silk stockings home to the wife. Maybe she'll let you back in her bed."

"They pay us to keep people out, Bill." There was no humor in the voice belonging to the first watchman. "We should go back. Meet up with Jack."

Bill sighed heavily. "Do what you want, Joe. I'm for my break." His footsteps faded away.

Joe hesitated, but moments later, the metal door clanged shut behind him. Presumably, he headed back to the power-house. And to look for Jack.

"Don't move," Thornton whispered. "We'll give Joe a few minutes. If he continues on, we grab our boots and make an escape."

His warm breath against her bare neck sent shivers running down her spine. She could feel the rise and fall of his chest, the thud of his heart. The press of his leather trousers against her through the thin satin of her skirt. She could feel every molded contour.

He was aroused. Impressively so.

Despite his words, despite his impassive face, here was the evidence he wanted her. That their kiss had not been a fleeting interest. The thought lit a fire in her blood. She could feel the heat of it now, rushing to the surface of her skin. Their predicament had put her exactly where she had so longed to be. She shifted, pushing backward against the hard column that pressed against her lower back.

"Amanda." He growled a low warning, the vibration against her neck sent a tingle of electric webs across her skin. Every nerve was on edge now, screaming to feel the brush of his skin against hers.

Hardly believing she dared, she rolled her hips suggestively, invitingly, and his erection pulsed against her. At last the advantage fell to her.

The fingers of his free hand dug into her hip, holding her motionless. "I won't take what belongs to another man," he warned.

She tipped her head back against his shoulder, looking up into his dark eyes. "I'm not his," she whispered. "Nor is there any... agreement."

"I'm not looking for a wife."

She dragged her lips across the rough stubble of his jaw. A thrill shot through her. "Noted."

Distant footsteps sounded on the factory floor.

They froze.

THE FOOTSTEPS FADED AWAY ONCE MORE, but still his heart pounded, propelling the liquid fire that was his blood everywhere except into his brain. He could no longer remember why, exactly, he'd been so intent on pushing Amanda away. Perhaps it was time to return the favor and give her a small taste of the flames she ignited in his veins.

He bent forward, dipping his head to her jaw, her neck, her throat, tasting her soft skin—and was rewarded with a soft gasp. He scraped his teeth gently over her shoulder, nipping lightly, and she shuddered in his arms.

Hot desire pulled in his groin. With one arm, he held her tightly against him, careful to keep the gypsy coins still and silent. He had no interest in discovery. "We could go now," he said softly, then nibbled her earlobe.

"Go?" She sounded confused.

"Back to the cart." He kissed his way along her jawline, then pulled back. "Is that a no?"

She whimpered.

"Amanda?" He wanted to hear her say it.

"Yes. No." She gripped his arm, the one that bound her to him, and gasped out, "We should stay... a bit longer."

The answer he wanted. His mouth stretched into a grin against her skin, a grin that was a touch feral. "Very well."

His free hand smoothed over the sinuous curve of her hip, upward across the smooth, bare skin of her stomach. Upward over the brocade of her vest, to slide beneath it, his palm cupping the full heaviness of her soft breast. Beneath the thin cotton of her shirt, her nipple was already pebbled with anticipation, waiting impatiently. He rolled the taut peak between his thumb and forefinger and was rewarded by the buck of her hips against his.

He pushed back, his groin hot and hard with lust.

She threw her head backward onto his shoulder, turning her face into his neck. "God, don't stop," she breathed.

He had no intention of stopping, not yet, not until he made her as wild as he felt. As his fingers pinched and tugged, he bent his head and covered her mouth with his, urging her lips apart, sweeping his tongue inside. She answered every stroke with one of her own.

Her hips rocked with increasing insistence, pushing against his throbbing erection, driving him slowly mad. He could feel her restlessness building, her hips moving in that primitive, urgent rhythm driven by biological instinct to seek fulfillment and relief. He knew, if he reached beneath her skirts, he'd find her hot and slick and ready.

His own body begged for release, and the large spool of cable wire before him beckoned. He wanted to bend her over it, lift her skirts and sink into her wet heat. But reason intruded, and he kept his desire firmly in check. Amanda was likely an innocent, and this was neither the time, nor the place.

Still, he could show her all-consuming desire. Even if it meant pushing the limits of his own control to the breaking point. He could make her come.

He pulled away from her demanding lips and looked at her. The pulse at her throat raced, her breath came in pants, her eyes were heavy with desire. Slowly, he slid his hand downward, splaying his fingers across her bare abdomen before hooking a finger under the edge of her belt, tugging a suggestion. "Do you want me to stop? Or do you want more?"

Her arms reached upward, hands threading fingers into his hair, and she breathed, "More."

His cock throbbed against the leather of his trousers. Blood pounded in his ears. He took a deep breath and, focusing only on the woman in his arms, slid his hand beneath the loose belt, her scarf, the waistband of her skirt, nearly losing all control when he discovered nothing but bare skin. His fingers brushed lightly over downy hair, dipping deeper to find her swollen and wet.

SHE JERKED in shock and mewled in pleasure as his fingers touched her core, where she was damp with pulsing need. He answered with a low hum of appreciation, his fingers setting up a slow, tortuous exploration of her folds. Circling, pressing, but never quite touching where she most wanted, needed the pressure.

She wanted to scream her frustration. Instead she ground backward against his erection.

He groaned and his teeth came down on her throat, scraping a warning. She gripped his hair in her fists, holding his hot, wet mouth pressed against her neck where it worked its magic. Kissing. Nibbling. Sucking. Sending new waves of heat between her legs where his fingers never stopped moving, addling her mind with desire.

Her heart hammered in her chest. His breath came in ragged, hot pants beside her ear. His leg pushed forward between hers, forcing her thighs apart, spreading her open to him. His fingers dragged mercilessly across her wet crease. She flexed and twisted her hips, demanding more, but he held her tight, continuing to explore her swollen folds.

Sweet torment.

If not for the threat of the watchman, she would twist

around, work the buttons at his waist until the hot length of him fell free in her hands. Drag him to the cold, stone floor. Though a virgin, primitive instinct ruled. She was desperate to feel him inside her.

As if he could read her mind, a finger slid deep inside her and she turned her face toward his neck, stifling a moan.

"Hush," he whispered in warning. "Or I'll be forced to stop."

He wouldn't dare.

She bit down on his throat, suppressing a feral scream.

Two fingers plunged inside her. Withdrew. And plunged again. Over and over as the base of his palm ground against her clitoris, her frantically bucking hips urging him on.

Her nails dug into the corded muscle of his neck as need grew. Muscles inside tightened about his fingers, seeking more pressure, straining for something just out of reach. She fought the urge to scream that built in her throat.

"Stop fighting it and let go." His low voice rumbled in her ear. Then his fingers thrust deep, his thumb pressed against her throbbing center, and his mouth covered her own, smothering her cry as her body shuddered and arched against his, clenching, pulsing as millions of tiny explosions shattered inside her.

Never had she ever experienced anything quite like this.

His arms shifted, holding her tight and safe as the tremors of bliss subsided, as the blood rushing through her body gradually slowed, leaving her limp and drained. He held her, pressing a kiss to her hair even as his own heart still pounded against her back, as the hard length of his desire still throbbed against her hip, but he made no move to sate his own needs.

What had just happened?

Embarrassed by her wanton, wild behavior, she didn't dare move. Dear God, she'd moaned and writhed and cried out as he touched her in ways no man ever had, dragging forth a pleasure so intense she'd cried out even under the threat of discovery. How could she ever look him in the eye again? Hold a rational conversation in his presence?

Overhead, rain began to drum on the windows, echoing her own growing distress. She listened as the rain outside gathered strength. Wind began to encourage the drops that fell, hurling them like sharp needles against the windows, against the skylight.

"No shame," he whispered into her hair as if reading her mind. "What we shared was amazing." Amanda flushed. She hadn't noticed much reciprocity. He continued, "If we didn't need to leave, and soon, I'd be tempted to repeat my performance."

Humiliation burned in her cheeks. She had no reply. She'd wanted this, asked for it, and it seemed he'd enjoyed it as well. But her heart was behaving in a most ungoverned manner, yearning for the man who held her. He made her feel alive. Physically. Mentally. Yet he would never be hers. He'd said as much.

This encounter might be all they ever shared. Was it enough?

Not nearly.

So for now, she would take anything and everything he was willing to give. For as long as he was willing.

His arms loosened as he whispered, "We should go now."

She didn't want to leave this moment behind, but it was time to venture out into the cold and wet of the dark night, out of the circle of his warmth. It was time to face what waited for them both outside. Responsibilities. Expectations.

"We should," she agreed, pulling away, moving as quickly as her unsteady legs would toward the exit.

CHAPTER TWENTY-SEVEN

T HORNTON SAT IN HIS OFFICE, listening to yet one more student try to explain why his case deserved special consideration.

God, he hated office hours.

And today's session was the worst. "No, Mr. Button," he said, cutting the man off mid-sentence. "I will not issue a reexamination. If you wish to raise your grade, I suggest you apply yourself more to your studies and less to your antics in the dissection room." The boy's mouth fell open. "Yes, Mr. Button. I am well aware of the reasons you and your friends spend such long hours with the cadavers. While there are no specific prohibitions against posing with dead bodies for the camera, I can assure you that the board of trustees is not at all pleased at the distribution of such images and is reconsidering your continued presence at this school."

The student, pale and shaking, jumped from the stiff-backed chair Thornton reluctantly provided for such student-centered encounters. "Sorry, my lord. I... we... it won't happen again."

"Good."

Mr. Button rushed from the room. Dare he hope that was the last of them?

Thornton closed his eyes and let his head fall into his hands. His headache pounded like a steam-driven piston against his skull. He'd barely slept last night. Instead, he'd lain there, aroused and frustrated until he'd at last taken matters into his own hands.

He wanted her.

If he were honest with himself, he'd wanted her since that first anatomy lecture. Certainly she'd registered as beautiful, as interested—her eyes had followed him as if he were something to be devoured—but her piercing insight into nerve conduction made her a woman to be pursued. He'd told himself he wanted her only for her mind, but that was a lie. He wanted her body and soul.

And she wanted him.

Watching her sit beside Sommersby in today's lecture —smiling at the man's comments, responding politely—all the while refusing to make eye contact with him had been nothing short of torture. Thornton wanted her to look up and see the heat in his eyes, see that he was remembering how he held her in his arms last night, making her writhe and twist and buck with pleasure and, at last, come with such force that even now he swelled at the memory. He wanted her complete and undivided attention.

Her continued proximity to Sommersby—to any male that expressed interest—set his teeth on edge.

When no further students entered, Thornton picked up the pile of correspondence he'd dragged with him from his townhome this morning. Invitations to balls, garden parties—and yes—even a tea, he threw in the bin. Then, recognizing Mother's loud, looping letters, he almost sent her missive behind the others, unopened.

With a sigh, he opened it, expecting the usual weekly exhortation to attend one event or another. But no, now she was arranging her own social events in hopes of forcing his presence. The countess informed him that he was expected at her upcoming house party in the country, that several young ladies were eager to make his acquaintance.

Wonderful how his own mother found him such a poor prospect that his marriage must be arranged. Alas, he'd only encouraged her by agreeing to the arrangement with Lady Anne. Now, it seemed, Mother had a mission.

"Was that the last of them?" Lady Huntley asked, strolling into his office.

"One can only hope."

"What's this?" Spying his mother's handwriting, she snatched the missive from his hand and backed away out of arm's reach.

He let her read it. She always did. Besides, his leg pained him too much to rise. "Left your manners at home this morning?" he grumbled.

"As did you. Besides, as your assistant, I am merely staying abreast of your affairs."

"More likely you view my mother's efforts as the weekly installation of a two-penny theater."

"Well," she said. "There is that. It's amusing to picture you with a quiet, pedigreed wife who will sit quietly, minding hearth and home."

"One who won't question my long hours in the... laboratory?" He almost said field. Though it was becoming increasingly difficult, even for him, to envision such a future.

"You could always pre-empt her. Perhaps Lady Amanda would be amenable to filling the position? No necessary white lies." Lady Huntley tipped her head, giving him a knowing look. "All of England does expect you to produce an heir. Producing one might be more interesting with a woman such as her by your side."

"Interesting, yes, but a damn sight more complicated. She is my student. Romantic entanglement is forbidden. And children are nothing but additional complications." His voice mocked, but his mind flashed an image of a small daughter, one with Amanda's features. He pushed the thought aside.

Lady Huntley glanced away, her response barely audible. "Entanglements and complications. I wanted them very much."

Immediately, he regretted his words.

John.

But there was no changing the past, only the future. To do that the eye doctor had to be stopped. He cleared his throat. "Lady Amanda, she is working in the laboratory?"

Lady Huntley nodded. "At this very moment. Henri

confirmed for me that the device is close to completion, requiring only a few more adjustments before it will be ready for rat trials." She paused. "Excepting, of course, the lack of an appropriate nerve agent. Is there any news on that front?"

He nodded. "The plant has been located. Lord Thistleton has been provided with a description and the location. He assures me it will soon flourish under his care."

"It still grows?" Her eyebrows rose.

"And blooms."

"Where did you manage to find this plant?" she asked.

"Growing alongside a factory chimney. Thank you, by the way, for suggesting to Lady Amanda that she ask her sister to provide a sketch."

"Of course, having dragged Lady Amanda out into the dark of night—this time unchaperoned—to find said plant," Black spoke from the doorway, "there will be unintended consequences. The Duke of Avesbury, who is capable of bestowing great power and funds upon your laboratory, requests your presence this evening." He cocked an eyebrow at Lady Huntley. "Care to wager? Pistols at dawn or the calling of banns?"

"You're late to that discussion," Lady Huntley said, then flicked a glance at Thornton. "Special license," she predicted.

Black laughed.

Thornton was not amused. "Enough," he said. "What brings you here, Black? Good news?"

The man's face sobered, and he let out a long sigh. "Alas,

it never is. Lady Huntley, I have the unwelcome task of posing a question to you concerning your former husband."

Lady Huntley frowned. "Ask away."

"Were you aware that Lord Huntley booked passage for two aboard the *Ada Reeve*?"

Thornton's brow furrowed. He and John had traveled aboard that airship en route to Belgium, but they'd each made separate travel arrangements. That meant...

"Yes. I was to accompany him, but an unexpected complication forced me to remain at home."

"I'm afraid I'm going to need more specifics," Black said.

Lady Huntley turned her face away, but not before Thornton caught the stricken look on her face and the shimmer of unshed tears in her eyes. "I miscarried. I lost quite a lot of blood."

The two men shared a look of absolute horror.

"I insisted upon remaining at home, to recover." She swallowed. "John tried to convince me to come; he outright begged. But I was adamant. Now, in retrospect..."

"You think he meant to take you with him, across the border into Germany," Thornton finished.

She nodded, her back stiff. "Is that all, Black?"

"Concerning your husband, yes. I'm afraid there's also bad news. There's another body."

"Gypsy?" she asked, turning.

Black shook his head. "Tony Spinolli, Lady Amanda's brother's therapist. Perhaps you could fetch Lady Amanda from Henri's side, Lady Huntley? We'll have need of her expertise."

"Right away," she said, departing.

Thornton opened his mouth, but Black held up a hand, listening keenly as the enormous gears on the iron door turned. Only when it clanged shut, did he speak. "You believe her?"

"You suspect she knew John was up to something?" Thornton countered.

Black shrugged. "My job is to tie off loose ends."

He thought back, trying to recall the days and weeks leading up to their ill-fated voyage. "I noticed nothing amiss, but Lady Huntley had yet to work in my laboratory. John seemed happy enough. Giddy, like most newlyweds. I suppose impending parenthood might have made him happier than usual, though, given his plans to sell our device to the enemy, I would have expected signs of stress." He paused. "John never mentioned that his wife would be joining us, though he did seem somewhat gloomy as we boarded the airship. At the time, I attributed it to leaving behind his bride. Now..."

"Perhaps his conscience was bothering him on multiple fronts."

"Perhaps," Thornton agreed. He hoped John had lain awake at night those three long days in the sky. "Bastard. Abandoning his wife like that."

"Agreed," Black said.

A few minutes later, Lady Huntley returned with Amanda.

"What has happened?" she asked.

Aside from her seeming inability to meet his eyes, she

appeared as always. Beautiful. Composed. Professional. Perfectly well rested.

Then again, he'd left her well sated. A satisfied smile tugged at his lips.

"You may wish to sit, Lady Amanda," Black said, waving his hand at the empty chair before Thornton's desk. "I'm afraid I have upsetting news."

She stiffened. "I'll stand."

"After your brother admitted to his involvement in our case, agents were alerted," Black said. "We've found Tony Spinolli. I'm afraid his body spent some time in the Thames before being washed ashore by the tides."

Amanda paled. "I believe I will sit after all." She lowered herself gingerly into the chair.

It was always harder when the individual was a personal acquaintance. Or a close friend turned traitor. "Was he altered?" Thornton asked.

"It appears, on the surface, to be another unsuccessful attempt," Black said. "The body is badly damaged." That anybody survived the kraken swarms was a miracle, making the Thames a favored dumping ground of murderers. "And bloated. Its smell is... indescribable..."

"It doesn't matter," Amanda said, but he detected a slight wrinkling of her nose. "We'll need to examine him."

"Let's go," he said, reaching for his cane.

"If you don't mind," Lady Huntley said, "I'll read the report this time."

"As will I," Black echoed.

"Cowards," Thornton teased. Though he was relieved to

part with them at the iron door, leaving him to accompany Amanda alone into the bowels of the building. "Amanda," he began, placing a hand at the small of her back.

She sidled away. "Not here," she hissed. "Anyone might be about."

"Very well. But soon." They would need to speak. He'd meant what he said about not wanting a wife. He wanted her, but only if she could accept that their relationship would need to remain a secret.

For now.

Perhaps in the future... He pushed the thought away. First he would need to speak to her father about Sommersby, about preventing that alliance from occurring.

They traveled to the autopsy suite in silence.

Amanda stepped into the room and gagged. "Dear God." She pressed a hand to her mouth and nose.

The stench of decay was overpowering and of such strength he feared it would set into their clothing, their hair, their very pores.

"This will require an hour's soak in a sodium bicarbonate bath to remove the smell," she gasped.

"At least." Thornton grabbed two OptiAir masks from their hooks, handing one to Amanda and pulling the other over his face. Only then could he enjoy the image that sprang to mind of her reclining in a tub, steam rising above her damp shoulders, wet tendrils of hair dangling about her face and neck.

He steeled himself to focus on the task at hand.

The India rubber seal prevented conversation, and so

they worked quietly and efficiently, taking samples and thoroughly examining the man's wounds—what the fish and kraken had left for them to examine—using hand signals.

Cause of death was not in question. The poor man's abdomen had been slit from stem to stern. Surgery in the eye socket had been attempted, but without a working nerve agent, failure had been unavoidable.

Still, there were multiple insertions of gold thread into the brainstem. But *this* neurachnid had not been able to negotiate the superior orbital fissure in a manner that would allow it to reach the appropriate ganglia clusters.

Time, however, worked against them. The longer it took to locate this mad scientist, this mad spy, the more likely it was that the eye doctor's independent modifications would succeed.

At last they slid the body into the refrigeration unit and retreated into the ascension chamber, pulling the rubber masks from their sweaty faces as the door slid shut.

Amanda fell backward against the wall, eyes closed, hair tossed and tumbled. "There is no evidence he has employed milligears, but there is every indication he has made other alterations to improve the stolen neurachnid. If he's not stopped, he may very well successfully refine my device."

Thornton didn't want to discuss the spider, not during one of the few moments they might have alone. He could fight temptation no longer. With two steps, he had her in his arms, his lips on hers, his body pressing her tightly against the chamber's walls.

Her lips parted, welcoming him in, her tongue tangling

hungrily with his, her arms wrapping about his waist, pulling him closer.

The distance the chamber traveled was all too short. It took every last ounce of his willpower to pull away, to reach the control panel before the doors slid open once more.

He reached the lever just in time, flipping it to "stop". They had mere moments before a disabled chamber would be noticed.

She stood there, face flushed, lips swollen, eyes wide.

"Ever since last night, I've not been able to think of anything but you, Amanda. I can't make you any promises, but if you'll have me..." He waited.

"Any way I can," she answered. Her cheeks burned an enticing crimson as she fought to speak past a measure of maidenly modesty. "But not here. Not in the school buildings."

"Not here," he agreed. A sense of triumph was quickly blunted by intense impatience. "Where?"

Her eyes dropped, and her voice fell to the merest whisper, fighting her embarrassment. "My laboratory. Tonight?"

"Tonight."

CHAPTER TWENTY-EIGHT

I T TOOK AMANDA OVER an hour in the bathtub—
washing her hair twice, scrubbing every inch of skin—
to finally drive every last trace of stench from her
pores. The gardenia-scented lotion was mere precaution.

"What happened to your feet?" Olivia gasped.

Her sister had burst into Amanda's room, catching her
applying salve to her feet. Amanda smiled to herself, holding
the memory of last night's adventure close.

With no time to lose, Thornton had scooped their boots
from the floor—and snagged a woolen coat from a peg to
wrap her in—as they ran barefoot from the building out into
a driving rain that had turned the road to mud. Mud studded
with foot-piercing gravel.

"They'll be fine," she said simply, rolling soft stockings
over her feet to hide the damage from Olivia's incredulous
eyes. If her sister but knew what Amanda planned

for *this* night. A flush rose to her cheeks. "What brings you to my door?"

"This." Olivia reached out and deposited a Babbage card on the table beside her. "You owe me much for those hours spent with an anatomy text. It was torture." She frowned. "Are you certain this is a good idea? I've only ever programmed steambots to do things *for* humans, not *to* them."

Amanda understood her trepidation. "Medical research is always scary. If it makes you feel any better, patients are always fully informed." Those that put themselves in Thornton's hands anyway. "Thank you."

"There's more." Her sister shifted uncomfortably on her feet. "I've come from Father's study."

"Carlton?"

Olivia sighed. "Best not to ask." A brittle smile formed on her lips. "It seems your turn has arrived. Father wishes to see you in his study. Mr. Sommersby has come to call."

Dread reached out and squeezed her stomach. "Is he still here?"

"Father sent him to wait in the library," Olivia answered, but tipped her head. "Don't tell me you intend to refuse him?" Her next words surprised Amanda. "Don't you want your own family? Your own household?"

Yes.

Except she did not want a husband any lesser than Thornton, and he did not want a wife. Therefore, she resolved, so long as he was in her life, she would do without a husband.

The only problem would be convincing Father.

Amanda stood, the many petticoats she wore fanning out about her legs. She finished dressing by donning a simple high-necked shirtwaist with tiny, pearl buttons and a skirt that gathered at the small of her back, giving only the faintest impression of a bustle. Last, she donned a soft, leather over-bust corset.

Then she sat before her mirror and reached up to pull her hair into a simple knot.

"Let me. I've a new style I'm working on for Steam Cora." Olivia moved behind her and began to plait and twist her hair. "What is wrong with Mr. Sommersby? A decent man from a good family with a modest income, which your dowry will augment considerably. You will live in comfort, and he will one day be a physician. Quite probably he will let you practice medicine as well. Is that not all you ever wanted?"

A few weeks ago, it had been. "Don't you ever want more, Olivia?" she asked.

As children, they'd been close, but the moment their skirts lengthened, the moment Mother began to groom them to catch a husband, a crack had formed, gradually widening and deepening until they could no longer reach each other. Now her sister threw a rope across the chasm.

"More?" Olivia laughed. "Romance is not for the daughters of dukes." She stabbed in a few hairpins. "Especially for those daughters who buck tradition and enroll themselves in medical school." She wrestled a final loose strand into a twist and pinned it in place. "There. Best hurry. Father was already pacing when I left."

Minutes later, she stood in front of his massive wooden desk.

Father stood behind it, his eyebrows disappearing into his hairline. That was a trick, considering his hair was on the retreat. "What do you mean, 'no'?" he bellowed. "I thought we had struck a deal. Have you someone else in mind? Lord Thornton perhaps?"

She fought a rising blush and shook her head. "No."

"Are you certain?" Father crossed his arms and narrowed his eyes. "All that time you've been spending with him late at night. Unchaperoned."

"You know romantic entanglements are against the rules."

He looked at her sharply. "If he's taken any unwanted liberties, I will bring him up to scratch."

"No, Father." Nothing Thornton had done was unwelcome or unwanted.

"Are you certain? Marriage, itself, is not expressly forbidden."

She stayed silent.

Father heaved a disgusted sigh. "At least consider Sommersby's offer."

"I don't think we suit."

He nearly choked at her response, but surprisingly, let it go. "On to other matters, then," he said. "Emily."

"As agreed, Father. I've told no one about Emily's whereabouts."

"No one but Lord Thornton."

Not revealing that Emily was a gypsy bride was one of the conditions she'd violated. Certainly Father would not force her from school for telling Lord Thornton? Amanda pressed a hand against a queasy stomach. "He needed to know."

"And now the Queen and many of her agents know." Father waved a hand. "However, so long as the *ton* remains unaware, I will overlook your indiscretion. Have a care, Amanda, *anyone* could follow you to her campsite. You've not the training to conceal your movements and are lucky Thornton intercepted you."

A lead ball fell into her stomach. She'd not been thinking of the ramifications. "I'm sorry."

"You should be. I promised not to interfere in her new life as a gypsy. She promised not to reveal herself. I'm doing my best to protect her *and* uphold my end of our bargain."

"She would be safer here at home, the baby too, if only..."

"You think I'm wrong to ban her from my household?" Father tipped his head back. "Emily is welcome here. All she has to do is admit she made a mistake, and she can return. Until then..." He threw a hand in the air. "A deal's a deal." He fixed her with a pointed stare. He began to pace. "She's gone native, gypsy style. No marriage contract. No church records. Just stated intentions and... and..." His voice dropped. "Evidence of their union." He poured a glass of scotch. Sipped. "Your mother would have an apoplexy if she discovers she's to become a grandmother to a gypsy baby."

Sad, but true. Likely her niece or nephew would know only one set of grandparents.

Father continued, "Nor would Olivia's engagement survive the news." After such news, no other *ton* male would have her. "Now." Father narrowed his eyes at her. "Sommersby and I have hashed out a tentative agreement. I could have you wed in mere weeks."

"No." Amanda took a step backward. "Can we not revisit our agreement, Father? I need more time."

"Time for what?" he asked. "You've had years. If you won't have Sommersby, *I* will find you a husband."

A terrifying thought.

"No?" Father's eyebrows rose at her expression. "I thought not. Off to the library, Amanda. Sommersby awaits your answer. I strongly advise you don't throw him beneath a steam carriage."

She stood in the hallway outside the library for a long time. At last she pasted a smile on her face and entered.

"Amanda," Simon stood, offering a tentative smile.

She moved to stand before the fireplace. "I've spoken with Father."

"And the result is such a grim face?" Simon looked pained. "Am I to be declined?"

She studied the man before her. He was tall. Handsome. Well-connected. Bright.

Yet so very, very dull.

With this man there would be no late-night dirigible rides in thick London fog. No crash landings into gypsy camps. No mysteries to unravel in the morgue. No late nights working side by side in a laboratory. No scampering across slick roofs or down muddy roads.

No passionate encounters that left her panting and sated.

Her toes curled in her slippers. "I'm sorry, Simon."

He reached out and lifted her hand. "I've agreed to everything you desire. You may remain in medical school, practice after graduation. I'll even build that laboratory in my basement for you. Though I hope you'll restrict your hours once children arrive."

Chances of finding another gentleman who would grant her such liberties were slim, but, his words made it clear he would not encourage her eccentricities; they were only to be tolerated.

"It's Lord Thornton, isn't it?" His mouth hardened. "That is why you won't accept my proposal."

She fought the instinct to look away. "No," she lied. "I want so much to be able to accept you, but..."

"But what?"

"Tell me, Simon. Do you feel any... chemistry between us?"

He leaned forward, tugging on her hand. "If it's romance you're after." His lips came down on hers. They were warm and soft—and trying far too hard.

She twisted away, feeling horribly disloyal.

Simon dropped her hand and stepped away. "Obviously, you do not."

"No." At the very least, she owed him honesty.

Undiscouraged, Simon pressed his suit. "Marriage is often one of alliances. I offer you all you want and more."

Amanda looked at him. His eyes were full of hope. How could he still want her? "You have," she said. "But..."

"Please, Amanda," Simon begged. "At least do me the courtesy of considering my offer."

AGAIN IT SEEMED he followed in Sommersby's wake.

Thornton fought back a sudden swell of jealousy as the man's carriage departed from her front door. He suppressed the tiny, niggling fear that Amanda had changed her mind.

Still, he could not leave; he had an audience with the duke.

His cane tapping on the stone floor of the hallway, he followed the odd—and old—steam butler into the duke's lair where a massive carved desk dominated one end of the room. Two plain, un-upholstered chairs stood before the desk. The duke's company was not expected to linger. He knew the trick well.

"Lord Thornton," the duke intoned. He was seated behind that desk and made no effort to rise. "*Several* nights have passed in which you've spent *several* hours in my daughter's company. Unchaperoned. I presume you're here to make an offer?"

Dread washed over him. If the Duke of Avesbury saw fit, he could trigger the parson's mousetrap with a single word. He could be a married man on the morrow. There was nothing to do but bluff his way through. "I think such an offer would take Lady Amanda by surprise."

"You do?"

"I do. Such long and uncommon hours were to be expected when you allowed her to work in my laboratory and with the Queen's agents. Murderers do not keep regular hours. Leads must be pursued as they arise."

The duke narrowed his eyes. "Make your report then. What is this I hear about flowers?"

Thornton explained the reason for the unexpected journey to Airship Sails, relating the events that had occurred that evening. Everything, that is, that wouldn't create an instant countess.

"Very good," the duke answered. "If that is all, you may go."

"There is one more thing," Thornton said. "I've a request to make."

The duke raised his eyebrows and waited.

"It has come to my attention that Lady Amanda has inescapable social obligations."

"Mmm." The duke crossed his arms.

"She is incredibly bright. Perhaps the most intelligent woman I have had the opportunity to work with. Lady Amanda could have a bright future in the medical sciences. When she is able to focus upon her studies, her grades exceed those of all others. Her laboratory work is stellar. Her insight into the eye doctor's progress essential." Thornton swallowed and brazened forward. "The requirement that she pursue marriage is negatively affecting both her studies and her work."

"Then end her social responsibilities. Make an offer. Marry her yourself. Problem solved."

Thornton's jaw slackened. Seconds passed before he was able to respond. "Your daughter should not be tossed to the first man to offer for her."

"Ha!" The duke looked genuinely amused. "You think you'd be the first? She's been turning gentlemen down for years. Fewer, recently, but still."

Thornton was too stunned to reply. She'd turned down Sommersby? The duke would consider him an acceptable son-in-law?

The duke cocked his head. "Ah, perhaps you think the board of directors would object? That rule was put in place to prevent instructors from taking undue advantage of unmarried females. However, should you marry..." When Thornton still did not speak, the duke went on, "Or perhaps you wish me to deny you?" He lowered his voice. "Perhaps it is my daughter who is making undesired advances?"

"No! Not at all, Your Grace." He wanted to run his hands through his hair, rip clumps out by their roots. "I want..." Thornton wanted Amanda by his side. At every possible opportunity. As a colleague. As a lover. But as a wife?

Did he dare?

No. It was too drastic a step. Marriage was not something to be rushed into without first contemplating all angles.

The duke began tapping the table with an index finger, a frown carving deep lines into his face. "You want?"

"I want you to grant her more time to choose a husband. Or, better, do not require her to marry at all."

The finger stopped. "No."

Irritation rose. "No? Will you not even consider my request?"

"Consider? You would do well to *consider* what will happen to Amanda if she does not marry and soon." The duke paused. "I've already delayed finding her a husband for several years, but now she has a limited amount of time before Emily's true whereabouts can no longer be concealed. After which, by association, Amanda will become tainted, disgraced in the eyes of the *ton*. All chances for a decent husband, a happy family gone." His eyes bored into Thornton's now. "Passion burns in Amanda. But when the *ton* cuts her, when they begin to actively shun her, and she finds her options severely limited, that flame will flicker and dim. She will become a bitter recluse, a slave to her work. And that, Lord Thornton, is no way for a woman—or a man—to live their lives. I have worked far too hard providing for my family, my children. I will not stand by and idly watch while another daughter ruins her life. My answer remains: no."

Thornton's fingers curled into fists. "If she goes against your wishes?"

"I will not force her to marry. Neither, however, will I allow her to continue at Lister University. She agreed to the terms of her enrollment."

"You left her no choice!"

"She tried to blackmail me. I returned the favor." The duke rose from his seat, leaning on fingertips over the great carved desk. "Mr. Sommersby has offered for her hand. I see him as the perfect solution. A good family, a good income, but not so good that his social status or finances will forbid her from following her chosen path. As to children," the duke shrugged, "I leave that to them."

Thornton was stiff with anger. Anger at the duke for tossing away someone as unique and special as his eldest daughter on someone like Sommersby. Anger at himself. For although every nerve in him screamed, "Mine!" Although he could give her everything that Sommersby offered—and more—he did not wish to be pressured into a hasty marriage.

He had known Amanda but two weeks, two weeks under strange and unusual circumstances. What would happen when normal, everyday life resumed? When they both returned to their separate pursuits involving long hours of work? When his leg failed?

"Then I will miss her." In his laboratory and in his arms. Gripping the head of his cane tightly, Thornton nodded and took his departure.

CHAPTER TWENTY-NINE

H E FOUND HIS AGENT standing guard in the chicken coop. Thornton had thought the man exaggerated when he'd described Amanda's laboratory, but beady-eyed hens did indeed scratch and peck about his agent's feet.

The man cast him a pained look.

Any other time on any other case, Thornton might have teased the man, mocked him for the fine coating of down and sawdust that covered his shoes, but learning of Amanda's impending engagement seemed to have paralyzed his every facial muscle. He neither smiled nor frowned. "Dismissed," he said.

"Sir?"

"I will take it from here." He and Lady Amanda required a private word.

"Yes, sir."

He knocked. A moment later, the door cracked open,

and her bright blue eyes appeared in the opening. "May I come in?" he asked, his voice carefully neutral.

"Yes, of course." A flush crept up from beneath her high-necked collar, and, as the door swung wide, her eyes flickered to a small, but neatly made up cot stuffed into the corner of her makeshift laboratory.

Before he could take a step, an orange cat slipped past his ankles, dropping a limp mouse at her feet, and yowled for her attention.

Thornton followed, stepping into the small, cramped space. He propped his cane against the wall and waited.

A large portion of her work surface was currently given over to chemistry equipment and a distiller. He recognized the *amatiflora* blooms that were submerged in water and boiling over an alcohol flame. Steam rose, then cooled, spiraling down glass coils before dripping into an amber collecting flask.

"Good work, Rufus," she praised, reaching down to scoop up the injured mouse and deposit him on a cotton pad. She twisted open a can of sardines for the monocled cat, who purred loudly in anticipation.

Did he imagine it, or was she avoiding his gaze? She wouldn't promise herself to another, to Sommersby, and still invite him to her... cot, would she?

Knowing it might be so, could he still accept?

It distressed him to realize the answer was, no, he could not. He would not take what had been promised to another. Disappointment settled over him like a low-hanging, sulfurous fog. "Amanda, is there something you'd like to tell me?"

"About the formula?" she asked, her voice pitched a touch too high. "You're early, but I expect to be done with the distillation soon. If you'd like to stay—"

"About Mr. Sommersby. Have you accepted his proposal?"

"How did you—?"

"I saw his carriage. Answer the question, Amanda. Should I leave?"

Her face burst into flame as she took his meaning. "I... no... I mean." She dragged in a deep breath. "Yes, Mr. Sommersby proposed. I declined." Amanda placed a hand on his arm. "Please don't leave."

He hadn't realized he'd been holding his breath, and the sudden rush of air into his lungs, the rush of oxygen to his brain provided stunning clarity. He wouldn't be her last lover, but he would be her first. He would do his damned best to make certain she would never forget him by staking his claim in the primitive manner mankind had done for thousands of years.

For tonight, at the very least, she was his.

He reached out with one hand and set loose the first tiny button beneath her chin. "The cot seems convenient," he teased. Another button fell free. And another.

She stepped forward, closing the space between them. Her hips bumped his as her fingers found his coat buttons. "Overnight distillation was my only option," she murmured. "I sometimes sleep here."

He unfastened the last button that peeked above her leather corset. "Sleeping wasn't what I had in mind." Hooking a finger over its edge, he tugged her forward. He was hot and hard and wanted her to know how badly he wanted her. "You're certain you want this?"

She nodded.

He ran his finger under the edge of her corset, brushing over the hardened peak of her nipple. She gasped, and he saw her pulse begin to race. He wanted more. "Say it," he demanded, deliberately holding his hand still.

"I want this," she whispered. Her arms wrapped around his waist, pulling him to her, pressing her stomach against the hard length of his straining erection. "I want you."

Satisfaction raced through him as he bent his head and claimed her lips with his own. They had all night and he meant to savor every minute.

A loud knock sounded at the door behind him. "Amanda? It's me, Ned."

With great effort—and soft swears—he pulled away.

Amanda reached up and threaded her fingers through his hair, tugging him back. "Ignore him. He'll go away." Her lips pressed to his throat.

Thornton growled his approval. His palms caressed the smooth leather of her corset, shaping the curves of her hips before dropping lower to cup the swell of her bottom.

The knocking grew louder and more insistent. "I know you're in there, Amanda. Open up. Father sent me."

It seemed the traitorous, over-privileged heir wasn't going away. Not without some forceful encouragement.

With a groan, Thornton pushed her away. He turned and, flicking the locks, yanked the door open. A young man wearing an ambulator cage that stretched from hips to toes stared back. "Lord Edward." Thornton addressed Amanda's brother, his tone anything but polite. "I'm afraid we are very busy. Busy solving *your* problem. Tomorrow would be a better time to visit your sister's laboratory."

"I'm certain you'd like that, Lord Thornton." Ned snorted. "Father indicated my sister might be up to something of interest. I never guessed—"

She cast her brother a dark look over her shoulder, cutting off his words. "Come in, Ned." Amanda stood before her workbench, making adjustments to the equipment. Aside from the stain in her cheeks, she was the picture of innocence. "Lord Thornton and I are working on reproducing Emily's original formula. Nadya pointed us in a new direction last night."

"Nadya? That old gypsy woman Emily was always hanging about? Wasn't she some relative of Luca's?" Ned asked, shouldering past Thornton, his mechanical steps heavy but sure.

It took every ounce of willpower not to shove Amanda's brother back out into the chicken coop. Though perhaps her tactic was sound. The sooner they answered Ned's questions, the sooner they could be rid of him. He focused on breathing deeply, on studying the sibling for whom Amanda went to such great lengths.

"Yes." Amanda kept her eyes on the equipment before

her. "She recalled a location where late-blooming *amati-flora* might be found. She was correct."

Her brother immediately brightened. "Any luck?"

Thornton eyed the steam-powered, exoskeletal device Ned wore with interest. The dials were within easy reach of the hands, the power packs small and compact, and the smoke it emitted minimal. The hinges and joints moved with only the slightest hiss of steam. Before long, he himself might require something similar. This morning, his ankle had begun to fail, twisting oddly beneath him.

"We'll know momentarily. I've enough distilled to run the test on one small subject." She waved a hand in the direction of the caged mouse. "Though if it works, there are only sufficient flowers to make enough for one vial of the nerve toxin."

Amanda pulled on protective goggles. Turning the stopcock, she shut off the steady drip of fluid. She pulled the amber collecting flask and, using a bulbed pipette, withdrew a measured amount of the distilled essence. Squeezing the bulb, she squirted the liquid into a waiting beaker, one that already contained an orange-red liquid. The solution shifted color as she swirled the glass, stabilizing at an odd yellowish-green color.

"Excellent," she said. "Exactly as Emily predicted." She glanced at him. "It's ready." She positioned the limp mouse on a steel tray before filling a glass syringe with a fraction of the fluid. With deft hands, she targeted the mouse's injury.

Several minutes passed during which no one spoke.

She slid her patient into the observation chamber of an

aetheroscope and manually activated the vacuum. With a quick adjustment to the magnification, the feline-induced wound to the rodent's legs came into sharp focus. Amanda inhaled deeply and held her breath. With a tungsten probe, she contacted the nerve and delivered a pulse of electricity.

His eyes were glued to the needle of the readout dial. It twitched, sweeping into the green zone before returning quickly to rest position. The barest of nerve response. Perfect for the neurachnid's probe.

"You've done it," he whispered, his lips pulling into an amazed smile.

"Done what?" Ned asked. "Did it work?"

Amanda turned around. Pulling off her goggles she gave them both a wide grin. "It did!"

Ned grabbed her in tight embrace, while Thornton fought the impulse to do the same. "My brilliant sister. Sisters!" He released Amanda. "Is the spider ready? Shall I cancel my appointment?"

Her face fell.

"Appointment?" Thornton asked.

Ned turned to him. "Ferrous replacements. Next week."

Ferrous replacements. A brutal, horrible surgery members of the *ton* turned to. Such a procedure worked. Barely. But it did allow gentlemen the appearance—if not the actuality—of normalcy.

"You can't manage a few more weeks?" Irritation laced Thornton's voice. Behind her brother, Amanda shook her head. He ignored her. "Have you any idea of the trouble you've caused?"

Ned had the sense to look ashamed. "I regret the trouble my decisions have caused."

"Regret." He barely managed to pry the word from between his clenched teeth.

Amanda stepped forward, laying a hand on his arm. Her eyes pleaded. "There are extenuating circumstances."

Ned nodded. "Georgina, the woman I would have as my wife, will be engaged to another man in a fortnight. Her father will accept my suit only if I am whole."

Thornton wanted to thunder that there were plenty of women who would have a future duke, broken or whole, but a glance at Amanda had him biting his tongue. He had an idea now what a man might sacrifice in order to possess the woman of his dreams. "There is protocol to follow," he said. "Rat studies will take, optimistically, a solid month. Long term outcomes," he waved a hand, "upwards of a year."

"A year!" Ned yelled. "No. Absolutely not." His eyes narrowed. "Ferrous replacements it will be." He stalked to the door, steam rising about him.

"Wait," Amanda pleaded. "Thornton, please." Her eyes brimmed with unshed tears. "Can an exception be made?"

Such an exception could cost him his career. A risk he found he was willing to take. For her and her alone. "Very well. The new neurachnid is complete. Can you wait three more days for us to make arrangements?"

"Yes." Ned nodded. "Thank you."

Thornton held up a hand. "You realize that the surgery may very well fail?"

"Of course."

"I have one condition." One look at Ned's face and Thornton knew the lordling would agree to anything. "You must have your father's permission. Know I will speak with him myself concerning the risks." Only then would he proceed, risking his career... All for one woman's happiness.

"Agreed." Ned turned to Amanda with pure glee in his face, seemingly convinced his sister's contraption was incapable of failure.

Thornton would speak with the Duke of Avesbury again and outline the terms of his son's surgery. If—when—the procedure worked, when the duke's heir walked again using his own nerves, his own muscles, Amanda would be free to marry on her own terms and on her own schedule.

CHAPTER THIRTY

WITH THORNTON'S PROMISE, Amanda didn't
have much trouble ridding herself of her trou-
blesome brother. He'd broken the mood by
barging in and then pushing Thornton to proceed with an
unapproved surgery.

She turned back to her workbench, arranging the various
bottles of solutions on the shelf, not quite daring to meet
Thornton's eyes. She felt guilty. Extremely so. It was wrong
of her to press him to break protocol in order to cosset the son
of a duke.

Ned's injury—if not his intended—could wait. He had
waited five years; he could wait another year if necessary.
But Thornton's injury could not. By her calculations, his
peroneal nerve was in danger of imminent failure. The *amatiflora* might not bloom in time to distill more essence for a
second procedure. If they were to break protocol to perform

experimental surgery on a human, it should be *his* injury they should attempt to repair.

"I'm sorry." Amanda kept her back to him, as she fought a growing tightness in her throat. "Perhaps another night." He'd looked so very angry, he couldn't possibly be interested in continuing what they'd begun earlier. After what she'd pressed him to do, he might never be interested.

He didn't answer.

She felt, rather than heard his approach, for he crossed the room without making a sound to stand behind her. She finished tidying the workbench and was about to turn around when his heavy hands fell on her waist.

"You have no idea what it does to me," his breath fell warm on the nape of her neck, "to watch you work. It's been such agony. To not be able to touch." His hands tugged at the laces of her corset, loosening them, pulling them free. "No. Another night won't do at all. Unless you tell me to stop, to leave, I've every intention of finishing what we started." His hands stilled, waiting.

He still wanted her? Even though Ned's surgery would mean his own leg would fail? She didn't want him to go. Ever.

"Stay," she whispered, setting his hands in motion once more.

Heat rushed over her. Her skin was on fire. Her nipples tightened, aching for his touch, straining against the thin shifting fabric of her shirtwaist as he yanked her corset free and tossed it to the ground. Her knees weakened and her world tipped off center.

Then his hands were exactly where she wanted them, cupping her breasts, squeezing them, plying her nipples with his fingers as she arched back against him.

"You like that?" He all but purred.

"God, yes." She wanted the fabric barrier between them gone. Wanted his hands directly on her skin.

His hands fell away, and her lips parted to object, but then those hands were on her hips, turning her to face him. One lifted, and the pad of his thumb touched the fragile skin beneath her eye. Her breath caught, and her heart stuttered at the tender gesture. "You need sleep. But," his lips pulled into a smile that promised all manner of delicious naughtiness, "not just yet."

She tipped her face into the warmth of his palm, felt its roughness against her smooth cheek. A warm, humming thrill rushed across her skin. "What I need is you." She let her gaze fall on those wide, oh-so-expressive lips.

He laughed, a low soft rumble. "Such directness. Such honesty." His hand wrapped around behind her skull, pulling her face toward him as his head dipped, catching her lips with his own. Warm and soft and gentle.

Emotions too complicated and unfamiliar to analyze surged through her. He felt so right. She lifted her arms, sliding her hands up his chest to his shoulders, exploring the hard muscles that lay beneath his waistcoat, beneath his shirt. Skin. She wanted to touch his skin. She pushed his coat from his shoulders.

He released her long enough to shrug the annoying garment to the ground, then stepped forward, pinning her against the workbench so she could feel the hard column of his arousal. He caught her mouth again, his tongue sweeping inward, stroking hers with suggestive thrusts. A mere taste, a mere promise of the carnal pleasures that would soon be theirs.

Heat pooled at the juncture of her thighs. She wanted more than mere kisses and promises. Her palms began a determined exploration of his muscled back, moving over the linen of his shirt, tapering downward to his hips and growing increasingly dissatisfied with the cotton and linen barriers that separated them. When her fingers met the waistband of his trousers, she growled her frustration and pushed hard against his chest.

Thornton stepped back, his breath ragged, his eyes questioning.

"Skin," she panted, reaching for the buttons of his waistcoat. She wanted to feel his warm skin brush hers as his body tensed and flexed. He assisted, making short work of his cravat, then the buttons that held his shirt in place. Moments later all his upper garments joined her corset and his coat on the floor.

For several long seconds, Amanda allowed herself to stare at the glorious, muscled torso that stood before her. She reached out and ran her palm over the crisp hairs that covered his chest.

"That's long enough," he growled and gripped her waist, lifting her, depositing her on the workbench. "Your turn. Finish what I started earlier." His voice, low and commanding, sent a ripple of electricity across her skin. He stepped back, ever so slightly, and crossed his arms.

He'd managed to make significant progress with the buttons at her neck before they were interrupted, but she'd had to undo some of that progress in deference to their guest. But this time he wanted to watch?

She smiled, softly and coyly, reveling under his intense focus as her fingers worked—slowly—to regain lost ground. Her nipples strained beneath the fine cotton, drawing his gaze to their hard peaks. But he did not touch. He waited as the cotton of her shirt parted, exposing a long, thin strip of bare skin. A few tangled strands of hair fell forward across her face.

Finally, he reached out, but not to touch her shirtwaist. Instead his fingers pulled first one hair pin free. Then another, and another. Lock after lock tumbled free over her shoulders, falling on the cotton that still covered the tops of her breasts.

It was torture, the waiting.

She drew in fast, shallow breaths as one long finger began to twist a lock of hair, the increasing tension tugging at her scalp, tipping her head backward, exposing her throat.

Enough.

She threaded her fingers through his own tousled curls and pulled his head to her throat.

He let out a low, satisfied laugh at her impatience.

At last he was touching her. His teeth scraped her neck, his mouth explored the column of her throat, his rough beard grazed her smooth skin which screamed in pleasure. A moan escaped her lips.

God, he was taking too long.

She tugged on his waistband, pulling him between her knees. Thornton stepped forward into the folds of her skirts. So many petticoats, all of them working against her. Desperate and bold, she caressed the hard column beneath his trousers.

Long and thick. There was so much of him, but all she wanted was him inside her.

He hissed out a wild sound, his hips flexing under her palm. He yanked open her shirtwaist and cupped both breasts, lifting them. He bent, sucking a taut nipple into his mouth, circling it with his tongue, pulling it gently between his teeth, all while his fingers toyed with the other tip.

Amanda arched her chest with a cry of pleasure, catching herself on her hands. This was what she wanted. Needed. She slid her hips forward on the workbench, wanting to feel the press of his arousal as his lips drove her into a frenzy, but the ridiculous volume of her skirts dulled all sensation.

Finally, she could stand it no longer. She needed more. Dragging his face to hers, she kissed him long and deep, pouring forth all the need she felt. Then, with her hands about his neck, she flexed her hips and slid from the work-bench, slid along his long, hard length until her toes reached the floor. She tugged at his waistband, her fingers searching for the catch. "More."

He laughed and tugged her toward the cot, with only a

slight hitch in his step. Then he turned, gathering her into his arms, kissing her forehead and murmuring into her hair, "I've wanted this from the moment you first spoke in lecture."

"You called me a fool."

"Secrets had to be kept."

"No more now."

"No more." He caught her lips again in a deep, soul-baring kiss. Then released her as his hands moved to his waistband.

His fingers moved quickly now, flying down his own buttons, tugging off his shoes. Amanda turned her attention to discarding her many skirts. Her drawers. But when she reached for her garters, he stopped her.

"Leave them."

Her heart stopped as she looked up. Thornton in all his glory.

In one hand he held a piece of brown paper. Inside it she knew she'd find a sheath. He'd come prepared. Strong, wide shoulders flexed as a muscled arm reached out for her, but her eyes were drawn to the crisp hairs that covered his chest, his abdomen, merging at the vee of a narrow waist and drawing attention to his large, rampant need.

All man.

An echoing need pulsed between her thighs, demanding fulfillment. She stepped forward, her hand brushing over his chest, her palm caressing its surface. She recalled his leg and glanced downward. Thin straps of jointed metal provided support. Beneath the brace, a jagged scar curved. "Sit," she said, pushing against his chest.

He frowned. "There's no pain. Not now."

"Please." She pressed again.

He sat, then fell backward onto the cot, dragging her with him. His erection pressed into her stomach. She slid herself over him, kissing him as she moved to straddle him, pressing her wetness against his need.

His hips bucked.

She bent forward, her hair falling in a curtain about their faces while she kissed him deeply, as the tips of her breasts brushed against his chest. Tongues tangled. Hips rocked.

At last the pressure building inside of her was so intense she could think only of release. She wanted him inside her, wanted him to fall apart beneath her as they both found their pleasure. She pulled back, sliding away, reaching for the brown paper packet, sliding the sheath she found inside over his thick member. Nerves flared and her hands shook.

"You're certain?" he whispered.

"More than anything."

His hands guided her hips back over him, over his thick column and onto its tip, nudging at her opening. It would hurt, she knew, but only for a moment. She hoped. Spreading her legs wider, she sank onto him, slowly, as he stretched her wide, and she had yet to take him entirely within.

"Fast? Or slow?" he hissed. His every muscle clenched with the effort to not move.

"Fast."

"Thank God." His fingers gripped her hips, and he thrust upward with a sudden surge, deep within her core, groaning in pleasure as he filled her tightly and completely.

She cried out at the sharp pinch, twisting at the burning sensation of being stretched so suddenly. Desire was ebbing away.

"Wait," he bit out through gritted teeth. "Stay. Give it a moment." He stroked the juncture of her thighs with the pad of his thumb.

Pain faded as pleasure returned and her body began to relax. He pulled her forward, sucking a nipple into his mouth and a bolt of desire shot through her to her center. Her hips bucked against him as she cried out. A sensation like she'd never experienced before took hold, a driving need to move against him.

She rocked her hips again.

"That's it," he moaned. His hands helped her hips find their rhythm, lifting her up, pulling her back down tightly against him. Each retreat left her empty, each plunge seated him deeply within her.

Her pulse raced, and her breath came in pants. He gripped her hips tighter now, his thrusts coming faster and harder as the primal need for release built. She rose. He plunged. Again and again and again. Tension coiled within her, all focusing tighter and tighter where they joined.

A low keen escaped her lips as her body seemed to pulse. He growled and drove into her, yanking her against him. Amanda threw her head back and let the spasm of pleasure wash over her. Thornton's fingers dug into her flesh, grinding his hips upward as he cried out his own release. She collapsed forward onto his chest, heart pounding, lungs heaving. What they'd found together—this sliver of paradise —was beyond anything she could have hoped.

At long last, she pushed herself upward and looked into his eyes. For a moment, she imagined she could see his soul. He held nothing back now, nothing was hidden. She felt a closeness, a completeness unlike any she could ever have imagined.

His hands caressed her back, smoothed her hair away, then pressed a kiss to her lips so tender her heart squeezed.

Amanda shifted to move beside him. Thornton's arm flexed, holding her tight against his side on the narrow cot. His eyes were closed, his face more relaxed than she'd ever seen before. She rested her head on his shoulder, and for a long moment, she lay still, content to do nothing but inhale his scent. She trailed her fingers along his jaw across the rough shadow of beard that darkened his face, feeling its stubble catch and release against the whorls of her fingertips.

If only she could stay like this forever, curled against his strength. Wrapped in his arms, the rest of the world faded. But she lifted her head, glancing over at her workbench. Duty beckoned.

"The drug can wait an hour. Rest now." His hand reached up, pulling her head down once more against his chest. How well he knew her. She smiled against his skin.

"An hour," she agreed, then, for the first time in weeks, drifted into blissful slumber.

She slept for nearly two.

Thornton was watching when Amanda's eyes fluttered open. He'd not slept a wink. Not with so many thoughts invading his mind.

The deep attraction he felt for this woman in his arms was more than lust. He'd thought their joining would satisfy him, but now he wanted more. She'd given him her trust, her virginity, her passion. She was his. He felt a driving, primitive need to let the world know exactly that. That she was off limits to all other men.

When she next arrived in the lecture theater, it would take all his self-control not to punch the first student whose eyes dropped to appreciate her feminine assets.

Mine! He wanted to cry the word aloud.

But would this last? Would she tire of a man who avoided society? Spent long hours holed up in a laboratory? Often disappeared for weeks? No. He wouldn't disappear. Not anymore. Not once his leg failed. That too presented a problem. He was soon to be a broken man.

Reluctantly, he moved away. He shifted to sit at the end of the cot and began to dress, pulling his trousers over the metal cage that guarded his lower leg.

"The pressure points worked well," she said, moving to sit beside him. "I can—"

"No. Thank you. It's fine." His words were polite, but his tone closed the topic.

She sighed, but tugged on her shirtwaist and began

ANNE RENWICK

pushing the tiny pearl buttons back into place. "Will you stay?" A slow blush that crept over her cheeks suggested she hoped for a repeat encounter.

He stroked her full lower lip with his thumb. "I think it's best if I don't, Amanda. Not tonight." They'd risked enough already, lying about in such a disheveled state. Questions might be asked, ones that would damage her reputation, perhaps even her career. "If you give me the vial of distilled essence, I can have it in the hands of the Lister chemists tonight. You've done amazing work here," he indicated her laboratory, "but with their equipment and knowledge, the drug will be—"

"Of higher quality," she nodded. "I know I'm not a chemist. No need to soothe my wounded, scientific soul."

"It will be better protected," he said. "And you will be safer with it removed from your keeping. If I work quickly tonight, there will be time to run the procedure tomorrow on a rat—at least once—in the laboratory, before we try it on your brother."

She nodded, her eyes not meeting his.

He tipped her chin upward. "Know that I already want you again, Amanda."

Now she looked deep into his eyes. "Then stay."

"If only I could," he said, then pressed his lips against hers, pouring his heart into the kiss, showing her what he could not say.

CHAPTER THIRTY-ONE

A MANDA WAS ON HER way to breakfast when her sister screamed.

A cacophony of blinking and hissing and whirring emerged from the breakfast room. She arrived at the door to find Steam Mary spinning in distressed circles and RT rolling back and forth across the floor, the teacups on his surface rattling and splashing. Burton stood, his jaw opening and closing without emitting any sound.

Mother had collapsed forward onto the dining table, her face buried in her arms. Before the table Olivia stood, or rather, swayed as she flapped a feathered fan at her face, her lungs struggling to cope beneath her too-tight corset; she wasn't far behind Mother.

"Sit, Olivia. Before you fall," she commanded.

Olivia's knees buckled, and she collapsed into her chair.

"Whatever is the matter?"

"It's over... everything's ruined..." The fan flapped faster.

"What?" she demanded.

"Emily." A trembling finger pointed at a gossip rag that had fallen to the floor.

Burton lifted it and handed it to Amanda.

She read.

'Lady E—, daughter of the great and powerful Duke of A—, was sighted last night in the company of those gypsies currently camping in Kensington Gardens. The colorful garb she wore, and her suspiciously rounded form, suggests she now lives among them as one of their own.'

The rag still in hand, Amanda sank into a chair beside her sister, wondering what—if anything—she ought do. The damage was done. Amanda lifted a half-empty teacup from RT's surface. She pressed the porcelain cup into her sister's trembling hand. "Drink some tea," she said, hoping the motion would slow Olivia's breaths.

A knock at the front door had Burton hurrying from the room. A caller at this hour could mean only one thing. Olivia turned toward Amanda, eyes wide with fear and apprehension.

"I will see the duke," a voice boomed. "Now."

Carlton.

Olivia dropped her teacup in her lap. Angry footsteps moved down the hall. Tears began to stream down Olivia's face.

As Steam Mary rushed to blot Olivia's skirts, Amanda took her sister's hand and squeezed. There were no words of comfort to offer her sister. She might not be sorry to see the last of Carlton, but all of Olivia's hopes and dreams, her efforts at securing a titled husband and her own household, had shattered.

Damp lashes and watery eyes looked back at Amanda. "It's over. No one will have me now. We're to end our lives in this house as two dried out old spinsters. Together."

A decided possibility. Though she didn't give it voice. She turned to the collection of steambots that had gathered in the doorway. Somehow their copper and bronze faces managed to convey worry. "Both women have had a shock and will be happier resting in their chambers." Metal necks creaked as heads nodded. "Steam Susan, please bring the bath chair for the duchess. Steam Joseph, if you would escort Lady Olivia to her room. Please see that their personal lady's maids are summoned."

Once her mother and her sister were taken care of, Amanda penned a quick note to Ned, who, she was informed, had left earlier for the Symphony House. She informed him the family was in crisis and suggested he return home at once. He could shoulder some of the burden while she labored in the laboratory on his behalf.

A KNOCK SOUNDED on Thornton's office door. "Enter!" he called, relieved that someone had arrived to rescue him from the tedium of neglected paperwork.

The necessary task was taking longer than normal as his mental efforts were hindered by the constant intrusion of thoughts of Amanda. Thoughts of her soft curves, of driving into her wet heat, of the look on her face as she shattered above him. Nothing had ever felt so good, so right. Last night, something inside him had broken free. A taste of her passion was no longer enough. He wanted more. Concentration was next to impossible.

The white-bearded face of Lord Thistleton appeared. "Good news, Thornton."

"That will make for a nice change. Come in."

The man laughed. "I sent a man to the powerhouse to collect the plant, roots and all. *Amatiflora* now grows in my greenhouse under lock and key. I've never seen its like, though I believe it a close relative of —" he waved a hand, "never mind. In a few weeks, I should be able to force a bloom."

"Excellent," Thornton said, trying to muster some enthusiasm. By then it would be too late for him. "And its essence?"

Lord Thistleton grinned. "More good news. The nerve agent was easily concocted in our laboratories. Your assistant, Lady Huntley was so kind as to assist. She brought us a rat." Lord Thistleton laughed. "The looks on the faces of my assistants. None of them are used to test subjects with faces and tails. In any case, she helped us with a trial run of your drug. The formula is impressive, quite effective. It does not suppress nerve transmission completely. It only calms the nerve. Lady Huntley assures me that this is exactly the outcome you hoped for?"

"It is." The neurachnid needed to test its connections as it wove its golden strands.

"Well, then, I'll be going. I'll send updates on the plant's status."

"Wait," Thornton said. "The drug?"

"I left the entire vial," Lord Thistleton grinned widely, "safe in your assistant's hands." The man nodded and left.

Good. Finally they made progress.

Black appeared in the doorway. "We have a problem."

A problem. He supposed good news was too much to hope for with a murderous spy on the loose. "What now?" he asked.

"Nasty rumors about Amanda's sister have begun to circulate."

Thornton swore.

"Exactly. It seems a party of gentlewomen, seeking to have their fortunes read, invaded the gypsy campsite in Kensington Gardens. One of the women recognized Lady Emily. Additional precautions are being taken." Black glanced over his shoulder. "Her sister, Lady Amanda, is, at this very moment, striding down the hallway with a decidedly fierce look upon her face."

Thornton stood. "If you'll wait for us in the laboratory?"

Black nodded, then ducked out.

Moments later, Amanda stepped into his office, her eyes dark with concern. She closed the door behind her with a shaking hand. "You've heard about my sister?"

"Black knows. He'll keep her safe."

"Nothing can undo the damage to my family's reputation. My mother and Olivia are beside themselves."

"Perhaps I should care more what society thinks." He moved to stand before her, raising a hand to stroke a finger alongside her jaw. "Yet I find I only care what *you* think."

"Think?" She stepped closer, and slid her arms about his waist. "Must we?" Her face lifted upward, her lips parting in invitation, offering sweet oblivion.

Attraction sparked to life, and he lowered his head, giving her what she asked for—an all-consuming kiss. Their tongues tangled in a maddening dance as he dragged her against him. Her hands ran up his back, holding him tight, crushing her soft breasts against his chest. Desire flared. He groaned into her mouth. Now. Here. No need to wait until the evening. The chair would do.

"Echem."

A loud noise intruded. Thornton pulled away, fighting the urge to growl his irritation like a feral beast. Amanda backed away from him quickly, her face aflame.

Black stood in the doorway, his head tipped backward as he stared discreetly at the ceiling. "Next time, lock the door. Please."

"What?"

"We may have a problem in the laboratory. Two of them."

"Stop being coy and spit it out," Thornton growled.

"You indicated both Lady Huntley and Henri were here?"

"Yes." He glanced at the clock. "They should both be at work."

Black shook his head. "They're not. Your technician, Samuel, indicated that they'd left in some haste. Together." He held out a slip of paper. "Henri left you this note."

Thornton snatched it from his hand, reading quickly. "It seems Henri's mother has taken a decided turn for the worse. This is notification that he is taking an indefinite leave of absence." He looked up. "A note. Why would he leave a note?" He shook his head. "Something is not right. Henri would speak to me first."

"Lady Huntley?" Amanda asked. "Why would she go with him?"

"No idea." He grabbed his cane and moved with as much speed as he could manage. Something nagged at the back of his mind as if he was missing some key piece of information. "I need to see the laboratory."

They arrived en masse and stood, turning slowly. Nothing seemed amiss. In the corner, the latest acoustico patient recovered. By his side was Samuel, the day technician who had reported the odd behaviors of his fellow technicians.

Amanda moved to the laboratory safe where her neurachnid was stored. Her fingers deftly spun the combination. The door swung open. "It's still here." Relief colored her voice. She lifted it from the safe and wrapped the neurachnid in a clean linen cloth before pushing it inside her reticule. He couldn't blame her for wanting to keep it close. The laboratory no longer seemed a secure location.

A frisson of unease ran down his spine. "Lady Huntley assisted Lord Thistleton this morning. They trialed the nerve agent. He left the drug in her care. Where is the vial?"

Amanda's face paled. "It would be a dark amber vial—or perhaps an opaque green—to protect the drug from light."

They turned about, searched shelves and cabinets, searched every likely storage. Nothing.

Dread balled in his stomach. "Samuel!" he bellowed. "Did either Henri or Lady Huntley take anything with them from the laboratory?" he asked when the technician stood before him, eyes wary.

Samuel shook his head. "Not that I noticed." But pockets could be deep. "Neither of them appeared pleased to be leaving," he continued, looking hurt. "I thought it odd that they left without so much as a word. Usually, I warrant at least a wave."

Black swore.

"One of them is a double agent," Thornton stated baldly.

"Henri?" Amanda asked in horror.

"Likely," Black answered. "And Lady Huntley his hostage."

"Why not take the neurachnid?" she asked. Then answered her own question. "He had my plans before him all along."

Thornton nodded. "Henri will have built his own spider, incorporating all our improvements. He had the knowledge and the tools and access to all the necessary pieces. He needed only the nerve agent."

"But... how?"

"An excellent question." He narrowed his eyes at Black. "How did Henri pass your background check? You assured me of his trustworthiness."

"Do not accuse me," Black shot back. "I stand by my work. You were the one who insisted on bringing a foreign national into this laboratory. Medicine knows no borders, you insisted. I did check. Deeply. Not one single red flag. The man was in deep." Black stomped across the room. "Let's go."

Thornton began to limp behind Black, leaning heavily on the cane. Pain shot upward through his leg with every step. Amanda followed. "No," Thornton said. "Stay here."

"Not likely," she snapped back. "You dragged me into this. I'll see it finished. Besides, with two top agents beside me, I am doubly safe."

Thornton glowered.

"Let her come," Black said. "At the moment, she's the only objective, clear mind we have." He stepped from Thornton's laboratory and began to bark orders to the agents who stood outside the building. A massive manhunt was organized within minutes. Borders. Ports. Airship stations. All were to be on high alert.

But the first order of business would be to search Henri's quarters.

Thornton watched with annoyance as Black handed Amanda into the crank hackney. It annoyed him that he too required assistance, if only a sharp tug into the vehicle. "If he was indeed as 'deep' as you say, what will be left to find?" he grumbled, the moment the crank hackney began to move.

"All spies make mistakes," Black threw back. "Many have personal weaknesses. Some even let their saviors work in their high security laboratories."

"Gentlemen!" Amanda yelled. "Focus."

They rode in silence the rest of the way.

The landlord made a fuss about the invasion, but all objections vanished when Thornton produced several pound notes, and they were allowed to climb the dark stairs to the second floor to Henri's room. Black bounded upward with Lady Amanda behind him. He followed, struggling to hide the effort each six-inch rise cost him.

All for nothing. Henri's apartments were stripped bare and completely unremarkable. One large simple room. A mattress on an iron frame. A table and chairs. A wardrobe. A small coal grate.

Disheartened, they began their descent.

"Wait," Amanda said, pausing at the landlord's door. She dug into her reticule, producing her own pound note and knocked. The landlord's eyes grew large at the sight of yet more money. "Did Henri ever have visitors? Or unusual correspondence?"

The man thought hard. "Yes." He frowned. "One visitor. Once. I didn't like it. They spoke German. A horrible, guttural language."

WASP HAD what was necessary now. One final experiment to confirm expectations, a quick detour to do a little gardening, and the return home would be triumphant.

Despite its perception, the last procedure had not been, in fact, a failure. It had served many purposes. It proved that milligears were necessary to space the multiple insertions of gold wire correctly through the superior orbital fissure. It eliminated Tony and, when the improvements to the spider were viewed in the morgue, it provided Lady Amanda with sufficient inspiration to complete both her work and her sister's.

Wasp surveyed this newest facility. Barely adequate, but given a rapidly approaching departure, it would suffice.

A quick check of a pocket watch indicated that the last patient would arrive at any moment. Time for final preparations. Wasp reached for the clockwork spider, opening the glass abdominal cavity and carefully filling it with the necessary nerve agent.

Wasp heard rapping at the door.

"Good evening," Wasp said, swinging the door wide.

"This is the one you wanted?" the man asked, pushing in a bath chair containing Wasp's newest and unconscious test subject.

"Precisely. If you will help position him on the table..."

Soon the gypsy was stretched across the makeshift operating table, wrists, ankles and waist tightly bound. Head clamped in place.

"That's it," the man said. "No more. I've done everything you asked. Lady Amanda remains untouched."

"As promised." Wasp palmed the transmitter from the tray before turning to walk the man to the door, sliding the device unseen into the man's coat pocket. "Provided you remain silent."

CHAPTER THIRTY-TWO

C LUTCHING HER RETICULE, Amanda paced the hall waiting for word from Thornton. And Ned. And Emily. All the while, men came and went from Father's study, dark looks upon their faces. None would look at her, let alone speak to her.

She knew agents combed through London, tracing Henri's every past move. It was a struggle, to wrap her mind around the idea that she'd known the eye doctor and held him in high esteem. Her stomach churned thinking of all the long hours they'd worked together building the neurachnid. All that time, she'd been assisting a spy. Now Henri possessed everything he needed to connect the artificial eye to the cranial nerves.

Amanda turned on her heel and paced away from the front door. She'd not spent the whole of the afternoon in such a useless fashion. No, she could feel matters coming to a head, and so she'd gathered what resources she could. In her reticule was the neurachnid, a selection of Babbage cards including the one most recently punched by Olivia. Even more importantly, she had a vial of the *amatiflora* nerve agent.

After Thornton had left her the night before, she'd been unable to rest, unwilling to return to her bed. She'd remained in her laboratory, putting the distillation equipment to work once more. The additional amatiflora essence she'd been able collect was minimal, but now she had a small amount of the necessary drug.

Like talismans, she held these three items tightly. Preparation was always key. If—when—the eye doctor was located, there was always the chance he would be interrupted mid-procedure. She wanted, needed to be ready to offer the victim any assistance she could.

A hue and cry broke out at the front door. Amanda heard a woman's voice objecting, then pleading with the men Father had stationed outside their town home.

"Let her through!" she yelled, recognizing Emily's voice.

"She's gypsy," one man objected and stepped in front of her to block her progress.

Amanda shoved hard at his chest. "She's my sister, you idiot, and the gypsies are the ones who've taken the brunt of the eye doctor's horrible experiments. Show some kindness."

A piercing whistle cut through the commotion. Black, dressed as a gypsy himself, stepped forward. "She's with me. We're to see the duke. Step aside."

A low murmur started through her father's men, but they parted. Black, it seemed, was well known to them.

Emily rushed forward into Amanda's arms. "He's got Luca!" she cried, then began to sob.

Dear God. She held her tight until Emily at last pulled away, tears streaming down her face. "These men won't tell me anything." She wept. "Is there any hope?"

Hope of recovering Luca unharmed? Little. "There is every hope the surgery might succeed," she whispered instead. She helped her sister into the study where Father stood at the far end of the room, surrounded by his men. He turned, and began to make his way to them.

Emily collapsed onto a chair, an arm about her stomach. "But little chance the eye doctor will let him live, even so." She dissolved once again into tears.

Ned appeared in the doorway, then crossed quickly to their side. "What in all holy hell is going on here?"

"Where have you been?" Amanda demanded. "I wrote to you *hours* ago."

He looked back with wide eyes. "It didn't sound urgent. Mother and Olivia are always in a fit about one thing or another. It's impossible to keep track as to what—"

The study doors burst open once more. "Traitors," Thornton said, "everywhere I turn." He shoved a beaten and bloody man into the room. It took her a moment to recognize him.

"Simon?" Amanda cried.

One eye was swollen shut, but the other seemed to plead with her. Multiple cuts to his lips and face oozed blood. His clothes were torn and stained. His words were garbled and it took her a moment to understand. "I did it for you," Simon was saying, over and over.

Amanda looked at him in disbelief. "Did what?"

Thornton crossed the room to her side, his gait unsteady. Without a word, he wrapped his arm about her, pulling her tight against him. His lips fell on her hair. "Thank God you're safe," he murmured.

She turned her face into his shoulder.

Father cleared his throat.

As if, remembering his location, Thornton released her and stepped several feet away. The loss of his strength and warmth was painful.

"What is the meaning of all this?" Father demanded.

"Your Grace," Thornton began. "Mr. Sommersby is involved. A transmitter from my laboratory came within range of my agents. Only two such acousticotransmitters are currently in use. They recognized the unauthorized transmission and apprehended him. This was found on Sommersby's person, in his pocket." Thornton held up the small device meant to be implanted in an agent's ear. "He has refused to speak, insisting upon first seeing Lady Amanda, to ensure her safety."

"You see her now, Sommersby," Father said. "Speak now and I might let you live."

Simon lifted his battered face toward her, his one eye full of remorse. "I was used as well, Amanda. Don't you see?" He stepped toward her.

She stepped backward, shaking her head. "Don't."

Thornton had already taken hold of Simon's shoulder, pinning him to the floor.

"It was Luca or you, Amanda," Simon whimpered. "I had to choose."

"You lured Luca to him?" Amanda gasped in sudden understanding. "You know where he is. Tell me. Tell us now!"

All along, Henri had been weaving a web of his own, and Luca was to be the final strand.

"I can't. I won't." Simon's face fell and he looked away. "At first it was only supplies. A few chemicals. Medical equipment. Then the demands grew." Mr. Sommersby fell to his knees at her feet. "I had no idea," he wailed. "None. I love you, Amanda. Please understand, I was given no choice."

"Enough!" Thornton's voice cracked through the air. "Your Grace, both my laboratory assistant and your son-in-law, Luca, are missing. With them, the eye doctor has everything he needs to conduct one final experiment. At the moment, I care not about motivation. I wish to locate Henri and stop him before Luca loses an eye. Or his life. We need answers."

Emily moaned.

"If you care at all for me," Amanda addressed Mr. Sommersby, doing her best to keep the venom of hate from her voice. They needed his cooperation. "You will tell me where to find Henri. Where to find Luca and Lady Huntley."

Simon shook his head. "I can't. I won't."

An agent strode into the room and whispered in Black's ear.

"We've found him," Black announced, yanking Simon to his feet. "A pathetic spy you'd make, Sommersby," he said. "The crank hackney you used was all too easy to find, the driver all too eager to talk. We've no further need of you." He shoved him in the direction of Father's men. "Do what you will," Black said, then turned toward Thornton. "Let's go."

Amanda started to follow them.

Her father objected. "Stay here, Amanda."

Thornton put his arm about her. "No. She comes. We might need her expertise. I might need her assistance if," he glanced in Emily's direction, "there is a medical situation."

"You would put her safety at risk?" Father asked Thornton.

"I am needed," Amanda countered. She could speak for herself. "I will follow, with or without your agreement."

Father regarded them with a long steady stare, then nodded. "Fine. Go."

They followed Black who had already exited and was barking orders to his men.

"When we arrive, Amanda, stay close," Thornton said as they followed. "East London is no place for a lady."

She glanced at his leg, worried. He was leaning heavily on his cane *and* limping. Time was running short for too many people.

CHAPTER THIRTY-THREE

THORNTON PINCHED THE bridge of his nose between his thumb and forefinger. To think he'd been so thoroughly manipulated, so many lives ruined. When had it all started? When John packed the phaoscope prototype in his trunk? When the air pirates attacked? Thornton's escape from that dirigible had been all too easy; had he been purposefully spared? Had Henri already been waiting on the ground below?

The crank hackney jerked to a halt. They'd arrived. The indicated warehouse squatted beside the Thames, it's dark windows giving it a hollow-eyed look. Wincing, he climbed down and assisted Amanda onto the cobblestone street.

Black took one look at Thornton, at his leg, and shook his head. "Stay here. You'll only be in the way." Without a backward glance, he directed their agents into the building.

"Let's go," he said to Amanda, ignoring Black's directive.

"But—"

"By the time I climb one flight of stairs, Black will have neutralized any threat. But if the victim, if Luca is still alive..." He didn't wish to explain to a pregnant woman why her child no longer had a father. "There is also Lady Huntley to consider. We've no idea what he may have done to—or with—her."

Amanda needed no further encouragement.

Together they pushed through the noisy crowds that teemed the docks even before dawn had fully broken. They dodged men rolling barrels, steam dockworkers hauling crates, and any number of odd machinery carrying loads hither and yon, and plunged into the dark warehouse and up its rickety stairs.

It took every last bit of his strength to keep up with her.

On the ride here, he'd injected his leg with a last dose of Somnic. *The* last dose. These past few days he'd far exceeded the recommended amount, injecting his leg nearly every hour just to maintain minimum function, to keep his foot— quite literally—beneath him. Failure was imminent. If not for the iron bands of his leg brace, he would even now require a crutch.

A loud commotion broke out above them.

Thornton forced himself to climb faster. They arrived on the second floor to find Black directing agents to a rear exit. Black himself was crouched on the ground, bending over a crumpled woman's form—Lady Huntley.

He quickly took in exposed bricks and beams. Dusty, clouded windows. Wide, roughly hewn floorboards. A space designed to hold cargo brought in by ships arriving at

London's docks. Lady Huntley was shackled to a support post. A man's form was strapped to an old wooden door propped on two barrels of rum.

"Is she hurt?" Thornton yelled, storming across the room.

At the same time Amanda cried out, "Luca!" She ran to the man's side.

"She's fine," Black answered. He yanked Captain Jack's Tension Torque from his pocket and reached for Lady Huntley's hands.

Angry, red welts encircled her wrists where the bizarre manacles binding her to the post had rubbed them raw. Lady Huntley looked up at him with tears in her eyes. "I'm so sorry, Thornton. I couldn't stop him. He forced me to hand over the latest phaoscope and the drug." She shuddered. "His spider is a horrible mockery of Lady Amanda's design."

Thornton glanced at the gypsy. "Did he...?"

"Only one eye. It worked, exactly as designed." She swallowed. "Henri disconnected it. Go, I'm fine. See to the poor gypsy boy, he's in so much pain."

At least Luca was alive.

Thornton turned on his rebelling limb and crossed the room to Amanda's side, taking in the horrible sight spread before him. A bioluminescent lamp hung from a rope over the makeshift operating table. A nearby barrel held a metal tray containing an array of surgical implements and a number of bloody rags.

Luca moaned, fighting against the leather strap that bound his head to the table. One eye remained. The other was gone leaving an empty socket, surprisingly devoid of blood. Fine gold threads woven in an intricate pattern extended around and behind the cauterized stub of the man's optic nerve.

The pain must be unbearable. He searched through a small collection of glass bottles, Henri's abandoned store of drugs, looking for something that would bring the man relief.

Amanda leaned in closely, her hand stroking his sweat-dampened forehead. "Hold still, Luca. It's me, Amanda. It's all over. Emily is fine. The baby is fine. Both are safe at Father's house. Please. Hold still. Let us help you."

There. He palmed an innocent-looking glass vial filled with a clear fluid. The label confirmed its contents. From the metal tray, he grabbed a syringe and drew a small amount into the barrel. "Amanda." She looked up, distress written on every feature. He handed her the vial and indicated the syringe. She raised her eyebrows. "A small dose. Just enough to sedate him until we can get him the help he needs."

She glanced at the label and nodded assent. He stepped forward, deftly slipping the fine, silver needle into a vein and sliding home the plunger. Seconds later, every muscle in the man's body relaxed, sending Luca into a painless sleep.

Thornton exhaled a breath he hadn't known he was holding.

"What now?" she whispered.

"Look closely. Lady Huntley says the cranial neurachnid performed as expected."

"How can you be thinking of such things at this

moment?" Her voice rose with each word. "We have to do something to help him!"

"We will. But *what* we do depends on the success, or failure of the neurachnid. Look closely," he repeated. "I want to confirm Lady Huntley's observation."

She stared at him a moment then grabbed magnifying eyeglasses from the tray. Lifting a blunt-nosed probe and angling the lamp, Amanda leaned in closely to examine the eye socket and study the configuration of the gold threads. A moment later, she looked up in amazement. "She's right. It worked."

He stared back. He'd hardly dared to hope.

She handed him the magnifying goggles, inviting him to confirm her findings.

He accepted. "Indeed," he said. "All three cranial nerves appear to have received diffuse insertions." He studied the crimped ends of the golden wires. "All evidence suggests Henri successfully connected the artificial eye."

"But he severed the connection," she said, her eyes searching the crude medical space and not finding what she sought. "The phaoscope, it's not here. Nor is his spider. Wherever Henri went, he took them both."

Lady Huntley moved to stand beside them, her wrists wrapped in ragged cotton strips. Blood seeped around the frayed edges.

Thornton raised his eyebrows.

"I'm fine. Or, rather, I will be," Lady Huntley said. "If we transport him to Lister University Hospital, we could implement protocol number 374."

"We could," Black agreed, moving to join them.

"What is protocol 374?" Amanda asked.

"Luca's original eye is lost," Thornton answered. "Due to the delicacies of blood supply, there's no reconnecting it. However, I can arrange for Luca to have the most technologically advanced artificial eye in all of England."

Amanda shook her head. "As a gypsy, Luca won't want that." A single tear escaped the corner of her eye.

"It won't be forced upon him. First, his condition must be stabilized." He lifted his hand to brush away the tear from her cheek. "Don't fret. We have as much time as we need."

Black cleared his throat and looked away, barking orders to the remaining agents who sprang into action. "Lady Huntley, you need to come as well. Those injuries should be properly treated."

Black and Lady Huntley stepped toward the door.

Amanda also moved to follow the makeshift stretcher. Thornton put a hand on her shoulder, stopping her. "Go without us," he said to Black. "I want to take a closer look around."

"Of course," Black answered, but glanced at his leg, frowning.

"I'll be fine," he growled. "Be sure you find Lord Thistleton and tell him to keep the *amatiflora* under tight guard. Henri does not have access to the greenhouse, but I doubt that will stop him from trying."

Black nodded and then he was alone with Amanda. Silently, he held out his hand. She stepped past his outstretched arm, burying her forehead in his chest. Without a thought, he wrapped his arms about her, pulling close the woman he loved.

Loved.

Amanda.

The thought left him stunned. He'd fallen in love. When had that happened? He'd meant for this to be a temporary affair. Something to satisfy both their needs and desires. Now he wasn't sure an affair would be enough. The primitive need to possess her, for her to belong to him and him alone, had reared its head. Was it possible she felt the same? He kissed her hair. "Luca will be fine." This wasn't the time to sort through the tangle of emotions knotted within his skull. Later, when this situation was resolved, when he was alone, he would unsnarl them with great care. "Right now, we need to focus on finding Henri."

She pulled away and nodded, blinking away the tears that still threatened.

"Henri knew we would be coming," Thornton said. "He planted that acousticotransmitter on Sommersby. Left Luca alive. All to keep us busy, distracted. The question is why." He swayed a bit. The Somnic was wearing off.

"To buy himself time to escape," Amanda said. "A little time is all anyone would need to slip into the crowds that line the docks. Someone trained to evade..."

Thornton shook his head. "Certainly true. Yet Luca was very deliberately chosen. Henri delays us even longer if we all rush back to the laboratory to oversee the surgery." Thornton limped back to the barrel that held the metal tray. He held up an empty amber vial, the one that once contained the nerve agent. "He has a neurachnid and the artificial eye. He does not…"

"Have any more nerve agent." Amanda began to pace. "If *amatiflora* is indigenous to the British Isles, Henri cannot risk leaving without it. He has the formula. He needs the plant." She looked at him. "You cut off his access to Lord Thistleton and the greenhouse, but there must be more of the plant still growing at the base of that chimney."

"We took the last flowering vines. He needs someone who can identify the plant from the leaves alone. So we must ask, who else can identify it? Me. You. Emily." They were all, momentarily, safe.

"Nadya. We must warn her." Grabbing her skirts in her fists, she started for the stairs.

Thornton forced his leg into motion, following as quickly as he could manage. "For their own safety, the gypsies were ordered to disband, to leave London when Luca was discovered missing."

Amanda paused on the steps to give him a look of disbelief.

"I know," he panted. "They have no respect for authority, and they won't have gone far. But how can we possibly find her, warn her?"

"Nicu is her brother. He'll know. We need to go to Clockwork Corridor." Amanda continued, "Nicu and I spoke of Nadya in Henri's presence. And Nicu *trusts* Henri. We need to warn him."

They stepped out onto the busy street. Thornton placed

a protective hand at the small of her back and flagged a crank hackney with his cane.

He wanted to be a man she could count on, but even now, he was running out of time. His leg tingled. A muscle twitched. The first symptoms informing him Somnic no longer had any effect. Thornton swore under his breath. He shouldn't have been so precipitous in sending Black away. They needed help. *He* needed help.

But they were gone. And there was no time to lose.

He handed Lady Amanda inside the rickety vehicle that stopped in front of them, barely managing to haul himself inside before directing the driver to Clockwork Corridor.

"Your leg?" Concern laced Amanda's voice.

"Is bad." It killed him to admit it, but she needed to know. "And I've no Somnic left."

"Then we'll go to Lister Hospital first." She lifted a hand to knock on the roof.

He shook his head. "There's no time and it won't work. I've used as much Somnic as I can. Too much." Black had had to forcibly wrest the last vials of the drug from the doctors' hands. They wouldn't be giving him any more. "The last dose barely lasted thirty minutes. I've an hour or two at best before my leg truly begins to rebel. We'll need to be quick."

It already felt as if someone were slicing a knife through the skin of his leg. Every nerve fired, every muscle clenched. Without Somnic to stop it, the delicate balance of sodium, potassium, chloride and other molecules were falling into disarray. Soon, more and more nerves and muscles that had been tangentially affected by the drug would begin to seize.

No one before him had ever used Somnic to such an extensive degree. There was no knowing how many nerves and muscles would be affected. Only this one leg? The other one as well? His torso? His arms? Would the entire musculature of his body clench as his body metabolized the last of the Somnic? And how long until homeostasis returned?

A headache crept upward, threatening to engulf his entire skull. He rubbed the back of his neck. The aftereffects of Somnic? Or simply the result of psychological tension? Either way, he needed to relax, to find a way to fight the muscle tension that threatened to overtake him.

"My God," Amanda stood and crossed the carriage to sit by his side, bending to pull his leg into her lap. Her fingers pressed down, finding the pressure points.

The pain receded, but only slightly. It would be back soon and at a level guaranteed to drop an elephant.

"You need a doctor," she said. "Someone who knows how to help."

"*This* helps." But he knew nothing short of general anesthesia was likely to stop the pain. He clasped her hand. "Inform Nicu of the threat to Nadya. Have him send word to Black." He reached inside his coat, drew his TTX pistol and pressed it into her hands. "Hold on to this."

She gasped. "I've never..."

He managed a wan smile. "Soon, your aim will be better than mine, Amanda. Point. Pull the trigger. Remember. One bullet to slow a man down."

"Two to drop him. Three to kill."

He nodded. "Good."

With a worried frown, and handling the gun as if it might sting her, she shoved it inside her bulging handbag. "Now, your leg. Tell me what to expect. What to do."

The blood drained from her face as he gave her a quick rundown of possible symptoms. "They should pass in four to six hours."

"Four to six," she repeated.

He nodded, trying not to let the pain show on his face. There was little to do that would ease the process. A bottle of laudanum rested on a table by his bedside. He'd planned on enduring this alone, but circumstances being what they were....

It would be ugly, there was no avoiding that. And, at the end, when his muscles finally relaxed, the damaged nerve would rapidly deteriorate. He'd used such high doses, he had no idea what damage he'd already done. Even if the *amatiflora* bloomed next week, it would be too late.

It was likely too late already.

CHAPTER THIRTY-FOUR

A MANDA NEARLY WEPT with relief when the driver finally located Nicu's maroon vardo. She had to shake Thornton awake. He'd been in and out of consciousness the entire trip, and his face was white with pain.

She helped him from the cab and, when his leg muscles refused to cooperate, nearly toppled under his solid weight. A few men passing by threw her looks of disgust or pity, but not a single one made an offer of help, the middle class dismissing him as yet another dissolute peer and her, with disheveled hair and a rumpled gown, as his mistress.

Amanda paid the driver, then handed Thornton his cane. He stood there as if frozen. A sheen of sweat dampened his forehead, and he surveyed the distance to the vardo —some five feet—as if a vast canyon yawned before him. "Let me help," she said, wrapping her arm around his waist, doing her best to steady him. His body tensed as he forced his bad leg to move, its foot refusing to cooperate.

At last they reached the wagon. Thornton looked at the curved wooden stairs that led to the vardo's door and shook his head. "I can't." He reached out to balance himself on the back wheel. "Go," he panted. "Find Nicu."

"I'll be right back."

He nodded.

"Nicu?" she called, pushing open the slightly ajar door.

"Lady Amanda." Nicu rose from a chair to greet her. "How can I be of help this fine day?"

So he'd not heard about Luca. There was no easy way to broach her news, no time to cushion the impact. "We need to warn Nadya about Henri."

He shook his head and frowned. "Warn Nadya about Henri?"

"Henri is the gypsy murderer."

Nicu gave her a long look, then swore in Romani. "There's more, isn't there?"

She nodded. "Lord Thornton waits outside. He needs help. Now."

"Why did you not say so? There are few such men who would lift so much as a finger to help a gypsy." Nicu rose and headed for the door.

With her determination and the old man's wiry strength, they propelled Thornton into the vardo and behind the partition separating the old man's clockwork business from his personal living space.

They lowered Thornton onto the raised bed. Amanda

dragged a low stool to sit beside him while Nicu lit a fire. "Warmth is good for the muscles," he said, pulling up another stool. "Now, tell me, what is to be done?"

"Black. Get a message to Black." Thornton spoke from between clenched teeth.

"Black?" Nicu looked at her.

"An agent of the Queen who can stop Henri," Amanda explained. "We convey our suspicions to him. His agents will monitor both the greenhouse and the factory where the plant is known to grow. They will also protect Nadya." She quickly informed Nicu of the plant's significance.

"Nadya can identify this plant?"

She nodded. "She sent us to find it. We need to stop Henri from getting hold of the plant. Once he has it, he will disappear."

"Disposing of my sister as well once she is no longer useful." Nicu opened a box, pulling forth a sheet of paper and a pencil. He handed them to Amanda. "Write your note to this Black. I will see it delivered into the right hands."

As Amanda scratched out a message, Thornton ground out directions as to how to contact Black or any one of his men. She handed Nicu the paper.

He stood. "A few minutes. I will be back." Nicu caught Amanda's eyes. "Then we discuss what to do about our other problem." Almost indiscernibly, his head tipped in Thornton's direction, then he was gone.

Amanda turned to Thornton, smoothing his hair from his forehead. She wished for cool water and a towel. "How bad is it?"

"Worse." He dragged in a breath and the rest came out in a rush. "Can't bear to be moved."

"We're not going anywhere," she reassured him. "But I have more questions." Ones she'd tried to ask in the crank hackney before he fell unconscious. "How long before the nerve is destroyed? A week?" She paused.

He shook his head.

"A day?" Nothing. "An hour?" Her voice sounded a touch panicked even to her own ears.

A ragged breath. "May be too late already."

This was much worse than she'd expected. She'd counted on time. Time to test the neurachnid. Time for the *amatiflora* to be forced into bloom. Time, a resource denied to them.

If there was nothing to lose...

Nicu appeared in the doorway. "Now. What is to be done?"

Thornton's face was contorted in a grimace, his breaths coming fast and shallow. Amanda stood and crossed to Nicu's side. She pulled the neurachnid from her reticule and held it out to him. Quietly, she outlined their current predicament.

He took the spider gingerly in his arthritic fingers, examining it closely from every angle. A smile carved itself into his face. "I taught you well."

"You did." She glanced at Thornton. "His injury, while old, is not deep or extensive. I have the spider. I have the necessary Babbage card." She shook her head. "I'm not certain if I have enough nerve agent, but the window of opportunity is closing."

He nodded. "If not closed already."

Doubt crept in, but she went bravely on. She loved Thornton and would do all she could to save his leg and see his career—in its entirety—saved. "What I do not have is a calm, relaxed patient. His nerves are irritated and his muscles are in a state of chronic tension and are becoming ischemic; no blood is flowing through them. For the spider to work, he must be relaxed."

"Opium," Nicu pronounced. Amanda stared in open-mouthed disbelief as Nicu turned and pulled a long pipe and a small lamp from a box. "I am an old man with many aches. Opium will relax. Calm. Stop the pain."

Thornton moaned, and she turned. The effects of withdrawal had spread to his arms. Bent at uncomfortable angles, they seemed to hover above the mattress, locked in position. She lowered herself onto the stool once more, turning his face toward hers. Stiff neck muscles resisted her efforts. "Listen. I have all I need to attempt a repair of your leg."

"No."

She held his head tight as he tried to pull away. "Why not?"

"No nerve agent." Sweat beaded on his forehead, his eyes over-bright.

Amanda pulled the vial from her reticule and held the green fluid before his eyes. "I have some. With the remaining extract, I mixed a small amount of the drug."

His head jerked to the side, neck muscles in a spasm. "Probably won't work. Not enough."

"There's no way to know without trying," she insisted. How could he believe she would give up and let him lose the function of his leg without attempting the procedure? Her stomach clenched. Ned. She'd put her brother ahead of him. Never again. "I had a Babbage card designed to correct your specific problem." Amanda thought it best not to mention that it was Olivia's first foray into anatomical matters. He didn't respond. "Nicu has some opium. Will you at least let us ease the pain?"

A jerk of the head. Yes.

The older man lit a small brass lamp and affixed a glass chimney to it. Amanda watched, fascinated, as he dropped a tiny amount of opium into a white, ceramic bowl attached to the long stem of the pipe and began to heat the opium. A sweet smoke began to rise from the pipe. He waved her away, taking her place by Thornton's side. "Breath this in, my lord," he said, holding the pipe to Thornton's mouth.

As the minutes passed, Thornton began to relax, his body seeming to sink more deeply into the mattress.

"Better, my lord?"

"Much," Thornton breathed, his eyes glassing over. "Thank you."

Nicu nodded. "Now. About this surgery. Sometimes promises must be broken."

"No." His voice sounded empty, as if he had given up.

Amanda wanted to scream her frustration. The stubborn man.

"What have you to lose?" Nicu asked. "If you decline, you will depend upon machinery to move freely. My Amanda is brilliant. I believe in this spider, as do you, you who took her into your laboratory. Trust her. Let the spider do its task. She tells me it works quickly." He shrugged. "What have you to do for the next few hours but lie about and wait?"

Thornton said nothing.

Nicu went on, "Would you leave me, an old man, to defend your woman while this Henri, this murderer, walks free?"

"Not mine." His eyes closed.

Amanda stepped forward.

Nicu held up a hand and shook his head, telling her to stay back. "I am no blind fool. She is yours. Do you think to keep her safe this way?" He paused and waited.

Thornton said nothing.

"Then you are the fool." Nicu pushed to his feet. "Leave the job to other men, better men. Sit back and wallow, while others do all the work. Perhaps the outcome will meet your expectations."

A rumble started deep in Thornton's chest. "Do it." But he did not open his eyes. He did not look at her. How it must hurt him to cede control, a man used to giving orders, not taking them. Used to solving problems, not being one. Used to performing experimental surgery, not being the subject.

Nicu nodded. "Good. I began to think Lady Amanda chose poorly." He turned back to her. "Now. What do we do?"

"He cannot move during the procedure; the spider must not be jarred. First, we make certain he's comfortable, as much as possible. Then we must tie him down." Together, they wrestled off Thornton's coat. His muscles responded oddly. Some seemed fixed and tense. Others were strangely pliable. "The brace on his leg must be removed. We need a blanket to fold beneath his leg. Alcohol—vodka will do— and a sharp knife. A flame." To both cleanse his skin and sterilize the blade. "And clean rags." For the inevitable blood.

"More opium," Nicu added.

"More opium," she agreed. "As much as you have."

She would never forgive herself if this didn't work.

THORNTON STRUGGLED to focus through the muddled haze that his mind had become. Between the aftereffects of the Somnic and the current effects of the opium, he could feel, but not move. Or, rather, move only with great effort and concentration and will.

But he was losing the will to try.

His arms were wrestled from his coat and bound to the bed. Sounds of fabric being rent reached his ears, and his lower leg met with warm air, then the chill of cold liquid. Vaguely, it occurred to him to be grateful that he'd instructed Amanda on the sterilizing properties of alcohol.

The pipe was pressed to his lips at regular intervals and he inhaled deeply, inviting in the sweet haze. Worry faded into soft bliss. Her soft hand was brushing across his damp brow, fingers threading through his hair. He smiled.

"Sebastian?"

"Mmm." Never had the sound of his given name sounded so wonderful.

"It's time."

"Mmm." Her fingers kept stroking his hair. It felt heavenly. All was right with her by his side. "Mine," he said.

The fingers paused. "What?" she whispered.

"Mine," he repeated, uncertain why he felt such a forceful need to claim her. "You're all mine. No one else."

The fingers began to move again. He struggled to move his arms, but couldn't seem to pull them from his side. His side. That was where she needed to be. Always. He forced open his weighted eyes and found her staring down at him, her expression unreadable. "Say it. Promise me. You're mine. All mine." The room spun, a whirl of color.

"I'm yours, Sebastian," she whispered back. She pressed a kiss against his forehead and his eyes slid shut. "Later we'll discuss if *you* are to be mine." Her tone grew harder. "This will hurt. We've bound you as securely as possible. Nicu will hold you still. Try not to fight him. Are you ready?"

"For?"

She sighed. "The neurachnid. The spider."

Right. Gold threads. Missing eyes. Betrayal.

She moved away. Took away her soft hands. Her voice. Her presence. Hard, rough and calloused hands bore down on him, pressing him into the bed.

Then, for a moment, he felt her soft hands again on his

bare leg. And then pain unlike any he'd ever known sliced through him. His heart pounded against his chest. Blood rushed past his ears and eyes, deafening him, blinding him. His lungs could not pull in enough air.

A pricking of the skin on his leg. Reason forced itself cruelly upon him. Amanda was repairing his leg. Or, rather, her neurachnid was. Tiny sharp needles seemed to grab hold, testing, prodding until they quite literally struck a nerve.

His eyes flew open, but saw only flashing lights and black spots. The pain was excruciating.

Then the spots spread like ink blots, melted into each other and began to flow across his mind bringing the blissful black of senselessness.

CHAPTER THIRTY-FIVE

ITH TINY, NEAT, PERFECT stitches, Amanda
closed the wound.
There was some muscle atrophy, and the
brace would be necessary until he regained his strength, a
week or two at most. All indications pointed to the spider
having rewoven the nerve successfully. Infection was the
only pressing concern. While Thornton was still mercifully
unconscious, she poured more vodka over the incision site
and bandaged his leg. She had every reason to believe the
procedure was successful, though she wouldn't know until
he woke.

"Thank you," she said to Nicu.

"You are very welcome," he answered. "Your family and
mine, we are tied by bonds that cannot be broken." A frown
cut into his features. "We will see Henri stopped. Justice will
be served."

Did the gypsies plan to assist in apprehending Henri?

Amanda's lips twitched at the thought of how Black and his men would react to the sudden swelling of their ranks.

There was a whistle from the front of the vardo, followed by a smattering of Romani. Nicu stood. "No news yet. I will wait outside. See he rests."

She lifted the knife she'd been given, but used it this time to cut the bindings holding Thornton's wrists in place. She caught up one hand and began to massage the stiff muscles, wishing the side effects of the Somnic could be willed away. Slowly, his long fingers relaxed, curling gently in her cupped palms. Encouraged, she moved on.

Her fingers worked a cufflink free, setting it carefully to the side. She rolled up his shirtsleeve, admiring his wide wrists and brushing her palm over the sprinkle of dark hairs that covered his forearms. Pressing her thumbs into the dense musculature there, she admired their quiescent strength, marveled at all he'd done with them. These were the arms, the hands, the fingers that worked magic in the laboratory. On her.

Her face grew hot.

But there was lust and there was love.

It occurred to her that somewhere along the way, at some time during these past two weeks, she'd managed to lose a part of her heart to this man.

She leaned forward, her fingers sliding beneath his rolled sleeves, pressing into thick muscles. His arm flexed, his hand curled about her hip. She glanced at his face. Beneath half-open, unfocused eyes, he seemed to watch. Her fingers stilled, but he was not truly awake. For a long moment she let herself stare back into those eyes and wonder.

What would it be like to truly belong to this man? To have him belong to her? To live a life together?

Of all the times to contemplate such questions. What a disaster her life was. Luca gravely injured. Emily panicked. Olivia and Mother hysterical at the social implications. Ned distraught at the effects of his own selfishness. Her own would-be-fiancé complicit with a murderer yet still having the nerve to declare his love for her. Father attempting damage control and quite probably regretting any free will he'd ever granted his children.

All while she'd absconded with her lover and mentor, performed experimental surgery in the back of a gypsy wagon and waited to assist in the apprehension of a murderous German spy.

There was nothing to do but press onward, see this thing through to its conclusion.

Mine. In a delirium of opiate-induced fog, he'd spoken words that cut right to the core of her.

Yes, she was his, but unless he'd also lost a piece of his heart to her, this, whatever it was between them, had to stop. She'd been wrong to think she could settle for status as his lover, to consent to an ongoing affair conducted in the shadows. One where she must constantly worry about discovery, worry that she would be cast out from the medical community in shame.

She would not press him for more. He'd been clear from the beginning, when she forced him to acknowledge the attraction between them, that he did not want a wife. When he emerged from this fog a whole man once more, she would step aside. Her research project was complete. Once the situation with Henri was resolved, they would go their separate ways, parting as friends and colleagues.

She would perform the surgery once more upon her brother, and if—when—Ned walked once more under his own power, her success in the medical community would be assured. Under the cloak of secrecy, Thornton and Lady Huntley would use her neurachnid to install their devices and, with his leg repaired, Thornton would once again accompany Black into the field.

His head jerked in her direction, his unfocused eyes open again, but this time, he spoke. "Sorry," he rasped. "So sorry."

"Sorry for what?" she prompted, curious.

But he only shook his head.

"Let me get you some water." She tried to pull away, but his fingers had curled around her elbow and held tight. She tried to maintain a clinical mindset, telling herself she was glad to feel the return of some muscle control. Yet as his dark blue eyes stared up at her, she found herself waiting. Waiting for... something.

"So many dead. My fault. I brought him here." His eyes fought a battle to stay open—but lost.

Ah, she understood now. Guilt. He felt responsible for Henri's actions, for the death of all the gypsies that died in the madman's quest to install the phaoscope.

"No. None of this is your fault." She smoothed the hair

from his brow. "You are not responsible for the evil actions of another. Not Lord Huntley's or Henri's deeds. This is not your fault," she repeated.

His head jerked away from her touch, then rocked on his pillow, disagreeing. "It is. Gypsies. Your family. You." He sighed, slipping deeper into his fog. "Mine. The woman I love. All ruined."

She shook his shoulder. She needed to hear it again. "The woman you love?"

"Mmm."

"Thornton?" She hesitated. "Sebastian?"

It was no good; he'd slipped back into his drugged sleep.

Amanda wanted to scream. She disliked this foggy, cryptic version of him. Terse but direct was vastly preferable.

Because he'd left her wondering. Could he possibly be speaking of her? Did he love her, fear he'd ruined her with their affair? Or did he speak of his former fiancée, who had cried off shortly after his injury occurred, wanting no future with a damaged man? Was it possible Thornton loved her, Lady Anne, despite her abandonment?

She pulled away from his limp grasp and stood. Anything was better than sitting there staring at the man she loved, wondering if her sentiments were returned.

Amanda stepped through the partition, walking past the hundreds of boxes containing an endless assortment of clockwork pieces, and climbed down the curved stairs onto the street.

A short distance away, Nicu stood beside another gypsy, Milosh, his assistant. Their heads were bent close together.

She could not understand the Romani they spoke, but their tightly controlled voices spoke of disagreement.

"What is wrong?" she asked.

Their heads jerked up. Nicu patted Milosh on his shoulder, pushing him away. He left, but not before she saw an intense look of dislike and distrust on his face. An all too common reaction to a *gadji* who made a nuisance of herself by hanging about gypsy vardos.

"A bit of trouble finding Nadya, that is all," Nicu answered.

Amanda's eyebrows rose. "Do you think...?"

He shook his head. "She was seen recently in the company of a woman who sought to have her future read in tea leaves. We will find her. Let us worry about it. Is your man recovering?"

Her man. Perhaps he was. For now. "Sleeping," she answered. "Has there been no word from Mr. Black?"

Nicu looked confused for a moment. "Your Queen's man, right?"

She nodded.

"No. Nothing. Perhaps he has already apprehended Henri and is busy with retribution."

She frowned. If Black had caught Henri, he, or one of his men, would have arrived with the news. No. Whatever kept Black from contacting them must be of the utmost importance. Unless he had also been unable to contact Father? She should send word, assure her family of her safety. "Will you send someone to my father's house? Let them know we are here?"

Nicu gestured to the clockwork horse attached to his vardo. "I could take you there, but should he be moved?"

"No," she said. "Probably not. A message should suffice." Likely Father's men would then arrive to assure themselves of her safety.

"Very well," he nodded. "I will send a boy." Nicu tipped his head. "Will you rest as well? Or is there something more?"

Just the general unease of being relegated to the fringes while others sought to apprehend the eye doctor. The unease of not knowing what developments had taken place. "No. Thank you. I'll see to Lord Thornton." She waved a hand in the air toward the door of the vardo.

Nicu nodded politely.

Inside, Amanda busied herself setting the small space to rights, then sat down again beside him on the low stool and spread a clean cloth across her lap. She set about cleaning the neurachnid in extreme detail. Each gear, each spring, each pincer. She tugged the Babbage card Olivia had punched free, returning it to her reticule. It had worked well. Like it or not, Olivia's talent with mechanical creatures, both steam and clockwork, showed much promise.

She rinsed the now empty abdominal vial. Perhaps Father could be persuaded to use some of his influence to delay Georgina's engagement long enough for the *amatiflora* to bloom once more. That was, provided Georgina's family could be persuaded to ignore the gossip about gypsies in favor of their daughter marrying a future duke.

An hour or more passed before he stirred again, before

his heavy lids once again lifted, fighting against the remaining opium fog. "Amanda?" His eyes were clearer this time, their focus on her face more pointed.

Did she dare ask? Could she bear to learn she was not the woman he loved? That what they shared merely served to quench primitive biological instincts through mutual physical pleasure? No. Better not to press. She'd only damage whatever friendship would be left between them after. Determined not to churn herself into emotional turmoil, she did her best to sound clinical and professional. "Does it hurt much?"

"A dull, diffuse ache," he rasped.

Now, while he was still under the influence of the opium, was the time to assess his leg. Any pain would be mitigated.

She pulled back the blanket, exposing the bandaged leg, and pressed her palm against the sole of his large foot. "Push," she commanded.

He did, weakly.

She conducted a complete examination. Plantarflexion, dorsiflexion, inversion, eversion. Weak responses, all of them.

"Did it work?" he asked.

"Yes." She should feel happier to announce such news. "You'll still need your brace for some time until the muscles regain their mass. You might have trouble walking at first, but on the whole, I'd say the procedure was a success."

"Good. May I please have some water?" His voice was hoarse.

Pouring a glass, she perched once more on the mattress

by his side. "Drink. Slowly." She held the glass to his lips. "You've lost a bit of blood."

He drank, then cleared his throat. "Any messages?" His deep voice was clearer now. And seemingly his mind.

Thank goodness she had not inquired about his feelings for her. It seemed he had no memory of his drug-induced ramblings. "Nicu sent word to Black when we arrived. He's not responded, not yet. I did have him send another message to my father, informing him of our safety." Strange. She'd thought one of Father's men would have arrived to check on them by now. Or have sent a message. "All has been quiet."

His brow furrowed with intense concentration. "How long have we been here?"

Could he be planning to leave already? Thornton needed time. Time to rest. Every additional minute gave him time to recover from the surgery, the drugs. Minutes during which her mind would continue circling around the question of whom he loved, her mind unable to force the question past her lips.

"About three hours," she answered. "Nicu did say Nadya was recently sighted in the company of a woman, but they can't seem to locate her."

"There's still time then," he said. Then, surrendering to the lingering effects of the opium, let his eyes slide shut once more. His arm stretched out and wrapped about her waist, tugging. "Come. You need rest."

"But..."

"Fieldwork rule. Sleep when you can." His arm flexed,

his palm shifting to press between her shoulder blades, pulling her against him.

She resisted. "Your leg."

"Your weight feels good."

Knowing this might be her last chance, the last time they might spend such time alone together, she caved. Stretching her body out alongside him on the feather-stuffed mattress, she let him tuck her into the crook of his arm. Her face fell on his shoulder, resting where his soft cotton shirt met the rougher wool of his waistcoat. She breathed in the male scent of him. Beneath her ear, his heart beat a comforting rhythm. Steady. Strong. Constant.

Her arm stretched across his flat stomach, rising and falling with each breath he took, and her body pressed against him, her soft curves fitting against his long angles, his warmth seeping into her while the weight of his arm held her fast, held her safe.

"Rest now," he said.

But how could she? To be held so closely, so tenderly by the man she loved was a moment to be treasured and captured in time. Moments to be stored against the inevitable moment when they must part.

Even as a fog of exhaustion began to engulf her, coaxing her mind to rest, tempting her with sleep, she fought it with every ounce of will that remained.

CHAPTER THIRTY-SIX

S OMETHING JOLTED HIM AWAKE.
Something was not right.
Vardo. He was in a gypsy vardo.

A brightly painted wooden canopy arched over him.
Orange curtains hung near his head. An overly soft feather
bed lay beneath him. Amanda was in his arms, her body
pressed to him, her head tucked beneath his chin.

That much was right.

Wisps of memories crept back.

Luca, kidnapped by Sommersby and handed over to the
eye doctor, Henri, who was his laboratory assistant. Luca and
Lady Huntley found in a riverside warehouse, alive. His leg
failing. A mission to protect the old gypsy lady. Sending
word to Black. Waiting.

He blinked and ran a hand across his rough face and
through his tangled hair as the last tendrils of an opium fog
lifted from his mind.

Opium.

That last memory slammed into him. Amanda had repaired his leg. Or at least she had tried.

He flexed his foot experimentally, the one on the damaged side, and felt an odd tingling. Yet the blanket above his foot moved. His foot had moved! "Amanda," he said. His mouth was parched and his voice sounded dry. "Amanda, wake up."

She stirred in his arms, groggily lifting her head. "You're awake." She pushed up onto her arms, her eyes turning toward his leg. "How do you feel?"

Every muscle ached. Every. Single. One. He might have injected the Somnic into a specific location, but its effects had been systemic, affecting every skeletal muscle, every nerve. Shortly after they'd arrived, there'd been a point at which he'd been unable to move. When even the simple act of breathing had become a daunting task. Each inhalation, each exhalation had begun to require conscious effort.

The gypsy and his opium might well have saved his life. Just as Amanda had saved his leg.

"Sore." He swung his legs over the edge of the bed to sit beside her. One leg of his trousers had been cut away. Cotton wrappings wound about his calf, covering the incision that would have been required for the neurachnid to weave its golden threads. He flexed his foot again, this time watching closely. "Amazing."

Despite all that had happened these past weeks, this past year, he let himself know a moment of personal relief. He'd been given a second chance. A chance he would not waste.

He reached out and pulled Amanda to him, planting a fast, hard kiss upon her lips. "Thank you."

She smiled back at him, her eyes alight with the thrill of success. He took in the disheveled mess she presented. Her clothes were rumpled and askew. Hair twisted and fell around a face that bore the red imprint of his shirtsleeves and waistcoat. She looked like a well-tumbled woman.

His well-tumbled woman.

Alas, this was neither the time nor the place. Not that inappropriate locations had stopped them before. Amazing how Amanda made him feel so very much more alive than he had in years. He opened his mouth to say something, and that's when he heard it again. The noise that had awoken him.

A faint creak. A squeak. The sound of wooden boards shifting past each other. The caravan shifted and rocked ever so slightly.

Amanda caught his gaze, the same questions written on her face. What happened outside? Were they preparing to move? Why?

How long—exactly—had he been asleep?

His fingers slid into his waistcoat pocket, drawing forth his watch. He flipped open the cover and peered at the time. Six hours had passed with no word from Black? Something was wrong. He knew better than to ignore his instincts, instincts that were beginning to scream that something was very wrong.

The vardo jerked into motion.

Where were they going? Thornton tried to stand, but his

leg buckled beneath him in pain and protest. He sat back down, clenching his teeth against the shock of pain that shot upward through his leg.

"It's too soon," Amanda gasped, reaching out to steady him. "The wound alone will take days to heal."

The pain subsided, and he hissed an answer. "We don't have days. We may not even have minutes." He jerked his head in the direction of the partition that separated Nicu's sleeping quarters from the rest of his wagon. "Take a look. Carefully."

She crept forward and peered around the partition. Then sat down beside him once more, her eyes wide. "The gypsy driving is not Nicu. It's Milosh, his assistant."

He raised his eyebrows.

"After your surgery, I stepped outside to ask Nicu to send a message to my father. He was talking to Milosh and…" Her lips pressed together. She knew something.

"What, Amanda?"

She shook her head. "It was probably nothing. He wasn't happy about our presence here, with Nicu."

"Unlikely," he said, his suspicions intensifying. Six hours without contact during an active manhunt was unheard of. His message to Black had never been delivered. Nor hers to the duke. "The gypsies have deliberately cut us off from outside contact." Likely they'd bypassed his agents entirely.

"Why would they do that?" she asked, her eyes round. "We've only tried to help."

"Gypsies distrust governments. Of all kinds. They prefer

to work outside and around anyone with direct ties to the Queen or the British government."

"You think they've gone after Henri themselves?"

"Yes. Nearly all the victims have been gypsy." All but Tony. "Can you blame them?"

She shook her head.

"I can't allow that. I need him alive. I have questions. Many. I cannot allow my—our—devices to fall into other hands." He wasn't used to explaining himself, but for Amanda... "I am not convinced of their ability to deal with a trained, foreign operative. If they act on their own, they put Nadya—and others—at risk. Henri may go to ground and finding him after today might prove impossible."

He reached for the metal brace that had kept his leg from outright rebellion for so many months. Wincing at the searing pain, he pulled the leather straps tightly about the bandaged surgical incision. There was no help for it. Wound healing and muscle atrophy required the one thing he did not have. Time.

"You shouldn't," Amanda objected.

"I know. Yet we have to assume Black—or the duke— never received our messages. For all we know, they are searching for us." Against his body's protest, Thornton stuffed his feet into his shoes, pulled on his coat. "If you will please return my pistol?"

The blood drained from her face as she reached for her reticule, pulling the weapon forth. "You're not going to... going to shoot Milosh? He's driving."

He took it from her. "We need answers." He shifted

forward. "If you'll hand me my cane, it's time to test your spider's work." Solid wood with a silver cap, it was more than simple support. Properly employed, it too served as a weapon.

With a frown, she passed it to him.

Gritting his teeth, he stood. The first step was like stepping on broken glass. Pain pulsed up his leg. He held his breath and took another step. Only slightly less painful. Yet despite the pain, his leg worked. Nerves carried complete messages. Each muscle responded to his brain's commands. With a deep breath, he wiped away any remaining expression of pain from his face and stepped around the partition.

Leaning a shoulder casually against the wall to compensate for the rocking motion of the caravan's iron-banded wheels as they rattled over uneven cobblestones, Thornton lifted his weapon and pointed it at the gypsy driving the clockwork horse. "Please pull to the side of the road."

The man glanced over his shoulder. His lip curled. Then he turned away. "You will not shoot," he said.

"Excuse me!" Amanda, her shoulders squared and her back stiff, moved into the room. "Where is Nicu?"

The gypsy shrugged, his glance at her insolent.

"Tell us what is going on," she insisted. "Or this man may have no choice."

"He will not shoot," the gypsy insisted.

"Can you steer the horse?" Thornton asked Amanda, leaning against the wall of the caravan.

She glanced at his pistol.

He gave a slight nod.

Her eyes widened and answered with a tentative, "Yes."

He hoped she meant it. "Last chance," he called to the gypsy.

The driver barked a derogatory laugh.

Leather boots were sometimes an impediment to the polymer bullets, so Thornton shot him in the thigh. The gypsy howled, grabbing his leg. Pain ran up his own leg as he lunged forward, wielding his cane to knock the man from his bench, sending him sprawling into wooden boxes piled upon yet more boxes. The old, dry wood shattered. Gears and pins and springs cascaded from their containers, burying the gypsy.

"Take the reins!" he yelled to Amanda, who stood frozen as the vardo began to careen widely into traffic

With a slightly panicked look, she scooped the leather straps from the floor and pulled. The vehicle shuddered as she slammed her foot down onto the wooden brake and steered them to the side of the road.

Relieved, Thornton lowered himself onto a nearby crate. From the floor, the gypsy let loose a string of what he suspected were especially colorful Romani curses.

"What have you done?" the gypsy yelled, when he finally regained the ability to speak in English. "I can't move my leg. I can't feel it."

"I did ask politely the first time. Now, answer my questions before I am forced to take this further. I'm told your name is Milosh?"

The gypsy spat at him.

Thornton sighed loudly and aimed his weapon at the gypsy's other thigh.

"Yes," the gypsy growled. "Milosh."

"Thank you. Let's start at the beginning. Did Nicu send word to the Queen's agents on my behalf?"

Milosh narrowed his eyes. "We take care of our own."

"Not an answer. I'm not in a mood to play games. Answer me."

"No."

"Where were you taking us?"

"To your hospital. Lister," Milosh grumbled. "I told Nicu never to trust a *gadjo*."

"Why?"

"Because you are all scum."

"Save your insults for later. Why Lister?" Thornton asked.

"Because your traitor, Henri, has been found."

"Found?" He lifted his eyebrows.

A nasty smile curled the corners of Milosh's lips. "Dead. Henri was found dead in Hyde Park. Floating in the Serpentine. Your people have him now."

Thornton kept his face blank. "Would you happen to know if they found any... devices in Henri's possession?"

Milosh looked blank. "Devices?"

Perhaps Henri had been working with someone, had passed the phaoscope and the neurachnid to a fellow German agent, but he had a strange feeling that something was wrong. He'd missed something. If the threat had been neutralized...

From the bench beside him, Amanda asked, "Where is Nicu?"

The gypsy looked away.

"Something is wrong," Amanda said, echoing his thoughts. "Has Nadya been found?"

Milosh swallowed. "No. She has not been found."

Amanda turned to him. "Nicu told me Nadya was last seen with a woman wanting her fortune told. How hard could it be to locate her?" Her voice rose with impatience and worry.

A flicker of something crossed the gypsy's face.

And it all fell into place. "Lady Huntley," he said. Speaking the words aloud hurt. The betrayal cut deep. "It's her. Not Henri."

"Lady Huntley?" Amanda asked. Her hand flew to her mouth. Her next words emerged on a breath of disbelief. "Lady Huntley is the eye doctor?"

He jerked his head.

It had been her all along. And John? Had he been guilty of anything? Anything more than falling in love with the wrong woman? Lady Huntley, scheduled to board their dirigible, crying off at the last minute, her husband conveniently dead and unable to be questioned. And he'd brought her into his laboratory. Trusted her with his most secret, groundbreaking research.

He pinched the bridge of his nose. Good Lord, he'd handed her everything she needed. Everything but human patients, which she'd obtained easily enough.

"Henri?" Amanda asked. "Was he friend or enemy?"

"Does it matter?" Milosh said. "Either way the spy emerges from your own nest. And you wonder why we do not trust *gadji*?"

Thornton raised his weapon once more, this time pointing it at the man's chest. "Answer quickly. Do my men know?"

"Ha!" Milosh said. "They certainly do not. The Roma do not wish for your interference. *They* can handle one woman."

"Airship Sails," Amanda said.

"If Lady Huntley has Nadya, how would they know?"

"Our note to Black. Or my sister. The Roma are her family. She would tell them." Amanda hesitated. "And not my father."

The gypsy smiled smugly. "Probably it is already done."

"What—exactly—is done?" Thornton demanded.

"Gypsies move about, everyone knows that." Milosh shrugged. "They also provide entertainment. Fortunes. Juggling. Fire swallowing. A tribe stopping for the afternoon by the side of the road to entertain those poor workers, locked up inside that large factory away from the sun and the stars, no one would think anything of it. If a few should slip through the gate to reclaim one of their own..." The gypsy shrugged again.

All hell would break loose.

"Thank you, for your cooperation," Thornton said. He shot the gypsy in his other thigh.

Milosh howled.

Amanda gasped.

He slid the weapon into an inner pocket of his coat and stood, swallowing the pain it took to do so. "In a few minutes," he informed the gypsy, "the numbness will spread. You will start to lose consciousness. You will wake up here, safe, hours from now. The side effects are minimal."

"Do not interfere," Milosh warned, his words already beginning to slur. "This is gypsy business. Your possessions will be returned to you. We have no need of them."

Thornton wanted more than what Lady Huntley had stolen. He wanted answers, perhaps a touch of revenge. "Will you drive, Amanda?" he asked, turning away from the gypsy. "I'm afraid I'm not quite up to it."

"Vauxhall Bridge?" she asked, shifting on the bench, throwing her weight onto the brake to release it. With a slap of the reins, the clockwork horse began to clomp forward.

"As quickly and as directly as possible."

Amanda slapped the reins again, and the horse slid into a trot.

"The gypsies and their antics might gain them access," he said. "Or they might provide the chaos Lady Huntley needs to escape unnoticed."

"Lady Huntley." Amanda shook her head, still in disbelief.

"Once Lady Huntley has that plant, the *amatiflora*, she'll disappear, and the fastest way for her to disappear is..."

"The submersible!"

"Exactly. The fastest way to exit London without being detected."

"But it was in poor repair. And what of the kraken?" Amanda objected. "They'd swarm one that size."

"A calculated risk, but by air or by land, she risks detection of her escape. Underwater, she can simply disappear." Thornton consulted his pocket watch again. "Dusk approaches, and high tide is in less than an hour. The water will be at peak height, no need for anyone to operate the lock system. As the currents shift downstream, she'll have a fast exit down the Thames. Once she enters that submersible and slides into the exit tube, it will be nearly impossible to stop her."

Amanda slapped the reins again, sending the horse into a rhythmic gallop.

CHAPTER THIRTY-SEVEN

BEFORE THEY REACHED the bridge, Amanda slowed down the mechanical beast long enough for Thornton to snag a messenger boy—a non-gypsy child. Thornton passed him a message scrawled on a scrap of paper and sent the boy in search of Black with the promise of a ridiculously generous reward if he succeeded in locating him within the next hour.

Though the boy ran away as fast as his legs would carry him, Amanda had little hope the cavalry would arrive in time to assist. If Lady Huntley really did intend to escape via submersible, there was nothing to prevent her from taking a hostage along with her to ensure a successful escape.

Vauxhall Bridge was almost straight when they began to cross; the tide was turning, the high waters sweeping past the damaged piers. They weren't the only vardo braving the crumbling bridge. Dozens of brightly covered gypsy caravans dotted its surface.

Thornton muttered under his breath about untrained civilians while he reloaded the cartridges of his pistol.

Amanda's stomach flip-flopped as the boards forming the surface of the bridge began to groan and creak. Ever so slowly, one section at a time, the structure began to bend with the tide, now favoring an eastward trajectory. She vowed this would be the last time she crossed the river at this point.

Near the far side, traffic slowed to a crawl. Shouts of anger, curses directed at the problem filled the air. The congestion, the commotion, all caused by an impromptu gypsy carnival outside the gates of Airship Sails.

"Pull over." Thornton pointed to a patch of dirt and weeds the moment they'd reached solid ground. "There's no chance we'll make it to the gates. No chance they'd listen to me either." He waved his hand at himself.

Amanda snorted. They made quite the pair. Lord Thornton, unshaven with a tangled mat of uncombed hair and red-rimmed eyes. A missing cravat, a wrinkled shirt, torn trousers and the accompanying bandages and brace. Her with hair tumbling about her shoulders, gown wrinkled beyond hope, a skirt stained with blood. No, they wouldn't be let past the gate looking like two asylum escapees.

With a glance at Milosh to assure herself of the continued rise and fall of his chest, she climbed down from the vardo, following Thornton to stand beside a section of the great iron fence that surrounded Airship Sails. She followed his gaze into the distance. There, beside the river was the gap in the fence where the submersible tube emptied into the river, its exit invisible at high tide. "Can you make it?" she asked.

His face was pale, and he'd flinched every time the carriage had hit the slightest bump. Since the surgery, he'd only managed to walk some ten feet, and half that was inside the vardo with his hand pressed against the wall. The gap in the fence was a good five hundred feet away. The submersible station itself, even further—and an uphill climb. "One step at a time. What other choice is there?" With gritted teeth, he set off toward the river, down the sloping riverbank, whacking weeds and brush out of their path with his cane.

Out on the river, various boats made their way seaward, following the tidal current. Standing at the front of each boat was a man armed with an air harpoon, ready to defend cargo from kraken.

She glanced down at her already ruined skirts and—grateful she'd worn half boots—plunged into the scrubby growth behind him. Branches caught and clawed at her stockings. Dips in the ground and unexpected rocks turned her ankles, threatening a sprain. Odd, scurrying sounds erupted from the underbrush, running—thankfully—away from her.

At last they reached the edge of the Thames. Less than a yard of the tidal flat remained—rocky, muddy and debris-strewn. Strange pale weeds grew at the water's edge. Her boot squished into the muck, and she stumbled, arms flailing in a desperate bid to regain her balance.

She lost and landed on her rump in the mud.

Mud, gravel, bone. That was as far as her mind allowed, before rebelling at classifying any further the components that constituted the Thames riverbank. Wet seeped through the folds of her skirts, and she very much regretted the absence of a bustle.

She twisted, looking for something—anything—to grab hold of in order to pull herself from the soggy, lumpy substance beneath her. There was nothing. "Thornton!" she called, her voice rising in distress.

Beside her in the... mud, lay a kraken, some five inches in total length. Its beak looked razor sharp, the hooks on the ends of its tentacles piercing. A tentacle flopped weakly, stretching toward her with hundreds of tiny suckers.

"Keep your hands out of the mud," Thornton ordered.

She obeyed, quite willing to await rescue. For less than a foot away from that kraken lay another. Then another. And another. Hundreds of kraken in various states of decay lay strewn across the exposed riverbed.

Perhaps the river men had cause for concern after all. One or two enormous kraken would be easier to deal with than thousands of these small ones.

She looked out at the crowded Vauxhall Bridge spanning the river's choppy waves, imagining thousands of the creatures fighting to make a home in the river, millions of tiny hooks eroding the bridge piers.

No, she would never cross that bridge again.

Thornton's boots squelched in the mud beside her and his shadow fell across her, one hand extended. "My lady."

She reached up, accepting his offer. "Many thanks." Her

hands went to her waist, quickly unhooking the overskirt. She let the damp silk folds slump to the ground. Her petticoats might be damp, but at least she wouldn't be dragging around who-knew-what behind her.

His eyes flashed approval.

"When did the kraken infestation grow so dire?" she asked, following him carefully and stealing horrified glances at the river's edge. Pale, suckered tentacles waved. She'd mistaken tentacles for weeds.

"It's only noticeable at certain locations. The cryptozoologists are studying the situation. Something about eddies and nutrient flow and proper habitat. But for us the key concern is this." He stopped at the edge of the water, pointing. "The kraken that live there."

Jutting out into the river some two feet below the water's surface lay a mussel-encrusted, curved iron structure: the submersible tube. Swimming about the opening of the tube were hundreds of the creatures, churning the water above them with their movements.

"They live in pipes?" She heard the horror in her own voice.

He nodded. "Apparently the female kraken have learned to use large pipes to replace sea caves. As they are sexually mature at five feet, it would appear London won the battle, not the war."

"Will it stop the submersible?"

"Impossible to know."

At low tide, passengers would board the submersible at the station. With the hatch sealed, the submersible entered into the lock, a gated and flooded, tub-like structure. Then, in one great motion, the riverside doors would open, releasing a great flood of water into the tube along with the submersible, shooting the vessel out through this tube into the Thames.

At high tide, when the tube's exit was submerged, the lock system was unnecessary. A submersible simply, well, submerged and quietly carried its passengers away. In the case of spies, never to be seen again. Unless the volume of kraken clogging the tube was sufficient to stop passage of the submersible?

Thornton turned and began limping up the riverbank, determination in every step.

With hopes of rescue, Amanda threw a final glance over her shoulder, scanning the river. None of the boats appeared to be official Navy craft—not that Black was likely to pilot a marked vessel—but neither did any appear headed in their direction. Timely assistance seemed less likely than ever. She followed Thornton up the riverbank along the path of disrupted river brush to stand by his side at the fence.

As the tube crested the riverbank, it erupted from the ground like an enormous annelid—wormlike and segmented —and passed through the vine-covered iron fence. In the distance, she could see it disappear into the low brick wall of the submersible tank.

A small building crouched on the edge of the tank. The submersible station. Not far beyond it sat the engine house, its chimney stretching up into the gray sky, belching great puffs of black smoke.

Near Airship Sail's official gates, a crowd gathered,

watching the gypsy's antics from inside the tall fence. Many yelled encouragement to the entertainers, but Amanda could also hear insults. A few threw pebbles from the ground at the performers.

Supervisors shouted at the distracted workers, waving their arms and pointing, unsuccessful at their attempts to direct employees back into the factory.

But some still worked diligently, moving about the factory yard, operating the machinery that carried in great rolls of silver airship fabric on enormous spools. Others drove wide steam wagons each loaded with a single large crate— one complete dirigible skin.

No one seemed particularly alarmed. No gypsies seemed to have breached the fence. None seemed to be Nicu or Nadya. Or in the company of Lady Huntley.

But in the gathering dusk, it was hard to be certain.

She turned to Thornton, "What..." The words died on her lips.

He was holding onto the iron bars of the fence with a white-knuckled grip. Her gaze dropped to his bandaged leg. Blood seeped through the linen strips.

For his sake, Amanda hoped Lady Huntley could be dropped to the ground from a distance with a well-aimed TTX bullet. For she knew he would not stop. Could not stop. Not until their technology was safely back in the hands of the British and Nadya returned to her family.

"A moment," he said, closing his eyes and lowering his forehead to rest on his arms. He pulled in several deep breaths, then lifted his face once more, tipping his head toward the fence. "We'll have to squeeze through. Careful-ly." He pulled a knife from his boot.

Sections of the iron fence struts had been cut away to create a roughly circular opening in the fence. It had been a hack job, leaving a gap between the tube and the iron bars. A thick growth of brambles arched over the tube and through the fence. Enough to discourage casual curiosity, but not enough to stop the truly determined.

The brambles were mostly leafless now, exposing their barbs to view. But if cut away, there was enough room to squeeze through.

She held out her hand for the knife. "Take the time to rest. Let me."

Thornton handed the blade over without hesitation.

Regretting deeply the lack of gloves, Amanda cut away the prickly brambles, branch by branch. By the time she was done, her hands stung and were crosshatched with scratches. She'd managed to avoid the sharp, rusty points of the fence, but not the brambles.

"Ready," she said at last. Then flattened herself against the tube, shuffling sideways through the narrow passageway, the fence catching at her clothing. "Careful," she warned Thornton, pointing at the sections of the fence that had been cut.

He slid through.

Together, they crossed to the wall of the tank and crouched behind a low thicket of evergreen scrub. Thornton caught her hand. Cleared his throat. "Amanda, if something happens to me, you should know..."

Her heart pounded in anticipation. A declaration? Now? Here?

A cry went up in the distance. "Stop!"

Dozens of gypsies swarmed the gates of Airship Sails, climbing over each other until several were able to scramble over the top and drop to inside. Chaos erupted.

"Stay close," Thornton commanded. He drew his weapon and moved at an angle through the brush.

CHAPTER THIRTY-EIGHT

T HOUGH EACH STEP STILL sent stabbing pain
though his leg, at least its muscles were once again
his to command. The blood loss was negligible.

Thornton crept as close as he could get to the rioting
crowd without discovery, then stopped and reached into his
waistcoat pocket to pull out his watch. He flipped open the
cover and slid out the crystal lens within, pushing it against
his eye. The crystalline structure, grown carefully under
high pressure, allowed a wafer thin lens to act as would a
telescope, seeming to draw far images near.

A number of gypsies had managed to breach the iron
gates, most only stopped by the very crowd they'd drawn
forth. But several gypsy men broke free, running out into the
factory yard.

"Nadya!" they called.

It was exactly as he'd feared. Incompetence. Lady
Huntley was certain to take advantage of the confusion.

Wait. He squinted. The gypsy men surrounded an old woman who was screaming and pointing at the great chimney. In her hand was a clump of dirt, a root ball from which protruded the *amatiflora* vine.

Nadya.

Seconds later, guards arrived, slapping the plant from her hand and dragging her and the others back toward the gate.

In the face of overwhelmingly bad odds, Lady Huntley seemed to have released her hostage. That made things both better... and worse. With no one to slow her down, her escape could be swift.

He quickly scanned the crowds, finding no sign of a small, petite blonde woman. She'd have to leave quickly, and now. From the number of gypsy vardos that had crossed the bridge, Thornton suspected the factory site was surrounded. Unless she planned to escape via dirigible, the submersible was her only other choice.

Now was his chance.

Thornton dropped the crystal lens into his pocket beside the watch and reached behind him, catching hold of Amanda's wrist. Tugging her behind him, they moved back along the line of bushes toward the brick wall of the submersible tank, stepping from their cover only when they had no choice. He pointed at the narrow iron ladder fixed to its side, leading upward to the boarding platform.

Amanda nodded.

As fast as he could manage, Thornton climbed upward, pausing at the top only long enough to ascertain that Lady

Huntley was not yet en route in their direction. If she was coming at all. He lowered a hand, helping Amanda to the platform, then pulling her hurriedly to the small submersible station. The door's lock was broken and swung open on rusty hinges with only the slightest creak.

Inside, the control room showed every sign of abandonment. Spiders had been busy spinning webs and draining prey for months. A rat's nest constructed from old newspapers, twine and rags and tucked beneath a distant desk looked recently occupied. Water-streaked dust coated the observation window.

Yet the control panel was wiped clean. Hoping to block Lady Huntley's escape, Thornton pushed at the levers responsible for releasing the first set of underwater doors, those that would allow the submersible to enter the lock. He encountered no resistance; the mechanism was broken. She had opened the doors, then severed the cable connection.

He would have done exactly the same.

Now the only thing standing between the submersible and escape into the Thames was the second set of doors, and those doors were controlled from within the submersible.

Thornton pushed more buttons. Nothing. There were no other options here. The entire control panel had been disabled. He turned his attention instead to the submersible, studying it through the grimy observation window. It seemed in working order, if somewhat poorly maintained. Tied to bollards, it bobbed gently in the holding tank's water, its top hatch slightly ajar.

To reach it, Lady Huntley would have to pass directly in front of the station's door.

"Amanda," he spoke in a low voice, telling her what he'd seen through his lens.

"Nadya, she looked unharmed?"

"Yes. But listen, a woman who has so callously taken the lives of one gypsy after another will not think twice about hurting you to ensure her escape." Lady Huntley was all too aware of his weakness where Amanda was concerned. She would not hesitate to use that to her advantage.

He wrenched a cast iron lever from the control panel and pressed it into her hand. "When Lady Huntley arrives, stay here. If I must step outside, use this to wedge the door shut behind me."

Amanda took the lever, but looked unconvinced. How could he persuade her?

"Promise me," he demanded. "I do not wish to worry about your safety." He gripped her by the chin and pressed a hard, demanding kiss against her lips. "Please. I need to know you are safe from harm." He needed to know the woman he loved wouldn't be in peril while he dealt with a dangerous threat.

"Thornton?" Her upturned face searched his.

Now was not the time or place to declare himself. "I..." He tried to turn away. There was a spy to neutralize. All else must wait.

But she reached up and gripped his head, pulling him back to her for another soul-searing kiss. "I need you to stay safe as well," she said, pressing her forehead against his. "I *also* need to help."

"Then help me watch." He tugged her against his side, very much wishing to continue where they'd left off, but not at the cost of missing Lady Huntley. "Any minute now, she should appear."

Together, they stared fixedly through the filthy window, every muscle tensed in anticipation. Time was passing. Too much. Had he guessed wrong? Was Lady Huntley crazy enough to attempt a dirigible escape?

His eyes lifted to the roof of Airship Sails. Would he stand here helpless while that woman flew away unhindered, carrying years of research with her?

But he saw nothing.

He'd wait three minutes more, then give pursuit.

Two minutes.

One.

Then he saw her.

She mounted the platform, but did not arrive alone. She had Amanda's sister.

Lady Huntley held Lady Emily's neck in a tight grip with one hand while pressing a pistol to her stomach with the other. Tears streamed down Emily's face.

Beside him Amanda smothered a cry of distress. He pushed her down, out of sight. This mission had gone terribly awry.

Lady Huntley boldly marched Amanda's pregnant sister out onto the submersible's launch deck. Over Lady Huntley's shoulder hung a bulging canvas satchel. She now had everything she needed to make a clean escape. Devices, the plant, and a hostage at whom no man in his right mind would fire.

How had she managed this?

He swore.

Luca.

Emily would have rushed to her husband's side. Where Lady Huntley lay in wait, unwittingly released to care for the very man who—Thornton resolved—would be her last victim.

All neatly orchestrated.

"I see you there, Thornton. Amanda," Lady Huntley called. "Stay where you are, and I promise to let Emily go. Safe and unharmed. Just as soon as I leave Britain behind. Think of it as a gift, in return for all you've given me."

"Look at me, Amanda," he whispered, ignoring the taunt. "We're going to save Emily. Even if it means losing everything else. Understand?"

Amanda nodded, concern and worry in her eyes.

He positioned himself behind the station door, crouching, TTX pistol at the ready. If killing multiple gypsies wasn't reason enough, the moment Lady Huntley had aimed a weapon at an unborn child, all his scruples about hurting a woman evaporated. He'd like answers and justice, but he'd be lying if he denied entertaining thoughts about firing a third bullet and dropping Lady Huntley dead to the ground.

He'd yet to fire a third bullet at anyone, male or female. As a physician, it was a matter of principle. One he would set aside to save Emily.

But stopping Lady Huntley was going to be harder than he'd like. Gone were the full black skirts, the tightly fitted bodice of cambric. His former laboratory assistant—once a docile and grieving widow—was now encased in thick, protective leather. Leather leggings, leather boots, leather gloves, as well as a padded leather coat with a high collar and a hood. Goggles covered her eyes.

Anyone but Thornton would have been hard-pressed to identify her, but they had spent the last year at each other's sides, working seamlessly together in his laboratory. He knew her height and build, he knew her stride, and he knew the color of her hair. Tendrils of it blew free about her face.

Try as he might, he could recall no indications she worked for a foreign government, yet he couldn't stop a certain rage that swelled inside his chest. She was responsible for the deaths of many, including his best friend.

Well aware of the technology possessed by the Queen's agents, she was prepared. All that leather might well hamper the penetration of the bullet, slowing—even stopping—the entry of the TTX into her system, but it would not stop him from trying.

Only the pregnant woman she dragged alongside her would. Emily would survive a bullet. The tetrodotoxin levels from one bullet weren't high enough to kill a woman her size, but a baby... there was no anti-toxin. He couldn't risk it.

Using Emily as a shield, Lady Huntley advanced slowly and steadily toward the submersible's hatch. Then Emily tripped, and Thornton grabbed the opportunity, taking swift aim and pulling the trigger. With a hiss, the TTX bullet shot through the air and lodged in Lady Huntley's thigh.

He ducked back behind the door.

With a howl of frustration, she returned fire. Her bullet missed, slamming into the door beside him with a small explosion. Fragments of scalding metal sprayed into Thornton's neck, seeming to bite with tiny teeth.

He ignored the stinging sensation even as his heart pounded a warning. One more hit and Lady Huntley would drop. This would all be over. He rotated the barrel locking another cartridge in place, waiting for her to release Emily.

But she didn't. She swung her arm wide, discharging her weapon. The observation window shattered. Amanda screamed.

Thornton looked. He had to. Amanda clutched her shoulder with one hand, her face contorted with pain. Blood blossomed across her sleeve. "Amanda!" he yelled, his hesitation costing him precious seconds.

"Go!" she yelled. "I'm fine. She's getting away."

With a slight hitch to her step now, and unable to control the bulk of her hostage, Lady Huntley shoved Emily aside and hurried toward the submersible.

Torn, he turned and lifted his weapon once more. Lady Huntley was moving too fast. He had no choice but to aim for the vast expanse of leather covering her torso. The cartridge struck her upper back, but Lady Huntley kept going. He spun the barrel and fired his last TTX bullet. He missed. With a curse, he charged after her.

Lady Huntley had just reached the submersible's hatch

and was about to step inside when Thornton grabbed her shoulder and shoved her back onto the platform, placing himself in the path of escape.

She raised her weapon and pointed it directly at him. "Let me pass," she said. "Your weapon holds only three cartridges. Mine possesses six."

All he could do was delay. Stall in the hope some of the poison passed through the skin into Lady Huntley's system. "Why?" he asked. "Why such betrayal?"

"I shoot your lady love and that's what you ask?" Lady Huntley laughed and rolled her shoulders, as if working out a certain stiffness. "Do you feel the back of your neck burning?" she asked. "An interesting chemical coats these bullets. You should attend to it immediately. To Lady Amanda."

He didn't look away. "Surrender now, and I will see you treated fairly."

"Fairly," she scoffed, her voice taking on a slight German accent. "I know how you view my extracurricular experiments. There will be nothing 'fair' about it. But it was necessary. You British, you are too slow to advance your science, wasting time working with rats and other such vermin. Better to be bold, to lose a life or two." She shrugged. "A culling of society's undesirables. Everyone wins."

"It seems even husbands are expendable." He bit the words out.

A sly grin spread across her face. "Ah, at last you ask what it is you really wish to know. Was John aware he carried the phaoscope?" Her hand twitched. "Was he tricked? Or did his beautiful, young wife seduce him to her cause? Let me pass and I'll tell you."

Thornton slowly shook his head.

"No? Not interested?" She lowered the pistol, pointing it at Thornton's recently repaired leg. "Very well, then. I must be on my way." She sighed dramatically. "It seems such a shame; Amanda's spider has proven stunningly successful."

Amanda burst from the submersible station, rushing at Lady Huntley with a wild scream, her arm waving the broken iron lever he'd handed her.

"No!" he yelled. What the hell was she thinking!

Lady Huntley knocked aside the iron bar. It spun across the platform, out of reach. She grabbed Amanda by the hair, tugging her head back, pointing the pistol directly into her neck. "That's enough of that."

Amanda's struggles quickly subsided. Though she whimpered, she threw Thornton a triumphant look.

Lady Huntley stepped forward, dragging her newest and most valuable hostage with her. "We'll be leaving now."

His eyes scanned the dock, looking for any advantage, when, from the folds of her petticoats, Amanda's fist emerged holding the very knife he'd given her to cut the brambles. Her technique was terrible, but the knife was sharp and her aim was true. The blade pierced the leather of Lady Huntley's leggings, cutting deeply into the musculature of the thigh. If Amanda hadn't punctured the femoral artery, she'd come damned close.

With a primal howl, Lady Huntley shoved Amanda violently away.

Except she wasn't so easily tossed aside. Amanda had somehow managed to thread her injured arm through the strap that held the canvas satchel over Lady Huntley's shoulder, and she wasn't letting go, no matter the pain written on her face.

Nor was Lady Huntley deterred from making her escape. She took aim at Thornton and fired. The bullet tore through his recently repaired leg. Flashes of searing white pain spotted his vision, and he staggered, momentarily off balance.

Amanda held on tightly, dragging behind Lady Huntley, refusing to let go of the bag. With the bloody knife still in her fist, she hacked at the strap until the fibers separated and frayed. There was a loud tearing sound and the strap pulled free from the bag. With her arms wrapped about the satchel, she collapsed on the platform.

Lady Huntley had lost all but her freedom. As she careened toward the submersible hatch, flinging herself through the opening, Thornton could only see one option.

He pitched himself through the hatch behind her.

—➤—⚜—◄—

A SHOT RANG OUT, making a horrible clanging sound inside the hull of the steel-plated submersible. Amanda shoved aside the satchel, pushing herself to her feet with the one arm that didn't feel as though it were on fire. She ran toward the hatch, but she was too slow.

An arm reached up—Lady Huntley's—and pulled the hatch door closed.

From the edge of the docking platform, she watched in horror as the propeller began to spin. Valves opened and hissed, and the long cigar-shaped vessel began to submerge in a cloud of bubbles, ripping the bollards from the dock.

She bent over, grabbing the broken iron lever and running toward the dock mechanism that controlled the final set of doors. Once they were open, there would be no stopping Lady Huntley, no rescuing Thornton.

With the one arm that still responded to her commands, she beat on the mechanism. Over and over and over. She heard screams, barely recognizing them as her own. A sudden hiss. A blast of steam from the mechanism. She jumped back. Had it worked?

No.

Gears turned and a winch twisted, yanking upward on the chain that raised the final set of doors. Lady Huntley must have control of the submersible, or it wouldn't be moving forward. A high-pitched mechanical whine filled the air. The propeller picked up speed, roiling and churning a great froth of water, and the submersible shot forth into the tube.

Behind her were footsteps and cries of alarm.

Emily.

Her sister needed assistance.

She cast a quick glance over her shoulder. Emily was safely wrapped in Nadya's arms. Beside them stood Nicu.

Factory workers surrounded all three. Several angry-looking men advanced in her direction.

Emily was fine, but Lady Huntley was carrying the man she loved out into the Thames, to the sea. And he was bleeding.

Panic gathered inside and rose into her throat. "No!" she screamed, running for the ladder that clung to the side of the tank. Flinging herself down it, falling to the ground, she rose and started running once more. She squeezed past the iron fence and stumbled down to the river's edge, not caring what might be underfoot.

Amanda stared at the opening of the tube into the Thames. Hundreds of small kraken churned the water with their tentacles waving, holding on to... pieces of other kraken. It was as if... as if the submersible had exploded outward, shredding all kraken in its way. She looked up and out, but there seemed no other evidence of the vessel's passage. Before her stretched nothing but an expanse of choppy river. No wake disturbed the water. No air bubbles rose to the surface. Boats moved past, going about their routine. Beyond it London sat, cloaked in the dull gray of the oncoming night.

Something inside her choked. Gone. Would she ever see him again? Her heart constricted as if uncertain it should continue to beat. She should have said something, declared her love, before it was too late. Before the opportunity was ripped away.

Out of the gathering darkness, from beneath Vauxhall Bridge, a single small boat fought its way upstream, against the prevailing currents, pointing itself in her direction.

Black and his agents? If so, they were too late. Far too late.

Wait. What was that? She struggled to focus through the gloom. There, on the surface of the water, the pattern of waves disrupted. And then she saw it, the metallic hump of the submersible rising in the Thames, water cascading down its sides.

The hatch opened.

And Thornton, his dark hair blowing in the wind, climbed out.

The world spun and grew dark as the kraken-strewn shore rushed up at her.

CHAPTER THIRTY-NINE

BRIGHT LIGHTS OVERHEAD blinded her before she even opened her eyes. Amanda turned her head away from the glare and cracked her eyelids. Where was she?

The room that swam into focus had a familiar feel. The same stark, utilitarian decor of Lister Laboratories. Yet she was in a hospital bed, the mattress thin beneath her, the pillow almost non-existent, and the wool blanket itched. A row of equally stark beds stretched away from her. All empty but for one. At the far end, beneath a blanket, slept a lone figure.

"Hello?" she called. Footsteps echoed on the tiled floor.

A moment later, a familiar face looked down. "About time," Black said. Amusement danced in his eyes. "Being shot by a German spy is no excuse for lying about unconscious for days on end."

Days? "Where, exactly, am I?"

"You're in the long-term hospital ward beneath the laboratories for those agents requiring round the clock care. No one was certain what effects the poison might have. That bullet was lodged in your shoulder blade for quite some time, its poisons seeping into your system. Surgery was required to remove it. It was touch and go there for a bit, Lady Amanda. You nearly stopped breathing." Black frowned. "The Chemistry Department is still struggling to determine exactly what toxin coated those bullets."

Amanda struggled to sit up; pain radiated through her shoulder, down her arm as the memories flooded back.

Shot.

Lady Huntley also shot Thornton, deliberately firing at his injured leg, underscoring the depth of her betrayal.

"Thornton?" Was that him at the far end of the room?

"He'll be fine." Black waved away her concern. "Lady Huntley's bullet only shredded some muscle as it passed through. The toxin made the wound a nasty mess, but it'll heal. Nice work, by the way. On the fly surgery in the back of a vardo. Once that new wound of Thornton's heals, the doctors say he'll soon be as good as new." He rocked back on his feet. "Ever consider field surgery?"

Amanda ignored his attempt at levity and sank back into the pillows. Thornton was fine. Yet not here at her side. She couldn't bring herself to ask if he'd visited. Likely he was back in the classroom, back in the laboratory. She ran her fingertips over the coarse wool blanket. Work and duty would always come first with him. He'd pushed her away when she'd first made her advances, warned her there was no place in his life for a wife. Except... those feverish words, the way he'd clung to her as if she were his lifeline. She was so certain he was about to make a declaration.

First, she needed to know what had happened inside that submersible. "I heard Lady Huntley's weapon discharge. I was so certain..."

"Would you like the whole story?"

"Tell me."

"Your messenger boy directed me to the Airship Sales factory. Apologies for not arriving sooner; I commandeered the first river patrol boat I could. My agents and I found you in a crumpled heap at the edge of the Thames, surrounded by gypsies. They caught you as you collapsed, sparing you a swim with the kraken. Impressive that you managed to stave off the effects of that German bullet long enough to run to the river's edge."

"Adrenaline." The only thing worse than the pain in her shoulder had been knowing that evil woman had the man she loved in her grips. Amanda closed her eyes. *The man I love.* She hadn't meant to let that happen, love. She'd warned herself against such feelings and yet there it was. She'd gone and fallen in love with him, body and soul, and lost a piece of her heart in the process.

His intelligence, his drive, his work. His loyalty to his country and those he cared about. And there was no discounting the physical attraction she felt. That low growl in his voice, those facile fingers, those curls that tumbled over his brow when he was lost in his work.

But that kiss in the submersible station, it had been their

last. It had to be. She'd grown too attached, wanting to keep Thornton for herself. But she wouldn't. She'd promised to lay no claim on him. She would let him go. Now, while she could still do so with dignity and without embarrassing him, without damaging either of their careers. It hurt. But she didn't regret her actions. Any of them.

The hole in her heart tore a little more.

"How?" she prompted, needing to distract herself from such unwelcome thoughts and feelings. She opened her eyes and looked up at Black. "If Thornton is fine, why didn't he stop the submersible from leaving the dock?"

"The tetrodotoxin from the bullets slowed her down, but Lady Huntley still managed to throw the vessel into autopilot before Thornton could reach her. There was a struggle. You can imagine what that must have been like inside such a small tin can. Thornton managed to grab Lady Huntley's arm in time to deflect the bullet, though it ricocheted around. It must have made quite some noise."

It had. A horrible clanging noise that had nearly stopped her heart from beating.

"By then, the submersible had entered the initial portion of the tube, and Thornton reasoned it was better to blast through at high velocity rather than risk getting stuck." Black had warmed to the story, his arm whipping through the air as if recreating Thornton's explosive launch into the Thames. "I gather the number of kraken you'd observed was cause for concern?"

She nodded. There'd been so, so many.

"The river patrol is quite pleased, by the way, that

another kraken nest has been located and destroyed." Black paused. "Lady Huntley required a few hours of assisted breathing, but is now, unfortunately, fine. I found her the darkest, dankest cell I could manage. So far, she is refusing to cooperate."

Amanda hoped she refused to cooperate for years. "Henri?"

"Exactly who he said he was," Black answered. "Thornton has seen that his mother will be well-cared for."

"Luca?" she asked. Then followed his gaze to the blanket-covered lump at the far end of the room. "Is it that bad?"

"A matter of perspective, I suppose. No gypsy wants artificial modifications. Gypsy and *ton* are a lot alike that way. So, from Luca's viewpoint, his artificial eye is an abomination. From a research standpoint, he's a miraculous success."

"And from the Queen's point of view?"

"There is quite some concern over his status as Romanichal gypsy." Black sighed. "Since he has declined to enter the Queen's service, the camera has been disabled. Therefore, only two options remain. He may return the eye."

Amanda sucked in a breath.

"Exactly," Black said. "Or he can sign an agreement to take on an entirely new identity, to prevent the technology from falling into enemy hands. No matter his choice, Luca will never be allowed to leave England's shores."

"A new identity. He has to go into hiding?" she asked.

Black nodded.

Amanda did not think Luca would agree. Gypsy identity

was tightly tied to family. "What does my sister have to say about all this?"

"Despite your father's many and colorful threats, they are not legally man and wife. The Queen herself has forbidden Lady Emily entry into this facility, and without a legal marriage she will not be offered the opportunity to disappear with Luca."

Emily must be beside herself with worry. "Not a healthy situation for the baby."

"I know, but my hands are tied."

"Take me to him." She struggled upright, then, looking down with alarm at the thin cotton gown she wore, she pulled the wool blanket about her shoulders, the most modesty she could manage.

Black averted his gaze. "He won't talk to anyone."

"He only need listen." Amanda's legs shook beneath her as she stood. A bullet wound and a hefty dose of an unknown toxin had left her physically weak, but her mind felt as clear as ever. And she needed something to think about besides Thornton.

The floor was cold beneath her bare feet and a draft blew about her ankles as she walked past the long row of beds. She counted six, wondering if they'd ever all been occupied simultaneously. The whole distance, Black's steadying hand was at her elbow.

He left her at Luca's bedside.

The light above his bed was off, casting Luca's beard-roughened face into shadow as he lay on his side, eyes closed. But there was no hiding the swollen tissue about his new eye.

It was purple and yellow and green and looked hideously painful.

"Luca," she said, lowering herself onto the edge of his bed. "Are you awake?"

"Go away, Amanda," he said. "Try to help Emily forget me. This agency, whatever it is, will never set me free. Not so long as I wish to have two eyes."

"Such melodrama, Luca. You've a wife with a child on the way."

"Not in the eyes of the law."

"Phfft." She brushed aside his objection. "A special license and a minister can take care of that in a heartbeat. All you need to do is agree to cooperate." She paused, waiting for a response. None came. Stubborn man; it was time to turn the screws. "Emily needs you, Luca. Your child needs you. Don't abandon them. Do you know what their lives will be like among the *ton* without a husband or a father? Don't abandon my sister when she needs you most."

His eyes slitted open. One brown and one blue. Apart from the color, no one would guess one was not his own.

She continued. "Emily left behind everything she knew to be with *you*, gave up her entire life for *you*. It's time for *you* to make your own sacrifice and do what is right. Together, you can begin again."

His eyes lost some of their distance. "Not as Roma."

"No. Not for now. But neither will you suffer the disgrace of becoming a peer." That made his lips twitch. "At least agree to marry her *gadjo* style. Then you can discuss—*together*—the value of two eyes."

A long moment passed.

"Agreed." She began to stand, but Luca caught her hand. "Thank you, Amanda. For stopping that awful woman. For caring what happened to my people."

She squeezed his hand. "Anything for my brother-in-law. Take good care of Emily and my niece or nephew."

"I will."

A MINISTER CONDUCTED a short ceremony the very next morning at Luca's bedside. Mr. Black, Father, and Amanda alone stood witness for the agency refused to grant Mother, Ned, or Olivia access.

Not that Mother or Olivia would have attended. News of Emily's appearance at the house, some six months pregnant and dressed in "gypsy rags" had torn through the *ton* like wildfire. Likely both women were prostrate with humiliation.

"It's only for five years," Amanda said, embracing her sister, losing the fight to hold back the trickle of tears trying to escape her eyes.

Though her mother and sister behaved abysmally, Father had promised much to the Queen so that his son-in-law might walk free with such a valuable device implanted in his thick skull. Heavens only knew what it had cost Father to convince the Queen to agree that Emily and Luca could return in five years when such technology would no longer be cutting edge.

Several minutes later, Emily wiped her own eyes and pulled away, wrapping an arm about her stomach. "I promise, the very next day, I will be on your doorstep with my son or daughter."

Black stood at the door, his eyes turned upward to study the ceiling as he rocked on his heels, their long goodbye clearly trying his patience. Beside him, Luca beckoned, anxious to leave. Four walls and a roof had never surrounded him for such an extended period of time.

With hope and love shining in her face, Emily walked toward her husband. Seconds later, they were gone.

FATHER WALKED beside her as they exited the building. "I'm told that gypsy weed has begun to bud," he said. "Lord Thornton anticipates scheduling Ned's surgery in a few weeks' time."

"That's wonderful." The expected response, though her words were flat. Thornton had yet to appear. He'd not sent even a simple message in her direction. She felt numb.

"You have proven yourself, Amanda. I was wrong to keep you from medical school. I trust you will assist with Ned's surgery?" Worry drew his eyebrows together.

A few weeks ago, Father's request would have puffed her chest with professional pride.

"Of course." She was a professional. Feelings had no place in the surgical suite. She and Thornton worked well together, and she would let nothing stand in the way of seeing Ned once again walk on two feet without mechanical assistance.

"Good."

Still, she felt strangely empty. Hollow. For too long her life had revolved around work and now that it was done... She should feel something more, having finally reached the goal she'd set herself some five years ago.

She straightened her shoulders. It was time to let go of the guilt that had driven her research and move forward. It was time to find a new passion, a new problem to solve. There was certainly no dearth of disease and injury about. She would select another research topic, something not involving neurophysiology. Rumor was Professor Rathsburn was encountering difficulty with a cell line designed to speed and promote healing of bone injuries. Perhaps he would consent to let her join his laboratory.

Father sighed. Father never sighed.

"What is it?" Amanda braced herself, waiting for him to name the man he'd chosen for her to marry. After the disaster with Simon, he likely had little confidence in her ability to choose for herself.

"After much thought and consideration," he began, "I have decided to release you from your obligation to marry."

"Excuse me?" Her feet stopped moving. Certainly she'd heard wrong.

"Your passion and dedication to medical research impress me. As do your results. I've instructed my solicitors to set aside funds to provide you with an allowance. It is enough that you may live alone if you so choose, though I hope you'll consider remaining at home."

Her mouth fell open. "I need not marry?"

"That is what I said." His eyebrows rose. "Of course, if you *want* to marry..."

"Not at this time," she said, looking away.

"About Mr. Sommersby. I'm sorry. Sorry to have pushed him on you." Father admitting culpability. It seemed today was a day for many firsts.

"I chose him," she conceded. "Shall we agree to bear culpability equally?"

He nodded, then drew a deep breath. "Unfortunately, before Mr. Sommersby was caught in illegal possession of Lister University technology, he lodged a complaint against Lord Thornton."

"A complaint." Amanda couldn't seem to inhale.

"There's to be an inquiry concerning improper behavior between a student and a professor. Tomorrow. First thing in the morning."

Right or wrong, the simple fact that she was female meant that, if there was fault to be found, it would land squarely on her shoulders.

Her hand flew to her chest. Was she to be expelled?

CHAPTER FORTY

I T WAS WITH A CURIOUS kind of relief that she finally
stood before the school's board of trustees. Her relationship with Thornton had come to light. Hours of
worry had paralyzed her, but now, for good or ill, judgment
would be passed.

From a wall of the dark paneled room, Joseph Lister
stared down at her from his portrait in seeming disapproval.
Five more frowning, white-haired, older gentlemen sat
behind a long, polished table. No chair was provided for her.

Dressed in a simple dove gray walking dress, her hair
pulled back from her face tightly twisted in a chignon,
Amanda clasped gloved hands demurely at her waist,
waiting for them to pronounce judgment.

Where was Thornton? How could he leave her to stand
here alone? She'd been certain he would at last present
himself.

She hated to admit it, but she missed him horribly.

Missed his arrogant confidence, the sound of his rumbling voice, the smell of his skin, the touch of his hands. She'd been hoping for one last glimpse. A chance to say goodbye.

A mustachioed and bespectacled man cleared his throat. It seemed they were starting without him. Amanda pulled back her shoulders.

"Lady Amanda," the man began. "A number of damaging accusations have been hurled in your direction suggesting that your relationship with Lord Thornton is of an improper nature, but given that the source of these allegations is untrustworthy at best, further investigation would be required."

She held her breath. Could it be that she was not to be expelled, that they would simply slap her hands and burn her ears with a warning?

"We are deeply disappointed in you, young lady."

Several other older gentlemen grumbled.

Though she met his gaze unashamed, Amanda's stomach soured as hope curdled.

"Prior to your association with Lord Thornton, you were top in your class." The mustachioed man lifted a pile of papers, tapping them into perfect alignment. "The *only* reason you will be afforded the opportunity to reclaim your place is because Lord Thornton has resigned his position at Lister University, effectively rendering any relationship between you irrelevant."

She gasped. *He'd done what?*

"That is correct, my lady." He leaned back in his chair. "I suggest you return with all due diligence to your studies and refrain from further intimate contact with anyone who might be perceived to be your superior." He slid his glasses down his nose, staring at her over their rims. "You may go, Lady Amanda. Quickly, before I change my mind."

She spun on her heel, exiting the room. Heart racing, she turned corners until she found herself inside Lister Laboratories, striding down its wide hallway. She came to a sudden stop outside Thornton's office.

Several feet away, the great iron door stood crowing its impenetrability. Her access was, no doubt, revoked. Amanda vowed it would be temporary. First, she had to stop Thornton from making a horrible mistake. She would not be the cause of the end of a great man's career.

It wasn't right, and it certainly wasn't fair.

THORNTON WAS PULLING YET another handful of books from his bookshelf when his office door opened. He spun around in time to watch it slam shut. He'd been expecting Black. The interrogation was to begin soon.

Instead, Amanda leaned backward against his door, looking quite unlike herself. He supposed he'd grown used to seeing her in high fashion. Or in complete disarray. But not like this. Her hair was ruthlessly scraped back from her face and twisted into a severe bun. Nor had he ever expected to see her in a gown with a starched neck so high it was likely to strangle its wearer. And gloves. Long black gloves that stretched beyond her elbow. Her eyes were narrowed and her chest heaved.

He should have known she'd come. He should have locked his door. "Can I help you, Lady Amanda?" He forced the title from his throat, tacitly agreeing to respect the distance her attire—if not her behavior—worked to establish.

"Stop," she spat. Her chin lifted. "Spare me the manners. No lord this and lady that. How could you let me face the board of trustees all alone?"

His ire rose to meet hers. "We're not partners, Amanda." She winced, but didn't look away. "There is no equality here. Not in the eyes of our larger world. We are—were—professor and student. Primary investigator and research assistant. Man and woman."

Didn't it boil down to just that problem? He was a man who could easily force her world to meet his desires. He would not do that. It wasn't right, and it wasn't fair. "My attendance was unnecessary." He struggled to keep all emotion from his voice. "We reached an agreement earlier, my resignation in return for your continued enrollment and an end to the investigation." He'd accepted all the blame for their indiscreet behavior. He had options; she had none.

His absence was calculated to injure. Intended to sever their connection with one clean blow. Yet here she stood, eyes blazing.

He met Amanda's incredulous gaze for a long moment, then turned abruptly back toward his bookshelf and resumed packing. "I've taken the position your father offered me. Director of a private laboratory." Far from the inconvenience of incompetent students, his employees all carefully vetted and handpicked by the duke. It was a desk job. He suspected he'd hate every minute of every day. In his new position, he would foster and direct new research projects—the projects of other scientists. Wouldn't that be a special kind of hell? "In return, the duke has agreed to release you from your agreement. You're free from all time constraints and may choose to marry—or not—on your own terms."

"You!" Her voice was incredulous, her stare pained. "*You* brokered a deal with my father? You did this for... me?"

"Yes." He jerked his head in a nod. He'd carved out his heart, set aside his own wants and desires. For her. Such brilliance should not be snuffed before it had a chance to burn bright.

"But your work!" She stomped a foot. "*Your* laboratory!"

He clenched his hands into fists. "What laboratory? I've lost every competent assistant."

"No. You can't leave." She shook her head. "You're a brilliant and famous neurophysiologist. Your research is groundbreaking. Even if the only ones who know it are sworn to secrecy. You can't just leave." Her voice cracked. "You can't sacrifice your career for *me*."

"Why not? Who's to say you're not the next brilliant mind? That your research won't save lives?" He dropped a lid on the crate, lifted a hammer, and viciously drove home one nail after another. He'd had his chance; she deserved hers. "Go, Amanda. Become a physician, a surgeon, a research scientist. Marry or don't. The choice is yours." He couldn't bring himself to look at her face. Instead, he picked up another nail.

Her next words, softly spoken, brought a whisper of hope. "What if the professor is married to the student? Would that still constitute an improper relationship?"

His hands froze. "No."

"Too bad you have no interest in acquiring a wife." Her words curled seductively about him.

He set the hammer down on his desk with extreme care. His mind raced. She was *teasing* him? Was it possible she *wanted* him to propose? He took a deep breath and straightened, turning to face her. "What if I said I'd changed my mind? What if I told you that there is one, and only one, woman I could marry? Only one woman that I love?"

"I would understand." Her eyes glistened. "For there's only one man I love, only one man I could marry."

He abandoned his books, moving closer. His heart hammered in his chest. Love. Something he'd never dared hope he'd find in a marriage, but there it was, shining in her eyes. "It nearly killed me to stay away."

"It was foolish of you to try." She pulled off one long, black glove and stepped forward closing the distance between them. Reaching out, she threaded her fingers through his hair, her blue eyes full of longing. "I've missed you. There's no one else I want. With you, I don't have to pretend to be what I'm not. You understand me without even trying."

Could it be that simple? Why not? He felt the same.

440

Every word she spoke resonated deep within him. He wanted her by his side. Always.

Thornton caught her face in his hands and drew her toward him, catching her lips with his own, pouring his heart into a tender kiss, doing his best to show what he feared words could not express.

He pulled away and stared into her eyes. No more hiding his thoughts from her. "Marry me." Taking a deep breath, he summoned the words forth. "Not to satisfy a group of stodgy old men, not to please your father, and not to save my laboratory. Marry me because I don't wish to live without you. You are what's been missing from my life. With you, I feel alive. Marry me because I love you." There it was, his heart laid bare, but once he'd begun, he couldn't seem to stop. "I find you beautiful, intelligent, exciting..."

"Exciting?" A small, teasing smile played about her lips. Her bare hand slid down over his neck, her fingers wrapped about his cravat, tugging as she stepped backward. "Will you show me?"

Desire flared hot and hard. He followed, step by step by step. Her back met the closed door, but still he didn't stop. Not until his legs—both now working—tangled in her skirts. He reached behind her and flipped the lock, ensuring complete privacy. His fingers began to work free the tiny buttons that held her throat in their grip. He brushed his mouth against her bare neck, feeling her pulse flutter beneath his lips. "Say yes, and I'll show you," he spoke against her skin. "Right here, against this very door."

"Now? Is your leg up to it?" Her words came with a hitch in her breath.

"You'll have to agree to marry me to find out."

Her low laugh drove him wild. "Yes, I'll marry you."

Gone was any thought of restraint. Buttons flew as he yanked open her bodice. He whispered a word of praise when he found that the corset beneath tipped her taut nipples upward.

She gasped as he closed his lips about one rosy peak, gently nipping. His hand palmed her other breast, rolling another pebbled nipple between his fingers. Her back arched against the door with her cry of encouragement. Then her own hands began to move, tracing a path down his chest to his waistband, tugging. "Please."

"Patience." He stepped back, reveling in the image of the woman he loved splayed bare-breasted against his office door as he freed himself. Then, kneeling at her feet, he slid his hands about her booted ankles, lifting her skirts as he moved his palms over tightly laced leather, upward to where they met silk stockings. He lifted the froth of ruffles yet higher and his thumbs brushed against her garters, the bare skin of her inner thighs. Only to be stopped by a silky undergarment edged in lace. "Open for me," he said, urging her thighs apart.

Her knees nearly buckled as she obliged.

His fingers found the slit in her undergarment, the soft curls underneath. They searched out her cleft and the tight knot of flesh within. He pressed.

Her hips bucked against him. A cry escaped her lips.

Parting her swollen flesh, he tasted her wet heat, holding her tight against his mouth as she writhed beneath him.

Her fingers flexed in his hair, tugging. "Stop. No more. Please. I want you inside me. Now."

Her hands clutched at his shoulders as he stood, gathering her skirts in his fists. Kissing her deeply, pushing her back against the door, he hooked one leg over his arm. With one thrust, he was inside. With another, he was deeper. He swept up her other leg and gripped her hips, surging into her, every last vestige of control lost.

Her nails dug into his shoulders, her legs wrapped tightly about his hips, boots against the back of his thighs urged him onward as she moaned in pleasure.

He drove into her over and over, until her body pulsed around him in tight waves. Once, twice more, blood thundering in his ears as his own release tore through him. Lost in the warmth of the woman he loved. A lifetime would not be enough.

For a few long moments, the most he could manage was to breathe. Then, slowly and without releasing her, he untangled their limbs. He lowered himself to the cold, hard floor and pulled her soft warmth over him, stroking the twists of her hair that tumbled across his chest.

He'd set her free to choose—his arm tightened around her as warmth flooded his chest—and she'd chosen him.

Though expected elsewhere, this was where he belonged, with the love of his life in his arms. Always.

Deep in the bowels of an imposing, official building some distance away, the Duke of Avesbury consulted his pocket watch. Again. "I don't believe he's coming," the duke stated.

Black snickered. Not here anyway.

"Something you'd like to share, Mr. Black?" the duke asked.

"Not really, Your Grace."

"Hmmph. I hope he realizes his absence will negate our deal."

Thornton had mentioned a promotion. He'd kept delaying his acceptance, pacing the hospital ward's hallways, waiting for Lady Amanda to wake from her drugged sleep.

"I suspect, Your Grace, that whatever deal you struck with Lord Thornton is no longer relevant. When I arrived to collect him for the interrogation, he was rather—er—preoccupied with your daughter."

From a distance, he'd watched Amanda crash through Thornton's door, slamming it behind her. Black had crept close enough only to confirm sounds of their... reconciliation. Then left with all due haste.

Lucky bastard.

The duke's eyes narrowed. "Tell Lord Thornton I expect him in my study with news of an engagement before midnight. Or he'll answer to both me and the board of trustees."

"Yes, Your Grace." Black fought a smile. He'd guessed right, then.

"Since I'm to lose the earl, perhaps you'd like to take his place?"

"For the interrogation?" Black nodded. "Very much so."

"If all goes well today, you may consider yourself his replacement on a permanent basis."

Black's eyebrows rose. "Thank you, Your Grace. It would be my honor."

"You may proceed." The duke waved him forward.

Black walked over to Lady Emily's side. After today, she and her husband would disappear into a dusty, forgotten corner of Britain. "It seems Lord Thornton won't be joining us, my lady. Shall we begin?"

Emily nodded. Pulling protective eyewear into place, she poured a final ingredient into a draught she'd prepared earlier. She swirled the blue liquid and a plume of white smoke erupted from the surface.

His hand hesitated.

"No worries," she said with a sly grin. "It won't kill her, only loosen her tongue."

Reflecting that Luca had best keep his wife content, Black accepted the glass and pulled open the heavy door before him. Inside, two agents stood on either side of a chair where a heavily shackled woman sat.

Lady Huntley's eyes flicked over the contents of the glass.

"Shall we begin?" Black asked, taking no pleasure in the thought of the hours that were to come. His trust, once broken, was impossible to repair. And answers were required. "Or will you speak freely?"

"No. Do your best." She raised her delicate, pointed chin in the air. "For the Fatherland."

Hours later, Black had all the information he needed. He and his agents exited the interrogation room, holding the door open for one last visitor.

"Five minutes," he warned.

The gypsy nodded. "I'll only need three," he said. And winked one blue mechanical eye.

EPILOGUE

"WALK WITH ME," her sister said, slipping an arm through Amanda's, dragging her away from the wedding breakfast crowd.

Ned's surgery, her spider, had been a resounding success. After five long years, he finally walked without mechanical assistance and, from the crush, it seemed all of London had turned out to witness his most recent walk down the church aisle to make Georgina his bride.

Amanda's own wedding several weeks earlier had been a small affair held in the front parlor and sparsely attended. "Is something wrong?" she asked as Olivia pulled her into a secluded alcove.

"I'm to be engaged tomorrow," Olivia stated flatly.

"Has Carlton changed his mind?"

She shook her head. A tear ran down her cheek. "No. Someone else has proposed. He is titled and willing to wed into our family despite..." Olivia swallowed.

Amanda's heart squeezed. "Do you want me to talk to Father about it?"

"No. It's for the best. I only wanted to apologize. If not for Carlton's public accusations, you would not have had to marry that..." Her hands flapped about in distress. "That *man* in such haste."

Amanda caught her sister's hands, steadying them. "Olivia, that man is my husband, and I love him with all my heart. I wish only the same for you."

With a sob, Olivia threw her arms about Amanda, hugging her tightly. Then, with a gasp, released her before turning to run down the hallway.

"Whatever is wrong?" Thornton inquired, his breath warm in her ear as his arms came about her waist, pulling her backward against his strong, lean form.

She leaned into his strength. "It seems my sister is under the impression I was forced into marriage with a mad ogre of a titled scientist."

Thornton nuzzled her neck. "Mad for you, perhaps. But ogre?"

His touch was too distracting. She would speak with Olivia later. "You do have a voracious appetite," she answered, tipping her head to provide a better angle. "And a tendency to growl."

"Mmm. An appetite which is currently unsatisfied. Shall we explore the gardens?" His low voice vibrated against her skin awakening every nerve ending.

"Did you not notice the dusting of snow, my earl?" A token objection for she knew he would keep her warm.

"I did, countess." He nudged her toward the terrace doors. "A decided advantage as I fully expect it to keep the other guests indoors."

ABOUT THE AUTHOR

Though ANNE RENWICK holds a Ph.D. in biology and greatly enjoyed tormenting the overburdened undergraduates who were her students, fiction has always been her first love. Today, she writes steampunk romance, placing a new kind of biotech in the hands of mad scientists, proper young ladies and determined villains.

Anne brings an unusual perspective to steampunk. A number of years spent locked inside the bowels of a biological research facility left her permanently altered. In her steampunk world, the Victorian fascination with all things anatomical led to a number of alarming biotechnological advances. Ones that the enemies of Britain would dearly love to possess.

www.AnneRenwick.com

instagram.com/anne_renwick
facebook.com/AnneRenwickAuthor
pinterest.com/AuthorAnneRenwick

www.ingramcontent.com/pod-product-compliance
Lightning Source LLC
Chambersburg PA
CBHW051205120726
47905CB00004B/993